The Devil's Descendants

by

Amylynn Bright

ISBN-13 9798367663860

ISBN-10 1477123456

Cover design by: Sweet 'n Spicy Designs

Library of Congress Control Number: 2018675309
Printed in the United States of America

If not for the brilliant ladies of Snark & Shenanigans, I'd never have pulled this off. They are everything that is brilliant, sarcastic, and humorous. I repeatedly thank the old gods and the new that I have access to the hive mind.

As for the next books, that's for future critique group to figure out.

Also, for Bug. She came up with the Stairway to Heaven idea and demanded mention.

We are each our own devil, and we make this world our hell.
—Oscar Wilde

1

EIGHTEEN YEARS AGO

L uke pulled at the collar of his brand-new dress shirt and
stretched his neck, grimacing in misery. Six other ten-year-olds
also milled about in the formal room of their ancestor's home, most
of them plucking nervously at their own fancy clothes.

He glanced at the double doors, thick and tall, stained dark
brown. They were locked and had been for almost a half an hour.
When he paced in front of them, which he'd done several times
already, he'd not heard anything. There had been no voices raised in
anger, no chanting, no screaming. He didn't know what to expect
exactly, but it seemed any decision this monumental would be louder.

"Are you scared?" His cousin Asher paused next to him, his hands
shoved in his trouser pockets, and stared at the massive oak doors.

Luke shifted his weight and sighed. "No," he lied.

"Me either," Asher said, but Luke could practically smell how full
of shit he was. "I do wish I'd eaten more, though. Now I'm starving."

That Luke could agree with. "Maybe they'll take us to get pizza
after."

Asher snorted. "If it's neither of our dads."

"It won't be." Luke sounded sure of himself. He was, mostly.
Sort of.

"It could be," Asher noted. "Odds are one in seven. It's gotta be one of them. I bet its Uncle Albert."

"Hey! I heard that." Benji lurched forward from his seat on the sofa. He'd just turned ten last month and was the youngest of the cousins by several months, He was also the scrappiest. "Take it back."

Asher shrugged. "I don't mean anything by it. It might be your dad, you know."

Benji raised his fists. "Take it back."

The rest of the boys looked on, waiting to see if their cousins would come to blows.

Luke stepped between the boys. "It's gonna be one of them, Ben. Your dad, or mine. Maybe Ash's. Probably not Seth's because it's his grandfather now. It's almost never a straight line. I mean it could be, but it probably won't." He glanced at Seth who wore a thin-lipped smile.

"Not in the last thirty-two ceremonies," Seth agreed. He looked remarkedly less edgy than the rest of them.

"But there's nothing that says he won't be," Jacob insisted. He was the oldest of the cousins and he always insisted that made him the smartest. "It could totally be your dad."

Seth's smile faltered and that seemed to satisfy Jacob.

"My dad's taking me to a baseball game tomorrow," Ian interjected. He said it fast and loud, like he had to get it out in order to make it true.

From the back of the room, Ethan snorted sarcastically. "Okay dude."

Asher shrugged again and Benji threw down his hands, the fight blown over that quickly. One more glance at the closed doors and Luke wandered over to sit with Seth. "So, what's it like?"

"What?" Seth asked like he didn't know what every single one of them was thinking. Five other faces gathered around and waited for enlightenment. Luke cocked his head and leveled his gaze on him. Seth picked at a button on the suede sofa. "I don't know. I don't think I ever met my grandfather."

"Oh." Luke wasn't the only one frustrated.

Ian kicked the leg of the sofa. "Dammit."

Even though the cousins had all grown up together, and their family history was well-known among them, none of them really understood the reality of what was happening tonight. The only thing that they were all certain of was that after this evening, one of their lives was going to completely change. Forever.

The boys all jumped and turned towards the doors as they opened. Their fathers filed from the inner sanctum one by one, and as each of the older men appeared, the boys visibly relaxed. Seth's father led the group and, as Luke had predicted, he had not been chosen. Neither were the fathers of Benji, Jacob, Ian or Ethan. There was an extended pause before, finally, Asher's father emerged, alone.

That left only Luke's father, Aaron.

Wearing the ceremonial red silk cape, Aaron Mephisto strode from the candlelit room, his expression grim but resigned. Luke shuddered and felt the tears coming. Or he was going to throw up?

His father put his hand on his shoulder, and it already felt heavier.

The old man, Seth's grandfather, the Devil who retired tonight, was the only one among them who seemed excited. He clapped his hands together and rubbed them with anticipation. "All right, boys. You're up. Let's get this show on the road." Like a fiendish wolf, he ushered the sheep-like boys into the room for the next part of the ceremony, a ritual that would also initiate them into their family curse. If there was a new Devil, there would be seven new Princes of Hell as well.

The man he'd known and loved all his life spoke in his ear. "Come on, Luke. This won't take long."

Was that supposed to be encouraging? He didn't care how long it took—five minutes, an hour, a week—he didn't want to do this at all. He for sure wasn't hungry anymore, but he wanted to go with his father and get some pizza. He wanted to do anything else but return to that mysterious room and go through with this. He wanted to do something normal. Even though he didn't really understand what all of this meant, he did know that normal would take on a very different meaning from now on.

His father's hand applied more pressure and Luke was urged

forward, propelled unwillingly toward the flickering, smoky light and a sense of diabolical foreboding.

When he faltered, his father whispered, "It's going to be okay, son." But the smell of brimstone said otherwise, and Luke suspected this was the first of many lies his father would tell.

No part of it was okay, but Luke and his father led the way and began the ceremony that would make Aaron the Devil of his generation.

2

EIGHTEEN YEARS LATER

W hen Stanley tapped on his office door, in that annoying cartoonish pattern that the managing partner thought was so damn funny, Luke knew nothing good was going to come from it.

"Hey there, big guy." Stanley leaned his shoulder on the door jamb. "Virtus Templum has called a meeting for this morning. I guess the old man is stepping away from the project and there's a new lead on their end." One look at Luke's expression and Stanley rushed to continue. "Shouldn't be a big deal. The whole project is still young enough that if they want to make a few little design changes it won't be a big deal."

A string of inventive curses ran though Luke's head like the sound check at a death metal concert. He clenched his jaw. "I'm in the middle of something."

"I'm sure you are." Stanley took a step into Luke's sanctuary and peered at what he was working on. "The Veritas Templum building will win you and our firm many awards. But that'll never happen if the project is never built because no one took the meeting and the client chose another architect." Stanley's expression morphed from jovial to no nonsense in the span of a heartbeat. "Put on your happy face and toddle out there. No happy face? Pretend until we can have Jeb order you one from Amazon. Look, no one else is available and, don't forget, this is supposed to be your—what did you call it—magnum opus? Let me be clear. The partners expect you to pull this off."

The men stared at each other for a long beat. Luke worked to subdue his temper. Stanley no doubt thought his position in their company meant he could push Luke around. Luke took quick inventory of the stakes at hand and knew he had to suck it up.

Luke blinked and relaxed his jaw. "What time?"

The smile returned on Stanley's face, and it was almost like he hadn't just left a threat hanging out there. Luke had heard the people around the office refer to Stanley during one of his fits as "being Satan," but he wasn't. Not even close. Nevertheless, the man was the managing partner and not to be ignored. "Ten. Big conference room. I understand their whole team is coming in."

He stood up and turned to his superior. "Fine."

"Oh, shit. I forgot. If they ask you about that"—he gestured to Luke's face as they turned to the door—"tell them you were rescuing babies from a burning building or something."

Looser jaw, Luke. "I'll take care of it."

Checking his watch showed he had half an hour. There was nothing he could do about his face, but he did pull a tie out of his bottom desk drawer as a nod to corporate propriety. It was a hideous brown silk with some wretched, red artsy-swirling design. It looked like a blood clot.

Jebediah, his "assistant," appeared at his elbow with the notes from the last meeting with the previous client team. Luke browsed them, and annoyance suffused his brain. These were his designs. He knew them better than anyone else. Sure, they were based off the wants and needs of the client, but the real beauty was all his inspiration. From his experience, client meetings only fucked things up, and a new team on this project sure as hell guaranteed it. A bunch of hundred-dollar haircuts coming in with some half-baked scheme that would require hours reworking the simple elegance of what he'd created. This was the design that was supposed to come up anytime someone googled his name. The picture on his Wikipedia page. His Fallingwater.

It wasn't just the imposition of this meeting that put Luke on edge

—or his arrogance, though his work was impeccable just as it was. It was also that Luke knew he was terrible at dealing with people. Usually he didn't care, but now, the idea of risking all that he'd created on his ability to appease an idiot filled his stomach with acid.

His assistant popped up in his eye line again. "I've pulled a couple of ties for you to choose from," he said. The ties in question lay draped across his forearm like he was a sommelier presenting a fine wine, not a denizen of hell disguised as a foppish, twenty-something assistant presenting fashionable torture devices.

Luke gave his suggestion a raised eyebrow, presented like a warning shot. "I already have a tie."

Jeb was not cowed. He was never cowed. "No, you have something tied around your neck that looks like it was used to mop up a crime scene. These ties"—he swept a graceful hand across the selection like a game show hostess—"are from the Versace collection." Of course he liked Versace; the logo had snakes.

"Get out of my office." Luke delivered the instruction in a low, steady voice that would have alarmed most people. Not Jeb. Nothing alarmed Jeb, the damn gargoyle. It was infuriating.

"All right," he said and turned on his heel. "I'll put them right here in the cabinet should you decide not to embarrass yourself."

Luke ignored him. "Get the presentation cued up in the conference room. And I'll need the specs printed—"

"Right here," Jeb strode confidently back into Luke's office with the information he needed. "I've already printed extras for the other attendees and had them bound and placed around the conference table. Also, I set the thermostat in the room to sixty-seven so it won't be too warm and make you sleepy." The young man paused with an expectant expression. "Do you need to tinkle before everyone arrives?"

"You're fired." Luke tossed the words out there as an angry aside, knowing that they meant nothing. Jeb wasn't going anywhere. No matter how often or loudly he said them, not even when bracketed by curses, there was no way Luke could phrase the words where they'd ever take effect. Jeb had been sent by Luke's father, and Luke would be cursed by his annoying, sycophantic presence forever. Besides, everyone other than Luke thought Jeb was the world's finest assistant. They couldn't see through the facade, past the perfectly creased khakis and crisp oxford button-down, to the twisted visage and polished granite of the lively gargoyle.

The people from Virtus Templum Pharmaceuticals sat at one end of the conference table. There were five of them, four men in pinstripes and one woman in a pale-yellow suit. Luke smeared on a professional smile and shook their hands in introduction. Each of the men gave Luke's black eye an interested glance, but the woman gaped at him before getting control of herself and extending her hand.

"Mia Hatcher. Nice to meet you," she murmured.

For an ice breaker, Luke explained that he'd been boxing earlier in the week and the black eye was evidence that the other guy had a decent jab. The male suits seemed to take this information as an entirely reasonable explanation.

"We should see the other guy, eh?" the one at the head of the table joked. His sideburns seemed…excessive.

"Right," Luke agreed. The truth was, he'd had his ass handed to him. Luke boxed and trained in mixed martial arts because it was a visceral way to deal with the anger that ruled his life. It was an outlet, a way to get through his day-to-day existence without going postal and actually killing someone. Managing his part of the family curse often left him battered and exhausted, which served his purpose beautifully.

"Did you win?" The lady in yellow did not stop staring.

"I didn't lose." On the projection screen, he pulled up the first set of schematics outlining the basic structure of the building. "These are the changes in the lower floors your team had requested at the last meeting."

"You should use cayenne pepper and Vaseline on that bruise. It'll make it fade faster." Sitting between two gentlemen, the woman was small enough to look like a teenager. She smiled at him. Her cheeks dimpled. With brown hair cut just shy of her shoulders and large brown eyes, she reminded him of an anime character.

"I'll take that under advisement."

The glass door to the conference room opened, and Jeb entered with a tray loaded with a fresh carafe of coffee and creamer and sugar.

For the next ten minutes, the meeting progressed like it was supposed to. The clients asked a question that made sense. He explained how his design maintained better air flow. Sideburns nodded in understanding. He relaxed. The whole thing wasn't going as badly as he'd expected.

Then the Disney Princess left the table for the credenza and filled a coffee cup. Luke explained the state-of-the-art ventilation system he'd designed while watching her from the corner of his eye as she doctored it with cream and sugar. Her forehead was screwed up in concentration while she stirred. He tracked her across the room, blowing on her coffee, her forehead still wrinkled up in concentration.

"That sounds really interesting. But I was thinking..." She paused long enough to take a tentative sip.

Ha, and just like that, Luke could feel the click, click, click of the anticipated climb as this meeting turned into a roller coaster.

She continued, "A state of the art ventilation system is certainly nice. But I was thinking that a large courtyard would accomplish the same thing and be much more attractive and beneficial to the employees in the building."

He somehow managed not to snort. "You mean an atrium?" He turned to look at the plans projected on the wall that most definitely did not include an atrium.

"More of a courtyard. One with trees."

"That's fine. When we speak with the landscape architect—"

"Hmmmm." Ms. Hatcher stood with her coffee cup at half mast, staring at the drawings on the projector but not actually seeing them. She had a faraway look in her eye that Luke found dubious. "I was envisioning a courtyard in the middle of the building. Right up the center with balconies all around so the employees have the sense of being in an orchard."

"Like an atrium?" He made an effort to control the annoyance in his voice.

She smiled and drew her focus back in the room, directing it at

Luke. "Yes, but much grander. Like an orchard," she repeated the ridiculous word.

"An orchard? With trees?" Sure, lots of buildings used flora to create the comfortable illusion that you weren't spending your life rotting away in an office building, but he had the sense that she wasn't talking about a couple of trees here.

"An orchard."

"An orchard," he parroted in disbelief. Why not add the gates of heaven at the entrance?

Sideburns chimed in. "Now that's an interesting idea. We should expand on that."

And just like that, the pixie spoke and the meeting went all to hell, and he knew Hell. By the time the meeting finished, he was completely redesigning his previously perfect building with a goddamned orchard right up the middle. He was so annoyed at everyone by the time the clients filed out of the room, every one of them chatting animatedly about atriums, courtyards and trees, that Luke was going to be hard-pressed not to slug Jeb when he saw him next.

Snow White paused at the door and smiled up at him. "Thank you for hearing me out today. I know it's going to require a lot of work on your part, but I think the project will be so much better for it."

Luke forced a smile to cover the seething frustration eddying in his gut. "I'll discuss it with the partners, and we'll see what we can do."

"We'll make another appointment, how about a week from now, to see how you're coming."

"That will be fine."

"Get yourself some cayenne pepper." She gestured up at his face. "It really will help."

At this point, he was probably going to have to go get the shit kicked out of him again just to get his equilibrium back.

CHAPTER THREE

M ick Jagger crooned "Sympathy for the Devil" from Luke's car stereo. Glancing down on the passenger seat, he saw his cousin Ethan's face fill his cell phone screen. He answered at the stop-light. "Hey, man. What's up?"

"Come meet us for a drink."

"Nah." It had been a very long day, and he was in a foul mood. But still, the only people on Earth who would understand were the six other people who shared his curse. "Who is 'us'?"

"What? Are you in the car? It's so damn loud I can barely hear you," Ethan yelled into the receiver like Luke couldn't hear him either.

Luke smiled despite himself. Unlike most of his cousins, Luke did not drive a sleek sports car or a padded luxury sedan. He gave the engine some gas and let the RPMs rise, loving the rumble of the big block engine in the '69 Chevelle Super Sport. The jackass in the Japanese import next to him at the light thought he was signaling a race. He revved up his own motor in response, but it sounded like he was running his exhaust through soup cans. Luke met his gaze and actually laughed at the kid, but he gave him the nod anyway.

"Yeah, I'm in the car. Hang on." The light turned green and Luke smashed his foot on the gas and left the light in a cloud of rubber and high-octane fuel. About even with his rear bumper, the rice burner struggled to keep up with the muscle car, and the Chevelle left him in the dust well before Luke dropped it into third.

God, he loved American heavy metal.

He'd almost forgotten about Ethan until he heard him laughing through the speakers.

"Did you win?" he asked.

"Of course, I fucking won."

"So, are you coming for a beer or what?"

Feeling less surly after the impromptu drag race win, he reconsidered. "Who's there?"

"Me, Benji, and Ashe." Ethan listed off two more of their cousins. Luke knew he'd feel better if he let off some steam with the boys.

"Where are you? I not going to some stupid frou-frou bar." He was not in any kind of mood to deal with prissy men and haughty women tonight.

"We're at Jugheads. Get your ornery ass over here and I'll buy the first round."

Luke turned left. "Give me twenty minutes to change my clothes."

"Thata boy," Ethan said and hung up.

Half an hour later, wearing worn Levi's, a favorite T-shirt, and boots, he parked the Chevelle next to Ethan's matte black Bugatti Chiron. The lot had a smattering of other cars and a collection of Harley Davidsons and Indian motorcycles. He could hear the band playing some old Bob Seger tune, "Night Moves," it sounded like, and he felt the grip of his tempestuous nature ease back. Relax. He was glad he'd come; this was just what he needed to settle his soul.

He swung open the door and was met with the aroma of stale beer and French fries.

"Hey, Dwayne," he greeted the bouncer, a behemoth of a man somewhere over three hundred pounds with an old ratty biker ponytail and scraggly beard that hid a frequent grin. "How you been, man?" They grasped each other's forearms and pulled in the top half of their bodies for a quick guy hug.

"Not too bad," Dwayne answered and waved away the five-dollar bill Luke offered for the cover charge. "You're good. The boys are in the back." He gestured with his head towards the far room where the pool tables were.

Striding through the crowd, he saluted the bartenders, two on for a Friday night, and nodded to a couple of other regulars he knew.

His cousins had already grabbed a pool table and a game was in progress. Ethan was talking cars with another guy while Benji lined up his shot, which hit off the far rail and easily kissed the ten-ball into the corner pocket. Benji was the best pool player he'd ever known. For a person who never did much of anything, the few things Benji participated in he did extremely well.

"Hey." Benji looked up from his position bent over the pool table. "Long time, no see."

Benji had just come home from almost a year abroad. Something to do with painting or sculpting or something while touring Italy. Their temperaments couldn't be further afield of each other. Luke was a Doberman pinscher where Benji was a basset hound. Luke had struggled with his volatile personality since he was ten years old and the cousins were indoctrinated into the family curse. Benji probably had his own demons to battle, but Luke thought being saddled with Sloth was a hell of a lot easier on a person than Wrath was.

His cousin mastered another complicated shot, dropping the six and fourteen balls in opposite pockets. "How have you been? I guess from the looks on your face you've been having some trouble coping."

Luke shrugged and touched the bruise under his eye. "Nah, this actually helps, believe it or not." He asked the waitress for a beer. "I do this every couple of months"—he indicated boxing by throwing a couple of shadow punches—"and then I can control it much better. Or at least it doesn't feel so much like it controls me, ya know?"

Benji nodded and cast his attention back to the two ball.

"What about you? What were you up to in Italy? Italy, right? Pretty women? Fast cars? All the spaghetti you can eat?"

The twelve-ball crashed into the far corner pocket. "Yeah, there were some pretty women. Fast cars aren't really my thing. Food was good, though." Benji straightened and leaned a blue jean-clad hip against the table while he chalked up his cue. "Toured a lot of museums. That's what I went for. To study art."

Ethan ambled up with four shot glasses full of amber liquid clinking together in his hands. "Did he tell you about how he spent all those weeks in the Vatican? Never burst into flames, not even once. That's probably a sign, huh?" he said with a hearty laugh. He passed one handful of glasses to Luke and Benji before looking around. "Where's Ashe?"

Benji rolled his eyes and tossed his head in the direction of the bathrooms. At that moment, Asher emerged from the dark corridor with his arm around a gorgeous, giggly woman. Typical. Fucking Asher. The two paused and their cousin pulled the girl in close to whisper something in her ear which caused her eyes to slide closed and her lips to part. Then he kissed her, one hand at the nape of her neck, the other pressing in at the small of her back. Sweet Jesus, the man was like a walking chick-flick hard-on.

The kiss finally ended, and the girl walked away with a grin on her face and a hip swinging swagger that implied promise.

Asher turned towards the three of them. "Is one of those for me?" he asked, indicating the shot glasses in Ethan's hand.

"Yeah." Ethan shoved one at him. "I thought this was a guy night."

"It is." Ash's expression was completely innocent. "Oh, you thought Lisa… No, man, I didn't do that." Ethan's eye roll implied that he didn't believe him. "No, really. I didn't do that. I didn't use the *push*. I can't help being this fuckable all on my own." Then Asher glanced at the pool table, "Damn, did you already run the table, Benji? Fine, rack 'em up again and let Luke have a go at you, fucking pool shark."

"Wait," Ethan demanded and raised his glass. "Four of the Seven."

They joined the salute and clinked glasses. Benji kept running the table, five more games, until Ethan and Luke demanded that he bow out.

"It's not like we're still out hustling like we're fifteen anymore. You sit and drink," Luke demanded, taking away his pool cue and shoving him towards a stool.

"Tell us about the beautiful Italian women." Asher nudged Benji in the shoulder.

Benji turned on him with a look of disbelief. "Surely you've had plenty of Italian women. What the hell do you expect an amateur like me to tell Lust that you don't already know?"

Ethan guffawed, spilling some whiskey neat over the rim of his highball. Luke broke the triangle of billiards balls, and they scattered across the table. Two stripes and a solid disappeared in the corner pockets.

"Now hold on," Luke said, leaning on his cue. "I wouldn't mind a quick rundown of your Italian festivities."

Asher grinned and did that stupid clichéd thing where he kissed his fingertips and then popped open his hand. "I. Am. Telling you," he started, "Italian women smell better than anyone else. Maybe it's all the basil and garlic, I don't know. But when you nuzzle in that great spot right at the nape of their neck and their hair falls around your face. Man." He groaned.

Shaking his head, Benji took a big gulp from his longneck bottle. "You're ridiculous."

"Or maybe it's the Sicilian sun. It toasts their skin to perfection and boosts the aroma of the Mediterranean."

Luke lined up his next shot. "Well, if that's the case, then Greek women would smell just as good since they're in the Mediterranean, too."

"I can speak to that," Ethan insisted. "I dated a girl from Greece. She smelled fucking fantastic."

Unbidden, Luke wondered what Mia-the-princess smelled like. Where the hell had that thought come from? She probably smelled like office. Then from somewhere in the back of his brain, the answer came to him; she smelled like fields, warm fruit, a soft breeze.

He blinked twice and felt vaguely light-headed.

"Dude?" Ethan asked with a raised eyebrow. "All right?"

He scoffed. "Sure."

Over the next several hours, they drank and got worse at eight-ball instead of better while they debated the lure of temptresses from around the globe. It was never decided which ones smelled the best. Or which ones had the softest skin. Or—when by the time they'd gone through four rounds of shots and the conversation had disintegrated to raunchier levels—which ones gave the best blow jobs.

By this time, Luke was feeling more relaxed than he had in weeks. Even better than he had right after the last MMA match. Hanging with his cousins, even when it was only a few of them and not all seven, when they got together, they connected on an elemental level and it eased their torment. None of them understood it. Not even their fathers could explain it, but it had been like that for them a generation before as well, and the generation before that, for as long as there had been generations of humans.

Always seven first-born sons, born the same year, each signifying one of the Seven Deadly Sins until the ceremony where the Devil of their generation would be chosen. And then they'd gift the curse to their sons. As the untold generations before them had done.

Luke propped his contented, drunk ass on a stool and put his elbows on the little round table. Ethan and Benji, drunkenly giggling about something, headed down the hall to hit the facilities. While Asher went to talk to the band to see if they'd play some Stones or AC/DC, Luke surveyed the bar. His attention was drawn to one particular guy who had his hand on the waitress's ass. He watched the scene play out with interest. A woman Luke could only suppose was the man's girlfriend spied them and marched over to the table. The waitress had the good sense to depart with alacrity, but it was too late. The girlfriend had already seen, and the beginnings of an argument surged forward. The man was on his feet now, towering above his girlfriend.

Ashe sidled up next to Luke and took a sip of his beer. "What's goin' on?"

Luke gave a brief rundown. When the woman burst into tears, Luke had to hold Asher back. "Your vibe is only going to make the situation worse," Luke assured him.

The girlfriend yelled something at the man and turned on her heel in a huff, preparing to storm away. The dude grabbed her by the arm and wrenched her back toward him with such force that she teetered on her heels. She couldn't even gain her balance before he was jerking her arm like a rag doll and screaming in her face. The argument escalated so quickly, her friends seemed unprepared to assist.

WRATH

"That's enough," Ashe announced, making to intervene, but Luke held him back again.

"Wait," Luke told him.

Asher threw up his hands in frustration. "What the hell are you—oh." Ashe turned back to the argument and waited to see how it would play out.

Luke concentrated on the girl, training his gaze on her, focused on her entirely. The pressure inside him burgeoned, enmity rose in him like bile until he pushed a bubble-sized amount of fury to her. Instantly her head came up and her expression changed. She twisted free of the man and turned on him in a rage. Filled with only the smallest amount of Luke's venom, she was like a Valkyrie.

But like many times Luke gave a push, especially when he was inebriated, the wrath wasn't contained. It was only seconds before the poisonous essence was everywhere, like a toxic spill. That corner of the bar at least was rapidly growing into its very own Chernobyl, and it would only be moments before the whole bar was reeking with it.

Which was why Luke hardly ever gave a *push*. This was why he ate the poison instead of distributing it far and wide as previous ancestors had done. This was why he so often took a beating in the ring—to find a modicum of relief.

About the time Ethan and Benji emerged from the bathroom, the brawl was in full swing.

"Oh no!" Ethan exclaimed. "Luke, what did you do?"

There was only one way to get rid of the rest of the sludge that boiled inside him. Luke shrugged and waded into the fray.

Hours later, the four of them sat in a cell at the county lock up with the rest of the bloodied brawlers.

Asher held the corner of his shirt to this forehead to stop the bleeding, but he still had a grin on his face. "It's been a long time since one of our nights out ended like this."

Benji grinned back at his cousin, then winced and gingerly touched his swollen lip. "I missed you guys. None of this ever happened at the Vatican."

Luke sat against the block wall with his arm in a makeshift sling.

He laughed. "This might actually be the first time I've ever dislocated a shoulder."

"No." Ethan shook his head. "Remember that time in Milwaukee?"

"Right." Luke nodded. "You look good with stitches."

"Dashing, right?"

"Totally."

An officer came around the corner. "Mephistos," he called out. "All of you. Your rides are here."

The lobby of the police station seemed smaller with four gargoyles waiting patiently. Clearly acting as the spokesmen, Jeb stepped forward. "Well, look at you."

Not even Jeb could annoy away Luke's good spirits.

Ethan's servant wore the livery of an English butler. He handed his master a clean, perfectly folded shirt. "Sir. I've taken the liberty."

"Thanks Mordecai. How'd you ever guess?"

"History suggested you might need one, sir."

Asher's spy had the guise of a hot woman, because of course his would be. She brought him coffee. And Benji's keeper, who looked and acted like a kindergarten teacher, gave him a big hug when he emerged.

And Luke was saddled with the bossy, gay assistant.

Jeb looked him over with a pursed-lipped expression of disapproval. "Did you have fun?"

Luke answered with a petulant pout. "As a matter of fact."

"You know you could have all taken care of this on your own. A little *push* from Benjamin and maybe a tweak from Asher and all of this would have gone away without dragging us all away from our own Friday night plans."

"I don't see a clean shirt or coffee or anything nice."

"Oh, for God's sake," Jeb launched himself at Luke and wrapped his granite arms around him and squeezed. He patted his back none too gently. "Better? Is this what you really need from me tonight? Really?"

The stone embrace was unmovable, and Luke was forced to stand there looking like an idiot. "All right, fine. I don't want a hug."

"Um-hmm." Jeb withdrew and the pursed-lip expression was

back. "You don't care about your clothes and it's too late for coffee. Besides, I'm angry at you for messing up my evening. I did have plans, you know, and bailing you needlessly out of jail wasn't part of them."

"Yeah." Luke rolled his eyes. "But I like it when you do it."

Mollified, Jeb linked his arm through Luke's and walked him out of the police station. "You're forgiven. Now, let's go get some pancakes because I know that's what you really need."

HEAVEN

THE CURSE

Once she'd discovered the fiercely guarded antiquities chambers in the very furthest corner of the massive Library of Heaven, Juliet concentrated on getting inside. The youthful angel puttered around in the stacks and pretended to peruse ancient Egyptian and Sanskrit documents, but there had always been one of the armor-wearing Authorities on patrol standing nearby. They were forbidding and stern, standing guard with gleaming shields and helmets. Their spears seemed a bit of overkill to Juliet considering that they were in Heaven, after all, but what did she know? Here she was plotting to go where she wasn't allowed. For all she knew, there were lots of Third Sphere angels just like her jockeying to get into places they didn't belong.

She'd had already gobbled up the sacred texts in the regular part of the celestial library, reading some of them more than once. There wasn't a lot to do in Heaven. It wasn't what a person had been led to expect. The library meant she hadn't been bored exactly. Juliet loved to read and, once she'd discovered the ancient collections, she really was in paradise. All the information the immortals could ever want to recall was there at their fingertips. Juliet started with the most recent documents, recent being a relative term when one was talking about the eons of time since creation. She'd browsed the censuses but they, like the reams and reams of parchment relating to the arrival of humans to Heaven and the assignment of angels to choirs, was dizzying.

There were shelves and shelves of decrees and proclamations and edicts. It seemed the angels found much to comment on. The section regarding Rome alone was colossal. Most of these Juliet found mind-numbingly dull. In deeper confines, she turned giddy when she discovered what appeared to be the transcript from the Burning Bush and notes on the actual Commandments. It seemed like there might have been an eleventh. She was going to have to find someone to ask, but the Authorities who ran the library were very intimidating.

She was fascinated by the inventories labeled Livestock, and Creeping Things, and Beasts of the Earth. There were copious, boring notes from when angels visited the humans. These were few and far between these days, as God frowned on the angels making appearances anymore. It seemed like things got out of hand pretty quickly. All angelic/mortal meetings were very highly regulated by the Dominions. Once Juliet asked if she could visit Earth and was given an enormous application packet to complete just for a mere twenty second drop-in that didn't even include talking. Juliet had given up. It was too daunting. Besides, what the heck was she going to say anyway? Heaven's nice, but bring a sweater for the evenings?

Still, when she was alive, tabloids had run a lot of sensational stories about angels appearing and talking to people. One tiny old Basque lady who lived next door from Juliet's parent's house swore on a stack of bibles that an angel had appeared in her kitchen and warned her of a train wreck. It didn't matter that no trains ever actually wrecked. Mrs. Arizmendi said it was because she'd convinced her husband to take the bus into work that day. Juliet wondered if her neighbor was in Heaven and what she did with her time up here.

Fortunately, Juliet had an eternity to wait for her opening to sneak into the antiquities room. She had to be patient. It wasn't like she could start a fire as a diversion or something. So she waited for her moment and, when it finally arrived in the form of a split second when the sentry was distracted by a kerfuffle outside that involved a tremendous amount of barking, she skittered past him and through the door in a blur.

This section of the library was more than ancient. Antediluvian certainly, older than time likely. Her fingers wiggled with excitement at the prospect of reading first accounts of God and his proclamations. The quest for knowledge thrummed through her in rapturous delight. She went to the furthest corner and selected the first scroll from the highest shelf.

The document was so ancient the velum it was written on crumbled around the edges when she unrolled it. The ink glimmered on the page like a living thing, purring with an enchanted pulse, the silvery whorls and swoops from the celestial quill breathing on the paper. Holding it made her fingertips tingle, as if cradling the document in her hands lent the merest suggestion of the power of God himself. She unfurled it slowly with reverence and awe.

The Curse

Lucifer wandered the garden looking for her. He'd seen her for the first time days before, wading hip-deep in cool spring water. Although he knew his father wouldn't like it, he stayed to watch her swim. The woman was lovelier than anything else in creation. From the shade of a tree, the angel spied as she dove under only to break the glassy surface with her face lifted to the sun. She swam with grace, her supple limbs stroking lazily across the lake only to rise at the base of a waterfall to let the water tumble over her. Humming with contentment, she allowed the clear water to sluice across her skin and run in rivulets down her breasts and her long legs. Lucifer felt stirrings. A need he did not recognize burgeoned in his chest and low in his belly, so he slunk further into the shadows and watched her, fascinated. Captivated by her beauty and innocence, he couldn't stay away from her.

Rachel.

Her name was Rachel, the daughter of the first man and woman. Along with her parents and brothers, she had the run of the garden.

When he found her that morning, she lazed on a small rise in a sun-soaked meadow surrounded by furry creatures and lazy blue flowers.

This would be the day. He would speak to her today. He must.

Unfurling his wings, he strained to stretch them to maximum effect. As he approached her, he allowed the feathers to trail over the flowers, knowing he looked magnificent. Certain of his masculine beauty and angelic perfection, his belly was no less filled with sharp apprehension when she sat up and noticed his arrival.

"An angel," she said in an awed whisper. Her crystal blue gaze explored him, taking in the glory of his wings, his face, his body.

Lucifer fluttered his wings ever so slightly, setting the wind to whiffle through his pearl-white feathers.

"I am Lucifer." He spoke the words like a proclamation, as if God himself had asked him to deliver the message, but Father had not, and wouldn't approve of this meeting.

She smiled, and his heart beat faster. "I am Rachel."

"I know who you are."

Her gaze trailed across his wings in fascination. "May..." She paused for a long heartbeat while Lucifer held his breath, waiting for her to continue. Finally, she pulled her gaze back to his face. "May I touch your wings?"

He exhaled in a heavy rush. He moved to stand taller, expand his chest deeper, push his shoulders out wider. "Of course."

She wasn't tentative. Her bare feet padded across the grass until she stood directly in front of him. She offered him a fistful of posies to free up her hands. Reaching near his elbow, she touched the rounded covert feathers, allowing her fingertips to drift along with their pattern. Lucifer tried to remain impassive even while he watched her expression move from curiosity to enthrallment. She reached up on her tiptoes to smooth her palm along the very top nearest his shoulder and a frission of euphoria rocked through him. He flexed his wings, almost an involuntary reflex to the pleasure her fingers brought him, and she gasped in wonderment. She followed the path of his wing to the ruffled primary feathers and then ducked underneath and continued her exploration from the back.

Lucifer closed his eyes and luxuriated in the sensation of her caress.

Skittering across the secondary feathers, she arrived at the space where his back was bare. He moaned softly when her fingers brushed the skin of his back before continuing on their journey across his left wing.

"I wish God had given me wings," she said once she came to stand before him again.

His hand rose to her face almost on its own, his need to touch her was so great. "Instead He made you the most beautiful being in all of His creation."

She smiled up at him and, impossibly, she was even more exquisite. Lucifer tucked a perfectly formed flower behind her ear. A flower that paled in comparison to his beautiful Rachel.

He found her in the same meadow the next day and the next. For weeks they met there or by the stream and rejoiced in being together.

"What does it feel like to fly?" she asked, staring up at the sky. She lay next to him in the midday sun, her body lazing across the feathers of his outstretched wings.

"Weightless," he said, and laced his fingers with hers.

"It must be wonderful."

It was. Lucifer loved flying—it was further proof of his divinity.

She turned her face towards his and asked, "How high can you go?"

"All the way to Heaven."

Her sigh was filled with wonder as she turned back to the sky. "What do the clouds feel like?"

Lucifer laughed. "I'll show you someday."

She rose to her knees, taking his hand in both of hers. "Will you?" She was breathy and wide-eyed. "I would love to fly with you."

"You won't be afraid?" he teased. "Being so high?"

Her eyebrows gathered and her forehead wrinkled. "You would never hurt me."

She sounded so certain, her faith in him, in his power, in his love. A rush of strength coursed through him, suffusing him with masculine vigor and potency.

He pulled her to her feet. "Put your arms around my neck," he instructed, and wrapped his own around her waist, pulling her naked curves flush with his body. Pleased with her squeal of pleasure when he unfurled his wings and pushed off from the ground, it was pure arrogance and a desire to further impress her that sent them streaking straight up to the clouds. She clung to him and grinned with joy. Beating his wings with angelic prowess, he spun them through clouds with air as soft as rabbit down. He pushed them higher to where the atmosphere grew thin, and then with a lazy roll, he turned them back to Earth. He flew low enough that Rachel could touch the tops of the trees with her fingertips. They skipped over the sea, his feathers brushing the *waves and splashing them with briny mist. They joined a flock of geese and passed through a kaleidoscope of butterflies.*

He enjoyed showing off. It was exhilarating. He was invincible when he was with her.

All the while, Rachel held on to him, trusting him with her life.

When they finally alit back in their meadow and Lucifer unwrapped his arms from her waist, she didn't let go.

"I knew it would be wonderful," she said. Her eyes sparkled with joy. "You're wonderful. Thank you."

Then she stretched on her toes and she kissed him. Soft lips and warm body in his arms. Lucifer's heart swelled. He pressed her softness against the hardness of his body and took her mouth. There, in their meadow, they explored each other's bodies and gave themselves to each other. Her declarations of love were a sermon to his soul. A revelation. An epiphany.

God's fury was more ferocious than Lucifer could have ever predicted.

"It is forbidden," He raged.

"I love her," Lucifer explained, but it was to no avail. God would not listen to explanations.

"It is forbidden." The final word on the matter was spoken, but Lucifer would not listen. Michael and Raphael, his archangel brethren, extolled his foolishness, but he would not heed their warnings and dire predictions either.

He flew down to her, and though Rachel was afraid of His wrath, her love for the angel was greater. They would leave the garden to be together. Lucifer would be her god now, confident that his divinity could sustain them.

But God saw their plan. Lucifer was banished from Heaven for the sin of his pride, sent to the underworld, to languish in the kingdom of the dead. Lucifer would be the king of all the sinners.

Rachel was inconsolable. God looked to the youngest of his glorious creations with a hardened heart.

"Please let me go with him," she begged. "I cannot live without him." She clung to her angel, her lover. "I'll give anything."

"Would you give your soul, my daughter? Would you sell your soul for this betrayer?"

"Every day," she professed through her tears.

"You'll give up everything for him? To never come home? To never come to my kingdom of Heaven?"

"I love him."

GOD'S FURY at Lucifer's betrayal and Rachel's faithlessness was insurmountable. No amount of pleading from Adam and Eve could persuade him. Lucifer's brothers appealed to their father, but it did no good.

Lucifer and Rachel were cast out. He wrapped his arms around his beloved, the woman who gave up everything for their love, and ferried them both to Hell where Lucifer's extravagant wings began to turn black, ebony starting at the tips, fading to gray, and eventually white at the top.

In his bitterness, Lucifer disguised himself as a snake and convinced Eve to eat the forbidden fruit, forcing God to punish his favorite children as well. If Rachel could not have the Garden, then no one would.

Lucifer did not think it possible that God's anger could grow, but once word came to him that Rachel had given birth to sons, his fury was indomitable. The Archangel Michael was sent to retrieve the children. The warrior angel beat back Hell's demons to take seven babies from Rachel's breast and deliver God's curse.

"Lucifer shall rule Hell and all of its denizens until his children reach adulthood. Then one shall descend and rule the underworld." Michael's voice thundered with the word of God. "Each generation shall give one male heir to rule Hell infinium. Lucifer shall ascend from Hell to spend the rest of his days in a cage of his own making, alone, separated from the woman he loves." The Heavenly Host wailed in misery, but Michael continued. "Rachel, the soulless mortal woman, is to remain in hell for all eternity, tormented without the angel she loves or the sons they made against Father's law."

Lucifer raged against the chains that bound him away. His gorgeous wings morphed darker as a reflection of his misery and fury. The Arch Angels wept fruitlessly at their brother's torment.

"We shall speak of this no more," Michael's voice of God declared.

Amen.

JULIET READ the timeless story of love and loss and sobbed, and then she read it again. Her young heart broke for the separated lovers and the anguish of a mother losing her children. This story was more wrenching than anything Shakespeare ever wrote, and this one was true. Or so she assumed. But how was it that no one knew about it? Okay, so it said at the end that God didn't want it spoken of again, but it seemed unreal that no one actually had.

People were terrible secret keepers. She knew because Charlene Butler had blurted Juliet's whole secret about her crush for Tommy Carmichael all over the sophomore class even after Charlene had sworn she wouldn't tell a soul. Everyone knew by third period. Everyone. How did literally no one know about Lucifer and Rachel? Was she still down there? Was Lucifer still up here?

Juliet pined to know more.

CHAPTER FOUR

Jeb bustled around Luke's office, straightening stacks of paper, adjusting the blinds. "That cute boy from accounting called two more times today. I can't take care of that stuff for you unless you give me your receipts."

Luke grunted. Accounting always got their underwear in a bunch when Luke didn't turn in his expense reports every month. Jeb would harass him endlessly about it, but Luke suspected his assistant loved taking the calls because then he could flirt on the phone with the accounting guy. Otherwise, Jeb would simply steal his wallet and turn in the reports himself.

He rubbed both thumbs against his temples and tuned out the babbling. The damned atrium had been retrofitted into Luke's design. It hadn't been easy. Load bearing beams had to be moved, the plumbing adjusted, and the schematics for the electrical systems had been a nightmare. He pulled up the three-dimensional view and set it to spin on the screen where it twirled like a concrete tornado. It wasn't what his original vision had been, but Luke could accept that the change didn't ruin it.

"Are you listening to me?" Jeb stood in the doorway, his arms crossed in irritation.

"I never listen to you." Luke closed the file and shut his laptop, then closed his eyes and rolled his neck to get the kinks out.

"I said," the voice closer now, "that I packed your iPad in your briefcase so you can show off the changes."

Strong fingers kneaded the tendons of Luke's neck. Luke jerked upright and swatted at Jeb's hands.

"Stop it. I can fix this. If you'd let me schedule you regular massages, you wouldn't get so knotted up."

Luke relented only because Jeb's granite-strong fingers really were amazingly talented. He allowed his head to be turned and manipulated and just when he was lulled into near bliss—*crack* —Jeb twisted Luke's head with one hand on his chin. It was terrifying but already his headache was loosening its grip.

Luke rolled his shoulders and moved his upper body like he had a bobblehead. "That actually feels good."

"It's my pleasure." Jeb patted both shoulders before moving away. "As I was saying, the iPad is in your briefcase. Don't forget to keep your receipts so you *can give them to me* in the morning. Now you promise me that you'll call an Uber if you drink too much."

He stopped pivoting his head and narrowed his eyes at his assistant. "What are you talking about?"

The smile didn't fool him. He knew that Jeb got a thrill every time he got to make Luke do something he didn't want to do.

"Your meeting with Mia Hatcher. It's tonight. Dinner meeting at Fletcher's." When Luke didn't register any hint that he recalled he had a meeting after work, Jeb continued, his tone altered so now it sounded like he was lecturing a petulant child. "Don't act like I never told you about it, Mr. Crabby. I've mentioned it twice; once on Tuesday after I set the meeting and this morning when I brought your coffee." He paused to look Luke up and down with one side of his mouth twisted in an appraising expression. "I guess since it's an after-hours meeting, you can get away with no tie"—he wiggled his fingers at what Luke was wearing—"but that polo shirt won't do."

He yanked open the bottom drawer of a two-drawer filing cabinet to expose an entire wardrobe Luke hadn't even known was in there. He stood to look at what appeared to be the men's section of Barney's department store. Jeb pulled out a freshly ironed, light-blue oxford and gave it a cursory shake. "Here put this on."

Instead, Luke popped the button on his jeans and tucked the tails of the red knit shirt into his pants. "I'm not changing my clothes."

Jeb's expression suggested he disagreed. "Yes, you are. I can't do anything about your attitude, but I will make you look presentable. You cannot, *cannot*, leave this office with a soy sauce stain on your shirt. Don't think I won't tackle you before you get to the elevator."

Soy sauce? He peered down and grimaced where he'd dribbled on himself during lunch. Shit. No, he couldn't go out like this, but he hated to give Jeb the win. "You have a white shirt in there instead?"

"I do, but you're not wearing white tonight." Jeb looked pointedly at Luke's dirty shirt and thrust the blue shirt at him again. "You're careless with your sauces and I'm trying to continue our good impression here. This one looks better with your eyes. You could be very handsome if you'd let me try."

Luke could not have cared less about being handsome at a business meeting. Or at any meeting. It wasn't even in his top five things to care about. Honestly, he wasn't even sure if there were five things he regarded highly enough to concern himself with on a day-to-day basis. He liked his job because he was good at it. He tolerated his cat, a mean Persian called Claw whose scowly expression matched Luke's most of the time. He was tight with his cousins, but they were bound by blood and the family curse, so that wasn't even by choice. He hated his father and he hated Jeb. Those were the only things he could think of and that wasn't even five.

Luke was taking too long, so Jeb approached and reached out as if he was going to assist him in the removal of his shirt. Luke growled. Jeb pursed his lips and raised an eyebrow. Then he wiggled the shirt impatiently. Luke whipped the polo over his head and threw it on the floor.

"There you go," Jeb smiled approvingly. "Leave the top two undone. You have a nice throat."

"Who says things like that? 'You have a nice throat'? What the hell does that even mean?" He did leave the buttons undone.

"I do. There are others in the Legion who think so, too."

"What?"

Now Jeb was squatting on the floor untying Luke's cross trainers. "Sure. They're always looking for gossip about the Seven. About you especially."

Luke didn't like the idea that his father's pets spent that much time thinking about him. "I catch wind you're gossiping about me, you're fired."

"Um-hmm." Jeb pulled off the athletic shoes and socks and set tan loafers in front of Luke's feet for him to slide into. He'd never seen them before, but they fit perfectly. One of the many outrageously annoying things about Jeb's perfectionism. "I don't tell them important things."

Luke couldn't imagine what qualified as important things. He never did anything but work and futilely try to get himself killed. It wasn't possible to do himself any lasting damage, at least not until the ceremony, but that didn't stop Luke from trying at every opportunity.

"Excellent," Jeb declared with a swift clap of his hands. "You look great. Very virile with the scruffy beard. I'm making an appointment to get your hair cut next week."

Luke was handed his briefcase and sent out the door in time for the meeting. Jeb had made a reservation in his name, and the *maître'd* told him his party had already arrived. He followed the man through the dining room until he reached a rounded booth.

Mia Hatcher was seated and had a glass of white wine in her hand and a notebook on the table.

"Hello." Luke said, as he slid into the booth opposite her and took a sip from the water glass. "I hope you haven't been waiting long."

"No." She smiled at him. "I just got here."

The waiter showed up and Luke ordered a Seven and Seven, rocks, two lemons.

"That sounded cool. Like a James Bond drink order." She lowered her voice to mimic his, "Seven and seven, rocks. Two lemons."

"I don't have a cool drink order. I don't even really know any drinks. I always just order a Chardonnay 'cause it's safe and sorta sounds like I know what I'm doing."

Luke was still trying to figure out the hierarchy of Virtus

Templum Pharmaceuticals. Her father was well-known, but Mia's name was not one he'd heard before. How did she get to be in charge of this important project? He'd asked his assistant for a rundown of who the players were, but he didn't know any more now than he did two weeks ago. He needed to know who was really in charge over there. Especially if Ms. Hatcher kept up with the arbor bullshit. Jeb was due for a blistering when he saw him next.

She leaned back against the leather upholstery and smiled at him again. Her cheeks dimpled. "How was your week?"

"It was fine. Busy. Working on your requested changes." It had been a damned nightmare. A lot of late nights. The best thing he could say about it was at least it was interesting work. Foolish, but a challenge.

"I'm excited." Damned if she didn't seem genuinely so. Tonight, she looked like Minnie Mouse complete with a black and red polka dot dress.

"Well then, let's order and then I'll show you what I've come up with."

"I've not been here in ages," the lady with the dimples said from behind her menu. "What do you recommend?"

Luke opened his own menu and stared at it. "Um, the porter house is my favorite. The salmon is good, and I know my cousin likes the cioppino."

"Hmm. Not a big red meat or fish girl. I think I'll have the pasta," she declared and closed the menu.

His drink arrived and Luke downed half of it in one gulp. Mia ordered pasta al pomodoro but asked to substitute angel hair pasta for the spaghetti and inquired if there were onions in the sauce. When the waiter told her there weren't, she asked if he was sure. He swore, no onions. "I'm allergic," she said as if apologizing. She added a Caesar salad.

Luke got the porterhouse, blue, and tossed in a salad, too. The waiter nodded, seemed to write everything down, told them they'd made excellent choices, and generally acted like a waiter.

"This is the first project I've been lead on. It's the chance I've been waiting for." She beamed at him from across the table. "My father landed a huge new client he needs to babysit, so I inherited the planning committee for the new headquarters."

Aha. Son of a douche waffle. Now this mess made a little more sense. A nepotistic cartoon character was ruining his life.

"Can I see the changes?" Mia asked and indicated the iPad with some excitement.

"Right." Luke brought up the renderings with the illustrated cross section of the building.

She pinched the screen and made the plans zoom in. "See, doesn't that make the whole thing nicer?"

Luke was only willing to admit that it didn't make it worse. Instead, he nodded and forced a smile.

She reviewed the changes in silence for a moment while Luke watched her and struggled to maintain a nonviolent expression.

"Hmmm," she said. "How much space have you allotted for the courtyard?"

When he described the area's dimensions, she drew her eyebrows together in a frown that looked out of place on her. Before she could vex him with more asinine suggestions, their salads arrived and she was momentarily distracted. After the waiter left, she asked him how long he'd been with his firm. Luke gave her the Reader's Digest version of his resume starting with college and ended with joining the firm.

"My team has really taken the state-of-the-art building to the next level. I'm sure you've heard of smart phones. I'm talking about smart office building. The technology is so exciting. Cognitive computers can run a building, controlling everything from regulating the temperature based on how many people are in a room to changing the art on the walls depending on who's present. Imagine an elevator that knows which floor you're going to or a desk that can adjust to your height."

Mia poked at a crouton with her fork. "That sounds a little scary. Like the Terminator or Big Brother or something."

Luke chuckled and then realized she wasn't kidding. "There's so much more. Office buildings that collect rainwater, or ones that create as much energy as they consume. The opportunities are only as endless as your imagination. The innovations are exciting."

This was the kind of stuff that made Luke's heart bubble up with excitement. So few people got the same kind of buzz from automation like he did.

"My father's very excited about that aspect." She wrinkled her forehead. "But that doesn't sound wonderful to me at all. It sounds cold and impersonal and the very opposite of where I'd want to spend the bulk of my waking hours."

Luke didn't have a defense for that. To him, that sounded like a perfect scenario—days spent doing something he enjoyed with very little human contact.

"I'd like to live in a Norman Rockwell kind of world. My idea of a perfect office building would be like home. There'd be lots of natural light and air." She took a wistful sip of her wine. "Creativity would be inspired by offices and conference rooms with access to a garden. Open office plans where employees can collaborate."

Luke retook possession of his iPad. "You know, the latest studies show that open office plans don't really work."

"Either way, I'd like to work in a building with lots of pet-friendly spaces, and I know other people do, too." She gazed at him expectantly, eyebrows raised as if waiting for him to swoon over her idea.

Swooning was out of the question. Pet friendly? Preposterous. Nothing like walking through dog shit while trying to get to the copier. It took every bit of self-control he possessed not to roll his eyes at her. "I do take a pet to work with me. My assistant is leash trained and has all of his shots."

Her laughter seemed forced. "It's important to me that our office building reflect certain values. Living things have merit. Not everything is made better by technology."

What she said next sent a shiver of terror down his spine.

"Let's get our teams together next week and go over a few other ideas I'd like you to consider."

Before he could ask what the hell she was talking about, the waiter appeared with their dinner and Mia's amusement evolved into dismay when he placed her plate in front of her. "T-bone for the lady and porterhouse for the gentleman. Can I bring you anything else?"

"Well…" Mia began and then faltered. "I ordered the pasta."

The waiter adopted the bored expression they always get when they've decided a customer is going to be a problem. "You ordered the Texas t-bone."

Luke considered Mia as she stared at the giant, bloody steak. Her expression read disgust and maybe even a bit of horror. One glance at the waiter told Luke that the man was too dense to interpret the signs correctly.

"I ordered the pasta." She didn't make eye contact with the waiter, just stared at the slab of meat.

"I'm sorry," the waiter said, but he wasn't. There was no attempt at making the situation right, either. The incompetent asshat turned to walk away, and she was going to let him.

Luke gaped at her. "You're not going to eat that, are you?"

"No. The blood…." Her face took on a green tint as she poked at the side of rice with her fork and prodded a baby carrot.

"Send it back."

"I'm all right. I had my salad – it was pretty big for a side salad. And there's the bread." Her smile was much too bright, and Luke wasn't falling for it.

"This is ridiculous. You're sending that back and you're getting your pasta."

"Don't make a fuss. I'm fine." Gamely, she popped a carrot in her mouth and made a show of chewing. "These are delicious."

"You've got to be kidding me." Heat licked at his throat and filled his stomach with ire. When it became abundantly clear that she wasn't going to stand up for herself, he dropped his hand heavy on the table. First, this crazy woman was changing his perfect plans with a whole lot of hippy-dippy hokum, and he was going to have to suck it up and make all the changes she could come up with or risk losing the project. He was looking at a major step back in his career, and she was too damn timid to send back a steak that made her sick? Tonight might very well be the night his head exploded. He considered giving her a push, just a little one, but thought better of it. Shifting in his seat, he looked around for the waiter. "Hey."

The server caught his eye and Luke bared his teeth in an animalistic show of aggression that passed for a smile. He crooked his finger at him until he changed directions and made his way back towards their table.

"Yes, sir?"

The man was truly an idiot.

"The lady ordered pasta." He pointed at her plate. "Is this pasta?"

"I don't think so, sir."

"Bingo." Luke pointed at his nose. "It is clearly not pasta."

"No, I meant that I don't think she ordered pasta." The fool worked a snotty attitude like the professional-level sphincter cruncher he was.

Mia raised her hand. "This is fine."

Luke turned his glare on her. "It is not fine. You're not going to eat that and we're not going to pay for it either." He aimed his ire back at the server. "Take that crap away and bring her what she ordered."

The waiter pulled out a note pad and looked at it. "My notes say porterhouse, rare." He looked pointedly at the plate in front of Luke. "And T-bone."

"Are you always this inept?"

"Now, Mr. Mephisto—" Mia interjected, but Luke cut her off with a slashing motion of his hand.

"I'm not ine—" Luke cut the waiter off, too.

"Well, the jury's still out on that. But just now, you have the opportunity to prove it to this lady."

The help looked less sure of himself now. "Sir, there's no reason to get mean."

"I think that bloody slab of meat gives me plenty of reasons."

Mia tried again. "It's okay, really."

"She did order the T-bone." The waiter said this to Mia. "You did."

In a burst of bravery, she ventured, "Well, actually…"

Luke waited. He counted five Mississippis to give her the chance to take a stand. When he realized she wasn't going to do it, he narrowed his gaze on her and the rest of the restaurant fell away. He wanted to flood her with rage—the asshole waiter deserved it—but Luke didn't. Instead he *pushed* her a blip, just a drop, of fury and waited for her to go to town on the guy. She blinked her eyes and twitched her nose. Luke leaned back in his chair, ready to watch a massacre. And then...

Nothing.

She clasped her hands together on her lap and pursed her lips together. Luke's jaw dropped open, and he stared at her. The push didn't take. That had never happened before except with the gargoyles and his cousins.

He'd have to figure that out later. Right now, someone needed a beatdown. He lowered his voice and trained a terrifying gaze at the waiter. "Say that she ordered the T-bone one more time. Please. I'm begging you."

The man clapped his mouth shut and whipped the plate of meat off the table so fast blood almost sloshed off the plate. Luke shifted back down into his seat and glanced over at Mia. Her already large eyes were as big as satellite dishes in her face, and her mouth hung slightly open. She did not appear grateful. No, actually, she looked...upset?

"You're welcome," he told her and folded his napkin back into his lap.

She didn't reply. She placed both hands briefly over her cheeks, then fiddled with her own napkin before turning the stem on her wine glass slightly counterclockwise. All of this was accomplished while avoiding eye contact with him. What the hell kind of reaction was this? She clearly didn't want to eat the rare meat, had certainly not ordered it, and wasn't going to do anything about it. Now that he had convinced the server to take care of the mistake, she was acting weirder than normal. Was this because of the *push*?

Luke sighed and searched for something to say that would fill the awkward silence. Topics off the table were clearly restaurants and office buildings. "So, then, do you have any pets?"

Her smile was forced and her tone extra chirpy. "Yes, I do. A rather enormous dog. His name is Godfrey, and he's a Great Dane." But then she visibly relaxed, settling into the topic of conversation that she obviously enjoyed. "Hold on a second. I have pictures." She fished out her phone and flicked her finger across the screen. "Here he is the day I got him, and here he is last summer in the park. Oh, this is one I took this morning."

Luke blinked at the sheer number of pictures that flashed by. What he saw was practically one of his father's Hounds of Hell. He'd bet a hundred dollars the dog outweighed his mistress by twenty-five pounds, if not more. She babbled away, her peace seeming restored. She didn't look at the waiter when he returned with a new plate, this one loaded with pasta and fresh sauce.

"Thank you," she said.

"Better," Luke told the waiter, then picked up his own knife and fork to dive into his steak.

She stirred her food with her fork. "That whole scene was unnecessary, you know."

So a thank-you was completely out of the question, then? She sure as fuck wasn't going to stand up for herself. Someone had to do it. He resisted the urge to say any of these things out loud.

"Enjoy your dinner, Mia."

They ate in silence for a moment while he wondered if he'd be able to manipulate her into dropping all of these insane ideas she had about her building.

She took a sip of her wine. "I like what you've done so far, but it's not big enough. The multi levels you designed are really interesting, but what I really want is double, maybe triple, the dimensions of what you planned out already."

The expensive porterhouse turned to rubber and lay there in on his tongue like a solid mass while he considered the absurdity of what she was requesting.

Gesturing at the design on his iPad, she continued. "I want it big enough for a grove of apple trees."

He chewed. And chewed. "How many is a grove?" He suspected it was more than ten, but it better be less than a hundred. He almost laughed. An entire floor of an office building taken up with trees. What the hell?

38

She smiled down at her plate while she spun noodles on her fork. "Let's start with thirty."

And we better end with thirty. He must have made a noise because she raised an eyebrow in his direction.

"I know you can design this, Mr. Mephisto. I have faith in you." Then she paused for a heartbeat. "However, if *you* don't think you're capable, I'll let my father know and we'll find another firm who is. That is the building I want."

Minnie Mouse got a backbone over trees but not over her dinner order? He didn't understand her at all. But he did understand the threat she was making, and he wasn't going to risk losing the project. Management had made their expectations very clear on that matter.

He should have let her eat the damn bloody steak.

CHAPTER FIVE

H er roommate was on the sofa watching reruns of *Sex and the City* when Mia got home.

"How did it go?" Cassandra asked without looking up from her project. Her current passion was wedding planning, and she was working as an assistant to the most sought-after organizer in the city. Mia gave it six more months before that job lost its bloom and fell to the wayside, along with real estate agent, department store merchandising, and stockbroker.

Mia dropped her purse on the floor, the carryout package on the coffee table, and then flopped herself on the other end of the sofa with a breathy flump. Her puppy Godfrey bounced over to greet her, stopped to inspect the to-go wrappings, and then clambered up onto the cushion and lay his head in her lap. She massaged his floppy Great Dane ears and he grunted.

"Uh-oh." Cassandra set aside the invitations she was stuffing. "I don't even have to take a reading. My spidey sense says it was bad."

"'Cause I'm stupid. I shouldn't let these things bother me this much." She lolled her head back against the cushion.

"Don't be so hard on yourself. What happened?"

She told her best friend about the scene with the waiter and how Luke had been over-bearing. "The whole dinner was tense. I couldn't even eat any of the darn pasta when it finally showed up." She pushed the remains of her dinner with her toe.

Cassie curled her legs underneath her. "So, don't get mad, but devil's advocate, it just sounds like this Luke guy was trying to get you the dinner you ordered, and that the waiter was the real problem."

"Oh, the waiter was a troll, no doubt about it."

"Then maybe he deserved his comeuppance." Cassie shrugged.

Mia sighed. "He definitely did. I wish it was me who gave it to him, but I was so busy freaking out I couldn't. There was this one minute when I was so angry. It was weird. All of a sudden, I was filled with this incredible ferocity. I actually thought I was going to create a scene, but I got control of myself. Still, it was awful. It was like I was at dinner with my dad, and I was seven years old again." She balled up her fist and punched the sofa cushion in a completely ineffective and rather absurd exhibition of anger. Nothing happened except a small puff of dog hair rose and circulated around with the air conditioning. "I'm tired of being such a wimp."

Cassie raised her eyebrows and nodded. "Uh-huh. I'm making tea. Something to settle your stomach." Cassie left Mia, defeated, on the couch, and headed into the kitchen.

"Maybe I need to get back into therapy," Mia said, even though she was already feeling the effects of being home, the quiet calmness that seemed to surround her when she was with best friend and her dog.

The response came from deeper in the house. "Or maybe you need some peppermint tea and some balls."

She flung her head back onto the cushion. "I know. I'm such a loser."

Cassie slapped her hand on the door jamb to the kitchen. "We talked about this. No more defeating language. You, Mia Hatcher, are not a loser. You're an intelligent, witty, and beautiful woman. Say it."

What was Mia thinking? She didn't need to pay a therapist. She had her very own new-age, affirmation-spouting counselor in her best friend. And she was free. Well, not exactly. Mia generally supported the two of them in that she paid the majority of the mort-gage and covered most of the bills. Cassie couldn't manage to get her life in order since college. It was like she simply couldn't figure out what she wanted to be when she grew up and her bachelor's degree in Women's Studies with a minor in French poetry didn't do much to help in the competitive job market, even if it was from an Ivy League university. So, she fluttered around from one fascinating career to the next, leaving when things got dull. Mia didn't care about any of this. Her best friend had been with her through everything for her entire life. Cassie and Mia had a shorthand that was worth more to Mia than any amount of rent could buy.

"Say it, Mia. Repeat after me. I am intelligent and witty and beautiful."

Mia repeated the words—Cassie wouldn't leave her alone until she did—but she didn't do it with any level of enthusiasm.

"Your problem, Millipede, is that you're all kinds of strong when it comes to work, but you can never manage to stand up for yourself when it's personal. It's your dad's fault." Cassie punctuated the air with a pointy index finger. "You'll do anything to please the old fart which manifests itself as perfectionism at work, but then you're a jellyfish when you don't want to offend anyone personally. What I don't understand is why it matters at all if you offend a waiter who screws up your order? What do you care?" The whistle on the tea kettle blasted off like a missile siren, and Cassie left to tend it. She called back over her shoulder, "You're way too damn nice."

How many times had they had this conversation? How many times had she wished that she could be more assertive? How many times had she thought of the perfect thing to say a half an hour or even a day too late? She was tired of caving in and pretending that what she wanted wasn't important.

Mia squished up her dog's face with both hands. "What do you think, Godfrey, my love? Do I just need some balls? You seem to be doing okay without yours and you are plenty assertive."

The dog rolled over on his back, all four feet in the air, and sneezed.

Cassandra emerged with a tray loaded with tea stuffs. "Godfrey is not the one to be taking assertiveness training from. He's terrified of bubble wrap. Seriously, I was doing some therapeutic popping earlier and it scared the shit out of him."

"My poor little pupper," Mia cooed to him in a baby voice. Godfrey sneezed again. She inhaled deeply through her nose and let the agitation fall away.

"Other than the waiter being an asshole, how was everything else? Did he make the changes you wanted?"

"Sort of. The beginning of the meeting went really well actually. He's smart and knows his stuff. He didn't blow off what I asked for. It wasn't enough yet, though, and I sent him back to make some more alterations."

"See, standing up for your building and then you cave over a bloody steak." Cassie shook her head and blew on the surface of her tea. "So next time the creepy Mr. Mephisto goes to steamroll the situation, what are you going to do?"

"He's not creepy." Crazy intense, yeah. Intimidating and fearsome, sure.

"Not creepy?" Cassandra's expression was skeptical. "Really?"

Mia shrugged.

"Let's see." Cassandra set her mug down and opened her laptop. "Shall we start with Google?"

Mia sipped and petted the dog who had dropped off to sleep with his head hanging off the side of the couch and his tongue reaching almost all the way to the floor.

"Oh." Cassie typed some more, then added, "He's not bad to look at, is he?"

Mia did think he was good looking in an overly masculine way. His features were precise and strong, with sharply sculpted lips and deep-set eyes. Both times she'd seen him it had looked like he hadn't shaved in two days. The man was built like a brick wall and his size was overwhelming.

Cassie pecked away at the keyboard some more and then paused while she scrolled along the page. "Did you know he does MMA fighting?"

"Um-hmm. He had a black eye the first time I met him."

Cassie turned her head slowly and with maximum drama. "And you didn't tell me about that? What the heck?"

Mia shrugged and gave her a half grin. "He said he'd gotten it in a boxing match."

Her friend stared at the computer and whistled long and low. "Hello there, Mr. Mephisto."

She turned the laptop to face Mia and she was confronted with a photo of Luke in boxing shorts and nothing else as he marched into the ring. Masculine didn't seem to be enough of a descriptor. The muscles on his chest and arms were rounded and bulging. Every single abdominal muscle was carved into his stomach like clay. A massive red tattoo of the devil stared out from his right pectoral. His expression was fierce.

"Sweet baby Jesus," Cassie said and tapped the screen.

Mia quite agreed.

THE NEXT MORNING, Mia was up early and drinking coffee as the sun came up. One hip leaning on the counter, she watched the sun appear over the top of the orchard and spread a thick blanket of pink and peach and rose across the sky. She was dressed in layers: well-worn jeans, T-shirt, and a sweatshirt under a workman's denim jacket. She was also wearing her rubber gardening boots with flowers and red-hatted gnomes all over them. They'd been a present from Cassie on her birthday and they suited Mia perfectly.

The steam from the brew warmed her face until the bagel popped out of the toaster. Godfrey lifted his head at the sound, but decided it wasn't worth getting up from the rug in front of the stove.

"You're not a morning dog, are you?" Mia asked and nudged him with the toe of her boot. He grunted in response, but that was all the effort he expended. It could have even been a snore. It was fine. He needed to conserve his energy now because when he came with her to the greenhouse and the orchard later, he'd be racing around like a lunatic, barking and chasing anything that would run.

She slathered her bagel with cream cheese and filled a travel mug with more coffee before heading out the back door. Just as she knew he would be, Godfrey was right behind her, already perking up and looking spunky.

He was delighted to jog along beside her when she drove her all-terrain vehicle the short distance to the greenhouse. While her neighborhood did make for a long commute to the city and her office, the enormous lot sizes and the fact that hers abutted farmland made it perfect.

She wanted to check on the tenderest tree clones in her nursery. She needed to make sure the grafts were taking before she brought them out to the orchard. The scion clippings she'd collected from what might well be the last remaining Saxon Priest apple tree on the entire planet had been dry and not as vigorous as she'd hoped.

Godfrey bounded into the nursery ahead of her and dashed off to check the far corners, barking with glee the whole way. He was such a joyful idiot that she couldn't help adoring him.

The plants were lined up in big troughs so she could easily transport them. The grafts were holding well, and it looked like the scion and stock were marrying up as they should. The Sisters would be delighted to hear it.

The Daughters of Eve convent were some of the leading apple detectives in the country. Mia had visited their convent in Washington State, touring their masterful gardens and orchards as part of her undergraduate degree. She had been so influenced by their mission to conserve and protect heirloom plants and vegetables that she had remained a partner in their efforts by offering her skills in micropropagation. The Sisters would send her a lead on a thought-to-be extinct Junaluskee or a Cox Orange Pippin, and Mia would gas up the car and tromp through abandoned orchards and forests to collect scions.

So far, the Sisters' orchards housed 456 varieties of heirloom apples, and Mia was very proud to say that she'd been fundamental in eighteen of them.

She checked the bindings and added some more asphalt compound on a few older projects. Nothing in her life gave her more pleasure than velvety green shoots emerging from a whip she'd nursed into health. She'd always had an affinity for gardening, one she couldn't explain as she certainly didn't have an example to emulate in her parents. Her mother nursed hangovers, not seedlings. And her father had never been in her life often enough for her to know if he appreciated plants or not, even before he moved out and her parents divorced when she was seven.

She was a city kid who did not belong to the 4H or Future Farmers of America, and yet window boxes bloomed under her care.

Cassie had grown up around the corner from Mia, and they'd been bosom buddies since the spring her father left for good. And while they seemed as unlikely a pair as any two girls could be, they'd been inseparable almost immediately. Cassie was a free spirit even then. While Mia twisted her hair in easily manageable braids and wore designer clothes that made her mother happy—or at least avoided her mother's attention—Cassie wore cut-off denim shorts and rock and roll concert T-shirts, her blond hair in wild waves down her back. Cassie danced and twirled through life, giving her opinions so loudly that everyone noticed her, while Mia smiled from the sidelines and apologized to those her friend may have offended.

Spring the year they were nine found Mia planting strawberries in her backyard garden while Cassie composed new jump rope songs. The summer they were twelve, Mia had harvested sunflower seeds while Cassie read aloud from Harry Potter. The year they were sixteen, her friend sunbathed in a bikini and answered the quizzes aloud from Cosmo, while Mia tried grafting roses for the first time.

Now, while Mia watered her newest plants, she remembered the tragic end her roses came to when her mother, drunk and seething from some argument with Mia's father, massacred the bushes in the middle of the night with the hedge trimmers. In the morning, Mia found her mother passed out in the living room with muddy feet. She knew what she'd find before she'd even gone to the yard to look. Her mother destroyed anything Mia loved eventually. Mia said nothing. She didn't even cry. Instead, she threw the clippings in the compost and scrubbed the footprints from the chintz. When her mother sobered up and apologized, Mia told her it was okay, she wasn't mad, she forgave her, because that's what Mia always said.

Bruce Hatcher traveled extensively as a captain of industry, but when he was home he took his daughter to dinner and gave her trinkets from his travels. He bragged that he had a perfect daughter who got perfect grades and never caused him a minute of trouble, and Mia made sure that was always true. Since her mother's good will was so mercurial, she couldn't afford to lose her father's affections as well. Mia took the adage to heart and was seen but not heard.

When they were eighteen, she and Cassie left for Bryn Mawr, where they shared a dorm room all four years. Mia got her degree in agronomy and microbiology, and Cassie tried a little bit of everything. Cassie told her every detail the night she lost her virginity to a hunky football player, and Mia quietly dated an accounting major from Villanova.

Even graduating with excellent grades, Mia couldn't seem to settle into a career. The economy was in turmoil and there simply wasn't employment opportunities that fit her specific area of study. It turned out, her temperament was wholly unsuited for dealing with the politics of a laboratory environment. She floundered.

"I told you that was an absurd degree," her mother had scolded and swirled ice cubes in a highball. "You should have done something useful. Well, you can always marry well."

Before she could really figure what to do with herself, her father made her a place at his firm. She wasn't equipped to tell him no. She'd never intentionally displeased her father in her entire life. Quite the opposite. Mia endeavored to the kind of perfection that made her invisible. Her work wasn't satisfying, but the efforts she put in with the Daughters of Eve and her home nursery filled her soul. She'd harvested three years' worth of heirloom carrots in her home garden and trudged along with her father's firm before she'd inherited the current task of completing the new Veritas Templum Pharmaceuticals headquarters.

And met Luke Mephisto.

Her last meeting with the architect had made her see that maybe she could make the office building of her dreams, a home away from home. Especially if the company's employee's homes had been anything like her own growing up. A place where people could be happy to spend more of their lives than they did with their families. Some of Luke's ideas would dovetail nicely with her own.

She hitched the little wagon trailer to her ATV and checked that her toolbox was stocked with grafting knives and pruning shears. She added some extra electrical tape which was great for binding the trees, tossed in her gloves and some rubbing alcohol, then clipped the latches shut. She nestled a chainsaw alongside the toolbox and hollered for Godfrey to stop rolling in the manure pile.

Heading out to the orchard in the early morning, her dopey dog bounding ahead of her, made her ridiculously happy. There was still dew on the grass and a rosy tint to the sky. Once Godfrey's bull-poop cologne was far enough ahead of her, she breathed deeply the aroma of green and grinned.

Her orchard was her own little slice of heaven.

CHAPTER SIX

"You can see why we need to upgrade our office space," Mia said with a smile as she escorted Luke and Jeb, who'd demanded to accompany Luke, to her office.

Luke glanced around the area as they walked through the outdated corporate offices of Virtus Templum Pharmaceuticals. It looked like every other corporate building. The lobby was fine and, he assumed, tastefully decorated. He glanced over at Jeb, and rethought the tasteful part based on his assistant's sour expression. Catching his eye, Jeb raised his eyebrows, pursed his lips, and crossed his arms.

Once they entered the inner sanctum however, it was clear the company had outgrown their space. Storage boxes lined the halls and people doubled-up in the cubicles.

Mia continued, "We're kind of packed in here like sardines."

"I see." Jeb sniffed and then continued in a stage whisper, "This is a tragedy."

Her laugh was surprisingly throaty, not at all what Luke was expecting. A woman who looked as cute as she did all the time with her flippy little skirts and polka dot sweaters should have a girlish giggle. Mia's sultry laugh sounded like that of a jazz singer.

She swept into her office, gesturing towards a large conference table at the other end of the room. Her office had the long table, her desk and another desk on an opposite wall.

"I just sort of took command of the conference room. I figured several of us in here would take up less room in the long run. This is Jason, my assistant."

Jason waved with the hand that wasn't holding the phone to his ear. Luke ignored Jeb who made some appreciative noises in Jason's general direction.

Jason finished his call and announced, "I'll be back with refreshments."

Jeb dropped Luke's laptop and notebooks on the conference table with alacrity. "I'll help." Jeb linked his arm with Mia's poor unsuspecting assistant, and he chattered away as they left.

While Mia gathered her papers, Luke glanced around the room. There were pictures of past projects on the walls. Luke recognized his company's work in some of them. Like the rest of the office, boxes were stacked in the corners, some of them two rows deep.

"How do you find anything with this filing system?" Luke asked.

"Oh, I don't find anything," she confessed. "If I were to start rummaging around, Jason would have a stroke. He's got a whole system happening over there."

He snorted. "Damn assistants."

"I'll bet you'd be lost without Jeb." She poked his shoulder with the eraser end of a pencil. "He seems to have a pretty good handle on you."

"I fire him at least once a day, but he won't leave."

He hadn't been consciously trying for another of her sexy chuckles, but there it was, tangoing around the room and through his head, and his nether region's reaction to it was unexpected. He turned away and strode towards the table where he selected a seat on the far side, the safe side. Away from her.

Mia grabbed a notebook and claimed the seat opposite him. "I wouldn't want to have to do any of this without Jason. Besides being the world's greatest assistant, he takes excellent care of me."

He avoided her gaze by taking out his laptop and pulling up the plans and specs for this ever-evolving project.

Jason and Jeb returned with a tray of coffee and another of bagels and fruit. Jeb had Mia's assistant jabbering away like long-lost best friends. Jeb was promising to take him to some club or another. Luke rolled his eyes and tried to ignore them.

Placing a mug of what was sure to be deeply complicated coffee in front of Mia, Jason took his seat all while giving Jeb moony eyes.

Jeb also placed a cup in front of Luke and took the spot between him and Jason.

The coffee was black and strong and a little sad. "Why don't you ever give me complicated coffee?" Luke asked Jeb, his voice low.

Tearing his eyes away from his new crush, Jeb raised an eyebrow in Luke's direction. "Do you want complicated coffee? I mean, I'll happily dump in some half and half, maybe a shot of espresso, and shave some roasted hazelnuts over it if that's what you want." He reached for the cup. "Give it and I'll go stir it with a chocolate spoon."

Luke snatched it out of Jeb's reach. "No."

"Um-hmm." His arched brow told him that his assistant had his number and they both knew it. "That's what I thought. Drink your lumberjack coffee." Then in a nicer tone, "I did fix your bagel like you like it." The bagel appeared: plain, sliced in half, one eighth of an inch of cream cheese schmeared on both halves, and then covered in sliced strawberries.

"Great. Thank you." Luke ran a palm down the front of his shirt, smoothing down his tie so that it lay flat. There had been an energetic conversation before he and Jeb left the office about whether or not Luke could wear the tie. Jeb described it as "an unholy" color of green. The adjective *vomitus* had been bandied about. The metro-sexual gargoyle had declared that the ensemble—he'd actually said ensemble—was aesthetically unpleasing.

"I'm telling you that people will retch when they see you." Jeb had delivered the critique with both hands over his eyes. "A person simply cannot wear tangerine linen with barf green silk. It's not done, unless it's in irony and, you sir, as gorgeous as you are, are never going to pull off irony on purpose."

"Says the dude with moss under his armpits."

Jeb had cast him a withering look. "I do not have moss under my armpits. My granite is impeccably maintained, and you know it. "

The crafty little spy was probably correct. Since he was not forcibly bound to a structure, odds were that he was in remarkably good condition for a stone creature almost a thousand years old. The reason the Devil favored gargoyles as spies was because they were insanely loyal and, once they'd mastered the art of guile, it was remarkably easy for them to blend in with humans. Luke had recognized him for what he was—an informant for the Devil—almost instantly. He gave himself away with his fawning compliments and obsequious doting. The Devil's pets were always too eager when it came to serving the Seven. He didn't know about his cousins and how they dealt with their own tattletales, but Luke barely tolerated Jeb in his life, and then only because if it wasn't that particular gargoyle, it would be another one. There was no way of getting around it. If his father wanted to keep tabs on him and the others, then he was going to. The Devil always got what he wanted.

Luke recognized people filing into the conference room-cum-Mia's office as the ones who'd attended the earlier meetings at his place. The seats around the table filled in, each person with coffee and something to nibble on.

"So, Luke," Mia began, "I did some research on what we talked about at the dinner meeting the other evening, and I'm really interested in discussing your ideas on utilizing reclaimed water. I can't design it, but that's what we have you for. To make my ideas reality."

Luke raised his eyebrows. "You did research?"

Jason pulled his attention from Jeb and his eyes flashed. "Mia loves research. She spent all of Monday Googling."

God love a loyal assistant.

She tossed Luke a distracted smile while she sorted through some notes, laying them on the table with crude drawings and sketches. "Yes. I was especially drawn to your suggestion that we capture rainwater. There are some really interesting ideas out there that I think we should pursue. There's a company in California that specializes in a system to reuse gray water. I don't know why I didn't think of it before. It's a brilliant way to irrigate the central garden—"

"Irrigate the central garden." It wasn't a question. He wasn't even aware he'd said it out loud, he'd just been trying to say the phrase to himself to the point where he could understand it. It was obvious that he wasn't going to get her to pull back on the wackier ideas. But if he could trade off a stupid garden by including a state-of-the-art water system, then he would have to look at that as a win.

"Uh-huh." Her grin made her face light up, and her blue eyes sparkled with excitement. "You keep saying 'courtyard' and 'atrium,' but you need to think bigger. Much bigger."

"And you're thinking of irrigating all of this"—he swept his hands over her notes scattered across the table—"with rainwater collection?"

Now she really smiled. "Yes. Something that will water the orchard area as well as the terraced gardens. Don't you think...I mean, I think it's a really forward plan." She paused and watched him for a second. "So I did some checking and there are several companies who have afford—"

"No." Luke shook his head and Mia stopped midsentence, midword, mid-thought and a brief flash of dismay skittered across her face. He felt the briefest shimmer of regret that he'd obviously hurt her feelings, but then outrage at the monstrosity she was making of his building swamped it. Disappearing were the cool exquisite lines of his design. He could barely see them anymore with all the God damned trees in the way. "No, I don't think it's a forward plan. I don't even think it's feasible. In fact, I think it's insane. You've hired my firm to design and build an office building for people to work in, not raise vegetables. I've done that. What you have before you is a structure that will win awards and spreads in magazines. Something to be proud of."

She was mucking up his legacy. He could practically feel acid eating at his stomach and inching up his throat. He'd created a modern technological masterpiece, and she was turning it into a 1964 hippie commune.

Jeb kicked his shoe. Sideburns cleared his throat.

Mia's eyes were downcast as she shuffled her notes. She took a deep breath, one that lifted her shoulders and brought her face up until she met his eyes. "I'm sorry—" She swallowed and began again, stronger this time. "I'm sorry, but I thought I was the client here." More note shuffling. "I will have Jason forward you my ideas. I'll expect to see some updated specs and cost breakdowns in, what? Two weeks? Or I should I get them to another firm?"

The room was unnaturally quiet as everyone waited to see what would happen next. He held her gaze. Luke registered anger coming off her in ribbons mixed with embarrassment and...anxiety. His skin practically tingled with the potent emotions streaming from her as they mixed with his own vitriol. Her fingers shook with the effort to stand up for herself. Luke was very aware of how intimidating he could be, he banked on it most of the time, wore it like an advertisement not to fuck with him. Nevertheless, the princess was doing it. She looked like she was going to throw up even while she maintained eye contact, her huge brown eyes trained defiantly on his.

"That will be unnecessary," he said in a neutral voice. The bile settled in his gut, extinguished by an interesting cocktail of new-found respect for her and unexpected lust. "Please have your assistant send them over. I'll review what you've researched and have some numbers for you soon."

What could it hurt to review her ideas and then give an outrageous cost sheet that would make it unfeasible?

She stood and Luke followed her to his feet. "Thank you for your time, Mr. Mephisto."

He hadn't tried to give her the *push* again. This was Mia, all Mia, all by herself, standing up to the Big Bad Wolf and asking for what she wanted.

She was the sexiest nutcase he'd ever met.

THE LOCKER ROOM at the gym smelled exactly like all locker rooms in gyms do, yet it relaxed Luke. The aroma of old sweat and deodorant soap brought to mind tired muscles. An exhausted body meant a quiet mind.

"You feelin' ready?" Ethan Mephisto, Luke's cousin, asked him. He didn't wait for Luke's answer before chattering on. "I heard Tank has been talking all kinds of shit. The way he's been going on I should make a killing on the odds after you beat his ass."

Luke pulled his shirt over his head and tossed it in the locker. "Yeah, Jeb told me." His super handy shadow kept up with the fighting news which was so incongruous as to be funny. "I'm not worried."

"You shouldn't be. I've rewatched all the tapes. He may have a strong chin, but his recovery is slow." Ethan rolled his neck and shoulders, limbering up as Luke changed his clothes. "I think for now we should concentrate on speed. You've totally got this guy; you've got three inches on him—"

"And I'm taller."

It was disconcerting how often his dick had been announcing himself lately. An unexpected image of Mia Hatcher sauntered through his head. He paused changing his shoes to recall the sway of her skirt as she walked away from him, still shaking from their argument. He'd noticed that whenever she was thinking she was also moving, which made for a sexy-as-hell view. Too bad when she was thinking she was coming up with balmy ways to screw up his building.

Ethan gave him a playful shove on his head. This cousin was probably the only person on the planet brave enough to attempt to manhandle Luke. "Jackass."

"But, I shouldn't take it for granted," Luke finished the previous thought. "Tank didn't get this far without some skill, and I'm sure he's watching my tapes, too."

"Well, yeah." Ethan snorted. "He wants to fight for a title. It's really too bad you can't."

Luke grunted in reply. Some would say the Seven had a lot of advantages. That immortality until you're forty thing would probably hold a lot of appeal to some. But the cons far outweighed the pros. Being a celebrity held no appeal to Luke, which was a damn fine thing since his dear old dad would never have allowed that.

The Devil remained inconspicuous, except when he wasn't.

Luke was happy being a journeyman fighter. He was well enough known that he was the one to beat to advance to a higher card, but a gatekeeper nevertheless. Luke had no desire for a title. His fighting had an entirely different purpose.

His high school football coach had started him on the road to working out his ever-present angry energy into something constructive that kept him out of trouble. Once Coach McGuinn found out the rowdy, troubled boy on his team was without a father he took him under his wing and worked tirelessly to provide him a good influence. Obviously, there had been no point. Luke was intimately related to the worst influence of them all. Still, Luke welcomed it even though he recognized the whole scenario was a cliché.

For God's sake, they were every sports movie ever made, but the truth of the matter was, Luke was desperate and had welcomed the coach's attention.

He couldn't explain to his coach why he lashed out. Why he got in fights in school. Why he didn't care if he got in trouble. Who would ever believe him? The aunt and uncle who raised him understood but couldn't make it better. His cousins, the rest of the Seven, had their own battles to fight.

Against all odds, Coach McGuinn managed to funnel some of his wrath into sports. First came football and rugby. Luke went to college on a full ride football scholarship and the brutal regimen of sports and scholastic pursuit kept the devil—so to speak—at bay for a while. A brawl at a rival fraternity his senior year led to his interest in mixed martial arts. It was there that he was able to best exercise his demons. Or maybe it was exorcized. Whatever. He relished the beating he would give and the one he'd receive. His masochism was a survival instinct.

He and Ethan worked out together for hours, until Luke was dripping and completely out of gas. He was of a mind to win this fight against The Tank, so he and Ethan concentrated on improving his speed to take advantage of the other fighter's weaknesses. Ethan insisted on going through the combinations again and again until Luke's shoulders screamed and his hips ached from kicking.

But it didn't work. His mind did not go blank with exhaustion like it usually did and he didn't feel the quiet in his soul that he longed for.

Instead, Luke kept imagining the twitch of a skirt hem. The way her expressive eyes would get that far away look to them when she was concentrating. He fought to control an erection when the memory of her husky laugh floated into his thoughts. That was his favorite distraction, reliving the first lurch of his cock when he'd heard her laugh.

Ethan complained. "Hey. You're not focusing, man. If you want to lose, keep it up."

He pushed himself harder. Ethan yelled in his face while he did sit-ups. He punched, lunged, and kicked for what seemed forever.

At the end of the workout, Ethan threw him an apple and gave a dire prediction. "If you don't pull your head out of your preoccupied ass, you might as well not bother to show up. Winning is going to take more than just being angry all the time."

Luke shrugged. "How's that Envy thing working out for you?"

Spiteful digs aside, Luke knew he was dangerously preoccupied, but had no idea how to extinguish this particular demon. Apple juice flooded his mouth and it occurred to him that maybe he didn't want to try

HEAVEN II

Hashmal gazed at her, patient and impassive. "Where are you supposed to be?"

Juliet shrugged and tried to be evasive. "The library. That's where I usually am, anyway."

The Dominion raised an eyebrow and opened his giant book. He ran his index finger down the seemingly endless column of names, turning pages until he paused, tapping at one of the figures. "The Celestial library," he confirmed, seeming surprised that she really had been assigned there.

She smiled, smug, and blinked at him.

"So why are you here? The Librarian has not mentioned that he is unhappy with your performance."

"I've been reading."

Hashmal closed the book. "As one does at the library."

"Yeah, I've read a lot. I mean a lot, a lot. It's totally okay because I love reading."

No living person would ever believe that angels could be sarcastic, but man, they sure were. "You can't possibly imagine how relieved all the of Dominion will be when I tell them that we assigned your duties so competently. It's as if we looked into your soul and were able to divine the perfect job for you."

She beamed at him. "You Second Sphere angels are really on it, you know."

The angel exhaled through his nose. "Juliet, do you have a point?"

"Sure, I do. I'm getting to it."

Now his fingers were steepled together under his chin, the portrait of celestial composure. "Um-hum."

"Like I said, I've read *everything.*" She tried to infuse the words with import and meaning. "And I have some questions."

"Questions about what?"

Juliet considered where she should start. Maybe small and build up to the big stuff. "Was there really an eleventh commandment?"

"Actually, there were fifteen."

Her eyes opened wide and her jaw dropped. "Fifteen," she squeaked. "What were they?"

"God decided that the ten were sufficient. That's all you need to worry about."

Tilting her head, she tossed him some side-eye. "Was there anything in there about not being stupid? There totally should have been. Being stupid should be a sin."

A glimpse of a smile quirked his lips. "Is that all? I have much to do and I'm sure you're expected back at your post."

"No, there's more. Can you tell me where my neighbor, Mrs. Arezmendi, is? I'd like to say hey."

"If I tell you where you can see your friend, will you go away?" Juliet grinned at him until he opened his book again. "Mrs Arezmendi is with the Seraphim." He closed the book with a thud and rose from his chair, clearly preparing to shoo her on her way, his wings rustling with agitation.

"Wow." She stretched the word out and punched the last syllable hard. "She's one of God's hype men. I can totally see that." She mimicked the old lady's Spanish accent, "The whole Earth is full of His glory."

"Indeed." Hashmal sighed.

"One last thing." She remained firmly in her seat. "I found a really old scroll. In the antiquities room." Hashmal raised an eyebrow. But remained silent. "I read it. It was a story about Lucifer an—"

"You had no business in that room. That's why there are guards."

"I'll give you that, but the deal is, I did read it, so it's kinda out of the bag, you know?" She paused while it looked like Hashmal was having an aneurism. "Was it real? Did that really happen?"

The angel sat back down with a teeth-shuddering crunch. "Doesn't it say at the end that no one is allowed to talk about it?"

"Yeah, but... It's real?"

Now his head dropped into his hands. "Oh, my stars."

"It's so sad." Juliet deflated in her chair. "So sad. How long were they apart from each other?"

She thought he said the word "still," but it was hard to tell with his face muffled in his hands like that. She gasped.

"Still?" She dropped her palms on the desk between them with a loud smack. "You're telling me Rachel is still in Hell? By herself? Oh my G—"

"Don't! You need to forget that you read that. Go back to your post in the library and behave yourself. You've seen what happens when you disobey our Father."

Juliet wasn't listening. "Lucifer left her down there?"

"He didn't *leave* her anywhere. Look you, I am not discussing this. God did what was best. Everything is in his plan." Hashmal had stood and was now rounding the desk towards her. "You are never to mention this again. I'm very serious. I cannot—I will not—protect you."

She allowed him to usher her from his office. She didn't even protest as she was too much in thought. Obviously, he was of no more use to her anyway. If Rachel was still in Hell and Lucifer was free in Heaven, well then, a horrible misjustice had been done.

Maybe this was her duty in Heaven. Maybe this was what she was supposed to be doing.

Step one: Find Lucifer.

CHAPTER SEVEN

"Please. Pretty please." Jason begged. "I really want to go."

"Well, then go," Mia told him as she pulled her purse from her bottom desk drawer. "I'm not stopping you."

He dropped his head back and made excessive whining noises. "I can't go by myself."

"This isn't really my thing," she said and paused the search in her purse for her keys. "It doesn't seem like this would really be your thing either."

"You know what is my thing?" Jason asked. "Mr. Mephisto's pretty assistant. Jeb asked me to go. Apparently, his boss is fighting. You have to come with me, so it won't be weird."

Luke was fighting? Visions of virile men in shorts doing manly sporty things warred with her memory of the Rocky movies. She seemed to recall that Sylvester Stallone always looked pretty mangled by the end of the film.

"No one else can go," he continued. Now his hands were steepled under his chin in the pantomime of a prayer. "Mia, I'm begging you. Please come with me. I'll do anything you ask. Anything. "

She narrowed her eyes at him. "You'll take my car for servicing." She wondered what Luke looked like in shorts and only shorts. The internet was one thing, but in person would be something entirely different.

He grinned. "Absolutely. No problem."

That was too easy. "And give Godfrey a bath." She bet he looked really good. How could he not? The man was as big as a tree.

Jason's face fell. He closed his eyes and gave a defeated sigh. "Fine."

Her cell phone twinkled. "Hi Cassie. I'm running a few minutes late."

"I'm starving," Cassie's voice already had an edge to it. Her bestie was notorious for getting hangry if she wasn't fed on a regular basis. "I missed lunch today. The Saltzman-Heedley wedding was a freaking disaster. Oh my God, you wouldn't believe it. Debbie Garson showed up. Do you remember her from Kappa Psi?" Mia let her ramble while she rummaged around for her keys. "Tall girl, bottle blonde hair. Anyway, I guess she used to date the groom and she showed up at the bachelor party… Can I just tell you all of this at dinner?"

"Yeah, except I can't find my keys."

"Did you lock them in your car again?"

"No, I didn't lock them in my car." She covered the speaker on her phone with her index finger and whispered to Jason, "Go see if I locked my keys in the car."

Jason hopped to his feet and dashed out the conference room door, more eager than ever to please.

"What are you doing tomorrow night?" Mia asked into the phone. "Do you have a date or a wedding or something?"

"Actually, I have nothing tomorrow. It's a freaking miracle. I'm going to take a long, hot bath and paint my toenails. Drink a bottle of wine. Watch a foreign film. Something French, I think. Call for Chinese food delivery. Why?"

"Do you want to come with Jason and me to a fight?" Mia had to admit she was sort of into the idea now. The prospect of checking Luke out when he couldn't see her doing it had a very real appeal.

"A fight? What are you talking about? Like boxing?"

"I guess so." Mia dumped her purse out on top of her desk. Among the regular items were the following detritus: four wadded up gum wrappers, a lip balm with no cap and purse lint stuck to it, three pairs of sunglasses, a complete set of Allen wrenches, and a paperback novel. Also, no keys. "It might be fun."

"Have you ever been to a fight before?" Cassie asked, her tone skeptical.

"No, but Jason is begging for me to go with him."

"Make him wash Godfrey."

"He's pretty desperate, because he already agreed to do that."

The dastardly cackling on the other end of the phone made Mia chuckle.

"That little boy doesn't stand a chance with your moose."

"So come with us."

"When did you become Jason's wingman?"

"I'm not. Here's the thing. Remember the architect slash boxer..." She paused for effect and to allow Cassie's mind to wander back to those photos online. "I kinda want to see him, you know, outside of his suit."

"I'll bet you do." There was more cackling from the other end. "I remember him. I'm in."

By the next afternoon, Jason was beside himself with nervous energy and driving Mia crazy. Unable to bear his bouncing around anymore, she sent him home at four o'clock. Yes, she was still going to go. Yes, she promised to pick him up at seven. Yes, with Cassie. No, she planned to wear jeans and a T-shirt. Then she shooed him out the door.

Several hours later and she was hollering for Cassie. "Come on. If we're late picking up Jason, he'll perish from a broken libido."

Right on cue her phone announced a text. She didn't even look at it so certain that it was her love-sick assistant.

"Okay, I'm ready," Cassie announced as she twirled into the hall in a cloud of perfume, wearing a flimsy sundress and spiky heels. She took one look at Mia and made a face. "Is that what you're wearing?"

Mia looked down. Everything she had on was clean and, in her opinion, cute. "Yeah."

"No."

She nodded with finality. "Yeah."

Cassie's pointed finger squiggled in front of Mia's outfit. "What exactly do you think you're going to catch with that?"

"I'm not fishing. I'm going to go watch some guys beat the snot out of each other. I think what I'm wearing is way more sensible than that trap you have on."

A feminine hand encircled with golden bangles bunched up its fist and perched itself on Cassie's hip. "You said you wanted to go check out Angry Man away from the office. That implies that you will actually see Angry Man, wherein he will also be seeing you away from the office. Is that the image you want to leave him with? Frumpy jeans and a Lost Tree Hard Cider shirt?"

"I didn't actually plan to 'see' him. I figured we'd stand in the back and scope him out. I don't want him to think I like him or anything."

"Oh my God, didn't we have this conversation in the seventh grade?

"He and I have to work together," Mia pointed out.

Cassie rolled her eyes and used that same pointed finger to direct Mia back to her room. "Go change and don't come out here without some nighttime boobs."

Mia stood firm. "What the hell are nighttime boobs?"

"Daytime boobs are dignified, stately, and safely put away in their shirt. Nighttime boobs are flashy, in your face, and ready for some fun." Cassie shimmied in her dress and Mia worried about the boobs actually staying in their assigned seats. "Oh I know, wear that fuchsia halter with the keyhole neckline."

Mia had obtained said blouse for a date with an old boyfriend, but she'd never actually worn it. It was too much, and Mia often thought she must have been possessed by the spirit of a high-rent hooker when she bought it. It was so far out of character that Mia felt like someone else when she had it on.

Maybe being someone else would be fun for an evening. It was already totally nuts to be going to a boxing match to begin with. Why not?

"You have a black lace bra?" Cassie shouted after her. "Wear that underneath in case, well, just in case."

Mia put on the black lace bra, but not in case of anything. She'd have long turned back into a pumpkin well before any "in case" circumstances turned up. She kept on the jeans but added high-heeled boots instead of the sneakers she'd had on before.

"Now there you go." Cassie nodded her approval. "I knew you had a pair of nighttime boobs."

Jason had on the guy version when they got to his place.

"Wow," Cassie said when he opened his apartment door. "You look gorgeous." She turned to Mia. "See, he's got on his fishing outfit." Then back to Jason. "Are you wearing mascara?"

"Yeah." He batted his eyes at them.

Cassie stared up at him while he locked the door. "What brand do you use? Jeez, your eyes look huge. I'd sell my soul for lashes like that."

While Mia drove, Cassie quizzed her assistant on Luke, Jeb, what little he knew about fighting, and his impressive knowledge on makeup contouring. The two of them were a Saturday Night Live skit that went off the rails. Anytime they were together, they babbled away like manic morning talk show hosts, goofing around and teasing each other until Mia's stomach hurt from laughing.

Jason turned serious as they swung into the parking lot of the arena. "Wow, there's a lot of people here. I had no idea this was so popular."

While Jason texted Jeb they had arrived, Mia circled the parking lot, finally giving up and going for the valet. She was still handing over the keys when Jeb emerged from the venue like royalty. He hugged Jason and whispered something in his ear that made her assistant blush. Then he allowed himself to be introduced to Cassie, finally rounding on Mia as she approached.

"*Mon cheri.*" He took both of her hands and kissed her on both cheeks. "*Tu es magnifique.*"

"*Merci,*" she replied. "*Tu parle français?*"

"*Oui,*" he told her and laughed, switching back to English. "I'm doing that now. It drives Luke crazy."

"I'll bet." Mia really didn't get the dynamic with these two. On one hand, their relationship was combative and full of animosity. It seemed like Luke wanted to kill Jeb on a regular basis and Jeb did everything he could to irritate his boss. But then it was clear that Jeb took very good care of Luke, and God knows Luke would be lost without him. It was weird.

Jeb flashed a badge hanging around his neck on a lanyard at the door and informed the ticket takers that they were "on the list." Just as the parking lot had suggested, the place was packed.

Once they entered the crowd, Mia cast her glances towards the walls, looking for a nice place to see the bout but where she could remain inconspicuous. Nighttime boobs or no, she didn't necessarily want Luke to know she was scoping him out. It was hard enough working with the man and all his gruff ideas without adding sexual tension to the mix. And if he was unaware of any sexual tension, she certainly didn't need to bring it to his attention. She would just keep her libido to herself.

There was a decent place against the far wall, and she turned in that direction.

"No, no, no," Jeb pointed to the front. "We don't sit with the rabble. I saved us four seats up front."

Jason, too giddy to think straight, grinned at her over his shoulder and followed the object of his desire through the crowd.

Mia turned to Cassie for help, but her friend had a strange expression on her face as she watched Jeb and Jason from behind.

"What's wrong?" Mia asked.

"Nothing," Cassie said, but she wasn't convincing.

"What?" Mia prodded. She wasn't able to read Cassie's face, so she turned back to stare at the back of Jeb's head. She didn't see anything beyond a well-shaped cranium and an expensive designer haircut.

"It's nothing," Cassie assured her and pointedly looked away from the guys and back to Mia.

Mia raised an eyebrow. "Is it your spidey sense?" Cassie was always getting "psychic readings" on people. Mia was used to it. If the worst thing you could say about her friend was that she was quirky, well then, that was brilliant.

"Yeah." She was back to staring at Jeb's head. "I'm just trying to figure out what he is."

Mia laughed. "It's so loud in here, I thought you said you were trying to figure out what he is."

Cassie blinked at Mia. "I did. It's weird, but I can't tell."

She tossed her a perplexed look. "Well, he's gay. Obviously."

"I know he's gay, fool. I'm just trying to figure out what he is."

"You mean like Italian or Jewish or something?" Mia furrowed her brow and peered at Jeb's back again.

"No. Who cares about that stuff? I'm talking about what kind of supernatural he is." Cassie waived her hand in a dismissive gesture and then her expression returned to her regular happy-go-lucky one. "Never mind. I'll figure it out or I won't."

Jeb paused at the head of a row and did an excellent game show hostess wave.

"Oh no, we can't sit here." Mia finally spied the seats Jeb had saved for them. They were literally in the front row. It was too late of course. Jason was already seated and chatting up the people around them. Cassie shrugged and plopped down which left the chair between her and Jeb available for Mia.

Except for the size of the crowd, the scene was pretty much what she expected. The ring in front of them was elevated on a stage. There was a padded steel frame around the perimeter with chain link fencing enclosing the entire thing. There wasn't even anybody inside, and it still looked ridiculously intimidating.

The crowd was excited, jabbering away enthusiastically while they mingled with each other, keeping the room at a dull roar. It was only a few minutes before official-looking people emerged and took places around the outside of the ring. Then some girls in bikinis holding huge number cards showed up to hoots and hollers from the crowd. Cassie rolled her eyes and Mia just laughed.

The lights dimmed and hip-hop music blasted over the sound system. From the side of the room a crowd of five or six people emerged from double doors and jostled through the vibrating crowd. The clump of people strode up three stairs and smashed open a door in the chain link and entered the ring. The guy wearing shorts and bouncing around and punching the air like a caffeinated jackrabbit must be Luke's competition. Any doubt was squashed when Jeb cupped his hands around his mouth and booed when the announcer identified him as The Tank. Pockets of the crowd joined Jeb, while other groups cheered.

Excitement ratcheted up the crowd. Even Mia felt it.

She couldn't help measuring the fighter up against what she expected of Luke and she worried for a moment. The Tank guy was big and....Could a person be square? He seemed to be all muscle and bones, like if a brick had arms and legs.

From somewhere in the distance, the deep sound of a church bell chimed. And then again a little louder. And another. The crowd all around Mia jumped to their feet and chanted Luke's last name. Me-phis-to. Me-phis-to. Another church bell rang out and then a lone guitar.

Caught up in the excitement thrumming through the crowd, Mia joined in the chanting. The doors swung open just as the singer from AC/DC started the lyrics to Hells Bells. From her vantage point in the front row, she saw him the minute he entered the arena, and it caught her breath. As opposed to the tiny gang who joined the other fighter for his entrance, Luke came out with only one other person.

"That's his cousin, Ethan," Jeb said into her ear as if reading her mind. "They train together."

She nodded without taking her eyes off Luke. Underneath his strange fashion combinations, Luke was every bit as magnificent as she'd imagined. Where his opponent was an unwieldy cube of a human, Luke Mephisto was a poetic triangle. Broad, rounded shoulders and a heroic chest tapered into a ridged stomach. His low-slung shorts allowed an unblinking view of abdominals that directed her eyes right into the bottom of the triangle.

Cassie looped her arm with Mia's and pulled her close. "My, my, my,"

"Yeah," Mia agreed. Her gaze molested him from afar. Everything about him was hot; his muscles, his razor-sharp jaw line, the vivid red devil tattooed on his chest.

Luke and his cousin strolled confidently through the crowd, his entrance music implying that he was a dangerous man to encounter. Maybe even Satan himself. His hard expression gave credence to the lyrics. He entered the ring with slow, controlled movements that were more menacing than all the other man's frenzied bouncing around.

The fighters met in the center of the ring while the referee recited the rules. Tank taunted and flexed and acted like a maniac. In contrast, Luke stood straight and tall, and never took his lethal gaze off the other man. It was scary as hell.

They broke and headed to their respective corners. Luke turned deliberately in a measured arc, a malevolent grin turning up one side of his mouth.

Until he saw Mia through the chain link.

CHAPTER EIGHT

Luke felt solid. Prepared. He'd pushed all his distractions aside. That included the work on Veritas Templum Pharmaceuticals. Ethan had been ruthless in getting Luke's head on straight, and his fascination with Mia had waned. Luke was a furious machine.

Until he'd walked back to his corner and seen her through the chain link.

She'd been biting a fingernail but when their gaze met, her lips had spread into a smile. Then she waved. She fucking waved. Jeb had been standing right beside her, leading the cheering like he always did when Luke fought. He had to have something to do with this.

Luke gave his head a shake to clear the fog and took the last several steps to his corner. Ethan had already followed his gaze and was watching Mia.

"Is that her?" his cousin asked.

"Who?" Luke hadn't told Ethan anything about Mia. What was he going to tell him? That he had a little lust problem with a fairy princess? Yeah, that really spoke to his ferocious reputation.

"The girl who's been in your head," Ethan said dismissively. He gave Luke an easy punch on the abs drawing his attention back to the ring and the business at hand. "Look at me. If you want to impress the pretty girl, you're going to need focus. Remember what we worked on. Fast combinations. Double them up."

Luke bowed his head and nodded. He moved his body so that his back was to her, trying to ease the temptation to lift his gaze and seek her out again. "Counting to four. I got it."

Everyone cleared out of the ring except for the fighters and the referee in anticipation of the bell. Luke rocked forward on his toes and rolled his neck, then his shoulders. He eyed his opponent and growled low in his throat, generating the wrath that pumped him up.

Except that he knew she was there. He could feel her behind him, an ethereal flower in a garden of trash.

The bell rang and he pushed off on his toes. He didn't give a second for Tank to put into action whatever game plan his corner had come up with. Luke charged, fists ready, and caught the other man on the shoulder with a hard right, sending him off balance. A quick follow-up punch tagged Tank's chin with a left uppercut and another powerful right on the side of his head. Tank's right knee hit the canvas and the crowd roared.

Luke raised his eyes for a split second and connected with Mia's instantly. Hers were wide with shock, and a fission of power surged through him. It was short-lived because Tank took the opportunity to jam one of his club-like fists into Luke's ribs. Back to his feet, the other man followed up with a kick to the same spot which Luke was able to block with his arm.

Attention back on Tank, the two of them moved around the ring, each looking for an opening. Tank let loose a couple of punches that went wide. Luke cursed himself for losing the upper hand on his first strike. Eventually Tank drove in and landed two sharp punches to his mid-section, but it gave Luke the chance to wrap his arms around the other man's hips and flip him over his shoulder. Tank landed hard on his back. Luke rolled over the other man's legs, catching them in a grappling hold that should have caused his opponent to tap out after several seconds of tension on his joints. But it didn't. Tank slipped loose and spun the hold on Luke instead.

Ethan was yelling his head off from behind the fencing. The crowd's voice was indecipherable, but the mood was vicious.

Tank wrenched his arm another quarter of an inch. Luke took a deep breath and ignored the pain. He twisted into the hold slightly and took the opportunity to kick out at Tank, connecting with a satisfying crunch. Tank's grip relaxed enough that Luke pulled out of the hold and surged to his feet. There were a few more half-hearted parries until finally the bell rang and the fighters broke to their respective corners.

"Don't you dare look at her," Ethan growled as he put a hand on Luke's chest and pushed him back deeper into his corner. He squirted some water in Luke's mouth. "You're going to be a laughingstock." He provided a bucket for Luke to spit into. "Look at me—no, not at her—look at me. You didn't win that round. You're going to lose this whole thing if you don't pull your head out of her cleavage and focus."

"I'm going to kill Jeb." Luke glanced back over to the area where the gargoyle and his entourage were seated. Jeb was leading their section in a series of rousing cheers. Mia was whooping right along with them, though her expression seemed more concerned than bloodthirsty.

"You're going to get killed," Ethan insisted. "Come on, I want to hear you counting. Maybe that will force you to concentrate."

The next round didn't go much better. He got in a couple of good shots and a leg sweep that could have ended it all, but no matter how much he tried to ignore it, he could feel her in the crowd. Though blood from a cut on his left eyebrow was bleeding into his eye.

"The ref's gonna stop this," Ethan threatened when he was back in his corner. "Fucking blood everywhere."

"No," Luke insisted, blinking furiously and wiping at his face with his forearm. "I can finish him."

Ethan's grunt of derision should have launched Luke into beast mode. Instead, a frisson of doubt crept into his mind. He'd been so confident. What had happened? Another quick glance in her direction proved that she was still there, still watching him, this time with one hand on her forehead. She seemed distressed. He lifted his bloody hand and stuck his fingers through the chain link to acknowledge her. He waggled them hoping to show her he was all right.

His cousin straightened up and glared at him. "Are you fucking kidding me right now?" Ethan stepped back, waving his arm in invitation. "Go ahead and get the shit kicked out of you."

Luke ignored him and charged out to the canvas intent on ending this. For the first time in his life, he couldn't get it up—wrathfully speaking.

The crowd was ecstatic as the Luke they had been waiting for all night took command of the fight. His combinations flew from his body and connected with furious power. The big man wobbled a bit but recovered well enough to get in a couple more licks of his own. None of that mattered, because this round was Luke's. This was the kind of fighting he had trained for. This win was his.

They sized each other up, Luke watching for an opening for the final salvo as they circled the ring. The yells and whistles of encouragement were drowned out by the fury soaking his muscles. Even the crowd was a blur. If asked a million times how it was possible he saw Mia at that moment, he couldn't have told you, but he did see her. Her big expressive eyes locked onto his, which is probably why he didn't see the roundhouse kick that knocked him out.

"I MADE YOU SOME TEA."

Luke opened one eye. The room was dark and cool. Like a crypt.

"It's chamomile. It's supposed to be good for a headache." Jeb tried to fluff Luke's pillow, but he smacked his hand away. "Here, take these." Jeb thrust a couple of pills at him.

Luke did take the pills, probably only aspirin though he wished it was something much stronger. The doctor in the emergency room where he'd ended up after the knockout was adamant that he remain for a CT scan and overnight observation. The neurologist told him horror stories and threatened to call psych for a consult. The nurse actually yelled a little. Ethan rolled his eyes and told him he got what he deserved.

Jeb, however, did what Jeb did best. He showed up at the hospital with Luke's insurance cards, his past medical records, and a clerical mastery that convinced the discharge nurse that Jeb was more than capable of making sure Luke didn't die of a brain bleed during the night.

What Luke, Jeb, and Ethan actually knew was that Luke couldn't die. Not of a brain bleed. Not of a gunshot. Not of an asteroid crashing into the earth in an extinction event. None of the Seven Princes of Hell could die, at least not until the ceremony to choose their generation's Devil came and went the winter they all turned forty.

Jeb brought Luke back to his own apartment and to the comfort of his own bed.

However, just because Luke wasn't in a hospital didn't mean that he didn't require around-the-clock nursing care. Jeb was remarkably good at dosing and fluffing and making people drink fluids. He kept a chart.

"Any double vision?"

"No," Luke growled.

"Excellent." He turned the lamp on next to the bed, and Luke flinched away from the light. "Hold still and let me look at the stitches." Stone cold fingers gently prodded his eyebrow. "They look pretty good. That doctor had me worried. I don't think you'll have a scar."

"Isn't that a shame."

A soft terrycloth package appeared before him. "Here's another icepack. Leave it on there for at least twenty minutes. I'll be timing you."

Luke settled the package on his forehead. He hated to admit that it felt good there, so he wouldn't let on. Jeb already knew anyway. He felt the foot of his bed sink under the deceptive weight of his assistant.

"So," Jeb began, "what the hell happened?"

Luke snarled and sank further into the pillow. "You sabotaged me, bringing that woman." That's what it was, plain and simple. He couldn't figure out why she was so distracting, but he was drawn to her from the minute he saw her in the crowd. Compelled. That's what it was. He was compelled to stare at her, to be aware of her.

"Mia?" Jeb said incredulously. "You think this"—he waved his hand up and down the length of Luke's bruised body—"was all about Mia? Ha! Isn't that rich."

"Why? It didn't feel natural," Luke insisted. "Maybe a witch put a spell on me or something." That sounded even more asinine when he said it out loud.

Jeb scoffed at him. "Witches aren't real, you dope. No one put a spell on you. I would know. And before you ask, the answer is no, your father had nothing to do with this."

"How do you know? This could be some plan he cooked up."

Rolling his eyes, Jeb asked, "For what purpose?"

Luke lifted the corner of the cold compress and narrowed a black and blue glare at his assistant. "I don't know. Just to be a dick. He is the Devil, you know. He's been known to fuck with people just because he can."

Jeb snorted through his nose and rose from the bed. "Well, not this time. I never heard anything about any machinations, and I would have. I always do. You're going to have to face the fact that you like this woman. You like her a lot. Wrath himself has a crush. Before you know it, you'll be pulling her pigtails in the gym."

"Fuck off." If he did have a thing for the woman, it was purely physical. It wasn't possible he was attracted to the kooky Disney princess in any other way than lustfully.

The doorbell rang, and Jeb chortled all the way out of Luke's bedroom. While he was gone, Luke took the opportunity to go to the bathroom by himself. All he had was a mild concussion, but Jeb was acting like he was an invalid.

Man, he looked like hell. His immortality didn't preclude his body from the need for recovery, it just hastened the process. The cut on his forehead bisected his eyebrow all the way down to the corner of his left eye. His head ached. Rolling it back on his neck felt good until he made himself dizzy and had to clutch onto the sink to keep from going down. Wouldn't Jeb love the drama of that?

He stood in the shower for several long minutes, just letting the scalding hot water loosen up the muscles of his shoulders and back. He moved slowly, like a statue come to life, cataloguing the aches and pains of his battered body.

He finally emerged from the bathroom in a cloud of steam with a towel wrapped around his waist, feeling mostly human again. Well, human enough to want to address the grumbling in his stomach.

"Hey, Jeb," he called out as he rounded the doorway into the kitchen. "I'm starving. Are there any eggs?" Already his unnatural powers were working to knit him back together.

"There are," Jeb said with a smirk. "Look who came over to make sure you're all right."

Now she was standing in his kitchen.

"Hi," Mia said with a small wave. "I wasn't sure what the etiquette is for visiting a sick person who got beat up on purpose. You don't really seem like the flower sort. If you were one of my girlfriends, I'd bring the latest Cosmo and a chocolate bar. That didn't seem like you either. I brought pie."

"Did you hear that, Luke?" Jeb asked him with huge, knowing eyes. "Mia made you an apple pie."

"I'll just leave it here." She placed the pie on his counter. "You don't seem like you're quite ready for visitors." She looked at his bare chest and towel-covered hips and blushed. "I just wanted to check and make sure you are okay."

Luke stood there like a half-naked idiot and stared at her.

"Actually," Jeb said as he pushed himself away from the counter, "I need to run a few errands this morning, and it would be really helpful if you could keep an eye on him for me. The doctors warned me not to leave him alone for the first day or so after a head wound."

"Oh. Sure," she said. "I can do that." Then to Luke, "You should get dressed, though."

Still not having said anything, Luke turned and left the kitchen. He pulled on a pair of sweatpants, finding fresh pain in his ribs when he bent over.

She was in his kitchen. He had no idea what to do with that information. Why did she get his head so fuzzy? For God's sake, she was just a woman. He knew lots of women. He'd slept with lots of women. He never thought about any of them again.

He needed to get rid of her. Out of his head and more immedi-

77

ately, out of his kitchen. He didn't have the time or energy to deal with this.

He padded back down the hall barefoot. He opened his mouth to tell her he was fine on his own except that she was pulling frying pans out of his cabinet. Eggs were already out on the counter.

"I'm happy to make you some eggs," she told his bare chest before she yanked her gaze up to meet his. "What kind do you like? Scrambled? Fried? How about an omelet?"

He crossed his arms. "You don't need to do that."

"I don't mind. Really."

He watched her warily as she moved about his kitchen, finding the cutting board and a knife. "Jeb is overreacting. He does that a lot."

From inside his refrigerator she said, "He cares about you. It's obvious."

She emerged with peppers, onions, and mushrooms, some pre-shredded cheddar cheese, and lunch meat.

"I'm a status symbol to him." Jeb had bragged one time about how being assigned to one of the Princes was a huge honor.

"Well, I can tell by your work on our building that you're brilliant. Your ideas are really fascinating. I'm excited to see how our two aesthetics will blend."

He frowned at her. Was she talking about the same project? From his perspective, his perfect office building was slowly morphing into some weird farming extravaganza with desks. It was only because he was able to integrate some forward-thinking water treatment ideas to her folly that he hadn't run shrieking from the whole project.

"I'll bet he learns a lot from working with you," she continued as she rinsed the peppers.

Luke didn't dignify that assumption with a retort. Jeb was there to keep an eye on him for his father, and Luke resented every minute of it. He leaned his butt against the counter and watched her chop the yellow peppers. She had on a vee neck T-shirt and jeans that looked soft from wear. Even in that simple getup she looked good enough to eat. The rolling motion of the knife made her boobs jiggle and Luke soon became mesmerized.

After a few beats of silence, Mia glanced up at him. "So that was a heck of a fight, huh? Is that what they're usually like? I mean the punching and kicking and grappling? I've never been to one before, but I didn't realize you could kick and stuff."

"You're thinking of boxing." He crossed his arms again and tried not to look at her chest, but it was goddamned hard not to.

"What?"

He shifted his weight to the other foot. "No kicking in boxing. I do MMA. Just about everything but biting and eye gouging is allowed."

"Oh." She raised her eyebrows. "I don't mean to be cruel or anything..." She glanced up at him again before grabbing a handful of mushrooms and took to slicing them. "Do they usually end in a knockout like that?"

Luke closed his eyes and sighed. "I've never been knocked out before."

"It was terrifying," she admitted. "I mean when you went down it was like a tree falling." She raised her arm and bent it at the elbow to imitate a tree going down. "Boom. I think your head bounced off the floor."

"Thanks for that visual. That's what I needed since I wasn't awake for the actual event." He allowed his gaze to flit back to her breasts.

"Oh, man." She stopped chopping and turned to face him. "I'm so sorry. That was really mean." Her brown eyes were fringed by heavy lashes and her lips glistened a rosy pink.

He shrugged and pushed off from the counter to pour himself a cup of coffee, black and strong with all the recommended daily caffeine a growing boy needed to keep his wits about him. "You brought me pie, so it's okay."

"And I'm making you breakfast," she pointed out.

"Right. There's that, too."

While she was beating eggs in a bowl, she asked, "Has your mother ever seen you fight? I can't imagine what she thinks. It must be horrible for her."

He took a big swig of coffee and burned his tongue. "My mother's dead."

She rolled her eyes up to heaven. "Well, I cannot win, can I? Good going, Mia."

With her head thrown back like that he noticed her graceful neck and jaw line. His fingers twitched with the desire to stroke from her ear to her collarbone.

The smell of sizzling butter wafted up from a skillet and brought him back to the conversation. "I should let you off the hook for that one. She died when I was three. I barely remember her." It only took two steps to bring him next to her at the stove where he could brush his elbow against her.

"Your father then?" she asked, her look was tentative like she was wandering around in a mine field but couldn't stop herself traipsing through. "Has he seen you box? Fight. Whatever you call it?"

Luke took another sip of the coffee, forgetting that it was the temperature of lava. "You know, I don't really know. Maybe? I'm certain he knows all about it. His people are everywhere."

She still gave him a questioning look as omelet-making commenced. "You don't know for sure?"

"We don't talk. It's complicated like you wouldn't believe." He was purposely crowding her a bit at the stove. He couldn't help it, so desperately did he want to touch her. "My father left for work when I was ten, and I've rarely seen him since."

"Ah, my dad left when I was seven." Mia nodded in understanding. "Raised by your grandparents, then?"

"No, with my cousin Ethan." His forearm brushed her bicep when she added the veggies to the pan. Now his arm radiated warmth.

"Oh, Jeb introduced him to me, you know, after…" She focused on the pan. "Want to grab some plates?"

He marshalled his senses and dragged himself away from her warmth to set his small kitchen table for two. He apologized for his dining attire, but he explained that he didn't think he could lift his arm high enough to put on a shirt. Her responding look of sympathy was gratifying. It wasn't exactly her fault that he was in the state he was, but it sorta was.

Her omelets were amazing—fluffy, cheesy and warm. Afterwards, he felt better than he should have, considering that every time he lifted his right arm the pain in his ribs took his breath away.

Lured from his hidey-hole by the smell of food, his cat, Claw, wandered into the kitchen, looking like something that had been reanimated last week. He'd been a stray who sort of demanded to be let into his house one rainy evening. The two of them were never actually fond of each other, but they'd coexisted in Luke's apartment in a sort of surly truce for the last five years. Luke didn't touch him for fear of more scratches, hence the name, and Claw didn't demand anything other than regularly scheduled meals. It was a one-sided relationship, and Luke still wasn't sure why he allowed the miscreant to live there.

"Oh, hey, I didn't know you had a cat." Mia put her hand down as an enticement for the beast to come over for pets.

Before Luke could warn her away from harm, the fiend was rubbing her leg and purring like a Harley Davidson. He didn't even know the damn cat knew how to purr. "Jerk," he told the feline who gave him a beady-eyed glare in return.

He'd only been sitting for a few minutes, but already his muscles protested when he tried to stand. Mia looked up at his groan and winced on his behalf. "Is there anything else I can do to help?"

Well actually, Luke could think of several things, all of them required her to be on top and do the hard work, but he didn't mention them. "Nah, there's not much that you can do for bruised ribs."

Instead, she offered to rub liniment into his shoulders and Luke foolishly allowed that to happen. He hadn't thought the process through. Like how her hands intentionally on his body was going to rev him up even more than a casual brush of her elbow had. But when she set herself on the couch and innocently spread her legs indicating that he should sit on the floor between them so she could rub his shoulders, he sat without thinking. From behind him she couldn't see his arousal but by the time she was finished his shoulders were looser and his sweatpants were tented.

"Don't move," she said and crawled out from behind him after a good thirty minutes of massaging his aches and pains. "I hope that helped a little bit."

His forearms lay across his lap in an effort not to terrify the princess. He nodded. "Thank you again for the omelet. And the pie. I almost forgot about the pie. That was really nice."

She was really nice. He couldn't imagine why he was so drawn to such a likable person when he was such a short-tempered bastard most of the time. They were a true example of Beauty and the Beast. It figured that he kept imagining her as a cartoon princess.

Mia slid her purse over her shoulder and Luke used his good arm to push himself, groaning loudly, to his feet. She put out a hand to assist. Not only did he sound like an ancient old man, now she was guiding him by his elbow.

She released his arm. "I'm sure Jeb will be back soon."

Luke felt a sneer coming on. "Great," he said, but anyone could tell he didn't mean it.

"Please call me if you need anything." She smiled and tucked her hair behind her ear. "I'm happy to help."

"Thanks again." They weren't moving any closer towards the door.

"It was really nice getting together with you away from the office."

He stepped closer and Beauty didn't run from the Beast. She even tilted her face towards him. And when he kissed her, she let him.

CHAPTER NINE

M ia held her breath as the big man stepped closer to her. The one thought she had before he bent his head and kissed her was that she shouldn't have put onions in their omelets. But then she didn't care. Her eyes locked with his as he dipped his head and came closer and then, just before his lips touched hers, her eyes drifted closed. His mouth was soft. A gentle brush of his skin against hers. An exploratory pass before settling there for a sweet moment.

His fingers brushed her upper arm, a soft caress that made her wish for more, before trailing down the length of her bare arm where his hand curled loosely around hers.

Luke was such an imposing colossus of a man, both in stature and attitude most of the time, that his tender approach to touching her left her more breathless than the actual kiss.

Her eyes remained closed when his mouth lifted from hers, his face hovering just inches above hers, his breath soft against her cheeks.

"Thank you for checking on me," he said, just above a whisper.

She opened her eyes and focused on his deep liquid gaze, a pool of warm hazel gray that would seem even lighter once the bruises really took hold.

"It turns out it was my pleasure," she replied with a smile.

His mouth spread in a mirroring grin as his gaze flicked back to her mouth. His head dipped again, moving in at a slight angle, and he kissed her with more pressure this time. His lips moved on hers, experimenting, testing how their mouths fit together like puzzle pieces. She let her free hand roam up the planes of his bare chest, palm flat against his pectoral muscle, fingers sliding along his collarbone.

Ever so slightly, he pulled her bottom lip between his before breaking the kiss.

"Aren't your lips bruised, too?" she asked, thinking his mouth must be sore.

"I don't care," he told her.

Kissing Luke was heady stuff, and they hadn't even really gotten serious yet. She pulled away from him even while he still held her hand.

"I don't know if Jeb would approve of all of this activity after a head injury," she teased. "I'm not a very responsible nurse."

That languid smile was back, the one that she'd rarely seen before, but that made him almost painfully handsome—even with the blossoming bruises.

"I feel much better already." He moved that sore arm again and made an obvious effort not to wince.

Mia chuckled, aware of how husky the sound was. He tugged gently on her hand, but she resisted. "I'm going to go. You get plenty of sleep and keep ice on that eye."

"It's boring here alone."

"Jeb will be back in a bit."

The grin was still there. "You're much prettier than Jeb."

She shook her head and laughed. "I can't stay."

His eyebrows gathered. "What if I feel faint or something?"

Now she really laughed. "Dear God, man. You don't think I can catch you, do you? Sheesh, I'd be squashed like a bug."

He took a step towards her. "What if I promise to be really gentle?"

Something deep inside of her actually clenched, and she swallowed hard. She extracted her hand from his grasp and used it to halt his advance with a pointy finger at his breastbone. "Okay." She drew the word out. "I'll check back in with Jeb later, to make sure you're still all right. Maybe to make sure you haven't keeled over and squashed *him* like a bug."

"No," he said while following her to his front door. "Call *me* later."

"Okay, I will." Mia stepped over the threshold and, she hoped, clear of his magnetism. Her head was fuzzy, and she was feeling a bit drunk. Wow. If that's what a couple of relatively chaste kisses with Luke was like, she couldn't even imagine what serious necking with him would do to her. Face burning with a blush, she pulled away from his house and steered her car towards the freeway.

She hadn't intended to spend all morning with Luke. It was supposed to have been a quick check. For no fathomable reason, she felt guilty about his loss and she'd hoped the apple pie would atone. It seemed to her that if they became friendlier, he'd be easier to work with. Perhaps, she could win him over and he wouldn't resist her ideas so vehemently.

She had places to be that morning. She had a couple of orchards to check out and her dog had an appointment at the vet in the afternoon. She couldn't spend all day massaging and kissing Luke Mephisto.

Not that she didn't want to. Bless her soul, he was beautiful. And scary. And hot. And, maybe most exciting and scariest of all, overwhelming.

Never in all her life had she been so attracted to a man with a personality like Luke's. Even Cassie had remarked on it. Mia's usual preferred companion was a great deal...nicer. What a lame word. Her last serious boyfriend, Warren, had been pleasant, unassertive, and certainly nonconfrontational.

Cassie said Mia stuck with Warren so long because he never created any drama in her life and Mia despised drama. When Mia protested this fact, Cassie gave her a look and asked who she thought she was fooling?

"How many times did you shy away from the hot guy who showed interest in you because he was, I don't know, a bit wild? It's not a flaw," Cassie insisted. "It's just a very Freudian response to your parent's marriage." Mia had rolled her eyes at that, but Cassie insisted. "What's wrong with that? Your parents are a walking, talking Dr. Phil episode. If I was you, I wouldn't want to repeat that bullshit either. The only problem is that the Warrens of the world don't really ring your chime either, you know?"

Deep in her heart of hearts, Mia did know that. But men like Luke were a huge risk.

"Don't forget that your mother had a hand in that marriage, too." Cassie reminded her with raised eyebrows. "Your daddy wasn't the only volatile one in that relationship. It takes two to tango."

That was an undeniable truth. While one domineered by proclamation, the other used a sneakier passive aggressive tactic. Also, Mia knew that was why she had such a hard time standing up for herself. The therapist she'd had in college had pointed that out in a tearful session when Mia had been devastated by what she felt had been an unfair grade from her biology professor. He'd encouraged her to protest it during the prof's office hours, but Mia had been much too intimidated to do anything about it. Instead, she'd suffered with the first C of her academic career and struggled for the rest of the class to bring her average up.

What that amounted to in the long term was that she got bullied into doing things by her father and guilted and maneuvered into doing them by her mother, and even when she recognized that it was happening, she felt powerless to stop it. So, she'd selected boyfriends who didn't push her or challenge her in any way. Cassie described them as mac and cheese: boring but comfortable.

Yet Mia was continually drawn to Luke. Maybe she was hungry because the food metaphor that came to mind for Luke was barbeque ribs: tough but meaty with a complicated tang that made her mouth water.

She spent the Saturday doing the errands that she'd had planned, and for those keeping score, she seemed totally normal. Inside her head, however, she relived those couple hours alone with Luke over and over. She couldn't stop her brain from rewinding the slow, imminent dip of his head as he bent to kiss her. Or the warmth on her arm when he stood close to her at the stove. Or the way his shoulders filled her hands when she rubbed them with liniment, so careful to avoid the areas bruising up. It was the funniest thing. It was like a highlight reel that kept rebooting. Not the whole thing in one long R-rated movie. More like the previews for some sexy new rom-com.

When she was home from the veterinarian and had checked all of her apple seedlings, she hesitated for about five seconds before calling Luke.

Just to check on him.

Uh huh.

The phone rang five times—just long enough to make her consider that she was a fool and disconnect—before it was answered.

"Mia, darling, don't hang up," said a voice that couldn't possibly have been Luke's.

'Umm, okay."

"It's Jeb."

Of course. She had known right away.

She let out a breath on a long calming exhale. "How is he?"

"Well, he's being an ass just now, but that's not really unexpected, is it?" His breath exited in a long-suffering huff. "He's been in a nasty mood all day."

"I'm sorry. He was fine when I left him." So fine. In fact, he had been on the verge of playful. Definitely flirty.

"Well of course he was, darling. You were here. He likes you."

He liked her? She felt a giggle coming on like she was thirteen. "Did he have a relapse or something? I'm sure he's very sore and probably has a heck of a headache."

Jeb snorted. "No, he's fine. He's just a very churlish person." He hummed into the phone, something she'd seen him do when he was frustrated with his boss.

Mia allowed sympathy to flow into her voice. "Oh, I'm so sorry you have to deal with him when he's like that."

"Oh pish," Jeb told her, and she could almost see his hand gesturing that it was nothing. "I'm used to it. Besides, I'll get a spa day out of it or a gift certificate to Prada or something. I'm guessing you'd like to talk to the handsome brute?"

"If you think he's up to it."

Jeb laughed. "He's up to it. He's in the bathroom just now, but he'll be along shortly." Just as he uttered the words, she heard a gruff voice in the background. Jeb muffled the phone but she could still vaguely hear the conversation if she held her breath and strained into the earpiece.

—Why *mumble* you still *mumble mumble?*

—*Mumble mumble* dinner.

—Are you on my phone?

—*mumble mumble* Mia *mumble.*

—You told her I was in the bathroom?

That last part was an incredulous roar that was incontestably Luke. There was more mumbling, much of it sounding outraged and the other indignant, but by now Mia had covered her mouth with her hand to stifle the laughter.

"Mia." This was definitely Luke's growly voice. "Sorry about that."

She struggled to contain herself. "You know, the two of you sound like brothers, the way you argue."

"I'd have smothered him in his sleep if he'd been my brother." Luke paused like he was switching gears. "How was your day?"

"It was fine, but more importantly, how are you?"

"I'm good, actually. A few bruises and I'm stiff, but I'm a very fast healer. Any chance you can come over tomorrow and make me another of your medicinal omelets?" His voice had melted from the rough bass she was used to into something smoother. Velvet over gravel. "Maybe I can talk you into another shoulder rub? I'll get rid of Mr. Nosey."

"I wish I could." She really, really wished she could. She closed her eyes and the wide, smooth expanse of Luke's tattooed shoulders floated in front of her eyes. "I have some orchards to visit and a couple of farmers markets to hit. I really should get to the Daughters of Eve convent by the end of the day."

"Jeez, if you don't want to come over," he teased, "you don't have to make up a lie."

She chuckled. "No, for real. I have to find a couple of orchards I heard about. I'm an apple detective." She knew that would only confuse him more, but it was a fun thing to tell people because it sounded insane. Her father thought it sounded idiotic.

There was a long pause before he said, "Okay. What does that entail?"

She laughed again at his skeptical tone. "It's a really long story. Essentially, I've heard about a couple of possible leads on missing apples that I need to go check out."

"What is a missing apple?" To his credit he sounded genuinely curious and not at all dismissive.

Where to start? Mia had spent years researching the fruit and its systemic extinction, trying to beat back the cruelty and unfortunate neglect of Mother Nature. Apples were ridiculously complicated fruit.

She tucked her toes underneath the solid body of her dog. Godfrey snored in the grassy sun of their back yard. "You know that pie I made you?"

"Best pie I ever had." She could hear the smile in his voice.

"Thank you. I made it with Melrose apples. You've never heard of them because they were thought to be extinct until about four years ago. I found one tree in an abandoned orchard in a forest in Ohio. I grafted a scion and successfully grew the first new Melrose apple tree in maybe fifty years. You are one of only maybe fifteen people alive who've ever tasted a Melrose."

"Wow. You're a wonder, Ms. Hatcher. I still don't know what any of that really means, but I'm impressed anyway."

The grass tickled the back of Mia's legs. "It's all a bit nerdy. I'm an apple nerd." She paused and wiggled her toes under the Great Dane. "So tomorrow I'll be tramping all over hell, searching for this mysterious remnant of orchard."

"Can I come?"

He wanted to go apple hunting? "Really? Are you sure? You're going to think it's really boring."

"No, I won't," he promised without any real knowledge of what kind of perdition he could be subjecting himself to.

"There'll be hiking. With hills. Are you sure you're strong enough to do that? I mean, you know, you looked pretty rough this morning."

Rough was putting it mildly. "You had an awful hard time moving around and everything." And yet, his lips had been more than up to the task. She suspected if she'd hung around, other parts of him would have presented themselves as willing and able, as well.

"I'll be fine. I'm strong as an ox," he assured her. "I want to see you apple-detecting. Hey, are there other people who do what you do?"

"Yeah, a few others scattered about the country." They had a handy little network set up, almost an internet tip line.

He chuckled and her toes curled. "I'll bet you're the cutest one."

HEAVEN III

When the angels didn't want something—or someone—found in Heaven, they were serious about it. What they hadn't counted on was an angsty teenage angel with eons of time on her hands.

Juliet latched on to the tale of Lucifer and Rachel. This was a romance full of more passion and loss than even the tragic love story she'd been named for. If Shakespeare had only known. Imagine the glory of their story told in iambic pentameter. The idea made her squishy with longing.

She had to believe that what she'd read in the ancient scroll was real. The way Hashmal had freaked out about it when she asked had to mean something. She'd never seen a Dominion act like that. As the angels in charge, they were like the office managers of Heaven. They were the ones who really ran the place, knew everything that was going on, and were the closest thing to an authority figure in the Elysian. While they didn't run around in armor like the Authorities or strut about wearing a crown and carrying a scepter like the self-important Principalities, the Dominion were, simply put, divinely beautiful. The most beautiful supermodels, only with wings and clipboards. So much of Heaven was a vague bureaucracy.

Hashmal had specifically told her to leave it be. Still, she had to know more. Were the lovers still separated? Was Rachel still trapped in Hell?

The problem was, she had no idea where to start.

She'd begun by casually mentioning Lucifer to other angels who frequented the library without telling any of them what she knew. Most of the Third Sphere angels were like Juliet; they didn't really know much beyond their specific purpose. Frankly, most of them didn't seem to care about that either. They were content with their jobs "fulfilling the divine ministry." Juliet didn't know what that meant exactly, nor did she care. She supposed if you were a dull person in life, you didn't change that much in the afterlife.

In fact, that would be her hell—an eternally prosaic existence.

Instead, she searched.

Heaven was an enormous place. Not one that was easily understood in the physical sense, either. From what Juliet could tell, the place was specific to everyone. For her, the places that made her happy were a magnificent library and a homey bedroom with stuffed animals and a comfy bed. When she asked other angels what Heaven looked like to them, some said beaches or ancient forests. There were even those in Heaven who wanted to spend eternity in a bustling city, or a family kitchen, or fishing at the lake. There was a tapestry of grandmothers who cared for all the babies, and they were never more content. Heaven was a changeable landscape that became whatever made you the happiest.

She wasn't sure what she should be looking for. Where would a "cage of his own making" be? What even was that, exactly? There were literally no resources in the library to fill in these blanks. No one she asked had any idea where to go.

She showed back up at Hashmal's.

"No. Whatever it is, the answer is no." The Dominion pointed a finger at the door. "Go away."

"Hi," Juliet said and ignored his insistent pointing. "It's good to see you, too."

His sublime face stretched tight from strain. "What do you want?"

"I just have a couple of questions and then I'll go away." Juliet held up three fingers in a Girl Scout salute. "I promise."

"I'm not answering any questions. I already told you to leave this alone."

She wiped her face of expression. "Leave what alone? Oh, you mean that old scroll thing. I'm totally not interested in that anymore. That's old news."

A perfectly sculptured eyebrow lifted as if he didn't believe her.

She walked around his unmoving body and took a chair in front of his desk. "Where would an angel go if they got in trouble?"

He rotated on his heel but remained by the door. "What do you mean in trouble? What did they do?"

"The worst thing, I guess." She ran an index finger over the titles of some of the scrolls on his desk. With a huff, he rounded the furniture and smacked her hand away.

"Don't touch anything." He stacked all his materials on the far side of the desk, out of her reach. "*Most* angels"—he looked pointedly at her—"don't get into trouble. *Most* angles behave themselves, that's how they got into Heaven in the first place."

Juliet shrugged one shoulder. "True. But not everyone is perfect. Surely there are rule breakers in Heaven."

"Other than yourself, you mean. I don't think so."

She smiled and asked the next question as innocently as she could muster. "Let's assume that there are a few risk takers up here. So where do these angels do their punishment? If they get caught?"

Arms crossed and leaning back in his chair, he stared at her. "Juliet, I'm telling you to leave this alone. If you're bored in the library, I'll find you another assignment. Something more...engaging. I have no idea what, but something."

"I love the library."

"Then go back there and do librarian stuff."

"You know what librarians do?" she asked. "Research. Research. And more research."

Arms still crossed. "Then stop asking me questions and do your own research."

"I thought you wanted me to leave this alone." She dramatically shook her head as if to clear a fog. "You Dominion are so confusing."

He narrowed his eyes. "If this hypothetical angel was unrepentant, they'd go to Purgatory. You should research that. Maybe in person."

"Oh," she said, and ignored the last part. "That makes sense. For other angels. But I don't think he's down there."

He was back to raising that one eyebrow again. "Who isn't?"

"Please, Hashmal. You know who I mean." She waited but he didn't show any recognition. "Lucifer."

"Oh, my stars!" he jumped up and closed the door. "You are the most stubborn, willful child. I will never understand how you landed here. I won't tell you again to leave this alone or you'll have to face very real consequences."

She dropped her hands on her lap in exasperation. "I'm not trying to get you in trouble. Or me. I don't want to go anywhere. I like it here." Hashmal still stood with his back to the door looking furious. "The story is really sad, don't you think? Two lovers divided for eternity. I just want to— I don't know. I guess I just want to know if they really loved each other. Are they still apart? Is Rachel still down there? Is Lucifer still in prison?" The Dominion actually flinched when she said their names. "I died before I got to be in love. I didn't even get to go to my own prom. No first kiss. I never even held a guy's hand. I just want to know it's real for someone."

The skin around his mouth was taut. "We never see Lucifer."

"You know him?" That seemed too much to hope for.

"No." He shook his head. "But when Father's angry... The Host has not been...patient with our brother."

Juliet leaned forward. "What does that mean? He's here, right? In Heaven?"

Hashmal leaned back. "Father said we were never to discuss it, *and we don't.*"

Even when she was alive, she'd been rash. Her rebellion against authority had not been to curse her parents or run with the fast kids. She was not the kind to stay out all night or get in trouble with the law. Instead, when she was eight and was told she couldn't read the books in the upperclassmen's library, she'd read each and every one. Those books weren't for children her age, the librarian had said.

She'd been told that pretty girls didn't take math and science, and she'd excelled in calculus and physics.

Juliet didn't act out, but she couldn't be told no, either. Her defiance ran deep. She had been every parent's dream: she made good grades and her teachers loved her, but she had always been a challenge.

If her mother had been present for Hashmal's warnings, she would have laughed and clapped her hand over her forehead. "You might as well give her the keys to the Kingdom," she would have said. "She'll never stop now."

Juliet stood. "So you're not going to help me in any way?"

The Dominion towered over her with his angelic beauty. "I *am* helping you. You go back to the library where you belong."

She sighed. "Thanks anyway."

Juliet pouted around the library, frustrated that she couldn't seem to get any further in her quest. She reread everything she'd found before about Lucifer with new eyes, searching for clues but nothing new showed itself. One afternoon after a fruitless day of searching, she opened a door she'd thought belonged to a closet only to find a dark room filled with maps and ancient atlases.

Locating the maps had been like finding the Rosetta Stone. They had been very confusing at first. She'd had to figure out the celestial charts and how they related with landmarks before she'd been able to sort out any locations. It wasn't like she could ask anyone else, either. She did heed Hashmal's warning enough to know that she didn't want to involve anyone else in the danger. While it made the search difficult and slow going, it also made it exciting and adventurous. Very cloak and dagger, in heaven, which was also a little weird.

And then one morning, it had all come clear. If ever there had been a time for an angel choir to sing in the background, this was it. How had she missed it? All she needed to do was figure out what Heaven meant to Lucifer before she could find him in it. She decided that she wasn't looking for an actual prison. The curse was kinda vague on that, but a "cage of his own making" didn't seem like an actual physical thing. What she remembered from Earth was that

Lucifer was the King in Hell, but now she knew that wasn't true either. If the story held true, Lucifer was a prisoner in Heaven. If he wasn't allowed to leave and no one had seen him, maybe he was hiding himself away. It only made sense that Heaven to Lucifer would be a sad, miserable place without Rachel. On a hunch, she snuck the map for the furthest quadrant of Heaven into her bag and firmly committed to defying God's orders.

JULIET HAD NEVER SEEN an Archangel before, but the minute she saw Lucifer she knew she was seeing one now. The Dominions were more beautiful than any human, but an Archangel was more spectacular, more radiant. Just more. And standing in a desert, alone on leagues of cracked earth, there was nothing to distract from his resplendency. Tall and slender, a perfect specimen the renaissance sculptors would have used as a model, with wings much larger than her own. Where hers, and every other angel she'd ever seen, were pure alabaster white, the Archangel's were ebony at the lowest point, gently gradating back to white at the top. The effect was to look like he'd dragged his wings through the mud. Uniquely miraculous.

"Excuse me." She cleared her throat and tried again, louder. "Excuse me?"

He moved his head, so she knew he heard her.

"Um, Hi. Are you Lucifer?"

The angel stared at her, his expression blank and unblinking. A sudden nervous giggle escaped her throat.

"I'm Juliet." She curtsied and then giggled again. "I've been looking and looking for you."

"Why?" The word came out like a croak. Like he hadn't used his voice in a millennium. Maybe he hadn't. He was a mess dressed in dingy, shredded rags.

"I read your story and it was the most beautiful thing I'd ever read. How you and Rachel gave up everything for each other." She clasped her hands to her heart. "And how God punished you for your love. So romantic."

"Go away."

"Okay, but I just wondered if Rachel was still down...there." She pointed downward to be helpful. "In Hell."

Lucifer narrowed his eyes at her. "I...don't...know. Maybe."

"You don't know?" she asked, incredulous. "How can you not know?"

"Who are you?"

"Juliet," she repeated.

He stared at her for several long beats before he continued, "But who are you?"

She looked down at herself. "I... I... I don't know what you're asking. I'm Juliet. I work in the library." She smiled at the Archangel hopefully. "Do you want backstory? I was sixteen when I came to heaven. Umm, I loved strawberry milkshakes and Shakespeare and a boy named Tommy. I think he's a grandfather now, isn't that funny?" She paused again. "Does that help?"

"You're an angel?"

She flapped her wings helpfully. "Yep."

"And you've been looking for me?" He seemed really confused. Like an Alzheimer's patient or something.

She approached him as slowly as she'd do an orphaned bear cub. She didn't want to startle him. "Uh, yeah. And you've been hard to find. Not a lot of angels were willing to help."

"No, I'm sure not. They never were." Finally, he expressed an emotion. Resignation, it sounded like. "But why you?"

She opened her mouth to answer him, but nothing came readily to mind. "Huh. I guess because I can't meet Tristan and Isolde or Lancelot and Guinevere. Your story was so romantic, I guess I wanted confirmation that it was real."

"Our story is real, but it's not a romance; it's a tragedy. Now go away and leave me to my punishment." He turned from her, towards the darkness that opened before him, his version of Heaven morphing into a terrifying forest like something out of Hansel and Gretel.

"Don't lock yourself away again," she called after him. "Besides you haven't answered my questions and it took me forever to find you." He paused, just a hitch in his step, but it made her gush on. "You

97

really haven't seen her ever again? Or your sons? Aren't you curious?"

"Curious? You ask me if I'm curious?" He was facing her again and now he seemed angry. "You want to know if Rachel is still down there? I don't know. I don't know anything. I have begged Father for leniency. I have beseeched my brothers to intervene. When they failed, I pleaded with them to get her a message, but they would not." Oh, yes, he was definitely angry, and it was possible he was growing larger. "Is she well? Is she even alive? Does she hate me now after all this time?"

Juliet swallowed hard. "Maybe I can help?"

"It is forbidden," Lucifer growled through gritted teeth.

She shrugged, only because a giant, roaring Archangel was crazy intimidating.

"How?" he demanded. "How can you, a tiny girl-angel, help when my brothers cannot. How?"

"I don't know." She gave him a hopeful smile. "But I found you, didn't I?"

CHAPTER TEN

Luke was peeved to realize that he didn't make coffee as well as Jeb did. He didn't know what the tediously competent gargoyle did to a Keurig pod to make the black bean juice so tasty, but there was no denying that when Luke made it himself, it wasn't as delicious. What could Jeb possibly add to black coffee that Luke himself hadn't done?

He was standing outside his building contemplating the recipe when Mia's old pickup trundled to a stop at the curb. He hadn't argued when she told him she'd drive. After all, he had no idea where they were going and, from the sound of it, it was nowhere he should be driving a classic hotrod anyway.

"Good morning." Minnie Mouse was sunshiny and adorable in a baseball cap, her crooked arm resting on the door as she called out the window. "I see you already have coffee."

The truck was old enough that he had to manually tug the locking mechanism before he could get the door open. The bench seat upholstery was patched with duct tape. On the seat between them sat a picnic basket.

"Good morning," he said and leaned across the wicker basket and pecked her on the cheek. He was rewarded with a pretty blush that was just a shade or two lighter than the pink of the sunrise. "Do you always detect for apples this early?"

She dropped the old Chevy in gear and pulled back out onto the nonexistent traffic on a Sunday morning. "Yep. Hidden orchards are never conveniently located. We're going to be tooling around in the boonies for quite a while." She raised her eyebrows. "Are you really sure you want to do this? Now's your chance to bail. No harm, no foul."

Luke had absolutely nothing to do today, and riding around with a pretty lady was a hell of a lot better than anything his cousins would be getting up to. Or putting up with another day of Jeb poking him and writing crap down in his charts. He took off his sunglasses and peeked into the cloth-covered basket.

"You packed us a lunch?" He plucked out a wine bottle. Merlot. Nice.

"Yeah. This isn't like fishing. You can't hope that you'll catch your dinner when you're hunting for apples. Best case is you find them and then all you have to eat are apples. This is hungry work." She looked over at him, inspecting the contents. "Wow, your face looks great."

"Ah, you'll make me blush." He made a noncommittal noise and then tried to brush off the comment by holding a long baguette up to his nose and inhaling the yeasty aroma.

"No, seriously. I would have expected you to look much worse. Yesterday you looked terrible." He raised one eyebrow and looked at her over the bread. "Well, I don't mean terrible exactly. You looked fine, you know, handsome, but sort of mangled. No, actually you looked terrible. You really did. But today—It's not nearly what—" She stopped babbling and smiled. "You know what I mean."

He smiled to let her off the hook. "I used that cayenne pepper thing you told me about that time."

"You did?" She sounded completely amazed. "And it worked?"

Laughing, he pulled out a jar of olives to inspect them. "No. I was just kidding. I'm a really fast healer."

She stared at him for a minute, her expression lost behind her own sunglasses. "Sure. That seems legit."

He shrugged. There wasn't anything else to say. He healed fast.

Immortality was handy that way. Still, that little nugget wasn't something he normally worked into conversation. "You pack a nice spread. I see roast beef, bread, wine, olives. Very Mediterranean. I approve. Ooh, brownies and berries."

Mia was back to watching the road. "If all goes well, we'll be starving by lunch."

Before he tucked the cover back over the basket, he found a map tucked inside. When he opened it up, he found some areas circled and notes written in red pen.

Seven miles on Old Route 17

Past the drainage ditch, trail is quarter mile on left

West side of 2nd hill after the water tower

"Is this where we're going?"

"Yeah, I got a call on one of the wanted posters I left at a farmers market last month."

He glanced at her over the top of the map. "A what poster?"

"Wanted." She chuckled, clearly amused at his confusion. "A wanted poster. I think I still have some in the glove box."

"Like for an old west gunfighter?" He couldn't resist. Rolled up inside the glovebox was a tube of papers. When unfurled, they were definitely wanted posters for an apple. He read aloud. "Wanted: Information on Pink Felicity."

It went on to describe the outside color as yellow with dark pink speckles, the stem length as short with a shallow cavity. There was a full color artist's rendering of what the Pink Felicity looked like. It even included a sliced open cross section showing the flesh as pink and mellow with a five-pointed star in the middle where the seeds collected.

He continued, "Last seen on the Johnson-McGruder's farm." He ruffled the sheaf of papers and saw there were other apples wanted on other sheets. "Sweet Susanna. Holmes Gallant. Pomme Rose. Who names apples? These are crazy."

Her smile was radiant. "They sound like poetry to me. One of my favorites is Summer Ladyfinger, and there's Maidens Blush and Yellow Bellflower and Bogdanoff Glass. When you develop the apple, you get to name it."

Luke shrugged with one shoulder. "That's fair." He rolled the posters up and tucked them back in the glovebox, then shifted in the seat to face her more fully. "So, what I don't get is why. If you want an apple, I can get you a dozen of them right now at any grocery store. It doesn't seem to me that they're all that scarce. Why all the detecting?"

Mia wrinkled her cute little nose. "Sure. Apples are everywhere. The supermarkets are lousy with 'em. If you want Red Delicious— which isn't, by the way. Or Granny Smith."

"Oh, I see." He sipped his coffee through a smile. "You're an apple snob."

"Heck, yeah. And you're going to become one, too, as soon as you start eating good apples." She inhaled a deep breath and let it out. "Did you know that North America alone was the home to more than fifteen thousand varieties of apples?" She looked to him with raised eyebrows. He shook his head and took another sip. "It's true. We've lost over eighty percent of the varietals. Each apple has a unique genetic code, and once it's lost, it's lost forever."

He cast her a dubious look from across the cab. "Fifteen *thousand* kinds of apples? That's sort of crazy."

She nodded enthusiastically while still keeping her eyes on the road. "Right? Some estimates had the number as high as seventeen thousand."

"So, what's the deal? Global warming?"

"No. The villain in this scenario is different. The blame fits squarely on industrial farming and the rise of refrigeration. Once refrigerated shipping was a thing, Americans started living further and further from the source of their food. It stopped being grown on small family farms, and the birth of industrial farming gave way to crop manipulation." She looked in the rearview mirror and used her blinker to signal a turn. "Apples have always captivated America. They're not the favorite pie for nothing, you know. But if the farmers were going to ship these apples further and further, from the country to the cities, they were going to have to be hearty fruit. They had to be sweet to meet the tastes of the common consumer, couldn't bruise easily, and they had to stay ripe for longer periods of time. And thus we have the rapid proliferation of Red Delicious."

Mia glanced over and noticed he was still watching her. He enjoyed watching her. She was a complex little thing. He'd assumed that regardless of how cute she was, she was also a bit balmy. What else was he supposed to think with all the changes she wanted to make long after they were done with the design? Insane requests like an indoor orchard. Ridiculous. Of course, it was still possible that she was crazy, but at least she was knowledgeable about her obsession. Also, a smart man wouldn't get caught up in any kind of relationship with a client. And yet, here he was at this ungodly hour on a Sunday, cataloging the ways she was cute and giving her nicknames in his head.

The scenery flashing by was more rural than it had been only twenty minutes before. Less strip malls and office buildings and more wild expanses and foliage.

"So, what? The Red Delicious—which tastes fine, by the way. It's right there in the name." He gave her a cheeky grin and a chuckle when she gave him some side eye. "It edges out all the other apples 'cause they get to market better?"

She shrugged. "Essentially."

He sat there for a second trying to understand. "So, where'd all the other apples go?"

"They disappeared. Family farms got parceled off or went back to seed. They weren't in demand anymore so..." She flicked the fingers of her right hand.

"I'm sure it's more complicated than this, but why can't you just plant some seeds? How hard can apple trees be to grow?"

"It's not difficult at all. The problem is that you can't just plant some seeds and expect the apples to be the same ones that came from the parent tree."

"What?"

She glanced across the cab at him. "Are you sure you want to hear all of this? It's kind of technical."

He shook his head. "No. I'm in. You have a captive audience here."

"You're going to be sorry you asked."

Spreading his arms wide, he said, "Educate me."

"All right. Remember, you wanted it. Apples are complicated. If you plant a seed from an apple, there's no guarantee you'll get a fruit that's similar. Most often, you get what's called a spitter. Those apples are usually really sour or bitter. If they're edible at all, they're used for hard cider or apple jack."

"Brilliant. I love hard cider."

"Me, too." She switched lanes and directed the truck onto an exit. "But say you're a farmer who wants to grow more trees that make apples like the one in your yard. Your wife makes a kick ass apple pie with it. You can't just drop an apple in the ground, water it, and hope for the best. You actually have to take a cutting from the tree and graft it onto another tree. Basically, you grow a clone. That's what we apple detectives do after we find the trees."

The truck bounced over a cattle guard and then on to dirt where the new State Route 17 diverted from the old road. If he hadn't been paying attention, he'd have missed it. It's a good thing Mia had a pretty decent idea where they were headed.

"That's cool." He propped his arm along the back of the bench seat. If he felt so inclined, he was close enough he could actually take a lock of her hair and wrap it around his finger. "So let me see if I get this. The farmers stopped growing the hard-to-transport apples, and they started to fade away. So now you and some other people are trying to resurrect these old apples before they disappear."

"Right! So we visit farmers markets and talk to the old timers in the area about the apples they remember growing up. People have a funny relationship with food. It gets all wrapped up in their memories. People remember the pie their grandmother made when they were kids. Or the fritters on Sundays, and it makes them feel warm and fuzzy, all nostalgic. You know what I mean? Food memories are emotional."

They trundled down the road with Mia steering the truck around giant potholes.

"Yeah." He thought about his childhood and remembered having cocoa with his grandmother. She would add whipped cream and chocolate shavings. Mia was right. Anytime he drank cocoa as an adult, he was briefly transported to childhood where snuggly laps and favorite stories were the most important things in life. He considered for a moment that he needed more cocoa in his life.

Mia went on to describe how she'd gotten the tip on the Pink Felicity. "Almost in our backyard," she told him with awe in her voice. "I can't believe no one has stumbled on it before."

Luke pointed out the obvious. "Probably lots of people have stumbled on it and had no idea what they'd found. Until today, I could have stumbled on it and had no idea."

"True." She nodded enthusiastically. "When I heard a rumor about it, I put up the flyers and got a tip really fast."

The old state route had nearly gone to seed way out here. Since it was no longer maintained, the foliage was steadily encroaching and the parts of it that were surrounded by trees had a cool tunnel effect that felt almost magical. He gave Mia a quick side glance and considered that spending time with Minnie Mouse was making him fanciful.

One big bump in the road bounced her head into the hand he had along the top of the seat. He gave her neck a gentle squeeze. She didn't react, so he left it there for a moment before sliding his fingers into the hair at her nape.

They rode like this for a few moments, feeling the undercurrent in the air, before the tree-lined road broke away from the overhang and a large meadow spread out before them. There was only the rattle of the old truck and sounds of nature.

She finally broke the silence. "We're about seven miles from where we left the black top. Doesn't that map say something about that?"

He had to take his hand back in order to fumble with the map. "Yeah. There should be a trail after the drainage ditch."

Mia slowed the truck down and they both looked out their prospective windows.

"Over there." He pointed to the right. "That looks like an old drainage ditch."

She pulled the truck off the dirt track and onto the grass. "All right, we're hiking from here then."

"Bring the basket?" He asked, pointing to the picnic supplies.

She nodded and slid from the cab. "I don't know how far we're going to have to go. We might be miles from the truck before we find what we're looking for."

"Then the basket comes. I'll carry it."

Already pulling down the tailgate, she hollered. "No worries. I have a wagon."

Before he could get back there, she was already hauling a rugged trail wagon down. It was canvas framed by lightweight, accordioned aluminum with rubber inflated tires. She took the basket from him with a smile and nestled it in the wagon with a roll of electrical tape, twine, a small hand saw, and garden shears.

He waggled his finger at the odd assortment of items. "If this were a movie of the week, I would be yelling at the guy on the TV not to go into the woods with that woman. Are you planning to kidnap and murder me out here?"

All five feet, two inches of her stood tall. "Shakespeare said it best, 'Though she is but little, she is fierce.'"

He took two steps closer and towered over her. "Should I be worried?"

"Even though you got your ass handed to you the other night—"

"Oh!" He tossed his head back and laughed. "You're mean."

Her laughter mingled with his, the rich and throaty sound that had so captivated his attention before. "I imagine you can take care of yourself."

He pulled the wagon, and she led the way with a walking stick and a backpack. The trail, such as it was, started where the map had suggested, a few yards to the side of the ditch. They followed it through the meadow and shortly it began an incline through some rolling hills. Luke felt like he was on a treasure hunt and was giddy to point out the water tower when it came into view.

Luke picked up his pace. "Just over that hill is where the map said."

"Don't get too excited," she warned. "The trees might not be there. Or they could be dead."

"No way, Debby Downer. This is my first apple hunt. Beginner's luck says I have to win."

She shrugged. "I hope you're right. I'm just saying..."

"Nope. I'm not listening."

Of course, he was a foot taller than her, so he was able to see over the hill before she could. He let out a whoop of victory as soon as he saw the yellow and pink fruit hanging heavy from the trees. There were four of them still brandishing fruit like painted ladies in a funeral parlor, the rest of the grove dead and brittle making up most of the congregation.

He plucked apples from the high branches while she pulled ancient seed and farming catalogues from her backpack.

"They're perfectly ripe," he said through a mouthful, and lay down on the grass next to where she was studying the fruit and the books. "If I didn't know better, I'd say God loves me. Finding apples on my very first try. The best apples, ever, in the history of fruit."

"Umm hmm." She used a pocketknife to half one and compared it to the pictures inside.

Rolling over on his belly, he chewed and watched her. Her hat was pushed back, and she had a pencil between her teeth while she read. Periodically she'd turn the page or stare at the fruit. Finally, she took a bite and contemplated her mouthful, still perusing the text. Her bottom lip glistened with apple juice. Even as sweet as the fruit was, his mouth went dry when her tongue flicked out and licked up the juice.

"Watcha thinkin'?" he asked.

Her gaze finally met his. The radiant smile she bestowed upon him made it uncomfortable to lay as he was.

She held up the apple. "I think you're a good luck charm. I believe this really is a Pink Felicity."

"Do I get a reward?"

CHAPTER ELEVEN

Mia knew kissing Luke—again—was a mistake. Conventional wisdom insisted that workplace romances were a terrible idea. The covers of Cosmo shrieked promises of salacious horror stories on that subject all the time, and every letter to a self-help column asking for advice with an office breakup suggested what everyone knew all along—office romances were bad news bears. Even her father with the wandering eye insisted so eloquently that a smart person did not "shit where they ate."

But Luke was hot.

And funny.

And most intriguing of all was that he seemed genuinely interested in her apple fixation and not in a placating way. He asked real questions and listened to the answers.

And he was so hot.

Flirting with him was easy. Outside of the office, he was a different man: interested in learning new things, open to suggestions, and not nearly as alpha male as he presented himself otherwise.

He'd found the Pink Felicity and now he was angling for a reward.

And, ooh, she wanted to give him one. She'd relived that kiss in his apartment to an almost excessive degree and, as foolish as her desire was, parts of her body were desperate to know what would happen after another kiss. Her good sense was losing serious traction.

"What kind of reward are you thinking?" she asked. "I could make you another pie."

Luke's smile was beguiling as he took another bite of apple. "You do make a fine apple pie."

Oh. He wanted pie. She guessed she should be flattered. "Sure. I'm not sure if the Pink Felicity is best for pie, but I'll give it a shot."

He chuckled and tossed the finished core into the field. "I don't want pie for my reward." He rose up on his hands and knees and crawled towards her.

Mia would have let out a little squeak if she'd been capable of making noise. His grin had morphed into something predatory, but she wasn't afraid. She put her notebooks down in anticipation and held her breath. He stopped in front of her and, while still on his knees, he took her hand and pulled her forward so she was on her knees before him. He pulled off her baseball cap and tossed it aside. As a reflex, she ran her hand through her hair, certain that it looked horrible from being in a cap all day.

Slipping an arm around her waist, he pulled her flush and dipped his lips to meet hers. His mouth was infused with sweet apple nectar.

Just like the last time, he took his time and kissed her with finesse, slowly and determined to leave her boneless. When he finally released her, it took several long heart beats before Mia opened her eyes. Instead, she allowed the breeze to cool her heated skin and ruffle her mussed hair. Intermixed with the aroma of wildflowers and sweet grass, the ambrosia of apples filled the air.

"That was a heck of a reward," she whispered. "I should give more of them."

A satisfied male grin pulled at his lips. "Apple detecting is an underappreciated skill. I figured you deserved a reward, too."

She ran her arms up the length of his biceps and twined her fingers around his neck. "If that's the metric, you should know that I have located a lot of apples."

His eyebrows rose. "How many is a lot?"

"Hmmm." She looked to the sky and thought about it. "I'd say fifteen is a safe number, but it might be higher. I could easily be forgetting some."

He dipped his head again, this time to nuzzle her neck and nip at her jawline. "Let's take them one at a time," he murmured the words against her skin.

She clutched on to his shoulders and, throwing caution to the wind, tilted her head back to encourage him to take what he wanted.

"What was the first apple you found?"

"Huh?" It was impossible to concentrate on his words when her earlobe was in his mouth.

He pulled away and she huffed in frustration. "What was the apple called?"

"Oh." She blinked and searched her brain. "Umm, Oxheart."

"Oxheart," he repeated. His lips brushed hers and a large palm slid down to mold around her butt. "Which one was next?"

"It was uhh...Bowmans Ruby."

A nip at her chin followed by a stream of kisses down the column of her throat. "Delicious."

"The apple?" she asked and curled her fingers into his hair.

"And the detective." He planted a kiss in the hollow of her throat.

"First Winter," she said and pulled his mouth back to hers. She could still taste the apple on his tongue. They settled there for a long moment, exploring with their lips and tongues and hands.

When they finally came up for air, he asked, "First Winter?"

"That was the third apple I found."

"Well done." He had one of the best grins she'd ever seen. When he looked at her like this it was hard to believe she'd ever thought he looked scary. "You say there are twelve more?"

"Maybe fifteen or twenty." She tickled her fingernails along his scalp. "I was trying not to brag."

He chuckled. "I'm going to need more sustenance than apples if I'm going to reward you for that many."

"Oh, the picnic," she said, remembering that they had toted their lunch with them. Luke's stomach growled and they both laughed.

Luke laid out a blanket on the grass while Mia unpacked the food. They ate and teased and somehow managed to touch each other constantly. She avoided the topic of work entirely. The day was too pleasant to ruin with an argument about their project. Besides, she was still hoping that today would change his mind about the orchard idea. Instead, she asked questions about his fighting career and his cousin she met earlier. He talked a lot about nothing. He mentioned his other cousins in passing and implied that they were a tight group of friends in addition to being related. When she asked follow-up questions about them, he deflected.

"Just a bunch of dumbasses I've known all my life. More like brothers," he told her and tore a hunk off the baguette.

"That's nice, though," she said and brushed his arm when she reached for the wine bottle. "I don't have any brothers or sisters, but I've known my best friend, Cassie, almost my whole life. She's like a sister to me. I would be a mess without her."

He grinned and nodded. "There's no one else in this world who would put up with the seven of us, either."

She'd forgotten wine glasses, so she took a swig straight from the bottle. "I don't know. I get the feeling that Jeb would be right there with you. I mean, I thought Jason was fantastic, but Jeb goes above and beyond."

Luke flopped over onto his back and dropped his head in her lap. "Jeb's very dedicated to his job, that's true. But he's not what he seems either."

"Hmmm." She ran her fingertips over his forehead to move the hair off his face. "You mean because he's gay. Do you think he has a crush on you?"

She was surprised by the burst of laughter that shook Luke. She'd thought he'd immediately defend his manhood in a knee jerk reaction to the possibility, but for some reason Luke was laughing. Watching him in surprise, she waited. Finally, he wiped his eyes and sighed.

"Does that mean he does or doesn't have a crush on you?" she asked.

"Oh, no," Luke assured her while still chortling. "Jeb would lose his pants faster than I can wink, if I ever went that way. I'm just thinking of how insufferable he'd be with the rest of his cronies if he ever bagged me. Their whole spooky cabal is full of one-upman-

AMYLYNN BRIGHT

ship and if he'd managed to land one of the Seven…well, shit, game over."

Mia didn't really know what he was talking about. Did assistants have a cabal? Was Jason aware? Was he in on it?

She finger-combed his hair. Even through the shade of the tree, the sunlight brought out a million shades of mahogany and red and gold. "I get the sense that he thinks he's irresistible. You never thought of throwing him a bone?" she said, goading him a bit.

He tilted his head and looked at her. "Pun intended?"

It took her a second to realize what she said. "Oh. Ha. Yeah."

"No," he told her with emphasis.

Ah there was the masculine hetero pride.

"Why," she teased and gently scratched his scalp with her finger-nails. "He's really very pretty. My assistant is gaga over him."

"This is an odd conversation with my head in your lap." He sat up and Mia was disappointed that maybe she'd spoiled the mood. But he didn't pull away. Instead, he leaned towards her, dropped one arm against her opposite hip and basically trapped her against the tree trunk. "Besides the fact that I'm straight and not interested in Jeb regardless of how pretty he is, I would never have…" he seemed to struggle finding the right word, "…a fling with anyone who worked for my father."

Mia's eyebrows rose. "I didn't realize. Your father owns your firm?"

His face was only inches from hers now, and her mouth had gone dry. How could he change the whole mood from light banter to charged sexual tension in less than a heartbeat?

He slowly shook his head. "No, but I don't want to talk about my father."

Her hair tangled in the bark of the apple tree when she nodded in understanding. "Sure. I get that." Her own father was a never-ending source of aggravation for her, so she got where he was coming from.

Now his mouth was so close she could feel puffs of air when he spoke. "Talking about my father makes me wrathful, and I don't want to be that way around you."

"Okay," she whispered.

His lips brushed hers as he murmured, "Fairy princesses shouldn't meet the lion."

Luke filled the wagon with apples while Mia used the hand saw and other tools to take several cuttings which she explained she'd graft onto another tree.

"How much stuff can we make with all these apples?" He asked as he tugged the wagon along the route back to where they left the truck. He was eating another one. He couldn't get over how delicious it was. The pale-pink flesh was sweet without being cloying, and he loved the snap and crunch when his teeth sunk in. Snow White had been on the nose when she told him he'd become an apple snob after this.

"I don't know. I have a zillion recipes I'll be happy to give you. You can experiment and let me know."

He looked down at her and batted his eyelashes. "What'll it take for you to make them for me?"

Mia rolled her eyes and smiled. "We'll leave the negotiations open."

He watched her as they hiked back to the road. They'd eaten their lunch under the shade of the apple trees and made out like teenagers. And that's where he forced himself to stop. Necking was bad enough. He'd reminded himself repeatedly that morning that messing around with a client was a horrible idea, but he couldn't manage to keep his hands—or his lips—off her. He couldn't define her draw, but she was like his catnip. The more he got to know her, the more his focus had shifted from keeping his employer happy to desperately wanting another taste of her.

As soon as he'd hear the firm's board of directors voices in his head threatening him if he screwed up this deal he'd back pedal his attraction to Mia, but then she'd say some flirty banter or lick her lips or something and he'd slip right back into carnal thoughts that could ruin everything. It was that much harder that Mia was a more-than-willing participant.

Nevertheless, a smart man didn't dally with the clients, and he sure as hell couldn't have any kind of relationship with her. He'd never had a real relationship with anyone other than his cousins. He had no other actual friends. He had no history of entanglements. He was a planet spinning around in his own fucking universe.

None of the Seven Princes of Hell bothered forging connections with other people—especially romantic ones. The risk was too great to fall in love. His cousins probably understood that in an academic sense, but Luke knew it from experience. He and his dad had been very close, especially after his mother died. It had been just the two of them for eight long years. If his dad had thought that would end after the ceremony, he didn't act like it. But all of it had ended when Luke was ten, when his father walked out of that room wearing the mantle of the Devil, both literally and figuratively.

It had nearly broken him. He never heard anything from his dad after that, although he heard plenty from his father. That's the way Luke compartmentalized it: Dad before; Father after. Loving parent verses the ruler of Hell. How cliché was it that Luke hated his father? Clichéd, banal, boring and factual.

Luke had the self-awareness to wonder how much of the bile he had for this father was due to being saddled with Wrath, but in the end it didn't matter. He hated his Father, and the curse and everything that his life could come to if he was chosen during his generation's ceremony.

Luke would never, ever do that to another person. There was a one in seven chance that he would have to leave this Earth and take on life-destroying responsibilities, and he had no plans to leave anyone behind if it came to that.

That didn't mean the princess didn't entice the hell out of him. Just because he didn't do relationships didn't mean he was celibate. It's not like he ran around like lusty Asher and nailed everything that moved, but he did all right for himself. There were plenty of women out there who weren't interested in a relationship either. As long as expectations were set early on, things worked out nicely. If his partners got too clingy and didn't play by the rules, well, generally Wrath took care of that, too. Luke would give a gentle *push* and the lady in question wouldn't be interested in putting up with his bullshit anymore. It worked out perfectly. He got laid and they got to use some self-righteous anger and feel empowered.

It's like he routinely performed a public service.

They had just arrived at the truck when Luke was trying to work out how he could play that scenario on Mia without losing the account and being fired.

Mia took an apple for the road before Luke hefted the wagon into the bed of the truck. "Before we get home, I need to stop at the Daughters of Eve, okay?" she said.

He buckled his seatbelt while giving her a look. "The convent?"

"Yeah, but I don't think convent is the right word. Monastery maybe. Or abbey. They're religious, but I honestly don't know what religion they are. Are druids still a thing?"

Luke hadn't heard of the Daughters of Eve in years. He only vaguely knew about them from learning his family's canon. Something about an all-female religious order that worshiped Eve, the first woman, and her daughter Rachel who had fallen in love with Lucifer and started this whole goddamned mess.

God damned. Literally.

Luke's curiosity was peaked. "What are we going to do there?"

"Maybe a commune is the right word. You know they're sort of like hippies." She shrugged. "I've been consulting with them on their gardens. They're all into organic farming and heirloom plants and stuff. Their grounds really are like Eden. They grow everything and it's all a little wild."

Intriguing. "I'm game."

Anything to extend the time with the princess, you selfish bastard.

"The nuns are pretty cool," Mia ventured. "I was a little leery of going there at first, you know, it being a religious place, even hypothetically. I didn't want to be steamrolled by a bunch of righteous nuts, you know? When they called me for a consult, I expected them to try to convert me from the instant I walked into the place, but they didn't."

Luke unrolled the window once they were back on the blacktop. The afternoon had warmed up nicely, and the breeze felt good tickling his hair. "Not a religious person, then?"

She shrugged again. "My family never really went to church. We only observed the religious holidays secularly. Easter bunny and Santa Claus. That kind of thing. My dad is too busy for church. My grandmother on my mother's side is very religious. She's always trying to get me to see the light, but I have a really hard time believing in that mythology. Maybe it's the scientist in me." She glanced at him from across the cab. "How about you?"

The Seven came at organized religion from a very different perspective than regular people. They happened to *know* that some of that mythology was true. For Luke and his cousins, learning how the universe worked happened as simply and easily as learning the alphabet. There was no mystery. Their whole lives were predicated on the fact that God was real. That the Devil was alive and well. That angels and demons lived and breathed. But who would ever believe them if they told them? What was the point in it? It wasn't like any of them could offer up proof.

Besides, the Devil wasn't really known for his sermonizing. Luke and his cousins weren't put on this earth to convert people or bring them to the truth.

"Well, it's complicated," he told her.

CHAPTER TWELVE

M ia nodded her head. "If it's complicated, then it sounds like you went to Catholic school."

Hardly. "Nothing like that, but my cousins and I had a very strict religious upbringing." He fiddled with the old-fashioned hand crank on the window.

Most important lesson in their education was that there were rules. God was very serious about the rules.

"Oh," she said, but it was an acknowledgment that said she didn't understand at all. She drove and he sat in silence for a long moment. Then she cast him a furtive glance across the cab. "What, were you in a cult or something?"

Luke snickered. "Nah. But kinda."

He'd inadvertently opened up the floodgates because now he could feel her boiling with the energy of unanswered questions. She'd think he was crazy if he told her the whole, unvarnished truth. He could just see her pulling over the ancient pickup on the side of the road and ejecting him from the cab while demanding that he spit out the apple.

He had to tell her something. It couldn't be the truth, but he didn't want to lie to her either. The usual evasive answer wouldn't be good enough. Not for her.

"Well," he began, choosing his words wisely. "We believe in God, but in an Old Testament kind of way." He glanced over at her, and she wore a wide-open expression of interest.

"Like the fire and brimstone kind of God?"

"Yes," he said with enthusiasm because she kind of nailed it there. "Definitely. The New Testament doesn't really come into play where the truth is concerned."

She raised her eyebrows while she contemplated this. "Are you an offshoot of the Jewish faith?"

He sighed. "Not exactly. There isn't a name, and we're pretty unique in that we have a different perspective than just about anyone else in the world. We're sorta all religions and none of them, all at the same time."

She kept her eyes on the road to avoid potholes. "Do you celebrate Christmas?"

"For the same reason you probably do. It's fun and we live in a mostly Christian society. Atheists celebrate it. My dad and later my aunt and uncle did the Santa thing."

They were back on the asphalt now and headed towards civilization or wherever the Daughters of Eve monastery was located.

"So, I'm confused." She said. "You're not Jewish. You're not Christian. You basically follow Christian holidays. You believe in the Bible—"

"Nope."

"Nope, what? What part did I get wrong?"

He should just shup up while he was ahead. Now it was going to get sticky. "Yeah, the Bible. Not so much."

"Really?" Now she looked at him.

He could feel his chest filling up with jaundiced self-righteousness. It was the weirdest thing. Anytime he became embroiled in a conversation about religion he got himself all riled up. He needed to chill out. It had been a good day, and she wasn't even arguing with him. He was either going to calmly say the words or he was changing the subject.

No, Luke, we don't growl at Minnie Mouse.

"The Bible was basically a book written by the church to further their causes—especially the New Testament onward."

She hesitated. "Yeah, I guess so. Sure. I guess I intellectually know that."

"It's true," he assured her. "Even the Catholic church admits that."

"Oh. Huh."

There was another long pause while she ruminated over that and he waited to find out what she'd ask next.

"Sooo, who's to say what was changed or left out or added?"

He didn't answer, just looked at her with raised eyebrows that might encourage her to continue that line of thought.

"Like, everyone screws up a game of telephone, right?" She blinked furiously at the road. "I mean that's the fun part of the game. No one ever gets it right." Another pause. "And stories change over time. After the fifth, tenth, twentieth time you tell them, they're totally different."

She was damned adorable while she was experiencing an epiphany.

Slapping her hand on her thigh, she looked at him. "Honest to God, I never thought about this stuff before. I've never given religion much thought at all, apparently."

He shrugged and smiled at her. The poisonous juices that had threatened to erupt ebbed and he felt the tightness loosen.

A small hand-painted sign on the highway indicated the Daughters of Eve monastery was on the left.

"Taking all of that into account, how do you all feel about Jesus?" she asked.

"Don't know. Never met the dude."

Barking out a laugh, she directed the truck across the highway. A long dirt driveway led to a parking area where she brought the truck to a stop. The area was heavily wooded with massive trees. The afternoon breeze smelled of warm pine and forest mulch. A formidable wall surrounded the building, at least from the front. If he stood on his tiptoes, he could have peeked over the edge, but flatfooted all he could see was the slate roof of a massive building.

She led him up to an imposing wooden gate with a bell pull. "One of these days, I want to hear more about all this. It's fascinating."

He gave a noncommittal grunt. When she yanked on the thick rope, a heavy bell clanged on the other side of the wall. "Wow. Intimidating," he said, taking in the fortress quality of the place.

She grinned. "Only from the outside. You'll see. These ladies are the exact opposite of intimidating."

There was a scuffle on the other side of the wall, and then the snout of some massive animal shoved itself into the crack between the wall and the gate. It snuffled hard and then expelled a muffled woof.

Mia's grin widened when Luke took an involuntary step back.

"Just surprised me, that's all," he told her and shoved his hands in his pockets.

"Harvey, on the other hand, is very intimidating," she told him with what he was pretty sure was bloodthirsty glee. He gave her a double take and took another step back. Her throaty laugh was the one that went straight to his pants.

Another voice joined the throng on the other side of the wall. "Move, you dogs, move. Harvey, get out of the way." There was loud grunting and then the nose disappeared. At last, the gate swung open and a lady wearing overalls and a chambray shirt presented herself with a pack of dogs. It was immediately apparent which one was Harvey. One dog towered above the rest. Dirty white fur with huge dark spots covered his considerable body. His broad head was level with the woman's elbow, and he kept pushing at her hip to come around in front of her, but she laid her hand flat on his forehead and pushed him back behind. "Get back, Harvey," she scolded. Then her voice rang out in a singsong. "Hello, Miss Mia. Oh, and friend." She used both hands to hold back the pack. "I'm Diana. Just ignore the dogs."

Luke twisted his wrist in a small wave while Mia introduced them. "He's helping me follow up on leads today."

"Luke Mephisto," the lady repeated, as if trying to recall the name. She blinked away her thoughts and swung the gate open for them to enter. The sea of wagging dogs parted, and Luke felt like Moses as he waded through them after Mia. Inside the courtyard it already felt like a garden. Enormous pots of herbs lined the walls and a white flower-covered trellis arched over a walkway that emerged into a massive garden. Rosemary and mint mingled with the smell of dog.

He carefully followed the ladies as they led the way out to the garden, picking his way around the smaller of the dogs who clustered around his feet. Harvey didn't growl or give any outward indication that he planned to eat Luke, but he did give off a vaguely menacing air and stayed strategically between him and the ladies.

The garden was laid out in acres upon acres of cleared land in a patchwork of colors. All the dogs except Harvey lost interest in him and sprang forward into the garden, racing and barking in a mad melee. Diana and Mia strode ahead with a purpose, chatting away about horticultural things.

"You're a big-assed dog," he told Harvey unnecessarily, but he felt like he should say something. The animal hadn't taken his eyes off him once since they'd met. "What kind of dog are you? If I had to guess, I'd say polar bear and, what, bull."

Harvey snorted through his nose and maintained his position.

"What's a big guy like you eat, huh?"

The dog didn't answer but Mia did. "Architects," she called over her shoulder.

Right on cue the dog raised his eyebrows and cocked his ears. One giant snaggle tooth stuck out of his lower jaw.

"Nice. Thanks for that," Luke called back. "I'm not really an architect," he told Harvey. "Actually, I know Cerberus. He's a friend. We go way back. I'll tell him you said hey."

He could still hear Mia laughing.

As they passed through the garden, Luke took in the lush vibrancy. Along the winding paths they encountered other women in work clothes and giant floppy hats trimming bushes or weeding rows of vegetables. They all raised a hand in salute or called greetings to Mia. In the distance somewhere, he heard a tractor.

At the eastern end of the property, fruit trees grew in abundance. Right in the front were about a dozen apples trees. Mia and Diana inspected the branches and discussed cross pollination and bloom periods all while Luke marveled at the uniqueness of the trees. The grandest one had a canopy at least twenty-five feet wide. Some of the branches had sections tied and bound with tape, and these branches seemed to have different fruit. This single tree had yellow and red and greenish apples. Some of the fruit were large and round, where others were misshapen and lopsided. Standing underneath, Luke looked up and saw at least nine distinct apples.

"What's with this Frankenstein tree?" he asked Mia.

She was climbing up into the branches and inspecting some of the taped areas. He positioned himself underneath her as if he'd catch her if she fell. She made him nervous the way she scrambled about up there, holding a handsaw the whole time.

"These are the grafts of all the missing apples we've found. I bring cuttings here to the Daughters and we graft them on to these mature trees and they work like an adoptive mother."

"That is pretty cool," he admitted.

"Here." She tossed down a fruit that was red on one side and soft yellowish green on the other. It was almost perfectly round. "You'll like this one. It's best eaten right from the tree."

"What's it called?" he asked before sinking his teeth into the soft flesh. Tangy sharp juice filled his mouth and finished with just a hint of bitterness.

"Scarlet Pimpernel," she told him. "Better than Red Delicious, right?"

"Yeah," he admitted, his mouth full. "I'm feeling snobby."

She laughed again and he shifted in his jeans. A convent was probably not the place to lay her down under an apple tree and taste her, but God knew he wanted to. Also, probably not with Harvey observing the entire tryst from less than five feet away. Luke saluted him with the Scarlet Pimpernel.

When she got low enough for him to grab her, he clasped his hands around Mia's waist and brought her down from the tree. Diana reappeared with a basket of assorted fruit.

"Some of the fruit of your labors," she said and handed Mia the basket. She insisted when it looked like Mia was going to refuse. "We

have bushels of them inside. Mavis has made countless jars of apple
butter and apple sauce and apple chutney. Even tried some apple sauer-
kraut this year. Turned out pretty good, to everyone's amazement."

"Thank you." Mia turned and gave the basket to Luke who was
happy to be of use.

"The new grafts are holding well and should take just fine. I
expect they'll bud next year and then we'll see what we get." Mia
dusted off her hands on her jeans. "Maybe up the fertilizer regimen,
but otherwise carry on. I'm going to go check the rest. I'll meet you
back up at the house."

On the way back, Diana turned to Luke. "How long have you been
working with our Miss Mia? She's amazing, isn't she?"

He sidestepped the question. "She is indeed. Certainly knows her
way around an apple, that's for sure. Speaking of amazing, this
garden is a wonder."

"Thank you," Diana said and gazed about her as if looking at all
they'd accomplished with fresh eyes. "We believe that humans
flourish the best when communing with nature. In our own little
slice of heaven here on Earth, we look to re-create the bounty that
was Eden. With what we can nurture from the ground, we can
nurture others' lives and souls. No one should be starved for food or
spiritual bounty."

Inwardly, Luke rolled his eyes. "It's a lovely sentiment if a bit
simplistic."

"Life doesn't have to be so complicated," she said with a knowing
smile.

Luke couldn't figure out how old she was. Still an attractive
woman, she could have been anywhere from thirty-five to sixty-five.
Clear blue eyes appraised him from underneath a straw hat with an
epic brim. It did an excellent job of keeping the sun off her face,
which explained why someone who spent all her time outside could
be relatively wrinkle-free. Still, her gaze and her mien gave her a
sense of experience and authority that younger, less worldly people
didn't usually have.

Harvey must have decided Luke wasn't going to do anything

nefarious in the immediate future because he trotted along the path before disappearing among some tomato vines.

"What do you do with all of this stuff?" he asked and indicated the vast expanse of garden with a nod of his head.

"We eat it, of course," she said with a laugh. "We have a storefront in town that sells everything from our jam to face creams. Felicity has set up an online shop now, too. Those sales go towards the upkeep of the monastery and the costs of farming. We give huge donations to the local food banks and soup kitchens from our fresh harvests. Even the poor can have farm-to-table goodness. Our mission is to bring humanity back to the bounty and peace that was the Garden of Eden."

Despite his reservations about the generally hippy dippy philosophy of the place, he thought it was a worthwhile endeavor. He should send them some money.

Pointing to various patches of garden, she continued, "We have had enormous success growing heirloom varieties of fruits and vegetables, but still we're constantly looking to utilize new methods of agriculture. The brilliant botanists like Mia who work so hard to keep the traditions alive are doing the really good works." They continued along the winding paths, their footsteps falling silently on the soft dirt. "Besides apples we have some ten varieties of carrots. Did you know carrots were originally purple?" When he gave her a disbelieving look, she nodded. "True story. We have red ones and yellow ones, too. They taste simply divine. There are over three hundred varieties of squash. Now, we don't grow them all here, only fifteen or so, but all three hundred are represented somewhere in our gardens worldwide."

"Wow. That's astonishing. I'll never look at a salad the same way again."

She nodded and smiled proudly. "While science uses gene therapy and other genetic testing to grow heartier vegetables, the Daughters of Eve believe that returning to the mother garden will resolve much of humanity's ills."

Luke didn't know about that, but he was certainly willing to eat.

"How many of you are there?" Luke had seen seven or eight women working outside since he'd arrived.

"We have garden sanctuaries all over the world. Did you mean how many are here in this house?" She stooped to retrieve a hoe that lay forgotten in the pathway. "My sisters are aging, and we don't have as many young women join our ranks as we used to, but there are still twenty-seven of us. Many more worldwide."

The house came into view again. A massive building made of grey limestone abutted by two towers with conical roofs. The main building was three stories with massive windows on the north face and a gabled slate roof. An ell connected on the far end into what Luke assumed were dormitories. Harvey lay on the brick courtyard, basking in the sun while keeping an ever-watchful eye out for their arrival. Mia joined them almost immediately. She arrived on a four-wheeler driven by a tiny old woman wearing the uniform of denim work clothes. Towed behind was a wagon loaded with potatoes and cabbages.

"Everything looks great in appleland." Mia told them. "Have you been indoctrinated into the cult of vegetables?" she asked with a teasing grin.

Diana smiled broadly. "Not quite. It was a pleasure, young Mr. Mephisto." She took off her gloves and stuck out her naked hand. The instant his hand clasped the sister's, skin to skin, a hot wind whipped through the groves, swiping hats from heads and kicking up a swirl of dust. Diana's smile froze and she tilted her head slightly as if to examine him. After a long moment, she said, "Hope to see you out here with our Miss Mia again soon."

Luke retrieved his hand and stuck it in his back pocket. "Me, too." The brief contact with the nun had him feeling examined, seen. Uneasy.

"That is one hell of a garden," Luke told Mia as they bounced back onto the highway.

"Right?" Mia looked across the cab at him. "

"I have learned more about fruit and vegetables today than I ever thought possible. I had literally no idea. I mean seriously. I have never given an ounce of thought about heirloom vegetables before. No idea apples were missing. Or that freaking carrots were purple. My mind is totally blown."

"That's exactly what I was hoping for." She reached across the bench seat and patted his shoulder.

"What do you mean?"

Her cheeks were flushed from the sun and her eyes sparkled with excitement. She even smelled good, infused with the aroma of sunshine and mulchy earth and fresh plants.

Sexy as hell.

"I just knew that if I got you out here, in the wilderness, and you saw how exciting it could be. How impressive the Daughters of Eve's garden is." Her grin grew. "I just knew you'd see how important the orchard is for our building."

"You still can't put an orchard in our building." His smile was gone. The wonder of the day brought to an immediate and erection-killing end.

"But you saw—"

"I saw really cool stuff today," he agreed. "You and these apples are amazing."

"And the Daughters of Eve?"

"Wholly unexpected. I have every intention of sending them a huge donation."

"So why? Imagine those amazing trees in our building." She was tenacious; he had to give her that.

"Because it's an office building, Mia, and I am an architect. It's for people to work in. It's not a damn greenhouse. You did not hire a farmer."

"Think how—"

He put up a hand to stop her. "No, think about the structure. How would we get the light? How are you going to properly irrigate a damn orchard? You can have the same kind of impact by putting the trees all around the outside." He wished he felt bad—she looked so crestfallen—but he didn't. His firm was selected because he delivered a certain kind of product: a building to be feared. His designs were the architectural equivalent of military shock and awe. He did not make Norman fucking Rockwell buildings. "We can place a few trees inside, on several levels. They'll be gorgeous. You'll get the same basic effect."

She shook her head. "I want an office building that doesn't feel like a building. One that doesn't feel like a prison all day long. I want the employees of Virtus to be happy."

"We cannot waste the space needed for that kind of folly. That's what that is, Mia. It's a fucking folly."

Not even fairy princesses got everything they wanted.

What a shitty end to a fabulous day.

Well, maybe this was the reason why he and the lovely Snow White were never going to hook up. It was probably a good thing.

Damn.

HEAVEN IV

L ucifer didn't have any idea how Juliet could get down into Hell to find Rachel.

"Well, you were there once," she gently reminded him. "Don't you remember anything about it?"

Though Juliet had plopped down in the dirt, the archangel was pacing. He'd made a thin path that ran about six feet between two trees just on the edge of a forest that, if it had been anywhere else in creation, would surely have been haunted. Lucifer's version of Heaven was dreadful.

"It's been millennia," he said. "I can't remember the specifics. And besides, it's probably changed by now."

Juliet hadn't considered that. She had the few celestial maps she'd lifted from the library—she did not call them stolen, not even in her mind. Stealing was a sin and Juliet wasn't ready to make any official residency changes. She'd spread them out on the ground and anchored them with rocks. The maps she had with her were of the outlying areas. She'd been looking for Lucifer after all, not thinking of a vacation down south.

"I personally have never been out of Heaven since I got here. I know that sometimes the Third Sphere Angels get sent down to

Earth, but I don't know the procedure." She pictured walking to the edge of Heaven and base jumping.

He paused. "I just used to wish myself down when I wanted to see her and there I'd be."

"Well, I don't know if that's because you were an Archangel or what, but us thirdies can't do that," she assured him. "Maybe when you did it, no one had done anything bad before. Maybe that's why you could just poof" —she popped her fingers out like a firework—"there you were. Maybe after, you know, that's when the Dominions tightened up the ship."

Pacing resumed.

"Now you have to fill out forms and be approved to go to Earth. I thought about it once, but it was just too much work. Hey, wait a minute." She rolled up to her hands and knees so she could scan the furthest corners of the maps. "We're not trying to go to Earth. We're trying to go to Hell."

Juliet knew there was communication between upstairs and downstairs. She'd seen stuff on Hashmal's desk the last time she was in his office. Some of those scrolls and lists had definitely come from Hell. There must be some administrative communication from the Dominions to their counterparts in Hell, right? When it came down to it, they were all still dealing with the same God and thus the same rules in the end.

Who delivered the mail? She was going to have to return to the Quire and figure this out.

She promised Lucifer she'd be back and begged him not to move his Heaven from this spot. Hopefully, if his version changed again, she'd still be able to locate him on the Celestial maps. In turn, he made her promise that she would be back, even if she couldn't figure it out.

Juliet decided he was well and truly pitiful. More than ever, she wanted to know if Rachel was still in Hell. For Lucifer's sake. For the sake of star-crossed lovers everywhere. And because she might be bored.

Her first stop was the Library. She checked all the usual sources for information on how information was delivered between the two realms and didn't get very far. She found an outdated instruction booklet, The New Third Sphere Dominion, which had the suggestion, *see transportation document 26-187.64,* and in another reference she found, *see also communication i.e.; Above & Abyss, service level agreements updated 1647, 1914.* Unfortunately, she wasn't able to find the items referenced. If she ever finished this project, she vowed that she'd get the library updated and cataloged. The Dewey Decimal guy must not have been assigned to the library when he got to Heaven. What a transcendent example of Elysian irony. Hashmal wasn't really a barrel of angelic laughs, though, and probably his cohorts weren't either. Maybe ole Dewey ended up in Hell.

It was well known there was an elaborate staircase near the Narthex, the grand lobby just inside Heaven. As soon as the novitiates passed through the tremendous scrolled gates, the first thing they saw was the epic marble staircase that rose up, up, up past what the eye could see, all the way to Empyrean, the true home of God. Often times, cherubim loitered on the steps, or flit about near the cloud cover. They were adorable, as one had always been led to believe they would be, but they were fairly useless as far as angels went. They and the Seraphim, wandering around with their harps and godly pronouncements, were only outside of God's palace for the sole purpose of impressing the novices. It totally worked.

What she'd never noticed before, as she wandered through the crowd of novices, was a smaller, less glamorous set of risers that led down. Down to Earth? Somehow she didn't think so. If all it took to wander back down to Earth was to traipse on down the stairs, then why would anyone bother applying for permission? No, Juliet suspected that was a way down to Hell.

The brand-new angels were perfect for people watching, even better than the county fair. She lingered in the crowd, scoping out the lesser staircase. It descended into a cloudy mist. Only about the first twenty feet of risers and gilded bannister were visible before they faded away into what seemed to be nothingness. Also, two intimidating silver-armored Authorities flanked either side, their massive wings unfurled slightly to indicate their size and strength. Juliet marveled. Wings were terribly heavy and unwieldy, and she imagined the strength needed to stand at attention all day with their ponderous weight on display.

While she was watching, a third strode towards the staircase, his arms laden with scrolls. She was too far away to overhear the conversation with the guards and the courier, and she couldn't see what he showed them that qualified him admittance, but they stepped aside and he continued on his way down until he faded into the shimmering clouds.

That seemed too easy. Maybe she could grab a bunch of scrolls and act like she knew what she was doing. When asked, she could fake like she lost whatever identification was issued. She had always been a pretty good fibber. That was what she decided she was going to do until a novitiate wandered over and attempted to descend. In a flash, swords were drawn. The Authorities wings, which had been impressive before, unfurled into glorious feathered barriers. One of the guards spoke sternly to the man. She wouldn't exactly say the new angel looked afraid—after all, they were in Heaven and there wasn't much up here to terrify anyone, but he was definitely startled. They turned the confused soul around and sent him bumbling on his way.

So that wasn't going to work. She needed to either figure how to get in with the couriers and get a badge or find another way altogether.

She was exhausted by all this subterfuge and frustrated that she didn't seem to be getting anywhere. She needed a break. One of her favorite things about Heaven was playing with the dogs who were waiting for their masters to cross over. Heaven had the most glorious dog park. Hundreds of pets romped in the fields and Juliet took many opportunities to frolic with them. She went to the kennels first to see Hugh, the Dominion who was in charge of the "beasties of Heaven" as he called them. He was one of her favorites. Hugh's whole demeanor was such a radical about-face from the other angels in charge. It was hard to believe that he and Hashmal were on the same level.

"Hello, Juliet," Hugh called and waved her in when he saw her. He was in one of the bays near the front. A Corgi bounced out to meet her with a quick lick on the knee, before rushing back inside.

131

"Hey," Juliet replied. There seemed to be a lot of activity at the back of the small room. "What's going on?"

"We got some puppies," Hugh exclaimed, knowing how excited she would be over that development. "But I need you to stay quiet about it."

She started to ask why, but then stopped short as soon as she saw the tiny wriggling animals. The Corgi mom settled back down in the bed of soft blankets and her babies nuzzled sleepily against her. Momma seemed quite proud of her little brood, and Juliet guessed she would be, too. How many times did a dog have a whole litter of puppies with two heads?

"What—? How—?" Juliet didn't even know what words to string together to ask the obvious question. She knelt next to the wriggling pile and stroked her fingers along their backs.

"Right," Hugh nodded. "Cerberus got loose again."

Juliet scooped the closest puppy into her hand and tucked it under her chin. It was soft and warm. One head nuzzled her throat while the other snored gently. "Cerberus? The three-headed dog in Hell?"

"Yep." Hugh set down a bowl of clean water for the momma dog. "I guess he was up here for a couple of hours before anyone noticed. Looks like he and Petunia here are an item."

Still holding the puppy, Juliet ogled the rest of the litter. They were so adorable, she could barely contain herself. Five little bodies and ten little heads. "I thought Cerberus had three heads."

Hugh nodded. "He does. This has never really happened before. I'm guessing when you have three heads mate with one head, you end up with two heads." He patted Petunia's one head. Poor doggy looked tired.

"Wow," is all she could say. She kissed both heads of the baby she was holding. It was already back to sleep. She nestled him back in with his siblings, and Petunia gave him a perfunctory lick. "A Corgi and a Hell Hound. Who'd have thought?"

The two angels watched the puppies for a few quiet moments when something important occurred to Juliet. "Hey, how did Cerberus get up here anyway? I thought demons couldn't get into Heaven, just like angels can't get into Hell."

He shrugged. "Cerberus isn't a demon. He's just a guard dog."

"Yeah, but how'd he get in? Wouldn't the Authorities at the staircase see him right away when he came up? I mean, a giant three-headed mastiff is a little noticeable."

Hugh picked up a bucket of tennis balls and headed for the fields. "I'm sure he came up the back stairs."

Back stairs? There were back stairs? It was all she could do not to start shrieking questions at him. She modulated her voice and asked almost as an aside. "Where are the back stairs?"

He waved behind him. "Behind the kitchens. Want to come throw some balls with me?" He already had a collection of thirty or so dogs excitedly jumping around his legs.

She was already moving towards the kitchen. "Not this time, but I'll see you later."

"Keep quiet about the babies, at least until I can figure out how to tell Ariel," he called.

Juliet couldn't wait to hear how the Archangel Ariel felt about this new development. "I will," she promised.

Juliet had to jerk hard on the doorknob before it finally opened with the screech of wood against wood. She poked her head inside and found a hallway to a stairwell that descended five steps then made a sharp left turn out of sight.

A quick glance behind showed no one would see her slip inside, and she pulled the door shut tight behind her.

CHAPTER THIRTEEN

L uke had been working on new engineering schematics for the better part of the day, trying to maneuver a way to successfully heat and cool an office building full of trees without losing the integrity of his previously state-of-the art design and not kill any trees. Ire and resentment at the mockery to his perfect blueprints swelled to almost bursting, and he knew no more good work was going to come out of him today.

Luke let the rage radiate out of him for a split second, the briefest pulse, long enough for the lightbulbs to explode in a shower of filament and glass, before he swallowed it back down and capped it off.

"What the Hell—" Jeb said when he threw open their connecting door. He took one look at the carpet and huffed out an aggrieved sigh. "Hold on. Let me call maintenance."

After Jeb sweet talked the maintenance guy into changing the light-bulbs and vacuuming up his mess, he turned to Luke. "I'm calling Ethan. He needs to find someone to beat you up or something. I cannot tolerate you in this office anymore this week." While Luke scowled, Jeb shoved the laptop in his messenger bag and steered him towards the door.

Ethan was all too happy to meet him at the gym for an afternoon of therapeutic pummeling. He took one look at Luke's grimace and said, "Jeb wasn't kidding. What's got you so unhinged? Oh, my God, it's that girl, right?"

"It's not the girl. It's my building. She's totally fucked it up." Luke had already been working the heavy bag for a hard twenty minutes before Ethan arrived.

His cousin blinked at him. "I don't mean to be obtuse here, but how does she fuck up a building?"

He hammered the bag with his left fist. "I designed the perfect building. The automation is revolutionary. I'm telling you it's everything. Austere. Symmetrical." Another punch, this time with the right, putting his entire shoulder into it. "Everything about it is progressive and clean. This was the building I wanted to be remembered for when, er, after... You know."

Ethan sighed and rolled his eyes. "Okay, I got it." He positioned himself behind the bag to provide support when Luke punched it again in a rapid combination. "So, what did she do to it?"

Luke barked out a mirthless laugh. "Trees. She insists on trees."

"I don't understand." Ethan grunted from the effort of holding the bag in place. "What do trees have to do with your building?"

"Not. A. Fucking. Thing." Luke emphasized each word with a punch to the bag. He wore himself out attacking the bag as he explained to his cousin how jacked up the whole project had become. "She's cluttering it all up with trees, growing all willy-nilly and dropping leaves and messing with the technological perfection."

Ethan hung on to the bag and listened patiently until Luke was panting from exertion. "So I'm going to say something here. Just a thought, don't rip my face off. What if you put yourself into designing the building the way she wants? No, wait. Hear me out. What you're describing sounds kind of amazing."

"It sounds bonkers!" Luke roared.

"Or," Ethan said with raised hands, "it sounds like a legacy."

"You don't know what you're talking about." Luke said with all the menace he could muster and glared at his cousin, hands on his hips, chest heaving. Had everyone lost their minds?

Ethan shrugged and stepped away from the bag. "You're right, of course. I'm only Envy. I'm not an award-winning architect with amazing skills and Ivy League education. Trees are stupid."

Teeth barred in rage, he threw his entire body into one last punch. The impact sent the bag careening off the chain and smashed against the cement wall. Sand ran from a tear in the seam and puddled on the floor.

Ethan took a step back and assessed him with troubled eyebrows. "I think I'll find someone else to spar with you today. I have a date tomorrow and I don't want to look like a punching bag."

Luke's arms hung heavy from the exertion, like weighted jelly. "Nah, I think I beat most of it out already. You'll be all right."

His cousin opened his mouth as if to say something, then snapped it shut again. He turned and reviewed who else was in the gym that afternoon. He saw what he was looking for and his face darkened with a grim smile. "Eddie, you up for some sparring?"

The behemoth called Eddie lumbered forward. "Maybe, but not with him," he said and pointed a churro roll finger at Luke.

Ethan reached up and put a hand on Eddie's shoulder. "Oh, come on. You're bigger than him. Besides, he's already half worn himself out."

Eddie narrowed his eyes and stared at Luke. "Last time I got my nose broke."

Nodding, Ethan said, "Well, there's always that danger with anyone, right big guy? You can wear head gear. No one will think less of you."

Luke thought it was entirely too late for Eddie to be concerned about losing brain cells. The man was big and dumb, and he was probably born that way.

"Head won't fit."

"Ahh." Ethan stood on his tiptoes to get a good grip on Goliath's shoulders. He massaged the thick muscles. "That makes sense." His eyes grew comically big when he looked to Luke. "How about we agree no hitting in the face then? No more broken noses."

"I guess that would be all right." Eddie nodded.

"Great! No hitting in the face," Ethan told Luke, and he nodded. He escorted Eddie into the sparring ring. "Now I want you to really give him hell, Ed. Really go for it, right? We've been working on his recovery from combinations."

"Speed isn't really what I'm good at," Eddie said as Ethan helped him into a pair of sparring gloves the size of Nebraska.

Ethan slapped a palm on the leviathan's chest. "You just do you then. It'll be fine."

Luke stood in the center of the ring and rolled his neck with his eyes closed, appraising his internal barometer. He was right; he had worked out some of the vitriol. Instead of fluid lava coursing through his system, it felt more like a cayenne slushy. As long as he didn't think of the goddamned building, he should be able to reduce the venom back to a regular sluggishly coursing sludge.

Later, after Eddie had done his job and Luke had allowed himself a thorough pummeling, he admitted to Ethan that he was starving.

"Feeling better then?" Ethan asked as they walked through the parking lot. Ethan's sleek black Bugatti was parked next to Luke's Chevelle.

"Yeah." The vitriol was subdued. The illogical hysteria clubbed out of him.

"That's great and I still look beautiful. Eddie to the rescue." He tossed his bag in the trunk. "Where do you want to eat?"

Luke shrugged. "I'm in the mood for a nice bloody steak."

"That doesn't sound helpful. Do I need to go back in and find someone else to beat you up? I can run over you with your car. I'm not doing it with mine, but yours should withstand a couple solid hits."

Luke rolled his eyes. "No, I'm just hungry. Let's see if the guys want to join us. I could use a night with the Seven." He didn't want to go home alone. He was likely to relapse right back into a fiery funk if he didn't have anything to distract him. His cousins and all their jack-assery were bound to get him over the hump.

Seth suggested a new steakhouse that proved the man really did know what was what when it came to food. Even Benji agreed it was a magnificent steak and you couldn't make Benji get excited about much of anything. Afterwards, Ashe bullied them all into going on some pub crawl with him. He insisted that what would make *everyone* feel better was sex. Luke wasn't so sure about that. At the mention of sex, his brain and his dick immediately went to a fairytale land of apple trees and girls in polka dotted skirts. That line of thinking was only going to frustrate him, but Luke allowed himself to be pulled along for the ride.

The pub crawl was in conjunction with the monthly outdoor event that happened downtown. A lively neighborhood was cordoned off, and there were blocks of street performers along with venders and fortunetellers set up along the sidewalks. The air was heavy with the aroma of food trucks and incense and the occasional whiff of marijuana. They walked in a loose clump, jostling and teasing each other like they'd been doing their entire lives. Their conversations were drowned out by the music coming from the open doors of the bars, sometimes deafening dance mixes and other times the sound of a live band. It was warm out, the heat still radiated from the pavement and Luke had no desire to squeeze his big body into an even sweatier club.

"Come on," Ashe cajoled. "I'll get you laid and you'll be totally relaxed."

Sometimes it was comforting that his cousins were so cliché in their proclivities. Still, it didn't matter how easily Asher could get him laid tonight, Luke wasn't interested in going that route with a stranger.

"It's always possible you'll find some sweet little thing who will take your mind off the other one," Ethan suggested and gestured to the line of cuties going into some anonymous club.

It was stupid and pointless and certainly aggravating, but Luke wasn't interested in a substitution. Missing the point entirely, Ashe vowed he'd find Luke a bed partner from the bevy of talented-looking ladies in the outside crowd instead.

He slugged his lustful cousin in the shoulder and laughed. If that was the mood Ashe was in, not much was going to pull him out of it unless he was looking to get out. Seth grabbed Luke by the arm and towed him towards a line of food trucks.

"I've had these kababs before," Seth told him with a toothy smile.

"They're an amazing fusion of Mexican and Japanese. You're going to love them."

"You have got to be kidding, man." Luke laughed when Seth shook his head. "There's no way I'm going to be able to eat that. God, I'm still stuffed from dinner. Let's walk around some and digest, then maybe."

Seth got a kabob anyway. To his credit, it did smell wonderful. They merged back into the crowd and found his cousin Jacob sitting at a card table under a barber's awning having his palm read. The fortune teller was dressed the part like she'd stepped out of a scene from a Scooby Doo cartoon complete with a scarf decorated with gold coins that jingled when she moved her arms. Her fingers were bejeweled with the requisite rings on each finger and her hair, not blonde but not gray either, curled wild about her face. She wasn't young but not exactly old, somewhere between the ages of his Aunt Clair and that old woman from Downton Abbey that Jeb was always quoting. The truth of her age was somewhere under a thick layer of glittery purple eye shadow.

Staring at his open hand, she drew her index finger down the middle of his palm. "Ah, nice big hands, huh. You know what that means." She flirted with him, and Jacob laughed obligingly. "Square fingers, an Earth hand. You're practical. But see this fate line, it's very deep. That suggests you're strongly controlled by fate."

Jacob snickered. "That's rich, eh?" and Luke snorted. She had no idea how right she was there.

The woman continued, pointing at the area by his littlest finger. "Look at this. This says you'll have much wealth in your life."

That made all of them laugh. "I'm not Greed for nothin'," Jacob told her and tossed a twenty-dollar bill on her table.

The fortune teller gestured to Luke. "You, yes, you. Come here. Let Madam Helena read your fortune. Find out what's troubling you."

"No thanks, ma'am." He told her. "I know exactly what's troubling me."

Ethan leaned over and said in a stage whisper, "He's got daddy issues."

The woman gestured again. "Come, let me see." She held out a deck of cards.

"Go on," Jacob urged. "It's fun. It's not like she can tell you anything worse than we already know, huh?"

Luke sat in the woman's empty chair. She told him to shuffle the cards and cut them. She retook the deck and fanned them out on top of the table.

"Chose three and flip them over," she said.

He plucked out three random cards and did as she directed without really paying attention.

Ethan tapped his shoulder. "Hey, while you do this, we're going to pop over there." He pointed toward a stage across the parking lot where a band was just starting up. And then they abandoned him.

"You've met someone." Madam Helena narrowed her eyes and studied him.

"I meet lots of people."

She smiled, knowingly. "But this person means something. Hmmm."

Luke snorted and looked down to the cards for the first time. He tried not to gasp out loud, but he knew the woman heard him. He didn't believe in fortune tellers or gypsies or any of this hoodoo. Luke knew what magic was real and what was bullshit. Didn't he? But these cards gave him pause.

"Do you see something here that's means something to you?"

He straightened his face. The deck was old and the faces looked to be hand painted, works of art, really. The first card had an old man with a lantern standing alone in a field. There was an apple tree in the distance. "Maybe."

She laughed. "No need to be cagey." She waggled her fingers over the cards. "I already know what they say. What makes tarot so interesting is that there are as many ways to read the cards as there are people in this world. While they mean something to me, they could mean something different to you." She winked a heavily made-up eye and touched her finger to the tip of that old man card. "I'll tell you what I see. This one tells me that you're trying to decide something.

It's important and you must look inside yourself and find the answer. We'll come back to this one."

The second card was as beautiful as the first. There was a cryptic circle with arcane symbols on it. Around the outside were an angel, a winged cow, a bird, and a snake. Some other strange red creature seemed suspended from the bottom, and a sphinx sat on top. All of them held books in one hand and an apple in the other. The sphinx, however, seemed to be grinning out at him from the face of the card, and a bite was missing from his apple. Luke felt a bit nauseated.

With a whisper of her lace sleeve over velvet, the lady's finger moved to touch it. "This is the Wheel of Fortune. It speaks of new beginnings. Some of these things are not in your control. Fate can take you by the hand and lead you to these beginnings."

Luke swallowed and gazed at the final card. It was obviously The Lovers, even he could see that. Two figures stood in a garden. They had strategically placed fig leaves, making the implication obvious. Eve was handing Adam an apple. While the fortune teller interpreted the meanings to him as she saw them, she couldn't possibly know the significance to him and his family history.

"So, this person you've met, a lady?" she asked with high eyebrows. When he nodded his head even the slightest amount, she proceeded. "The lovers card doesn't always mean exactly what you think, but in this case I sense that it does. A change in your life is coming. Is there something in your future you are worried about?" She stared at him, and he made a concentrated effort not to show any emotion but, apparently, she got what confirmation she wanted. "She is going to play very prominently in whatever the winds of fate have in store for you."

Yeah, sure. "Okay," he said, and nodded with a smirk. "Lucky guess. It's all fairly vague, though, isn't it?"

Madam Helena narrowed her eyes at him again. She pointed to the fanned-out deck. "Pick another card. This one will represent your future."

"Sure." Luke picked a random card and slid it across the velvet, face down.

"Ready?" she asked with dramatic flair and flipped over the card.

"Mother fucker," Luke spit out in surprise.

The card on the table depicted the Devil. It was completely insane and totally impossible, but the man with the horns looked remarkably like his father. And to tie it all together, his feet were invisible, buried under hundreds of rotten apples.

The fortune teller stroked the face of the devil card, her face screwed up in concentration. Luke watched in horrified fascination as her face dissolved into that of an ancient crone, her skin wrinkled, loose, and creased, folding around her eyes and neck. It was only a split second, back to her old self by the time he blinked. He couldn't actually be certain that it had happened at all.

She cast him a shrewd glance. "The devil usually means entrapment. He can be looked on as a forewarning. A chance to avoid being ensnared."

What the actual fuck? It could mean some hocus pocus like she was describing, or it could mean a whole lot more. Was this an actual prediction?

"I don't believe in fortune tellers," he told her, like he was trying to convince her and remind himself that all of this was bullshit.

"Sure," she gave him a placating half smile. "For a guy who doesn't believe, you seem pretty rattled by this card. Why don't you pull one more so we don't end your reading on this note?"

This time he stared at the fanned deck of cards that remained. Picking the right one seemed very important. Finally, he pulled a card. He held his breath.

Madame Helene lingered with her fingertips on the card still face down on the table. "Remember the cards can be interpreted many ways."

When she flipped it over a huge yellow sun shone down on a baby riding a horse with a wreath of apple blossoms around its neck.

"Oh, this is a good one." She patted his hand. "The Sun. This means everything is going to work out."

It was really too bad he didn't believe in any of this sorcery.

L uke left Madame Helene's table outside the barber shop on the verge of an anxiety attack. What had that crazy woman just read in his future? He knew damn well she was a fake, a fraud, a charlatan. But even if she was, the cards he'd selected were an uncanny glimpse into everything he feared.

Everything in those cards spelled out his doom.

A piercing whistle caught his attention. When he looked up, Ethan was waving him over to where his cousins stood at the back of a crowd watching a three-piece acoustic band. He had been so far inside his head that he nearly walked past his cousins in a daze.

"What's wrong with you?" Ethan asked.

Luke blinked at him. He didn't even know where to start. "It's going to be me."

His cousin narrowed his gaze at him. "What makes you say that?"

Of course, Ethan knew that Luke was referring to the curse with that one short, enigmatic sentence. That was damn near all the Seven of them ever thought about. They had a shorthand about it that didn't require any explanation, a damned language of their own, like a hive brain or something.

Still, Luke suspected Ethan was going to make fun of him. Hell, he'd make fun of him if he hadn't been the one it happened to. That was Ethan's way, though. To tease when he was afraid. Luke shrugged, unable to bring himself to speak.

"Shit. Did that crazy woman tell you that?"

"No, because how could she know anything? But the cards did." Those cards had been spooky. Apples and Devils. Damn it, he couldn't suck in any air and his chest hurt.

Ethan stepped closer so that Luke's voice wasn't so loud. "What did they say?"

Luke grabbed his cousin by the arm and pulled him further from the crowd. "She said I had a decision to make, but that fate was in control of my life."

Shaking his head, Ethan visibly relaxed. "That's all? Calm down, man."

"No, that's not all!" Luke yelled. It didn't matter how far away they got from the crowd, people were noticing them now. "She told me to pick a card for my future and I picked the Devil card. The fucking Devil card. It even looked like my father a little."

Ethan blinked. "Oh." A spectacular example of his stunning eloquence as he grasped the situation.

Luke nodded furiously.

"Well, just breathe. She's a bullshit street fair fortune teller. It's a quack reading." Ethan demonstrated calm breathing by rolling his hands slowly in front of his chest while filling his lungs with air and then purposefully exhaling.

Luke was going to punch him in the face. Instead he put his hands on his hips and leaned his head back and practiced breathing until he felt lightheaded. "There's more," he finally said.

Ethan's expression remained placid. He was trying to be a calming influence, but all it did was make Luke grit his teeth. "Let's hear it," his cousin said.

"Mia was all over those cards."

"Who the hell is Mia? Oh!" Realization dawning on him, Ethan opened his eyes wide. "The chick. What do you mean she was on the cards?"

"I also pulled the Lover's card and Madame Helene said that it represented change, but there were apples all over the cards, every one of them. The Wheel of Fortune, the old dude with the lantern, even the Devil. Apples everywhere. The last goddamned card had a baby on it. With apples."

He wasn't used to this shortness of breath and racing heart. Was this a panic attack? Son of a bitch, he was going to pass out. Breathing, breathing. In and out.

Benji came over and dropped his hand on Luke's shoulder. "What's going on?"

"Luke's freaking out about that fortune teller." Ethan helpfully downplayed Luke's state.

Benji, who expressed so little interest in anything, perked up. "What'd she say?"

Ethan gave the Reader's Digest version of what Luke had told him, including the existence of Mia, the office building, and how Luke had lost his last fight because of her.

"What's the deal with the apples?" Benji asked.

Ethan shrugged. "I'm not sure exactly."

"They represent Mia," Luke explained. When both of his cousins crinkled their foreheads in question, Luke continued. "Trust me. Apples and Mia are a thing."

"Is it a kinky thing?" Asher chuckled from behind Luke where he'd obviously overheard the whole conversation.

He whirled around and glared at Asher. "This isn't a joke."

Ashe put his hands up in surrender and laughed. "Okay, I'm sorry." When Luke stood down, he continued. "So do we believe in fortune tellers now? She said things that freaked you out, but that's what they always do. It's sort of comes with the territory. She could have said the exact same thing to anyone and they would have interpreted it to fit their life."

"Not everyone has a one in seven chance of becoming the Devil," Luke stated the obvious. "Besides, it wasn't what she said, it was the cards themselves. I'm telling you, the Devil card looked exactly like my father. And all of those apples were eerie. She said the lady I had met would figure into what fate had in store for me."

"You think Mia is the mother of your child?" Benji asked, his question more ominous than it should be.

"No." The thought was ridiculous. Maybe. Probably, if the cards were to be believed.

"So let me play Devil's Advocate here." Asher paused and smirked when the rest of them groaned. "If Mia is the woman in the cards because of the apple connection, and the woman in the cards plays into your fate, why are you fighting it? I mean, you're either going to be picked next or you're not. You're going to have a kid in a couple of years no matter what you do to try and stop it. I say get with the chick."

With a roll of his eyes, Benji said, "You're just saying that because you'll screw anything that moves slower than you."

"Such is my fate," Asher noted, all evidence of his smirk gone. "We've each got our own shit to deal with, man. I'm just saying, if you're succumbing to the principle of fate, then go all in. What do you have to lose?"

"Everything." Luke threw his hands in the air. "I can lose absolutely fucking everything. I'm not doing that to someone who loves me. You assholes don't know what that was like, what it's been like. When my dad left, I lost it all. I know what the curse is, and that I have to contribute to it, but I'm not going to drag some woman who loves me down with me. I don't see you running around and letting people fall in love with you." He pointed at Ashe.

Asher shrugged nonchalantly. "It'll probably happen eventually."

Luke hit him square in the jaw. He hadn't even known he was going to do it. Ashe had said it so casually, as if devastating an innocent person was no big deal, that Luke's fist had fired at him like a piston. In his rage, all he could see was himself at ten-years-old, abandoned and heartbroken, everything in his life upended due to his family's curse.

Luke would do anything to avoid devastating another unsuspecting soul that way.

The thought of Mia, so generous of spirit and good and kind... It made him physically ill to think of bludgeoning that out of her, and his family's curse would certainly do that.

"Holy shit!" Ethan exclaimed while Benji propped Asher up.

"I might be the next Devil, but you're a bigger bastard than I'll ever be, and that's saying a lot." Luke brandished his index finger at Ashe, rage making his skin itch from the inside out. "But I'm going down with a clear conscience."

He turned and stomped off, wanting to be away from his cousins, from everyone. He needed some time alone to get himself under control. Whatever was holding him together was as flimsy as dental floss, and he didn't want to be with anyone when he finally broke apart.

Ethan started to come after him, but he heard Asher stop him. "Let him go before he starts a riot here or something. He'll be fine in a while."

"I'm calling Jebediah," Ethan said, like he was threatening to call Luke's mom.

After that, Luke was too far gone to hear them.

"Aren't you glad I made you come?" Cassie looped her arm through Mia's as they traversed a crosswalk with a large herd of boisterous street fair revelers.

Mia rolled her eyes with exaggerated movements. "I guess so."

She had been in a funk all week. She hadn't felt like doing anything. Not even working in the greenhouse was enough entice- ment to get her off the couch. She'd gone to work in her crowded, squished office building where she was supposed to be in the ecstatic throes of erecting the new home for her company. Instead, she was in development hell.

Initially she'd been so excited when her father assigned her to take over the project. This was a chance to finally contribute something worthwhile to Veritas Templum Pharmaceuticals. Up to this point, she'd felt like a latent appendage to her father, that loathsome crea- ture, "the boss's kid," who only got hired due to nepotism. Granted, she had a college degree, it just wasn't in anything useful. So, essen- tially, she was useless. The one thing she was good at was getting to know the employees. She probably would have been an excellent Human Resources person. She knew everyone's name, marital status, number of children, and hobbies. She got invited to weddings and graduation parties and, she was damn proud to say, it wasn't because her last name was Hatcher. She was granted access to their lives because the employees liked her. It might even be her superpower. She may have no idea what to do about a profit and loss statement, but she provided a service to her father he probably didn't even know he needed: she made his company human. She gave it a pulse.

With the opportunity to take the shell of a building where all of these people worked and turn it into a place worthy of spending more time in than their homes, Mia found a purpose. Her concept wasn't just about comfort, although that certainly played a big part. She wanted the building to live and breathe with them. She wanted a sanctuary. A place that inspired a person's soul, not just their wallet. She had a vision.

It was going to be a lot of work. The plans would need to be changed, and she'd have to convince Luke to see the beauty of what she saw. She'd assumed any architect would be excited about being part of something so revolutionary.

Except that she had a huge budget and an unwilling architect.

She didn't know what else to do to make him see the light. She thought for sure taking Luke out on a hunt and letting him be the one to find the lost grove would do it. It sure seemed like he'd had fun. He'd really gotten into the treasure hunt aspect of the whole thing. The Daughters of Eve had been properly impressive. How was it possible he still couldn't see her vision?

And there'd been kissing. Not that participating in kissing with Luke was a hardship. In fact, now it was harder than ever to keep her mind on whatever task she was supposed to be doing. Instead, Jason was constantly blinking at her, waiting for her to answer a question she'd never heard, or Cassie was tossing popcorn at her from the opposite end of the couch to get her attention. Godfrey had never gotten so much junk food in his life than while Mia was busy daydreaming about the grumpy architect.

After the disastrous ending to their fabulous day, all the effervescence had left her bubble. The building was going to end up just being another office tower. Of course, it would be an architecturally amazing building designed by an award-winning firm, but it would still be just a building. Luke would grudgingly shove some trees in the lobby, maybe put in a bank of windows and call it a day. It would probably win contests and be featured in magazines, but it wouldn't matter. Ultimately, it would be four pretty walls and a roof where people spent their lives.

So, she'd spent the last week pouting and moping.

"Idle hands are the Devil's workshop, and you've been idle long enough," Cassie had said that afternoon and demanded, "Haul your ass up and get dressed. We're going out."

Mia had made a face and leaned around her roommate's body to see the television. "I'm watching a House Hunters marathon. I'm very invested."

Cassie snatched the remote and turned it off. "Spoiler. They all want granite, the carpet is ugly, and they'll pick the wrong house."

"Hey," Mia protested.

"Um-hmm, go get dressed. First we're going to go water your stupid trees and the—"

"They're not stupid trees."

Cassie grinned. "No, they're not. They're fabulous trees. Sadly, not everyone appreciates a perfect tree. But we get up, we get dressed, and we live to water another day."

Despite her best efforts, Mia snorted and couldn't hide a laugh. "You're a dope."

"Yep, and that's why you love me." She curtsied, holding out a pretend skirt. "Seriously, chop-chop, I have plans."

These plans consisted of Cassie following Mia around the greenhouse with a hose and then getting manicures. Mia really did feel better after showering and doing something productive. By the time they met their friends at the street fair, Mia was back to her usual optimistic self. She vowed to herself that she wasn't giving up on Luke. That man needed whimsy in his life more than anyone she'd ever met. Apple-flavored whimsy.

Cassie, Mia, and a few of their old sorority sisters shopped the booths and listened to the bands. Lucy wanted to see the fortune teller but there was always a line. Beth tried some kabobs from a crazy Mexican/Asian food truck. She swore they tasted great, but Mia wrinkled her nose dubiously.

"Here's a real treat," Mia insisted when she saw a booth with the Daughters of Eve. Three of the Sisters manned a space beside the fire station. Lotions filled baskets and tables were lined with shampoos and salves. They also sold infused oils, herbs, and fresh honey. What Mia was most interested in was the display of fresh berry tarts and cakes. They bought a couple to share and went out to the square to listen to an acoustic band.

Mia was savoring a bite of strawberry tart when Cassie nudged her with her elbow. "Isn't that your crabby architect?"

She followed her gaze across the lot and spied Luke stomping through the crowd. Even from twenty yards away, she could see that he was nearly vibrating with agitation. Together they watched him as he noticed the Daughters of Eve booth. He came to an abrupt halt, mouth open, arms hanging at his sides, and he stared at it. By this point, he was close enough to her that she could clearly read his facial expressions.

He didn't look okay. Something was off. Normally, Luke was confident and sure of himself, cocky even, but right now he appeared to be on the verge of a meltdown.

"Hold this for me, will you?" Mia kept her eye on him and gave her fork to Lucy.

Cassie put her hand on Mia's arm to hold her back. "He looks like he's about to freak out, doesn't he?"

She shook off her friend's hand. "Yeah. I'm going to go see if he's all right."

Ignoring the protests of her friends, Mia headed across the macadam, keeping an eye on Luke as she threaded through the clumps of people. Things were advancing rapidly towards a full-on wigging out. His laser attention was still focused on the Daughters, but now he was muttering to himself and gesturing at their booth. She called his name, but he didn't hear her. A few steps further and she was almost close enough to touch him.

"Luke?" This time she said it softly, eyebrows raised in question.

"Apples everywhere," he said, but he still hadn't noticed her.

She was next to him now. A gentle hand on his bicep, she said his name. "Are you okay?"

He startled, jerked out of his reverie, and she dropped her hand and jumped a bit herself. "Mia," he said. "Of course, here you are."

She gave him a tentative smile, a gentle, questioning one that hopefully wouldn't push him any further towards whatever brink he was nearing. "What's going on?"

He simply stared at her. Not saying anything for several long beats, he stared. She blinked. A couple of times he opened his mouth like he was going to say something but didn't. Expressions she couldn't decipher shifted across his face.

Finally, she said, "You're kind of weirding me out here. Do you want to sit down?"

"No."

"Umm-kay. What can I do for you then?"

Moving slowly, like a drunken sloth, Luke shook his head. "Nothing. I'm lost."

Her eyebrows jammed together as she tried to decode what the heck that meant. He was definitely scaring her now. Was he on drugs? Did he have some kind of medical condition? "Should I call someone? Jeb, maybe?" Surely her own assistant had his assistant's phone number. She thought they might be dating or something by now.

Another slow shake of his head. Reaching for his hand, she clasped it in her own. His gaze shifted from her face to where his huge hand eclipsed hers. Somehow that seemed to shift him from his stupor. He squeezed gently. When his gaze came back to meet hers, Luke was clearly present.

"Hi," she said with relief, as if they hadn't been talking for the last couple of seconds.

With the smallest smile, he reassured her. Looking from her, over to the Daughters of Eve, then towards the street and the crowd around the fortune teller, then back to her.

"I didn't expect to see you here," he told her.

She shrugged. "I'm here with friends," she said, pointing to her little grouping of ladies. Three sets of eyes stared back at them with unease. She waved to alleviate their concern.

He widened his smile and nodded to her friends in greeting. "I'm here with my cousins."

When Mia looked behind him, she did see a clump of men, all staring at them in much the same way her friends had been. She waggled her fingers at them and the one she recognized from Luke's fight the other night waved back.

"Are you going to be all right?" she asked him. He seemed fine now, if a little out of it, but mostly there.

This time when he nodded it wasn't vague. There was a definite, intentional movement. She stared up at his eyes and he *saw* her. She was satisfied. Whatever had been wrong before, he seemed recovered from it now. She moved to take a step back and release his hand, but he didn't let go.

"Do you believe in fate?" he asked her.

CHAPTER FIFTEEN

M ia stared up at him, soft brown eyes filled with questions. "Fate? I don't know."

"I do. I think I do. I just saw a fortune teller." He pointed out Madame Helene. She had a new victim in her chair and, unbelievably, what looked like a crystal ball on her table. "She told me all about you. It was nuts. She had this whole crazy deck of cards and every single one of them had apples on them."

She blinked at him. "Apples?"

He nodded, still unable to shake the otherworldly sense of intervention that placed her in his path at that exact moment. "Inconceivable, right? Every card. Old men with apples. Horses and babies with apples. Some weird wheel thing with a Sphinx eating an apple." He ticked the instances off on his fingers. "Even the Devil had an apple, but I don't want to talk about that right now. The point is, there were so many goddamned apples. I flipped this card with Adam and Eve, and they held an apple. Of course, they did. It's Adam and Eve and they're the apple people, right? The fortune teller told me what the cards said, but I know what they really meant." He paused in his rapid-fire babble and inhaled. "At first it really freaked me out, right? One card would have been a funny coincidence. Two might have been weird. But all of them?" He gestured expansively and yelled that last line at the sky. "I mean, that woman couldn't possibly know how significant your damn apples are, and it pissed me off. And that was before I flipped the fucking Devil card. I know exactly what that means. What am I supposed to take away from all this? Is it a message? A warning? A prophecy?

Mia's eyes were wide as she stared at him, mouth slightly agape. "I..I..I don't know."

He squeezed her hand. "Of course, you don't, Mia. It was a rhetorical question. You couldn't possibly know, but I do. At first, I thought it was a warning to stay away, but then I saw the Daughters," he said, and gestured to their booth.

The Daughters of Eve showing up in the middle of his spiritual cataclysm threw his deeply entrenched moral covenant off kilter. The card reading had been as muddy as any prophesy given by the Oracle of Delphi, and Luke's knee-jerk reaction to it had been entirely negative. The appearance of the farming nuns turned that upside down and sent him looking at the predictions though something less dire, like the lens of a crystal goblet. Everything was disjointed, but beautiful. He knew at that moment that fate would propel him forward according to its whims.

If this was his new truth, then Mia was his destiny whether he would become the Devil or not.

Mia stared at him, perplexed, for a heartbeat and then said with raised eyebrows, "That was a pretty intense tarot reading, then, huh?"

She couldn't possibly understand how intense. He closed his mouth and swallowed away the rest of his rant. He inhaled and the breeze was full of her scent, filling him with visions of meadows and sweet fruit. He wished his head would stop spinning.

A shy smile pulled at the corners of her mouth. "Are you all right now?"

He squeezed her hands and hummed his assent. This was right. He had been wrong to be freaked out about her before. Not about the Devil part, but about her. The powers that be had spoken and sent the apples. "I'm great."

"You seemed a little out of it there for a bit, but you do look better now."

High, that's how he felt. Like he was on some sort of psychedelic mushroom, only Mia was the drug.

Giving a confused burst of laughter, she squeezed back. "I'll let you get back to...whatever."

There was no way in hell he was letting her get away from him. The world and all its sea of torments were out there, waiting to pull him down in every way imaginable. He wanted to lash himself to her like a lighthouse, where it was calm and protected. His demons couldn't get to him if he held on tight enough.

"No, you see, I pulled the Lover card and the apples were on it. You're my fate. You're my destiny. I didn't really believe it because I was so freaked about the other stuff, but then I saw the Daughters right there, like they were an omen or something. It kind of scared me, you know? That Madame Helene would say those things and the cards would look like they did and then, holy shit, there were the Daughters."

Mia's eyebrows were smooshed together while she intently tried to follow his explosive explanation. My god, she was adorable. He impulsively kissed her because he couldn't resist. It was quick and spontaneous but full of revelatory importance.

He whispered and she leaned in. "And there you were, as if I'd conjured you, the apple goddess." Now Mia was the one to look mesmerized. He grinned. "Fate."

Eyebrows in a tight bunch on her forehead, she said, "I thought you were mad at me, you know, for wasting your time on that apple expedition."

Oh, he had been plenty mad—furious actually—about the damned building and angry about her pig-headedness, not because he'd "wasted time" with her. But he didn't want to think about their project right now. At this moment, he wanted the fairy princess and whatever magic elixir she offered.

"Fate." Jerking his head to the side, he pulled her hand. "Come with me."

"I'm here with my friends." Mia gestured back at her girlfriends.

He'd forgotten they were there. Actually, he'd forgotten everyone was there. Two women watched with obvious interest, but a third scowled at him. "I shouldn't ditch them."

Luke whispered to her, "Tell me this doesn't feel right."

Her body answered when her eyes drifted closed and she swayed towards him.

He turned his gaze to the blonde friend, the one with the frown. "I'm stealing your friend. I'll make sure she gets home safe."

"Mia—" her friend implored. "No. This is not a good idea. Use your head."

"I'll be fine, Cassie. It's fate," Mia interrupted, laughing, but allowed herself to be towed away. "I'll text you later. I promise."

"You better or I'm calling the police," her friend called after her. "I'm serious."

Luke waved to his cousins who stood in a mystified clump, watching in bemusement. Fortunately, it wasn't too far to where he'd parked his car. He opened the passenger door for her, but before he let her in, he kissed her again. Still spontaneous, this one lingered a moment longer. He cupped the back of her head with one hand and pressed his lips to hers. She wasn't caught so off guard this time. Both of her fists clutched handfuls of his shirt at his waist. They were both breathless and giddy as they broke apart.

Once he'd pulled the car into traffic, she asked him, "Where are we going?"

"Somewhere quiet. Where we can talk, okay?" She had come willingly, but he didn't want to frighten her. He recognized that he was coming on very strong. "Your house?" he suggested.

She shook her head. "No, Cassie will be home soon." She glanced at him from the side of her eye. "Your place would be better."

He turned at the next light and pointed the car in the direction of his home.

She pulled out her phone. "I'm just going to text Cassie where I'll be so she won't worry. I know her. She'll be blowing up my phone if I don't."

In moments they arrived at Luke's house, and he was opening the door to his dark, empty condo. "Are you hungry? Thirsty? I'm not sure what pairs well with epiphanies."

Mia laughed. "No, I'm fine."

"I feel like I want a drink," he said. Jeb kept his bar well stocked. It seemed like a quick drink of something might settle him down. He was still flying high with revelations. Eventually he suspected he was going to crash, like a sugar high gone really, really bad, but not yet.

"Oh, if you're making yourself one, then I'll have one, too." She followed him to the liquor cabinet and watched while he poured a shot of amber liquid in two crystal glasses. "I'm a little nervous. I've never been someone's fate before."

He watched her over the rim of his glass as she took a tentative sip before putting the glass back on the bar. He went ahead and knocked his back, hoping it would bring him back to Earth.

The curtains were open and the only light that filtered into the room came from the moon. Mia stepped to the window and took in the lights of the city. "You have a beautiful view."

He had been standing very close behind her, so when she turned she slipped right into an embrace. "And you are damn near edible," he murmured into the hair on the side of her neck.

Running his fingers along her nape and lifting the hair away from her skin, he took in her scent. As he'd remembered in his dreams, her hair smelled of floral shampoo, but the skin underneath was warm sugar. He ran his nose along the tendon in her neck, enjoying the way her breath hitched at the contact.

"I almost hate to bring this up," she said, and from the way she was clutching at his shirt, she really did hate to bring up whatever it was.

"Hmmm?" Luke had a mouthful of earlobe and a questioning hum was the best he could do just now.

"We have this work thing and it's going to make it that much harder to design our building if we keep this up." She tilted her head to make her neck more accessible.

Using his thumb, he encouraged her to lean her head back so he could lick the hollow at the base of her throat, then skate his lips along that sensitive skin up to her chin.

"I don't want to talk about work." He pressed his lips against hers as a tactile example of how they couldn't talk right now. Slipping his tongue along the seam of her lips, he waited patiently for her to invite him in. When she did, he only touched the tip of his tongue to hers, enjoying the agony of the delay too much to rush in.

She was the one who took control of the kiss. She adjusted her head to a better angle and forged ahead, tangling her tongue with his as she gripped his shirt in tight fists and pressed herself flush to his chest.

Panting heavily when they finally came apart, Mia let out a stymied whine because she needed help with his shirt buttons. He almost laughed at how hard she was tugging at his shirt and growling in frustration. He didn't though. His princess had a fiery determination that was as sexy as anything he'd ever seen. He pushed her fingers away and undid the buttons, relishing in the way she devoured each piece of skin with her gaze.

Reaching high to push the material from his shoulders, she rubbed her palms over his chest and pressed open mouth kisses along his breastbone and between his pecs, stopping at his collarbone because that's as high as she could reach her lips, even on her tip toes, without him bending down. She wrapped her fingers around his neck and pulled his mouth to hers in another passionate kiss.

Somewhere he'd lost the upper hand in this seduction, not that he was complaining in the least. Mia had never been the aggressor when they kissed before, but this turnabout was hot as hell. While he kissed her back he gave his hands the freedom to roam her body like she did to him. All the times he'd kissed her before, in this very room and again in the apple orchard, he'd not taken the liberty of caressing her body. He was eager to rest his fingers in the indent of her waist and feel how the curve of her ass fit perfectly into his palm. He ached to test the weight of her breasts and stroke the length of her short but shapely legs up to where they ended and led the way to heaven.

Now she was pulling on his belt. Each tug brought his hips against her in jerky simulation of the rhythmed thrusting he was hard for.

"You want to take this to the bedroom?" he asked with a grin.

Mia was flushed. The color rising up her chest all the way to her cheeks proved her arousal as much as the heat in her eyes and swollen lips. "I don't care. In a minute I'm going to climb you like a tree regardless."

He chuckled, low and throaty, which only urged her on. Clutching his shoulders, she jumped and wrapped her legs around his middle. He cradled her ass in one hand and wrapped the fingers of his other in her hair to hold her mouth to his. He left his shirt on the floor in the living room. She whipped her top off and tossed it on the floor in the hall. Her bra dangled off the doorknob to the bathroom.

Stopping when his knees hit the bed, he dumped her flat on the mattress.

He barely had the opportunity to admire the beautiful shape of her breasts before she was demanding the removal of his pants. He playfully smacked away her hands when she sat up and reached for his fly.

With a naughty grin, he told her, "What's your hurry?"

Even while her eagerness had him harder than lead, he wanted to draw it out, tease her. He popped the button on his jeans and then slowly raised his gaze to meet hers. Then while she watched he drew the zipper down, slowly, one tooth at a time. She moved restlessly on the bed, her breathing heavy as she watched. His cock pushed against the cotton of his boxer briefs as eager to get to her as he was. When he set his hand on his hips to push the denim and cotton to the floor, she started to rise again, but he stopped, took two steps back, and shook his head until she settled back against the comforter.

Once his pants and boxers hit the floor, he stood tall and took her in. If he hadn't known better, Luke would have thought Asher's lust trick had touched her. Her creamy skin was flush with passion, her chest rising and falling with erratic breaths, and her gaze intense with want.

"You're gorgeous," she told him while her eyes roamed over his body, pausing on his own hand stroking his length.

He stalked to the bed. "That's my line."

Leaning down he unbuttoned her jeans and tucked his fingers under the waistband and tugged them down the length of her legs. She wiggled her hips to help until he was able to pull them off her legs and dump them on the floor next to his own pants.

Out of her clothes, laying on his bed clad only in pink silk underwear, she looked nothing like the fairy princess she usually did. Maybe an x-rated princess. No matter what shape she took, she looked like his destiny.

"Come here," she demanded.

He crawled up the bed between the cradle of her legs and leaned over her body. "Are you going to taste like apples?"

"What?" she asked while she twined her fingers in his hair.

He chuckled. "Let me see." He kissed the soft flesh of her stomach beside her navel then at her sternum before gently nipping her side in the hollow where her ribs ended and her hip began. Her fingers tangled in his hair so that he acquiesced when she urged him higher. Angling his head, he kissed her, his tongue slipping past her lips to stroke the inside of her mouth. She arched her chest and kissed him back, humming a sexy purr that went straight to his cock. "Yumm," he told her when he broke the kiss.

"Like apples?" she said through a laugh.

"Don't know. I need more samples."

He kissed her chin, her throat, ran his tongue along the top of her collar bone. He nipped the flesh where her shoulder curved into her neck. "You do taste good."

Her responding sighs urged him on. Spilling kisses and flicks of his tongue down her chest. He filled his hands with her breasts and closed her nipples between his forefingers and thumbs. She gasped and arched her back again. He covered one nipple with his mouth, soothing and sucking the bud until it was tight. Switching breasts, he did the same to the other nipple.

"My God, you do taste good." He settled there, between her legs and worshiped at the altar of Mia, alternating nipples and massaging her breasts. He didn't think it was possible for her to actually taste like apples, but she was sweet and warm and he couldn't get enough.

Eventually he moved lower, urged on by her encouraging moans of pleasure. With his tongue, he drew a long line down her stomach until he reached the boarder of the lacy waistband of her panties. He kissed her mound as he captured her gaze over the silk, and she grasped fistfuls of coverlet.

"Luke," she purred, her voice barely above a whisper.

He slipped a finger inside the silken barrier and traced her opening. Mia dropped her head back and moaned, a pleading invitation. Desperate to be inside her, he slipped her panties down her legs to reveal her entrance. She pulled at his arms to bring him closer, urging him with open legs to fill her. He grabbed a condom from the bedside table and sheathed himself before he grabbed her under her knees and yanked her to the edge of the bed.

Her skin radiated warm heat like a promise. Luke understood at an elemental level, a knowledge as old as time, that within Mia lay the path to either darkness or light.

Sliding his hands underneath her butt and with his feet planted firmly on the floor, he positioned himself at her opening and with one smooth movement, he slid home. She gasped and tossed her head to the side with a long arch of her back.

He paused for a moment, euphoria spilling over him. He closed his eyes, lifted his face to the ceiling, and allowed the light to fill his soul. The sensation lasted for only a moment, but it was a profound one. Brought back to reality when Mia called his name, she implored him to move with the rhythm of her own body. Meeting her thrusts with his own, he pushed towards a climax. The light was growing, something almost tangible that he could touch.

"Now," Mia cried, and with two more deep thrusts, he pushed them both over the edge.

Light exploded all around, like a sunburst or a super nova. A climax like none he'd ever experienced before. And then as the light faded, a serenity settled around him and a different kind of lightness enveloped him.

He unwound her legs from his waist, tossed the condom in the nearby trash, and crawled onto the bed, pulling her up with him and tucked her sultry, heated body next to his.

"Is all fate-sex like that?" she asked and laced her fingers with his.

He kissed the side of her neck under her ear. "No way, that was all me. I'm just that good."

She giggled and turned in his arms, hooking a leg over his hip. "You think you can do it again?"

"I wonder what the fortune teller would say." He smoothed his palm over her ass.

Mia glanced down between their bodies and said with a coy grin, "All signs point to yes."

She pushed him flat on the mattress and straddled him. She did all the work the second time the Devil's son saw heaven that night.

HEAVEN & HELL V

Neil hid behind the chimney and waited. He couldn't evade Duke Valefor or his creepy little goblin henchman forever, but a break would be nice. The solid stone at his back was hot enough to burn his fingers if he wasn't careful. Still, he crouched as close to it as he dared until the he was certain the coast was clear.

He'd only turned his back on the damn dog for a minute before he'd disappeared. He had no idea how he'd gotten himself wrangled with watching the horrid thing, but he had and now he'd lost Cerberus. Again.

It was so tempting to rattle off a long list of curse words, but when you were already in Hell they really didn't hold as much power as they used to. One of the many, many personal reasons Hell sucked, as far as Neil was concerned. He had been a "truly outstanding connoisseur of the blasphemous invective," as the old nun who punished him for it daily used to put it. Sister Agnes who taught second grade at Angelwood State School for Boys had been the first of many nuns who'd not been able to save Neil, but he'd hated her the least.

He peeked around the corner and spied the goblin, Scourge, disappearing around the far side of the barracks. Neil was exhausted so, instead of sneaking back out to continue the search, he slumped down with a weary sigh and dug around in his pockets for something to eat.

That was another thing to hate about Hell. Neil was always hungry. No matter what he ate, or how much of it, it was never enough to fill the hole. That was how he'd started out in life—lying, cheating, and stealing to eat had been what set him on his criminal path—and now he got to live with it for eternity.

Soggy boloney sandwich. Revolting, but he ate it anyway because his stomach was growling.

He never finished high school, so he didn't know if it was actually irony or just plain tragedy that while alive he'd finally earned a reputation as a banger with status, one who could afford to order filet mignon and drink the good beer, only to die and spend it slowly starving on rotten food.

Grudgingly, he got to his feet. Scourge hadn't doubled back yet, so Neil went the long way through the furnaces, past the chimneys and ground vents, even though he knew the three-headed dog wouldn't be there where it was the hottest. It was still the fastest way to the garbage dumps. That was where Neil had found the big, dumb beast several times before, anyway. Cerberus would follow his noses right to the mountains of rotting garbage and have a field day.

The stench was unbelievable. Warm, fermenting swill. Wasn't Hell grand?

"Ha!" Scourge popped out behind a mountain of putrid fruit. "I finds you."

Neil didn't give the goblin the pleasure of acting surprised. "Good for you." A quick glance around the dump did not reveal a massive dog. "If I had a milk bone, I'd throw it to you."

The goblin danced a little jig while he sang, "Duke Valefor giveses rewards for Neil."

Neil shuddered at the thought of what the goblin would get for a reward for bringing him in. "That's exciting, it is. Can't come with you though. I'm busy."

"No." The celebratory dance came to an abrupt stop. "You comes now."

Neil considered punting the greasy-haired creature into the

garbage heap, but he knew that would only delay his punishment. It would also seriously piss off the already nasty goblin. As Duke Valefor's pet, Scourge had the opportunity to inflict a hell of a lot of pain on him if he wanted to. Scourge always wanted to. Goblins weren't smart, but they had the focus of a brain surgeon when torture was involved.

"If I come with you now," Neil told Scourge, "I can't find the dog."

The goblin sneered. "I hates the doggie."

Neil laughed, which surely earned him a few more moments of torture, but it was worth it. "But the doggie loves you, doesn't he? Still have that bite on your ass?"

The Guard Dog of Hell didn't like goblins, especially Scourge.

With narrowed eyes, Scourge pointed away from the dump and back towards the main stockade and the Duke's nest.

Neil slouched off in that direction like it was no big deal, the creature prodding him in the back with a pokey finger. "It doesn't seem like you're limping as badly anymore." He gave a little chuckle. "Man, that dog sure did take a chunk of hide though, huh? That middle head just went CHOMP." This time he laughed for real, doubled over a bit, and smacked his thigh loudly for good measure. "And the way you yelped, dude, all high-pitched like a baby." He pitched his voice in a wavering falsetto and squealed in imitation. "That shit was funny."

Scourge shoved him, but it was pretty ineffective. Goblins were short and skinny. Compared to Neil's height, which had been above average in life, it was like being attacked by a seven-year-old kid. One on one, Goblins didn't stand a chance, but if you found yourself in the midst of a horde of them...

"You not laughs so much when his lordship is dones with you," the goblin promised. "You cries then."

Neil liked to think that he wouldn't cry, but who knew. Hell was not the kind of place where you could make promises to yourself and expect to keep them. At least, Neil's Hell wasn't. The decisions one made in life led to so many fresh paths of dread in Hell.

Duke Valefor's nest was roasting hot, as one would expect, but plush. Upholstered furniture filled his quarters with thick rugs underneath. Cigar smoke scented the room as well as a faint odor of decay. Littering the floor lay a multitude of small bones, and half-drunk goblets of wine—Neil heartily hoped it was wine—sat upon the tables. The duke did enjoy his comforts, especially when others weren't able to enjoy them. It was petty, but then of course it was.

Scourge bowed when he entered. Neil did not. Instead, he concentrated on avoiding eye contact and keeping his nervous hands still. The demon grinned. He barely moved in his chair, a giant high-backed throne. Was it unimaginative that it was constructed from bones? Maybe it was, but that didn't make it any less horrifying. The front legs of the chair were formed by enormous spinal columns curled all the way up to form the arms. He had no idea what creatures had been sacrificed for the sake of the Duke's ego, but they'd been humongous.

"Well done." Duke Valefor patted Scourge. The imp lingered, probably expecting his reward right away, but the demon was already focused on Neil. "You lost the King's dog. Again."

Neil blinked several times before answering, a lame attempt at keeping his voice even and apathetic. "I did not lose him, your lordship. He wandered off."

If you looked at Duke Valefor just right, you could glimpse his true form: a lion with a man's head. It always made Neil nauseated.

Valefor said nothing, just let his gaze bore into him, allowing the silence to linger until it became almost unbearable. Neil refused to fidget, but the goblin couldn't take it.

"He lets doggie runs away."

With a flash of movement, a hand—*a paw*—lashed out and swiped Scourge across the room. The goblin hit the wall with a crinkly thud, like eggshells wrapped in paper. One of the dozens of cats in the room wandered over and prodded him gingerly with a soft foot, but the goblin lay still in the heap where he landed. The cat climbed up the meager height his crumpled form provided, wrapped his tail around his body, and watched the proceedings with bored eyes.

"You lost the dog," Duke Valefor repeated.

Neil didn't deny it again, but he didn't admit to it either. He gave a practiced shrug and tried not to shit himself.

Duke Valefor leaned forward and scooped up another lazy feline.

He sat back in his giant red velvet throne and stoked a fat black cat with yellow eyes. It was so cliché as to be comical, but Neil definitely did not laugh. If there was any chance of talking his way out of this trouble, it would be toast if he giggled, even if it was from nervous terror.

The Duke seemed to be talking to the cat. His voice slipped into Neil's ears like warm oil, leaving him feeling unpleasant and dirty. "How hard is it to watch a dog? Honestly, tell me. It would seem that any idiot could keep an eye on it, the giant, stupid beast." He paused as if an idea struck him. "Are you an idiot, Neil?"

"No, sir." He exhaled through his nose. "Cerberus is—"

A long-fingernailed hand rose up in a quelling motion. "I don't care. What I do care about is Mastema finding out that the damned dog is missing and thinking that I had anything to do with it."

Neil pursed his lips. He didn't want anything to do with Mastema either. All the Dukes answered to Mastema, and he answered only to the Devil himself. Neil had the nickname of Head Master with the bangers in his crew because he was afraid of nothing and carefully thought shit through. His boys would never have believed it if they'd seen their old Head Master the only time he'd encountered Mastema. He might have pissed his pants. He'd rather avoid that again if at all possible.

A rangy orange tabby pushed what Neil was pretty sure was a human child's skull off a table ledge, then glanced over with interest as it rolled awkwardly back and forth.

Neil nodded and swallowed down his nausea. "I'll find the dog."

"Yes." The Duke's oily tone heated, oil that could blister. "You will."

Neil got the hell out of there. He moved away from the barracks as quickly as possible, past the dumps and the heat from the furnaces towards the outer circles of Hell, before he bent over and barfed up that miserable baloney sandwich. He finally stood, wiped the drool from his chin, and scanned the horizon.

He didn't know where the dog was, only where he wasn't.

It was impossible to tell time in Hell. Everything was a fucking eternity. But he'd been looking for the dog for a considerable period when he heard the rough chatter of goblins. He didn't have the energy to deal with an unruly horde. He turned into the sewers where the heat and the stench multiplied, thinking he could hide out until they passed. He opened a door and ducked inside, crouching low so he could watch through the keyhole.

There were fifteen or twenty of them, wearing the colors of a different Duke's Legion, most of them scrawny. He glanced around at the room where he found himself. It was hot, of course, but the smell wasn't so bad as to burn your nose hairs. A concrete stairwell rose up from the far side of the room. And most interestingly of all, there was a considerable amount of dog hair on the floor.

"Oh Cerberus," he called up the stairs. It was the first good lead he'd found, and he followed it up the stairs, hot on his trail.

CHAPTER SIXTEEN

Mia looked around her. She couldn't see much, the darkness was as heavy as the air, falling like dank velvet curtains. Claustrophobia hugged her, settled on her chest, squeezed. Hard to get a full breath, the air was so humid and heavy. Still none of that was as unsettling as the temperature. Oppressive. Like being in a kiln.

She turned in a slow circle and peered into the dark void. As she concentrated, she realized the darkness wasn't as complete as she'd originally thought. It was an illusion created by deep shadows on top of shadows. Like an old fashion camera trick. Inky black apparitions shifting over slate.

Something was moving around her. As her eyes adjusted further, the indistinct wisps took on outlines and coalesced into shapes which only lasted for moments before they dissolved into smoke again.

The heat pressed against her as if it was a living thing she could feel and touch. A scratchy caress from a calloused hand. Or an old woolen blanket that prickled.

Like an onion, another layer of the place revealed itself. Accompanying the heat came the funk of something burning, something foul. Maybe wet wool. She couldn't quite place it. And then the answer skittered across her mind as if someone had whispered it in her ear:

burning hair. Revulsion roiled in her gut as she realized it was how she'd expect the smell of the fires of concentration camps would be.

"Mia Hatcher, what an unexpected pleasure." The voice was low and seductive, a man's voice which sounded vaguely familiar.

She glanced around her, looking for the source, but it was still out of sight, disguised by the fetid darkness. "Where are you?"

The man laughed, a low rumble in his chest. "I am here. I am everywhere." Now the voice seemed to be coming from her left.

Mia turned in that direction and repeated, "Who are you?"

"Have you not guessed?

A low, mournful wail sounded in the distance. It was the very sound of misery. Impossibly, the heat intensified, causing her eyeballs to sting. "I don't know who you are or where I am. I don't know what's real."

Coming out of the darkness like a ghost, something brushed by her, then disappeared back into the void. She jumped, and a strangled shriek escaped her throat.

"I'll be honest. Of course, I will; I'm always honest," the voice said, this time from behind her. "I'm surprised to see you down here." Suddenly, the voice came from her right shoulder. "Not that I'm not thrilled to see you. There is such satisfaction when the inherently good make the journey down."

Abruptly, a wave of nausea brought her to her knees. The floor burned her legs where her skin touched as if the ground beneath her was the source of all heat in the universe. Gasping and clutching her stomach, tears dried on her cheeks almost the very instant they left her stinging eyes.

A hand appeared before her, held out with genteel civility to assist her to her feet. "Poor Mia. This place does affect some worse than others."

She took the offered hand, the man it belonged to coming into focus as if the smoke and darkness coalesced into solid form. Tall and thin, he wore an exquisitely cut suit that emphasized his broad shoulders and trim waist. Everything from his bespoke shoes to his jeweled cuff links were of the finest quality. He was so handsome she was almost mesmerized. He had the look of old Hollywood; glossy black hair parted on the left, eyes so dark they were almost black, fringed with thick eyelashes, a mouth framed by a lush lower lip and a perfect, bowed upper one. Yet, even though the catalogue of his parts was beautiful, the man was masculinity personified. Just like his voice, his face seemed oddly familiar.

Back to her feet, he slipped her hand in the crook of his elbow and led her into the darkness. Almost instantly, the nausea vanished. As they moved forward, a glowing light illuminated the way.

I'm dreaming. The thought filled her head in a desperate attempt to explain what was happening. *Nothing here is real.*

"Do I know you?" she asked, the sound of her words sounding distant in her ears.

"I know you," he told her without answering her question. A bustle of creatures scattered around their feet as they walked, like a pack of dogs that were distinctly not dogs. "Although we have not met."

Like any dream, inexplicable things happened. "Who am I?" she asked, although Mia thought she already knew who she was.

The handsome man looked down at her with a smile that went all the way to his eyes. "You're a very important lady, Mia."

He knows my name, she thought with a thrill. "Who am I?" she repeated.

"You're the perfect mate for my son. I couldn't have chosen anyone better for him." He patted her hand, resting in the crook of his elbow. He looked so familiar. She wished she could remember where she'd seen him. "You will be the mother of my grandson."

"I'm having a baby?" she asked in wonder.

"No, not tomorrow, but eventually. When the time is right." The handsome man laughed. For the first time, she noticed he had horns. Mia ogled and it occurred to her she should be afraid.

As if he knew her thoughts, he shook his head. "You're my guest here. I won't allow any of my pets to harm you."

He kicked out a foot and cleared the path of some of the creatures cavorting in their way. The animals squealed and trotted away, some of them on more legs than the usual four.

Another wave of heat blasted the air like jet exhaust. One of the beasts lingered close—some kind of monster she couldn't identify. The longer she studied it, the more her head ached. A grayish-green toad's head sat on the body of a large insect. A disgustingly fiendish mashup that made no sense. It trained its bulging-eyed gaze on her, opened its mouth, and vomited a dead rat at her feet. The pain in her head intensified, and she felt herself losing consciousness.

"Sleep tight, Mia."

Already she felt cooler, and the blinding pain ebbed from her brain. It took a huge effort to open her eyes, but when she did, she found herself in bed. Luke's bed. He was still asleep on his stomach, his face turned towards her. There were no creepy animals in the room. The handsome man with the horns was gone. The room smelled like cotton, man, and sex. Needing to touch him, she stroked her palm down his bicep. He stirred just enough to wrap his arm around her middle and drag her close to him. She drifted back to sleep with relief.

CHAPTER SEVENTEEN

S everal hours later, when she woke up again, she was alone in the bed. She sat up and wrapped the bedsheet around her and took stock. Except for Luke's giant cat, who was giving himself a bath near her feet, she was alone in the room.

"Good morning, Claw," she said, and tickled him under the chin. In response, the cat purred like a motorboat. "Any chance I'm going to be able to get out of here with any dignity this morning? Yeah, probably not."

She heard water running in the bathroom and figured this was her chance to at least get some clothes on before she saw Luke again. There was no way she wanted to face him naked. Not that she would have minded seeing him naked again. That man was built like a god. Renaissance sculptors did his form in marble. Religions could be formed for the sole purpose of praising his body.

She couldn't wait to tell Cassie all about it—with some edits of course. She wasn't sure she'd be able to confess how she'd behaved.

"I don't know what happened," she admitted to the cat as she slid out of the bed, sheet wrapped around her body like a toga, and searched for her clothes. "I was like a maniac."

Claw extended one leg, spread his toes wide, and commenced licking. If he was listening, he didn't show it.

Her panties and jeans were still wadded up on the floor by the bed. "I couldn't keep my hands off him." She pulled on her underpants and hopped up and down to get her jeans up over her ass, made more complicated with a king-sized sheet in the way. "The things I did, cat, oh my God, and begged him to do. So embarrassing. I can't even believe it was me."

The sound of running water coming from behind the bathroom door stopped, and she froze. It started up again, and she exhaled. "Have you seen my top anywhere? And a bra. I know I was wearing one when I came over here."

Claw switched legs and did not reply.

A drop to the plank wood floor did not reveal the rest of her clothes under the bed. She surveyed the rest of the room. It was furnished in a minimal style, something that seemed completely typical of what she knew of Luke's esthetic. The only furniture was the massive bed she'd become so acquainted with, mid-century bedside tables, and a large television mounted on a wall. Presumably, everything else was in the walk-in closet off the bathroom. The sheet she wore and the rest of the bed clothes matched the gray flannel upholstered headboard. The walls were dove gray with the exception of one navy blue accent wall. Over the headboard hung a Mondrian and the opposite wall had a Pollack. She was pretty sure they were originals.

The only thing about the room that wasn't neat as a pin was stacks of books on the floor around one of the nightstands. While she was down on the floor, she took a look at the titles. What did a man like Luke read in bed? There were the titles one would expect; some Clancy and Cussler, old school Stephen King, but also James Joyce, some philosophy texts, Harry Potter and the Sorcerer's Stone threw her for a loop, and a dog-eared copy of Dante's Inferno.

"As you do, you know, for light bedtime reading," she told the uninterested cat.

Yet, there was still no sign of her bra and shirt. A vague recollection of the previous evening's sexy-time events suggested the rest of her stuff might be in the living room. She closed her eyes for a second and rubbed her forehead, searching for explanations. She hadn't been drunk and there wasn't any subsequent hangover. She was one hundred percent certain she hadn't been drugged because she was distressingly aware of all her shocking behavior. These were all decisions she'd intentionally made. But all of them were so unlike her. It's just that the whole night, from the minute she'd seen Luke in the street during his nervous breakdown to this morning, had felt surreal. Like she'd starred in a movie of her wildest fantasies. She'd certainly had plenty of daydreams where she played the vixen and aggressively demanded sex the way she had last night, but it wasn't something she imagined ever doing in real life. She wasn't a prude by any means, but she also wasn't the sexpot type. She knew exactly what Cassie would say. None of her previous dull-as-dishwater boyfriends had inspired a sexpot.

The water stopped running again. Mia let out a squeak, "Eep!"

Rushing, she opened the bedroom door, and there on the floor were her clothes. Neatly folded, the bra sat atop her T-shirt which rested on her sandals. Who did this? Luke wouldn't have fetched her clothes and then left them outside the room, would he? Oh, my God, he must have a cleaning lady or something. How mortifying.

She was just pulling the shirt on over her head when the bathroom door opened. He wore jeans hanging low on his hips and that was all. Damn near all seventeen feet of him available for her to ogle. His hair was ruffled and there was shadow on his cheeks and jaw where his beard had started to come in. A heavy drop of water ran from his collarbone through the valley of his pectorals and disappeared into the line of hair that started at his belly button and traveled to destinations south.

His right pectoral was decorated with a brilliant black and red neo-traditional tattoo of the devil. The man was handsome in the old school style, with strong features, a sculpted mouth, and lush black hair complete with horns poking through. The artist had given him expressive eyes which appeared to be laughing at an inside joke.

Even though this tempting vision of Luke explained a lot about her behavior, it was still damned embarrassing. When she reminded herself that she still had to design a building with this man, she wanted to kill herself. How had that not seemed so important last night?

"Good morning." His voice was sexy gravel. Maybe he had a hang-over. Last night she would have said he'd been stone cold sober, but who knew?

"Hi," she said tearing her eyes from his abdomen and plucked the giant sheet off the floor. Not knowing what else to do with herself, she started to fold it.

Luke ducked his head and gave her a brief kiss on the lips. He smelled like toothpaste which helpfully reminded her that she hadn't brushed her own teeth. Yet another reason to want to die this morn-ing. "I can try to make you coffee?"

Who tries to make coffee? "Umm, yeah."

He unwound the sheet from her hands and she reluctantly released it when he tugged. Without looking, he tossed it on the bed, enveloping the cat in yards of fabric. Muffled meows of protest were ignored.

She followed Luke down the hallway to the kitchen she remem-bered from her first visit to his home. Now that she knew him a little better, she took a better look at her surroundings than she had before. Nothing had changed in his kitchen from the first time she'd been there. Cleared countertops and stainless-steel appliances revealed nothing about the man, except that he liked things clean and simple. And maybe a little intimidating if you took the complicated commercial-looking espresso maker into account.

Eyebrows raised in amazement, she said, "Wow, that's some machine."

He shrugged. "I don't know how to use it. Jeb fancies himself some kind of barista or something." To her disappointment, he pulled out a Keurig and plopped a canister in the hopper. Noting her frown, he promised, "I do have real cream."

She waved her hand at the percolating pot. "Oh, that's great. Thanks. I'm going to look around for my purse and stuff." Then she headed off for the living room, but sensed him following along.

Her purse sat on the coffee table. The bar had been cleaned up, the liquor bottle put away and the glasses removed. Everything neat as a showroom. The grey theme continued in this room as well. Above a modern leather sofa, she spied—

"Is that a Miro?" she asked with a squeak.

"It is," he said. His hands were jammed in his pockets and he nodded at the painting with a smile. "My cousin Benjamin found that one for me in Milan."

"Amazing," she said. "Is he a dealer or something?"

He turned his hazel gaze to her. "Benji? No. He doesn't do much of anything, actually."

"Your collection is pretty amazing." Mia wandered the room and wondered what other treasures she'd find. She paused at the fireplace to look at the few photos on the mantle.

"Are these your parents?" she asked, holding up a family portrait. It had that out-of-date look that family pictures got when the clothes and hairstyles were compared against the current trends.

"Yeah," he said. "Just the three of us."

"Your mother was gorgeous." Mia ran her index finger over the baby in the photo before focusing on the man. "Your father is handsome, too. You look a lot like him." She stared at the photo, something niggling at the back of her brain. "He looks so familiar. I wonder if I've ever met him."

Luke took the photo from her hand and laid it face-down on the mantle. "I'm certain you've never met him."

"Hmmm." She reset the frame on its legs and positioned it back where she'd found it. "Maybe an acquaintance of my father?"

"I doubt it." His tone was curt, and she tossed him a questioning glace.

She looped her purse strap over her shoulder and gave the photo one last glance, only this time a trick of the light seemed to give Luke's father horns. When she looked closer, they were gone, but even that split second tied everything together.

He looked exactly like the man in her dream.

Memories of it were fading, and she couldn't remember exactly what happened during it, but that man had most definitely been there. She started to say something to Luke about it, to laugh about how weird subconscious thoughts were, but the look on his face suggested that she shouldn't. So instead they stood around awkwardly for a second while she tried to think of something to say.

"You think that coffee's ready yet?"

The hard lines of his face softened into a sexy half-smile and he gave a little shrug. "I don't know, but we can go glare at it. That's what I usually do."

She followed him back to the kitchen while inventorying the many muscles in his back and shoulders.

"Hey," he said, actually sounding delighted, and she smiled at how incongruous that was with his normally gruff exterior. "The coffee's done."

Mia stood behind him while he poured cream in hers. Captivated by the valley of his spine nestled between the planes of muscles, she followed it with her eyes from way up past her head at the base of his neck until it curved into his cute little round ass. She licked her bottom lip and extended her fingers to skim across the warm, tanned skin between his shoulder blades. Barely touching him, she traced her fingertips downward along the ridges of his spine.

Luke shivered and sighed.

She dropped a kiss in the middle of his back and inhaled deeply. His scent was there under the mask of Ivory soap and shampoo, base notes of spice and that intangible Luke medley.

He set the mugs back on the counter and turned to face her. "Would you prefer to do this in the kitchen or go back to bed?"

She shrugged. "Drink coffee? Wherever you want. Fair warning: I'm a spiller so we might get it on the sheets."

In one shockingly quick movement, he wrapped his hands around her waist and lifted her onto the counter. He wedged himself between her thighs and yanked her hips flush against him. "Coffee later," he growled into the side of her neck.

If she'd started to squeal in surprise at his quick movements, it was detoured into a moan as soon as his lips started moving across her skin. One hand was wrapped in her hair and the other was already wending its way under her T-shirt. Mia wrapped her legs around his waist and locked her ankles together. Heat radiated from his skin where her palms smoothed over his ribs and biceps. She grabbed on to his shoulders when he pulled her head back to get better access to her neck.

"Luke." It sounded breathy and came out as a whisper. She swallowed and tried again. "Luke."

"Umm-hmm." The rumble of his voice vibrated against her throat. She could feel it everywhere.

"The kitchen is fine."

He brought his head up and have her a questioning look. "Huh?"

"Let's do it in the kitchen, cleaning lady be damned." She popped the top button of his jeans.

Her shirt was coming over her head, when he admitted, "I don't have a cleaning lady."

Then who cleaned up last night's mess and folded her clothes? It was difficult to think about, or even really care, when he was pulling off her bra and flinging it into the sink. What difference did it make if she got butt prints on the counter?

LATER LUKE WORE boxer briefs and Mia had on only a bib apron that said Hot Damn in flaming letters. They had moved to the dining room and were eating grilled cheese sandwiches with tomato.

"These are good but would have been better with bacon," Luke said around a mouthful of sourdough and cheddar.

"Honey," Mia said in all seriousness, "you cannot cook bacon naked. I'm going to want to use you again later and I don't want you damaged."

"But, bacon."

She giggled. "You know, they used to call tomatoes love apples."

"What?" He pulled the bread away from his teeth, stringing cheese for at least ten inches before the strand finally broke and fell back against his chin.

"They did." She nodded. "I've heard lots of reasons why. Maybe just as simple as they're sorta heart shaped."

He raised a skeptical eyebrow. "That's a stretch."

"Yeah. Maybe because they resemble another plant that was considered an aphrodisiac."

Luke had sliced these beefsteak tomatoes on the thick side so they held up under the weight of the cheese and bread. It was an excellent sandwich. Mia took a swig from a bottle of water they were sharing.

"I don't really need an aphrodisiac," he told her and stretched across the table to kiss her.

"They were also called the Devil's Apple—" she kissed him again "—and were blamed for witchcraft."

"Tell me more," he purred, his voice low and husky. God, he was going to kill her.

She lowered her voice to sound as much like a phone sex operator as possible. "So suspicious, Americans didn't really start eating them until the Civil War. People even believed they could turn you into a werewolf."

Luke threw back his head and howled. Mia waited patiently until he was done. He grinned at her wolfishly. "What cool stuff do you have in that fascinating head of yours about bacon?"

She shrugged and popped the last of her sandwich in her mouth. "Nothing really. I'm a just a plant girl."

He reached for her plate and the empty water bottle. "Not *just* a plant girl." He carried the dishes to the kitchen, and she followed along behind. "My girl is the Apple Queen."

His girl, he'd said. The thought made her warm all over.

SOMETIME THAT AFTERNOON, Mia hopped out of bed, where they'd spent the afternoon wrapped in sheets and binge-watching Doctor Who, to get something to drink and something to nibble on besides each other.

"I'm sure there are pretzels in there," he called after her, watching her nearly naked body tip toe away from the bed. She'd stolen the sheet to wrap around herself, leaving him reclining in their squishy, warm pillow fort bare-ass naked.

"Don't turn it back on without me," she called back.

"Then hurry." He chuckled at the sound of her barefoot, running feet and stretched his arms and legs, wiggled his toes. He encountered Claw at the end of the bed and nudged the sleepy animal with a toe.

He didn't budge, much less put forth enough fierce energy to bite, scratch, or maul his leg. Maybe this wasn't even his cat.

He turned to face the side of the bed Mia had claimed as her own. Feeling like a teenager, he pressed his face into her pillow and inhaled the scent of warm linen and herbal shampoo. His cock thickened of its own accord, a jerking reaction to the promise of burying his nose in her hair while sinking into the depths of her.

This had been the best day since...maybe ever. He couldn't recall a time when he was so relaxed and comfortable and yet in a state of arousal that only abated immediately after sex. They'd done nothing all day but doze, watch television, and fuck.

Luke never wanted it to end.

"What's taking so l—"

Mia appeared in the bedroom doorway, the sheet wadded up in a tangle around her body, with two beer bottles and a bag of pretzels. She looked annoyed.

"What's wrong?" he asked, sitting up, dread filling his gut in that way that usually brewed fury.

"You said you didn't have a cleaning lady." Her mouth was set in a firm line. "All the dishes are done in the kitchen and there are steaks thawing in the fridge. I know you didn't do it, so who did?"

Luke exhaled and the brewing firestorm abated. "Oh. You had me freaked out there for a second. It was Jeb, I'm sure."

One eyebrow thawed out enough to rise above the other and she moved towards the bed again, maintaining the posture of a lady miffed. "I don't know why that makes me feel better, but it does."

He took the beverages from her so she could more easily navigate her way on the bed with the swaddled sheet hampering her process. "Why would it have been a problem if there was a cleaning lady?"

"Well, we're not exactly being discrete here." She waved a hand over the rumpled bed. She took in his nakedness and blushed prettily, something he would have thought she'd have gotten past considering the things they'd done to each other all day. "I don't need someone thinking I'm a tramp."

He tried to follow this logic. "But Jeb won't?"

Thinking for a moment, she shook her head. "No. And Jeb's gay, so it wouldn't matter if he saw me running around in a sheet."

"But it wouldn't be okay if a cleaning lady did?"

"I have no idea why, but yes." She opened the pretzels. "Why does your assistant do all this for you? I mean, I love Jason and all, and he's a stellar assistant, but he doesn't come to my house and pick up after me or set out my dinner. That's a bit beyond his job description, isn't it? And let's be frank, you're pretty mean to Jeb all the time."

Luke filled his mouth with pretzels as a deflection. What could he possibly tell her about his supernatural assistant that she would believe? The truth was out of the question—at least at this point. He'd already sprung a fortune teller and fate on her, and she'd gone along with that, but where was the tipping point? On the other hand, maybe he should tell her the truth—Jebediah was an ageless, magical gargoyle, just like the ones each of the cousins was given to help them navigate through the terrible, complicated life that being one of the Seven was doomed to endure. She'd only think he was kidding, anyway, and that would be one less lie he'd have to tell her.

"I've known Jeb almost my whole life. We met when I was ten and we've been together ever since. Jeb is just always...there." He made a sweeping gesture meant to convey everywhere, all the time. "He's not really an employee of the company. Well, he is, but he's really mine."

She scowled at him in a way that was unbearably charming, and he laughed. "You're describing indentured servitude or slavery or something," she said.

"Totally not." From what Luke understood, being a gargoyle who served the Seven was an honor. To be the servant of the one ultimately chosen to be the Devil—well, that was damn near rapturous. His father's gargoyle, Ezra, was held in the highest possible esteem. "He's with me because he wants to be."

She raised a skeptical eyebrow. "I don't know why. You're so harsh with him."

Luke rolled his eyes. "Well, Hells bells, you've met him. He's fucking annoying." When Mia flinched, he paused and started again, knowing he could do better. "Jeb gets me. I've got some anger issues," putting it mildly, "and he understands. He knows my family history and what I have to deal with on a regular basis. I may give him a hard time, but he's okay with it." Trying to explain their relationship to someone who couldn't possibly understand was making him feel weirdly sentimental about the fool. "He takes care of everything. Been keeping me out of trouble since college, well, before college actually, but especially college."

Popping another pretzel in her mouth, she asked, "You guys even went to college together?"

He watched her chew, distracted by the tip of her tongue licking salt from the corner of her lip. "Yeah. I'm telling you, he's just always been there. He runs my entire life."

This time she fed him a pretzel. He nipped her finger playfully.

"Did he study architecture, too?" she asked. The sheet slipped from its wrap around her breasts, and she didn't fix it.

Taking the beer from her hand, he placed both of them on the nightstand. It was probably going to get rowdy in this bed shortly and they would make a mess. "No. Jeb was a political science major." He hung a pretzel from her furled nipple and then used his mouth to remove it.

She made a noise of approval and let the sheet fall completely away. "And yet he hangs out with you. Well, at least that explains why he's so good at handling you, all that political mastery and such."

"Yep, that's Jeb. Riding shotgun through my life." He pulled the pretzel bag away and tossed it on the floor.

When he pushed her flat on the bed and crawled over the top of her, she squealed and said, "I thought we were watching the Doctor?"

"Or," he purred against her neck, "we could play doctor."

SUNDAY EVENTUALLY ROLLED AROUND, and thoughts of the real world forced Mia from their love nest. She snuck out of his bed, got dressed, and brushed her teeth with a fresh packaged toothbrush she found in the bathroom.

When she emerged, he was up and wearing only those jeans again.

"I've gotta go," she said. "I have a million things to do today since nothing got done yesterday."

He pulled her back against the length of his body and wrapped his arms around her. "You're wrong. Lots of things got done yesterday."

She snorted and probably blushed, amazed that she still had that reaction to him after all the gymnastics they'd done. "It's a miracle we can walk," she teased back, but then finished with regret. "But still, I have a dog to walk and the greenhouse to check on. I was supposed to go out to the Daughters of Eve today. I'm trying to remember that I'm an adult. Lots of chores to get done."

"You don't have your car." He reminded her as he walked her down the hall.

"I'm going to call an Uber." She wished he'd put a shirt on or something because she was trying to hold it together and act like the well-behaved young woman she was and not like the wanton who'd taken over her body and wanted to climb him again.

"Let me make some coffee and I'll go with you," he said with finality. "Let me just grab a shirt and some shoes."

She beamed at him. "Okay."

He disappeared down the hall in a quick trot. She watched him go, enjoying the play of muscle under tan skin as he moved. There weren't enough superlatives available to her sex-addled brain to describe his glorious body.

"Good morning. I see you found all your clothes."

Mia whipped around to find Jeb with raised eyebrows and a smirk. "That *was* you?"

He gave a shallow bow. "Indeed." He raised a pink bakery box. "I have muffins."

"Oh, good. Luke's making coffee."

Jeb shook his head. "No, he's not."

"Yeah, he is."

He screwed up his mouth in distaste. "That swill he brews in that machine—" he said the word with utter contempt "—is not fit for pigs. He won't bother to learn how to m—"

"What are you doing here?" Luke appeared, his gorgeous physique covered.

Jeb rolled his eyes. "Saving you from boiling hot swamp water. And bringing muffins."

Knowing how most of Luke and Jeb's conversations went, Mia intervened. She gave Luke a look. "Be nice." Then to Jeb, she said, "I'd love to stay and listen to you both bicker, but I'm lying."

"We're on our way out." Luke growled and dangled his keys as evidence. He sounded unreasonably angry and Mia blinked at him, confused at how quickly it had happened.

"Actually," Jeb held up his hand. "Besides the muffins, I bring a message from your father." It looked like Luke flinched. "He wants to talk to you."

Luke's jaw clenched tight. "I'll call him later."

"Riiight." Jeb stretched the word out. "'Cause he's always so indulgent about waiting. He is demanding a face to face." He plucked two muffins out and handed one to Mia. "Never fear. I'll take you home and our boy here can respond to his summons from his paterfamilias."

"Damn it," Luke thundered and threw his keys back down the hallway. "Let Jeb take you home." He turned a hard eye to Jeb until the man excused himself. She heard the front door open and close. Luke laced his fingers through hers and walked her to the foyer. "I'm really sorry." His tone had modulated down, and he spoke to her in a soft voice that made her tingle.

"It's fine. It's just a bunch of plant stuff. And a dopey dog. And some nuns. You're not missing anything exciting."

"I'll miss *you*." He squeezed her hand. "I'll call you later, okay?"

She tilted her face up to kiss him. "Holy shit, is that an Alexander Calder?" She pointed at the ceiling where a mobile hung just over Luke's head. Brightly colored amoeba-shaped discs hung in a mobile sculpture at all kinds of perfectly balanced angles.

"It is. Impressed you recognize it."

"I know more than apples," she said and smacked him with a flat hand on his stomach.

He recaptured her hand and pressed it against his lips. "I know that," he said with a smile. "You also know about tomatoes."

"Your cousin again?" she asked, too busy staring at the artwork in amazement to flirt back. She really wanted to meet this cousin.

"Not this time. Picked it up at auction last week."

She didn't remember seeing a security keypad at the front door "You've got some kind of collection. Don't you ever worry about being robbed or something?"

He shook his head. "No. No one is ever going to rob me. I promise." Before she could protest, he pulled her into his arms for a sweet until-later kiss that squished her muffin.

"Tell your father hello for me," she teased and waved to him as she walked to Jeb's car.

"Oh, I'm sure he already knows all about you," Luke said with a wave.

She pondered his last statement for the rest of the day.

CHAPTER EIGHTEEN

T he note Jeb had left on his counter was short and to the point.
Your father wants to see you. Noon. He'll send the car.

Luke stared at the note but didn't touch it. Three very short sentences, and yet they had the power to enrage him. Every ounce of peace that he'd found with Mia evaporated.

He pulled the cup from the Keurig and drank the shitty coffee black. The acid from the drink mingled with the already bilious contents of his stomach and he could sense his barometer rising. He flipped the pink cardboard lid from the bakery box Jeb had also left on the counter and glared at the pastries. He ripped the top off a blueberry muffin and shoved it in his mouth with no ceremony as he stalked out of the kitchen. He chewed the dainty muffin like it was leather instead of cake, mulling over what he was going to do about this command performance.

He could always refuse to see his father. He'd never actually done that, but there was a first time for everything. He didn't know what the Devil would do to him if he flat out declined the summons. It's not like he could hide from the man. He was the Devil, after all. He didn't have the powers of God to be omnipotent or anything, but he had spies everywhere, and there would certainly be a punishment for defying his father.

Damn it.

It hadn't been long enough since the last time his father demanded an audience. That time the Devil had wanted to put in his two cents about Luke's collegiate academic performance. This time, Luke suspected the timing was too significantly close to the revelations about Mia to be about anything but that.

He lingered at the picture of his family Mia had found so fascinating. He stared at his parents. Seeing them all together, a cheerfully smiling trio posed in some ridiculous studio setting like a bunch of ignorant schmucks, ignited the slow fuse burning in his gut. He plucked the frame from the mantle and heaved it at the opposite wall with a roar. The glass shattered and the wood splintered but it didn't give him any relief.

Neither did the coffee mug when it shattered against the same wall. A chunk was missing from the plaster and the coffee dribbled down the wall to puddle on the floor surrounded by the glass and wood of the frame.

A flash of sanity urged him to save the photo from the mess. He couldn't bear to have it ruined, if for no other reason than it was of his mother. He didn't own enough photos of her that he could irresponsibly destroy one on a whim. He clung to the few keepsakes he had because the pitiful truth was, he had no real memories of her. He'd been only three when she'd died. The only recollections he had, he couldn't be sure weren't false. That they hadn't been planted there by his family—stories about how much she'd loved him substituting for actual memories.

He sank to the sofa, staring at the photo. She'd been the lucky one, getting out before everything went to shit. He hated her a little for that, too. He didn't know if he'd ever see her again. She was most certainly in Heaven, and who knew where he'd end up.

How much had she known about the curse before she'd married Aaron Mephisto? Had his father come clean to her before they got married? Had she been aware of what she was doing when she and his father had conceived Luke? Or had his dad kept the dark truth from her until it was too late?

By all accounts, Felicity Mephisto had been a caring, loving wife and mother. A tender soul, his dad had called her. His Aunt Claire, Ethan's mother, had confessed to him that she'd been crushed when Felicity had died. They'd been especially close friends, almost like sisters. It was hard to reconcile someone described with such compassion as being willing to love the Devil and, even more, to possibly give birth to the next one. Maybe she had been completely ignorant.

Luke couldn't do that to Mia.

He never discussed his mother with anyone, not since he was ten and the devastating losses really started piling up. It occurred to him that Aunt Claire would have some answers. He was going to need some advice from someone on how to proceed with Mia. The timing was excellent to finally demand some answers from his Father about this damn family curse.

Felicity Mephisto stared back at him from the static photograph, but now he could see judgment in her gaze. *You're going to ruin a woman's life*, she said. *You should be ashamed. Maybe she'll be lucky enough to provide the cursed heir and then die like I did. Then she'll never have to deal with the consequences.*

He turned the photo face down on the coffee table, then stormed down the hall to his bedroom, where he changed out of the jeans and into sweats and laced up his running shoes. He was going to have to see his father. There was no real way around it, but he was going to make this work to his advantage. He figured he better exhaust himself before the time came or he'd never get through it, and there was too much at stake. Fifteen miles ought to do it.

When he got back two and a half hours later, his legs weighed a thousand pounds and each breath felt like inhaling a welding touch. But at least for now, he didn't have the energy to kill anyone.

Not even Jeb, who waited for him in the foyer with a bottle of water, tapping his foot impatiently.

"Feel better?" he asked.

Luke nodded while guzzling. He wiped the dribbling water from his chin with his shoulder. "What time is it?"

"You've got time to hit the showers, which I highly recommend."

He thrust the bottle back at Jeb, sloshing the contents onto Jeb's shirt and the floor. "Don't aggravate me. I just sprinted to the moon and back to wear myself out. I don't need you revving me back up."

Jeb gave a little bow. "You're right. Carry on."

He peeled his shirt off on the way, noticing as he passed the living room that the evidence of his earlier rage had been cleared away. Even the photo was back in a frame and settled into its place on the mantle.

Rounding the corner to his bedroom, he was stuck with the fanciful notion that the bedroom might still smell like Mia. But Jeb had been in here, too. The bed had been stripped and remade, and all the clothes and the damp towel he'd left on the floor had been removed. Now the room smelled like clean cotton instead of a vague fruity aroma and warm woman.

He finished stripping, stepped into the hot shower, and let the steam and pounding water ease some of the tension he'd purposefully worked into his muscles. He closed his eyes and rolled his shoulders and stretched his neck. Working to keep the anxiety of seeing his father at bay, his mind naturally drifted back to Mia and the revelations from the night before.

Like a kick in the face, the Daughters of Eve materialized after the fortune teller... followed by Mia, appearing as if fate, destiny, or God himself had placed her directly in his path. Would that have been God, or the handy work of the Devil? Did it matter?

The flirtation they'd shared had not led him to believe their sex would be so epic. Kissing Mia those times before had been excellent, but sex had been spectacular, portentous—sublime, even. There simply weren't enough superlatives. Never before in his life had sex been so much like religious fervor. Was it because of the metaphysical nature of their joining? Or was it simply because Mia was...what? His fated mate? That was fucking ridiculous. Was it because Mia completed him perfectly? The yin to his yang? Was it that simple?

Just thinking about her got him hard again. He eased the ache with a handful of soap and pretended it was her.

While he was toweling off, three quick raps sounded on the bathroom door. "Close your eyes, I'm coming in." Jeb tossed open the door and walked in like it wasn't at all weird.

"Hey," Luke barked, and made sure his towel was secure.

"Oh, please," Jeb said with a wave of his hand. "If I see something I haven't seen before I'll let you know." He scooted past Luke and into his closet. "You need to shave."

"What the hell?"

Jeb answered from deep inside the closet. "There are certain standards. I cannot have you showing up to meet your father looking like a ragamuffin. You shave and I'll pick out your clothes. I just wish we'd had time to get your hair cut, but you were out running instead."

Like a petulant child, Luke grabbed his razor. He had been planning to shave, but now that Jeb was giving him direction like a nanny, he resented the inclination. "If I hadn't gone running—"

"I know. It's probably good that you did." Jeb stuck his head out and scanned the mostly naked length of Luke's body in a squint. "I just want everything to be perfect."

Luke scraped away at his chin while Jeb muttered from the depths of the closet. The sound of falling boxes was accompanied by a brief shriek. Luke nicked his chin trying not to laugh.

Jeb called, "Hey, what did you do with those black Ferragamos with the double monk strap?"

"I don't know what the fuck you're talking about. I'm wearing my usual dress shoes like I do every day."

Jeb said sounded winded. "You know the one's I'm talking about. The Ferragamos. You wore them to your cousin Cecily's wedding last year. They're black with—never mind, here they are."

Luke was rinsing his face and straightened, only to have Jeb's sudden appearance in the mirror behind him startle the shit out of him.

"Oh, calm down," Jeb said, in a ridiculous change of their usual roles. Then he reached out and ran his fingers through Luke's hair. "Such a pity we didn't have time for a haircut."

Luke slapped his hand away. "Get off me."

Jeb clucked his tongue, lamenting the state of Luke's head, before making his way out to the bedroom with his arms laden with clothes like an eighteenth-century valet. Luke stared at his hair. It looked fine. He wasn't meeting the Queen of England or anything. Jeez, it was just his father. So he was the King of Hell. He probably didn't have as many etiquette guidelines as the British royals did, anyway.

He ran a comb through it. It feathered around his ears and looked a bit shaggy. He curled his lip, annoyed that he allowed himself to let Jeb's paranoia seep in. He looked fine.

Out on the bed, Jeb had laid out a charcoal grey Dolce & Gabanna suit, white dress shirt, and socks. The shoes he'd nearly killed himself for sat on the floor. He passed Luke on his way back into the closet.

"There's no underwear. Am I freeballin' it?"

"Hell's bells," Jeb swore. A pair of boxers were flung from the closet door. "I thought you could handle your own damned underwear."

"Sorry," Luke said, not at all sorry. "I didn't know if there was special Devil visitation underwear I should be wearing."

Jeb appeared back in the doorway with a look of exasperation. "Look, try to cooperate here. I take very good care of you. Would it kill you to throw me a bone?"

Luke didn't answer, but he did put on the underwear without further comment. The gargoyle pursed his lips and added a royal blue silk tie to the array on the bed. Luke reached for the pants.

"No!"

He raised his eyebrows and looked at Jeb. "You're going to have to calm down."

"Put your socks on so that you don't wrinkle the pants."

Here he was, standing in his bedroom in his underwear, arguing with his father's gargoyle spy. "You understand that I'm not going to stand up all day, right? At some point, I plan to bend and shit is going to wrinkle."

Jeb pinched the bridge of his nose. "Please put your socks on first."

Luke snatched up the socks and glared at Jeb. "Holy shit, are you going to cry?"

"No."

He put on his socks while Jeb did some weird New Age breathing. "Now can I put on my pants?"

Jeb clenched his jaw, dramatically turned on his heel, and stormed back into the closet. Wow, that dude was a lunatic today. Pants on,

Luke slipped his arms into the pressed shirt and buttoned up the placket.

"Here," Jeb said and thrust a pair of platinum and blue cuff links at him. "These are calming and soothing with a balancing effect."

"What are?"

"Sapphires. You're going to need all the help you can get."

Luke stared him in the eye while Jeb's swift fingers lifted his collar and threaded the silk tie around his neck. He tried not to fidget while Jeb meticulously executed a trinity knot.

Jeb stood back and sized him up. "I did good." Jeb finally had a smile on his face. He handed him a watch. "I brought the Piaget," he said, then held up the jacket for him to slide his arms in. He moved behind Luke and brushed his hands across his shoulders, removing imaginary lint. Fingers tugged the fabric at his shoulders then tracked down his back and adjusted the vent below his waist. Luke felt like he was still at the tailor's. "This is excellent. You look very dignified, the proper son of a king."

Luke rolled his eyes. "I'm going to bend down now and put on my shoes. I'm warning you because I don't want you to have a stroke."

Jeb cast him a baleful expression that was more like his usual self. "I'll do it," he said and squatted before him to hold out a shoe, then did up the buckles. Then he stood up to face Luke and once more evaluated his masterpiece.

"You're gorgeous."

"You're a crackpot."

"The car is here."

Luke glanced at his watch. Twelve o'clock straight up. Shit. A small earthquake rocked this calm.

Jeb followed him down the hall, tossing out dubiously helpful hints. "Don't order anything with a red sauce. Don't forget to unbutton your suit coat when you sit. For the love of all that's holy, be respectful."

"Shut up, Jeb."

"I'm just saying. You know he doesn't come up here that often. Something important must be happening for him to want to see you

193

out of the blue like this. Usually Ezra just takes care of all the family stuff." Jeb's look of concern gave Luke a moment of pause.

"Whatever it is, I'll deal with it." And he would. Luke deserved some damned answers. Besides, the man might be the Devil but, somewhere underneath all that evil shit, his dad was in there.

HEAVEN & HELL VI

N eil climbed.
    The stairway up was narrow and dark and stiflingly hot.
Neil didn't know why his brain always had to mention the fact that it
was hot. He was in fucking Hell. Of course it was hot. Enough
already.

He'd been steadily rising for a while now and still couldn't figure
where the stairway came out. It just marched on, decrepit steps
perpetually threading upwards with no doorway to exit. The only
way out was either at the top or back down at the bottom. He'd
mentally searched what he knew of the layout of these buildings, and
he couldn't think of anywhere that would account for how far he'd
already climbed. He kept going, though, because there was evidence
—in the way of dog hair and slimy drool—that Cerberus was somewhere ahead.

Switchback after switchback, the stairs rose. Ten steps, turn at the
switchback, up ten more, repeat. Periodically, he'd pause to catch his
breath and strain his ears to listen for the dog. Once he called out the
stupid animal's name, but his voice just rang against the walls,
making a hollow sound. It was depressing and he didn't do it again.

The longer he climbed, the neater the stairwell got. After what felt
like a million stairs, he noticed that the cobwebs didn't cling in every

corner and the soot didn't stain the walls as thickly as it had at the bottom. The concrete stairs weren't as crumbly. The smell had vastly improved as well. Instead of the usual eye-stinging stench of rotting bodies, the odor was more dumpster fire and getting better as he rose. It was probably impossible, but the heat didn't feel quite so oppressive.

He also thought it unusual he hadn't come across another soul the whole time he'd been in there. Few hiding places in the underworld weren't already occupied by some other wretched creature looking for respite, and so far, he'd encountered no hint that anyone knew about this place other than Cerberus. Maybe the goblin patrols had already cleared it out? It was possible, he guessed, but no goblin horde was ambitious enough to climb this high just to collect a bounty. Not even Scourge would put forth that much effort. He was going to have to remember this place to hide out in. Shit, he might even move his stuff in here and take up residence on one of the landings.

It occurred to him that maybe this place had no end. What if he'd stumbled into someone else's fucked-up Sisyphean hell? Some poor bastard who spent eternity climbing an endless stairwell. Whatever. Neil was pretty sure that Cerberus had come in here, and since it wasn't like the mutt could have gotten out along the way, and he sure as blazes hadn't passed him going back down, Neil plodded along after him.

Hell was a relentless nightmare that broke you down and withered away even the vaguest memory of hope. But something about the clear light leaking down the endless tunnel of stairwell from wherever the damned thing finally let out made him feel a shiver of giddy expectation.

Another ten or fifteen floors and Neil knew for a fact that there was no place in his Hell that could account for a stairwell like this one. He'd been climbing for what felt like forever. By this point, the cement structure had taken on the generic quality of a municipal parking garage, minus the giant numbers painted on the walls to indicate what floor you were parked on.

How fucking funny would it be if he turned the corner of one of these landings and stumbled upon a vending machine? What he wouldn't give for a bag of Doritos and an ice-cold Coke. He been a resident of the infernal regions long enough to know that fantasizing about food would only make things worse, so he rarely allowed it. He'd been burned by vending machines before. One of the dukes found out he had a weakness for them and he put them everywhere, but the snacks inside were always moldy and wormy. One time the bastard filled the machine with fresh food: corn chips and cookies, Hostess Ding Dongs and Twinkies, a Snickers. A goddamned Snickers. Neil's mouth watered at the candy and his stomach growled. The Hell of it was he had no change to buy any of it. In a frenzy, he'd thrown himself at the machine like a lunatic, kicking and punching at the glass, knocking the machine over in a desperate attempt to get at what was inside. He got nothing. The machine was impervious to anything he could do to get into it. The duke and his goblins mocked him endlessly about it.

And yet, he seemed to think if he came across one in this stairway he might be able to get something out of it.

The humidity was mostly gone, and Neil was stunned to realize that the air was decidedly cooler. He even felt a breeze when he reversed the last switchback. Maybe he'd well and truly gone insane, but he thought he could smell something besides sulphur. He'd assumed that rancid smell was permanently glued to his nostrils, but something else was slipping through.

Renewed vigor had him mounting the steps faster than he had in a long while, chasing the scent and grasping towards the breeze.

When he lurched around another corner, he never in a million lifetimes expected to run into the soft body of a girl.

JULIET HAD LEFT her cardigan on the railing a while ago. She'd suspected she wasn't going to need it if these stairs let out where she was pretty sure they did. As she descended, she was grateful her dress didn't have sleeves, either, because it was definitely getting warmer. She pulled her hair high off her neck and plodded downward.

There was no plan.

If the stairs really did let out in Hell, what then? Certainly Hell was as big a place as Heaven. How in the world was she ever going to find the place where Rachel was being held? In addition, she had no inkling how the place even worked. What were the rules of Hell?

Sheesh, she didn't even know if she could get in when she got down there.

She'd already come so far it seemed stupid to turn back now. Maybe she was doing what the robbers did in those old heist movies her brother had loved so much: casing the joint. That sounded pretty romantic and awfully cool.

She was casing the joint. Excellent.

Here was the plan so far.

1. Go all the way down the stairs.
2. See if you can open the door.
3. Regroup.

What if there were scary things down there, like spiders and stuff? It was Hell; it only stood to reason that there'd be icky stuff. Certainly there were murderers and Jack the Ripper and other terrible people. Yeah, but the Ripper, as horrific as he was, had the appropriate number of legs at two. It was the crawly things with eight legs that really—

No, she wasn't going to think about spiders.

Down, down, down.

The air was starting to feel worse than the summer she'd spent in Arizona. She'd been like nine or ten, and she'd never forget the thermometer at the hotel had read 115°. When they'd gone outside it had felt like the skin on her face melted and her hair caught on fire.

Sweat trickled down her back, but she kept propelling herself downward.

Mindlessly counting the steps, she didn't even notice she was doing it until she hit three hundred. She'd started way too late to get an accurate count, anyway. By then, she'd revised her opinion of the temperature and recalled how miserable Florida had been during July when she went there for a school trip. *That* was hot; all that moisture in the air making you feel like you were growing hot fungus in your armpits.

And now something was getting a bit stinky. The sultry, wet air wafting up the stairwell had a stale campfire odor that had her wrinkling her nose. To revise: a wet dog who'd dried by a smoky campfire. *Thanks for that, Cerberus.* Still, he had a fur coat. How much worse would the heat be if she had to wear fur? Maybe that's why he had three heads. For all that panting.

Thank Heaven she was only visiting and didn't have to live here. Exactly what she'd remembered thinking about Arizona and Florida.

And now that she thought of it, deserts and swamps also had scary spiders. She cracked herself up thinking that she'd already been to Hell on Earth.

Down. So many stairs. Stairs she was going to have to come back up again—unless she got stuck down there. Yeesh.

She was bored. Epically bored. It turned out that climbing down stairs was a lot like meditating. A person could completely turn off their brain and just mechanically put one foot in front of the other. She practiced this, eyes shut, sweat gathering in the crinkle of her eyelids. She traced her fingertips on the wall so she wouldn't trip and fall endlessly down the stairs and break her head open.

Lord only knew how much worse it would be when she was all the way there. And Juliet hadn't even met any of the occupants of Hell yet. The lower she went, the more likely it was she'd meet some demon eventually. Poor Rachel had been prisoner down here in this steamy heat and noxious stench literally forever, being tortured by who knew how many beasts with who knew how many legs. And here Juliet was, complaining like a spoiled baby because she was a little warm. And a little afraid. She was disgusted at herself.

She renewed her determination to do anything she could to rescue Rachel and make sure she was reunited with the angel who loved her. She used the heel of her hand like a squeegee on her forehead and picked up the pace.

When she careened around another corner, she couldn't say she was exactly surprised to finally run into something from Hell, but she screamed anyway.

CHAPTER NINETEEN

A black Rolls Royce Phantom idled at the curb outside Luke's place. Sleek and mysterious, its windows tinted pitch black, it inhabited the space like a gorgeous but dreadful scarab beetle. As he approached, the driver emerged and opened the back door for Luke. Standing at least as tall as him, the man provided an unnecessary element of menace.

"Good afternoon, sir," the man said, his voice tinted with an accent Luke never could place.

"Hello, Ezra." Luke slid along the plush red leather seats. He was shocked to find the car empty. "Where's my father?"

When the driver got back behind the wheel, he said, "He had some business to tend to. He'll join you at the restaurant." Luke knew better than to ask any questions. There was always the risk that Ezra might actually tell you.

The cup holder next to his seat held a crystal highball filled with a light amber liquid and one perfectly square ice cube. As gently as a ghost in a graveyard, the car moved away from the curb. The ice cube didn't even hit the side of the glass. He watched Ezra's rear profile as the man drove.

He'd known his father's favorite gargoyle his entire life. Ezra had been with his father from the beginning, just like Jeb had been with Luke. He never changed. He'd had the same weathered, square face as long as Luke had known him. Heavy brows over black eyes, thin lips, slightly overgrown military haircut. Ezra was as stalwart, dependable, and discreet as the major domo for the Devil would be expected to be. If you needed to contact the Devil, you called Ezra.

"How have you been?" Luke asked. "I haven't seen you in months."

"The same, thank you."

"Anything new and exciting?" He took a mouthful of whiskey and soda and let it burn on the way down.

"No."

Sigh. "No gossip or anything?"

"Nothing to speak of, sir."

Luke finished off the drink and contemplated the lone cube at the bottom of the glass.

"The bottle is in the bar if you find you need another."

True enough, when Luke checked, a crystal decanter with a silver label engraved with "whiskey" sat nestled next to a silver ice bucket full of those perfect cubes.

"Hey, Ezra," he called, as he added another two fingers' worth of liquid to the glass. "Can you tell me how the Devil can make such perfect ice cubes? It seems improbable, don't you think? It's like they were measured with a protractor and cut with a laser or something."

Ezra met his eyes in the rearview mirror. "I make them."

"Of course you do." He was going to have to nurse this drink. No matter how tempting it would be, it was foolish to get drunk when he needed his wits about him.

"Any idea what my father wants to see me about? Any hints from the Dark Lord himself?"

"No."

Luke wanted to kick the back of his seat. "Have you been instructed not to tell me?"

"No, I simply do not know why. Perhaps he just wants to see you."

He laughed, maybe a bit too loudly. It sounded nearly hysterical, even to his own ears. He threw out his earlier conviction and swallowed another heavy gulp of whiskey just to settle his nerves a bit more. They sat in silence for a few moments. Luke listened to the sound of his own breathing and watched the traffic roll by.

Finally, he asked. "You knew my mother, didn't you?"

Their eyes met in the mirror again. "Of course."

"Did she know who he was?" Luke stared at the side of his head as the driver navigated a turn.

"I'm not sure what you mean, sir." They stopped at a red light and Ezra turned to face Luke. "Your father was Avarice when they met."

He had forgotten that—that his father was Avarice. "Do you know how they met?"

The gargoyle sighed. "It's been a long time," he said by way of evasion. "Perhaps this is a conversation you should be having with your father."

"I intend to. I was just wondering what you remembered about her." He put the glass down, determined not to drink anymore.

The Rolls glided to a stop and Luke realized they'd arrived at Infernos. The restaurant had opened the previous year to rave reviews and scintillating word of mouth. Now there was a three month wait for reservations. Luke hadn't been yet. He didn't find the décor at all intriguing, but Seth had, and he reported back that the food was outstanding. "I didn't realize that my father..."

"No, your father doesn't own this place. He just appreciates the irony." Ezra held the door open for Luke. "Enjoy your lunch."

"Fat chance."

The interior was actually a lot less garish than the name had led him to believe. He'd half imagined cocktail waitresses in red satin hot pants and devil horns. Yes, the booths were red and there was a subtle flame motif, but at least there weren't imps and demons running around the place.

The dining room was crowded, with overflow loitering in the foyer waiting for tables. The hostess led Luke to a booth in the middle of the room, exactly where one would expect to find a narcissistic Prince of Darkness. He was on the phone. Luke slid in and stared at his father, allowing icy rancor to wash over him while he was being ignored. The man looked like he hadn't aged at all. He didn't look any older than forty-five. In fact, they looked like they could be brothers, the familial resemblance was so apparent. Not a single gray hair anywhere on his head. Not a single wrinkle. Pretty remarkable for a man almost sixty. Luke was pleased to see that he'd been right to allow Jeb to choose his clothes. The other man also wore a suit, although one more classic than trendy. He'd be sure to let Jeb know that the Devil's hair had recently been tended to by a barber. That'd be sure to irritate the hell out of him.

The waitress came by, and Luke ordered iced tea. His father held up a finger and indicated one more of whatever he was drinking. He ended his call and set the phone on the table.

"Luke," the Devil said and swung his full attention on him. The atmosphere around the table burgeoned with heat.

"Father." He laughed to himself how much it felt like he was talking to Darth Vader. Both heroes were named Luke, after all.

"You look good."

Luke rolled his eyes. "I look just like you."

"Right." His father's face broke in to a wide, toothy grin. "Handsome devil."

Lacing his fingers together in his lap, Luke asked, "I'd like to say that it's good to see you, but"—he shrugged—"you know how it is. So what brings you up to the land of the living? A bunch of soul contracts come due or something? Thought you'd make a daytrip of it?"

The Devil lifted one side of his mouth in an indulgent smile and leaned back against the padded upholstery, looking very much like a wicked cat. "No. The Lords of Hell are more than capable of handling most of those kinds of transactions. They have their quotas. I only get involved with that type of thing when it is especially juicy." He looked away, as if searching for a memory. "I cannot recall the last time I even went to the Crossroads. Perhaps I should visit once in a while, just for old time's sake."

"Yeah," Luke said dryly. "I was just wondering the other day if that bicycle thing was true. I'd probably fall right off one these days."

The waitress reappeared and placed the Devil's drink on the table. "Macallan 25, neat," she said.

He grasped the drink gently in his palm and raised the glass to his nose. He breathed in and closed his eyes. He purred on an exhale. "Mmm. Orange and pear," the Devil drawled before taking a sip. "This is my idea of Heaven."

Luke snorted.

The Devil slowly opened his eyes and trained his terrible gaze on his son. "Spicy with a smoky finish."

Luke wiped the smirk from his face. Until he knew what his father wanted, it was probably best not to poke the bear.

"May I tell you the specials?" the waitress asked, undeterred or oblivious to the unspoken exchange. She gave each of them a professional smile and launched into describing the entrees the chef had created that day. Her gaze flitted between both men as she discussed the preparation of a fresh fish. The Devil placed his elbow on the table, raised his hand to his mouth, and settled his chin in the curve of his thumb. Luke watched, fascinated, as the woman's focus shifted from delivering the menu to them both to speaking entirely to his father as if enraptured. Her descriptions petered out like she ran out of gas.

"We'll start with the smoked salmon and some olives with hummus. Then two porterhouses, blue. Do not bring a steak out here that's one millisecond overcooked, or I will be very disappointed." His voice was soft, his expression plain, but the tone commanded obedience with the hint of danger.

"No, sir," she said, coming back to herself as if emerging from a fugue state.

"I saw lobster on the menu, but you did not mention it. Is that fresh?—Excellent, two of those. Also, the duck breast with gastrique á l'orange sounded divine."

The French rolled off his tongue like he was a native speaker, but of course he was, wasn't he? The Devil knew all languages, and how convenient was that?

"Can I bring you salads to start?" the waitress asked.

Luke didn't bother to answer since his father was doing all the ordering anyway.

The Devil waved his hand dismissively. "I am not interested in green food. But I do want you to send over the dessert menu."

"Absolutely." She backed several steps away from their table, her gaze never leaving the Devil's. If she hadn't brought Luke's iced tea, he would have thought she'd forgotten he was there.

His father turned his dark gaze back to Luke. It actually felt like the air was heavier in their booth, pushing on his shoulders, bringing him down. "You never did say what you're doing here."

The Devil shrugged. "I come up more often than you think. There are many irons in the fire, so to speak. Business is always good."

How often was that exactly? Twice a year? Once a month? What were they talking about? And he never felt the urge to see his own son? Luke found himself in that typical Catch-22 whenever his father came around. He despised the Devil, but missed his father, and could never quite give up hope that he'd see a sliver of his dad still hidden inside. It was childish and stupid, and he should have outgrown it already.

"So why am I here? Does one of those irons have to do with me?" He resented feeling out of control.

"Indirectly."

"Great. Just so you know, no one likes a vague Devil."

The Devil acknowledged the dig with a quick tilt of his head and a half smile. "You will know what you need to know when I decide you need to know it."

These command performances were never for the purposes of catching up. The Devil had spies everywhere. It was always assumed the gargoyles reported anything noteworthy. "What do you want from me, then? Surely there's something."

"I am reminding a contractee of the nature of the terms he agreed to," he said with a hint of diabolical menace, then added with false innocence, "You know, I believe you are erecting a building for him." Luke narrowed his eyes at his father. "His daughter had not been involved with our agreement, but what a serendipitous accident that turned out to be. Young love. How precious." He arched one smug brow.

All the alcohol Luke consumed in the car threatened to come up. "What are you saying?"

"I met your young woman."

Luke's heart seized and his stomach dropped. Bile roiled around like a fetid cyclone in his gut. He swallowed hard and stared at his father. "What do you mean?"

The fiend smiled, both indulgent and dodgy at the same time. "I wish I had thought to include her in the original deal, but this works out better in the end, hmm? Regardless, I found her to be quite charming."

"What do you mean?" Luke repeated. The thought of this bastard even being near Mia... "When did you see her?"

He struggled to control himself, and he swallowed reflexively as if that simple action could suppress the wrath that threatened to surge from his body like toxic fumes. The gentlemen at the table behind them began a ferocious argument, and before Luke could pull it back, a passing waiter dumped an entire plate of food on their heads.

The Devil ignored the tussle completely. Instead, he adjusted the cuff on his right wrist, fondling the cufflink shaped like a goat head. "Well, naturally I was curious. How often does your son find his soulmate?"

"I'm going to kill Jeb." Luke could almost feel the fucking gargoyle's neck breaking in his clenched hands already.

His father scoffed. "Your gargoyle? Do you honestly think he is the only spy who reports on you?" He circled the rim of his glass with a long index finger. "No, Jeb is surprisingly loyal to you."

If not Jeb, then who?

"Frankly, he continues to shock me. Ezra felt certain Jeb was an up-and-comer who would do anything to improve his station, but it turns out, no." The Devil took another long, savoring sip on his scotch, then licked his lips. "If he belonged to anyone other than you, I would switch him out. It's terrible the way I play favorites."

Favorites? The demon was delusional.

"Are you telling me I don't have to be saddled with that syco-phantic jackass?" For one brief moment, Luke considered the option of trading Jeb in for someone less annoying, but the thought of training anyone else to make his coffee the way Jeb did pushed it away.

The Devil picked up his fork and inspected it. "It makes no matter to me which asset I have with you, but I sense you have formed an attachment."

Luke actually let that last dig go. He recognized the evil bastard was trying to get a rise out of him, and he had to play this smart. "Never mind, he's fine." Luke was self-aware enough to know life would suck without Jeb. "Besides, knowing how you work, his replacement would be horrendous."

His father smirked. "Most likely."

Sure, he was totally the Devil's favorite.

The waitress returned to the table with the dessert menu and a basket of warm bread. She nodded towards the nearly empty tumbler. "May I get you another?"

The Devil relaxed against the table, his forearms crossed over the wood. His gaze captured the waitress's and then, with an almost imperceptible flick of his wrist, Luke saw the woman's awareness slip away. It was obscene. She fastened her attention on his father as if he were the nucleus of her world.

"Not right now," he said, and the acrid odor of something burning filled Luke's nostrils, "but my son needs your attention."

"Oh," she said, and like a child sleepwalking, she turned her focus to Luke. She homed in her brown-eyed stare on him, and Luke felt an involuntary shiver. "I'm yours," she told him earnestly. "What can I do for you?"

"I'm fine, thank you." Luke crossed his arms. And darted a glance at his father. only to find that the man was studying him back.

"Don't give up that easily," his father encouraged her. "There must be something he needs."

The woman wore a wedding ring, but it didn't bother The Devil in the least. In fact, that was probably part of the twisted fun he got out of it. Another movement of his fingers and the waitress's hands rose to her breast.

"Stop it," Luke demanded of his father. His eyes darted around the room, but no one else in the crowded dining room seemed to notice. "Just stop it."

Without breaking eye contact with Luke, the Devil's lips curled in a smug smile. "You can go," he told the waitress.

Her hand dropped and her awareness slid back into place. "I'll check back with you in a bit, then."

Through clenched teeth, Luke demanded, "What the hell was that all about?"

"Being the origin of all sins does have its perks. You should see when I really turn it on. One weekend, just for fun, I showed up at a tent revival in the Bible Belt..." The Devil laughed, deep and potent, and for just a second Luke had a flash of naked bodies, writhing. "This generation of Sins aren't as fun as they used to be."

"Don't involve me in your hobbies."

The Devil raised one eyebrow. He seemed satisfied that he'd gotten a rise out of his son. "None of that has anything to do with your Mia," he continued. "I do approve of her. I have seen in her soul; she will be an excellent mother for my grandson."

The fury returned, crimson flames licking the inside of Luke's brain. "You didn't say how you know her."

"I met her in her dreams last night. She didn't tell you?" When Luke didn't respond, the Devil smiled knowingly. "Interesting. She did very well in Hell, better than I thought she would, actually."

"Why?" Luke leaned forward and hissed the words. "If she's not a part of your agreement with her father, why would you bother with her?"

All amusement disappeared from the Devil's supernatural face and his tone turned serious. Luke felt the claws of dread pass over him and settle heavily in the air. "It is my prerogative, Luke. Do not forget who you are talking to here."

Luke sat backward, hard against the leather. There was a line you didn't cross with the Devil—maybe even more so when the Devil was your father. Skirting that line, he allowed his wrath to bubble to the surface.

"Forget? How the hell could I forget? Everything about my life constantly reminds me who I am, who you are, who all of us are.

Seriously? I have a constant rage bubbling under the surface of my skin. My cousins are tortured by their own demons every day—lust, greed, sloth, pride, envy and gluttony ruling their lives. I have a gargoyle who follows me every fucking place so he can spy on me to my father, the Devil. How the fuck can I forget who you are?" His father raised a sardonic eyebrow which only incensed him more. "And I'm going to be next. I know it. You probably know it already, which is why you're up here."

"None of us knows who's next. Not until the ceremony and you have, what, twelve years before that happens? There has never been any way to predict who gets chosen, and you know it. Just because you are immortal right now does not mean you will not give yourself a heart attack." The Devil snorted. "Whatever gave you the impression that you are next?"

"A fortune teller." The minute it came out of Luke's mouth, he knew it was stupid to tell him. He waited, supremely annoyed, until his father stopped laughing.

"The hell you say," the Devil managed to get out before he guffawed again. "Some crackpot in a tent somewhere saw you with horns in her crystal ball?" A carefully manicured hand slapped the table, a heavy ring clanged against the wood.

"No. Tarot."

That disclosure only renewed the Devil's peals of laughter. Their entire restaurant was focused on his father at this point. The room was filled with uncomfortable guffaws as the diners and waitstaff unwittingly joined in. Their waitress's expression was of someone uncomfortably laughing at an off-color joke.

"Never mind. Just drop it," Luke told him. "Let's get back to Mia. I want to talk to my dad about her. And my mother. Is that possible?"

"I doubt it."

Damn it. You never knew if you were getting the truth when you were talking to the Devil. He lied about everything. "I have questions that need answers."

The man looked intrigued. "Proceed."

"Did my mother know who you were when she married you?"

"Ah, Felicity. Aaron Mephisto had loved her," he said, referring to his previous life, talking about himself like he was a different person. The Devil's lips spread in what seemed to Luke to be a genuine smile as he recalled his mortal wife. "They were very happy together until she died."

From everything he'd heard, Luke believed that was true. "If she hadn't died, did she understand her fate? Did she marry you knowing you might be the Devil one day? And that she had a one in seven chance of her son being the Devil, too?"

The Devil didn't say anything, not right away. He stared at Luke for a long beat. "Felicity knew that there was something unique about our family."

Luke sagged a bit in his seat. "She didn't know."

"Aaron did not reveal the whole truth to her, no. Odds were decent he would not be the chosen one. Why risk his happiness by telling her?"

Luke recalled how Ezra had said Aaron represented Greed. That explained so much. If Aaron had wanted something, he would have done anything necessary to get it.

"What if she had lived? What would you have done then? You did get picked. She would have been destroyed." Just like he had been.

"I would have done my duty." The Devil told him this with a face completely free of emotion. Totally blank. Void of feeling. Zero remorse.

Luke never felt more disconnected from his father than he did right now. He suppressed the craving to roar and overturn the table. Instead, he was able to contain his ire to their booth. His hands balled up into fists in his lap, and all the glasses shook and sloshed out their liquid. "You might have broken her. You broke me."

The man who looked so much like him shrugged. "You seem to be doing fine. Even if that is not true, there are certain truths about your life you cannot change. You will have a son, whether with Mia or not. You will stand in the ring when the time comes and, if you are chosen, you will step up and accept the horns. Do not think for one minute you have any say in the matter."

Scrubbing his hand across his mouth, Luke realized there was nothing here for him. This man wasn't his dad and there didn't seem to be any of the man he had loved left in there. Aaron might have been Avarice, but he'd managed to put that aside well enough to be a good father. He'd believed he wouldn't be chosen, and he'd lived his life that way. Luke knew better. He couldn't stumble around blindly and hope.

He couldn't do that to Mia.

He wouldn't do that to her.

B y the time Monday morning rolled around and she still hadn't heard from Luke, Mia was certain that she wouldn't. Except that they were still working on her building project, so they were going to have to work together. Only now the whole thing was going to be unbearably uncomfortable. She lamented this fact to Godfrey while he gamboled around the greenhouse with her at sunrise.

"Hey, spit that out," she yelled at the dog, and then continued talking to him in a normal tone. "Seriously, you'd think this was my first time or something, the way I'm acting. I should know better, he, it, just seemed so different, you know?" Godfrey did not know. He ran past her at top speed, tongue hanging out, and knocked over a stack of terra cotta pots. "I mean how, many times can I call? How many messages can I leave before I look desperate?" The dog clearly didn't know. He was crouched in a full bow, his front legs spread straight out in front of him and his giant black and white butt wiggling in the air. "The answer is two. It is always two. Three reads as clingy."

She squirted the dog with the hose and he yelped in glee, then spun around in a complete circle before dashing off through the trees.

"You're a buffoon," she said and laughed as he romped around the perimeter of the garden.

"I knew better than to get involved with a client." She rolled her eyes to herself. "If Daddy finds out, he'll kill me." She raised her face to the heavens as if some benevolent force up there could guide her. As if her father were going to be paying attention. It's just that you never knew with him. There were so many times when he just seemed to be in on information that he shouldn't be.

Godfrey ran by at dangerous velocity for someone who couldn't control his legs.

"Don't knock over—" Too late. A crash of tools sounded at the front of the greenhouse.

Checking her watch and turning off the hose, she started for the door. She restacked the tumbled pots on her way and gathered the shovels and spades next to the worktable.

Godfrey was stretched out on the gravel in front of the door, panting. "Did you wear yourself out? You big lovable doofus." She nudged his rump with the toe of her boot and signaled toward home with a tip of her head. "Come on."

Back at the house, the dog climbed up on her bed and took over the entire middle of the mattress with his gangly limbs. He was snoring in seconds. She changed for work, smoothed down her hair, and put on some makeup. A look at the person in the mirror suggested that maybe she wasn't the type of woman that men have epiphanies over. At least not men like Luke. She sighed and shook her head.

"Good morning," Cassie said, and hovered over the coffee maker while Mia made herself a travel cup.

Mia made a face at her.

"You know he was never going to call on Sunday. Not the day *after*. That would be sheer lunacy." Cassie leaned her hip against the cabinet and crossed her arms over her bathrobe. "And honestly, millipede, don't get too upset if he doesn't call at all. He gives off all kinds of player vibes."

Mia reached around her and grabbed the full pot. She did not tell her best friend that she'd called and left two messages that had not been returned. Feeling playful the day before, she'd sent a silly selfie with Godfrey and inquired how his lunch went with his father. There had been no reciprocation. She'd had the weirdest dreams and had barely slept, so now she wasn't in the mood for Cassie's admonishments and another recitation of the Cardinal Rules of Dating. "What are you even doing up?"

It took a moment for Cassie to respond since she became involved in a yawn so epic she shivered afterwards. "I'm meeting a bride at her venue to go over her theme. Unicorns, I think." Her friend rolled her eyes. "Can you believe a grown-ass woman wants her wedding to be a unicorn theme? I mean, good god, I'm not even that whimsical."

Mia agreed, it sounded horrible.

"Yep, but we'll take her money and unicorn the shit out of that thing," Cassie said as she poured four heaping teaspoons of sugar into her coffee mug.

"Make sure you get lots of pictures of that." Mia waved as she headed for the front door.

"You betcha." Cassie tasted her concoction and grimaced. She added another spoonful of sugar. "Hey, text me if you hear from your dude."

"Apparently, he's not my dude," Mia grumbled and pulled the door closed behind her.

She told herself to stop thinking about it. It's just that you shouldn't bandy the word *fate* around if you don't mean it.

While she sat at a light, she flipped through her preselected radio stations. She paused for a moment on "Shout at the Devil" Mötley Crüe and yelled the chorus with Vince. Next, the Eighties station was playing Van Halen, "Runnin' With the Devil." She spun the selector dial and let it land wherever it wanted, playing musical roulette. It only took a second to recognize "The Devil Went Down to Georgia." Surprised that she could still remember all the lyrics, she joined Charlie and urged Johnny to rosin up his bow. By the time that song had finished, she'd only advanced about fifty feet, not much progress. She turned back to the radio. She went back to the preset channels and the first song that popped up was "Devil Inside," by INXS. Man, she missed that old band.

Traffic finally started moving and, when she arrived, she parked in her spot right on time. The radio had done its trick, and she was feeling looser by the time she dropped her purse and tote bag on her desk. She hummed along with the song in her head, moving her shoulders a little to the tune while she switched on her computer and sorted through her day.

"What's that song?" Jason asked as he set her coffee on her blotter.

"Hmmm?" Mia looked up, not realizing that she'd been quite that loud.

"No, don't tell me. Let me guess. Keep going." Jason's forehead wrinkled in concentration. He joined her and hummed a little part until they got to the hook, then recognition nabbed him. He rolled his shoulders up a bit and swiveled his hips. Doing a pretty good Elvis impression, he sang, "You're the Devil in disguise."

They finished the chorus together in deep baritones and giggled.

Mia spent the first part of her day cleaning up the unfinished things from Friday and the minutiae that Monday brings. She scanned her emails for anything important and stopped on a request for an appointment. The mouse hovered over the "Accept" button. "There's a meeting on the building project today?"

Jason's voice came from behind his computer monitor. "Yeah. Luke Mephisto's assistant requested something for late today."

Her shoulders tensed up again. Elvis had left the building and taken all the fun with him. "What for?"

Her assistant's head and shoulders appeared to the right of his monitor as he leaned around to look at her. "I assume to talk about the building."

She gave him a withering look. "Obviously. But we weren't supposed to get together again to go over the changes Luke isn't going to let me have for another week."

Jason shrugged.

Was this the bastard's plan? Did he think he could pretend that nothing happened on Friday night and just shove a work meeting in her face right away Monday morning to get her back to the status quo? If all he wanted was a one-night fling, then what was with all the seducing? Why use words like fate and destiny? What kind of a hateful person did that? She probably wouldn't have gone for a one-night, slam-bam-thank you-ma'am date because she was a damned grownup who knew better, but he'd acted so weird, like he had been under a spell or something.

That was what he was going to claim. She was sure of it. He was going to say temporary insanity caused him to say all that crazy nonsense.

Oh, hell no.

She clicked her mouse on the "Accept" button with all the force her index finger could muster. She vowed she would not go away quietly. She didn't know what she was going to do about it, exactly, but she had hours until this so-called meeting today to think on it.

It was one of the new junior executive's birthday, so at ten that morning everyone gathered around his cramped cubicle to sing Happy Birthday and share cake.

"That was really sweet of you to do," Margorie, the office manager, told Mia. "You're always so on top of this stuff."

"Sure." Mia smiled and let the knife sink into the frosting. "When I went to the bakery today all they had was Devil's food."

"Sounds wonderful," Marjorie said, and took a slice. "Oh my gosh, this is so good. I need to get the name of the bakery."

"It's a new place just opened around the corner. From Scratch, I think it's called. Strange little lady owns it, but she sure knows how to bake."

Her day progressed with little excitement and there wasn't much to distract her from contemplating the afternoon meeting. During lunch, which she ate at her desk, she reviewed Jason's notes from the last meeting and did some more research on the internet, looking for ways to thwart Luke. By the time four o'clock came around, she had a legal pad full of ideas, statistics, and thoughts she hoped would arm her in whatever showdown he planned.

The receptionist buzzed Jason that their appointment had arrived, and she excused herself to the bathroom to make sure she looked all right. After all, she was seeing the man she'd just recently had mind-blowing sex with and, if he was going to dump her, she wanted him to regret it. She tried to think what Cassie would have done in the circumstances. Probably loiter around in there for fifteen minutes, keeping them all waiting for her, and then make a grand entrance. Mia didn't really think she would be able to pull that off. Besides, she was too antsy and could only hold out for three minutes. She washed her hands and told her reflection to be strong before pushing out the door and into the fray.

Mia jumped when she realized Jeb was waiting for her just outside. Was this an ambush?

"There you are, gorgeous." Jeb stepped in sync with her.

"Umm, hi," she said. "Are you all here?" She didn't know what else to say.

"With bells on," he said and then pushed her into a janitor's closet and closed the door behind him.

"Eeep!" Mia stumbled into a shelving unit and tripped over the mop bucket before she grabbed onto something solid and caught her balance. "What—"

"Hold on until I find the light."

She held on to a pillar or something while Jeb slapped around at the wall for the switch. Fluorescent light flickered several times as it came on until it fully committed to working. Mia realized she was holding on to Jeb, not a random pillar, and immediately let go.

"Sorry," she said. Holy crap, he must work out. He was a lot more solid than his lean frame would suggest.

"You're fine." He brushed away her embarrassment at grabbing him. Instead, he took a step backward, shuffling against the mops and brooms, and gave her an assessing look. "Cute as hell," he confirmed.

"Uh, thanks," she said, utterly confused.

He opened up the messenger bag he had slung across his chest and rummaged around in there for a second, emerging with a tube of lip gloss.

Reflexively her hand flew to her hair. "I already checked, and I look all right."

Jeb nodded. "Yes, you do. You're like the world's tiniest super-model. Here, do this with your lips." He opened his lips in an "O" as an example.

She drew her eyebrows together and eyed him, but opened her

mouth as suggested. Jeb drew on some clear gloss and then smacked his lips together like he wanted her to do.

"Nice," he said and shoved the wand back in the tube. That went back into the bag, and he rummaged around some more.

"What's going on here?" she demanded

The handle of a giant push broom slid slowly down the wall and plinked loudly off the floor.

"Getting you ready," he said, staring into the satchel. "I would have thought Jason would have done this for you, but I'm kinda glad he didn't. I'd just have to redo it anyway."

"Redo what?" she asked. This was singularly the most bizarre thing that had ever happened to her.

"You're already a doll," he stated in a tone that suggested she should be paying attention. "Just making you even better." His hand emerged triumphant with a bottle of perfume.

She put up her hands and backed away—not far, because the shelves were right behind her. A cascade of cleaning supplies tumbled down. Plastic spray bottles jumbled on the floor and some fluid seeped out, spreading a ring of blue toward the wall.

"Stop." She said the words loudly and clearly like her college karate teacher had told her to do at an oncoming attacker.

He stood there, one hand on his hip and the other wrapped around the perfume bottle, index finger on the plunger. "Look, honey, you're the one for him, and I'm just making sure he doesn't do anything stupid."

"That all sounds very nice of you and I appreciate your help. It also sounds totally insane. Don't you think Luke can make his own decisions?"

Now he dropped his chin and looked at her from the top of his eyes. "Really?" He rolled those same eyes and snorted. "The man is a disaster. Has been ever since he saw—. Since he saw his father. He thinks he knows what's going to happen in the end, but for now he's just being clueless. All I want to do is wrap this whole affair up without any more needless angst." He raised the bottle and turned his hand in a big circle. "Spin."

Confused by all the words coming out of Jeb's mouth, she didn't even know how to refuse, so she twirled. A light musky mist rained on her skin.

"This doesn't seem very loyal of you," she noted. The perfume was really nice, nice enough to buy some for herself.

Jeb plucked a stray thread from her blouse and gave her another once over. Apparently satisfied, he explained, "I am one hundred percent loyal to Luke. Beyond a doubt. Always will be. Sometimes loyalty just looks different when you're on the outside. Come on, now. You're perfect."

Mia didn't know what to say to that. Instead, she closed her glossy lips and followed Jeb from the closet. Her office was full of people and yet remarkably quiet and tense. Jeb greeted Jason affectionately and passed out smiles to the rest of Mia's staff. Luke narrowed his eyes at Jeb before turning his gaze to her. His hard glare softened almost imperceptibly before he blinked and turned back to his laptop. At the sight of him, her body went on high alert. While her brain was irritated that he was ignoring her, her body seemed willing to drop her panties at the first inviting look.

"I have some new virtual walk-throughs I think you're going to like." There was nothing to hint at his mood in his tone.

He was outfitted in a dark blue suit that fit across the wide expanse of his shoulders like second skin. His hair was tousled like he'd had his hands in it a lot. He was unfairly beautiful. Mia watched him specifically not watching her, and her heart sank.

She took a seat next to him. If he was going to do this, she didn't want to make it any easier on him. It was a stupid move. She should just let him go. It would be simpler in the long run, and certainly less embarrassing.

She watched as Luke opened a virtual representation of the new headquarters of Virtus Templum Pharmaceuticals. He clicked another button and the view moved from the exterior into the lobby. Mia gasped. Inside where there had been a modern lobby only last week now showed a great expansive space with trees lining the perimeter. A flagstone floor gave the impression of a giant courtyard, but the trees really sold it. The virtual camera zoomed up and showed the building was open all the way to the twentieth floor to a massive glass ceiling. Virtual sunlight streamed in, highlighting that each floor ended on a balcony overlooking the lobby. More trees rimmed the balconies. It was almost exactly what she'd been asking for that he'd been refusing.

"This is beautiful," she exclaimed, her voice breathy. She watched the tour in awe and swallowed back a lump in her throat. "Just what I envisioned."

The rest of her team gathered around, expounded on the tour, and talked excitedly amongst themselves.

Luke stepped back and nodded. Mia beamed at him. She wanted to kiss him—would have done if he'd not looked so imposing and unapproachable.

"I knew you could do it." She left the table and walked the several feet to where he stood alone.

"Yes, well. I have the mockups I wanted to show you right away." He crossed his arms. "The cost analysis will follow by Friday. It will be substantially different from our original numbers."

"Fine," she said and looked at her feet. The sounds of excited conversation filled the room except in their odd little bubble where the air ceased to move.

He cleared his throat. "I'm sorry. About this weekend." A long pause stopped time while she waited for him to continue. "I didn't mean... I can't—"

She caved. She was a coward. "It's fine," she said. It turns out she couldn't stand the agony and the humiliation of his denial. He'd dragged her into this crazy fantasy of fate and destiny and now she just wanted the hell out.

"My life is really complicated right now," he said in a low voice.

Somehow that flipped her switch, and she felt her face flush with anger. Keeping her voice at a fierce whisper so the rest of the room wouldn't hear, she hissed, "You started this."

"I know," he said. When she glanced at him, he had the decency to look miserable. "I really don't want you to get hurt."

You've have got to be kidding me. "Who's writing your dialogue? Hallmark?"

He didn't defend himself, which was something at least. He shifted his weight to his other leg and sighed. "I'm sorry."

"Please. 'Do you believe in fate'," she mocked his line from the other night. Her vehemence shocked her, but she loved the power of it. "Just do my building, but otherwise, you can go to hell."

With the best last words of her life, she snatched up her purse and strode out of her office, leaving him standing there looking like the aggrieved party for once.

HEAVEN AND HELL VII

THE STAIRWAY TO HEAVEN

N eil wrapped his arms around the girl to keep them both from tumbling down the stairs. As it was, they stumbled and he had to swing her body around to avoid slamming her into the wall where the stairwell turned downward. Instead he took the hit, smooshed between the wall at his back and her soft body.

"Oof," she said on an exhale.

Once they were steady, he lowered her to the ground where she stood an inch or two shorter than him. He waited to see what she looked like until she'd gathered the mass of hair that had fallen over her face from their impact and pulled it back into a ponytail.

It had been worth the wait.

She was young, somewhere around his own age. And she was pretty, really pretty. Soft and girly, just the way he liked them, but not in a creeper way. He'd just always liked girls better who didn't try too hard. The mass of hair was the color of milk chocolate and it hung long down her back. Her features were delicate; big, blue eyes, little nose, wide mouth. Her body had felt soft in his arms.

"Whoa," she said. "Who are you?"

Her voice sounded just like he thought it would—gentle and breathy.

"Neil." He stood a little taller and pushed his own contrary hair off his forehead. "What about you?"

She tilted her head and smiled at him. "Juliet." She stuck out her hand to shake.

He clasped his fingers around hers and held on. It had been so long since he'd seen something beautiful that he couldn't let go. A zing of what felt like an electrical jolt ripped up his arm. It wasn't bad —not like an electrical fence or a taser. It was more like the zap you got when you dragged your feet on the carpet but times five. It didn't hurt, but it was strong enough that he felt it in his teeth.

"What are you doing in here?" she asked, and gently extracted her hand.

Leaning back against the wall, he tucked his own hand safely away in his jeans pockets, his fingers closed around his palm to hold in the feeling. "Going up."

"From where? Are you from—" she pointed downward and whispered the last word "—Hell?"

"Maybe."

She pulled her lips to one side and eyed him up and down. He knew what she saw: a dude in torn up jeans, scuffed boots, a ratty old T-shirt, and, stupidest of all, a leather jacket. Yeah. In Hell. You were in death what you were in life. Taking it off would not have made the temperature any more tolerable anyway.

She, on the other hand, had on one of those pretty sundresses girls wore in the summer with the straps on her shoulders and buttons over her tits—which also looked perfect, by the way. It came to just above her knees and cute strappy sandals covered her feet.

"And you're from—" he pointed iup, teasing her, "—Heaven?"

"I am." She was back to smiling, which he liked better than skeptical. "I wasn't sure where these stairs ended."

He narrowed his eyes and took a deeper look at the pretty girl. "You're an angel, right?"

"Yes," she said, and then sounding less sure even while bobbing her head up and down, "Sorta. Mostly."

He raised an eyebrow. "What does that mean?"

"I'm an angel. You know, like, I live in Heaven and stuff." She used lots of gestures.

Neil pushed himself off the wall and took a step closer to her. He wanted to know what she smelled like. "So what's the problem?" he asked.

She shrugged. "I just don't feel very official. There are others up there who are way more angel-y than me."

Cinnamon rolls. Did everyone in Heaven smell like this? Was it always baked goods or did you get to pick your flavor? Like maybe flowers sometimes or summer rain? Man, everything in Hell smelled horrible, decaying fish carcass was the best case scenario and he'd smelled much worse than that. A lot of the time it was the gummy stench of rot that filled his nostrils, and you never got used to it. He leaned into her and inhaled through his nose. She craned her neck backwards and cast him a concerned side-eye glance.

"You got wings?" He leaned to the left, ostensibly to look behind her.

"Um hmm," she hummed, and took another step to the side, evading him.

He raised that eyebrow again like he didn't believe her. Her mouth dropped open and she made a little noise of incredulity that said how dare he not trust her. She stood up straighter and showed the slightest strain of effort about her eyes before pure white feathered wings unfurled behind her. Even though they were broader than her shoulders and the tips of them extended well beyond her head, they were smallish. Lovely, but dainty. There was a theme here, he reckoned.

"Just because you've got wings doesn't mean you're an angel." Neil maintained a completely neutral expression while he unfurled his own wings. Not beautiful like hers, but impressive just the same.

She gasped and, despite any earlier misgivings, she stepped closer. He could really see the blue of her eyes this close. It was a deep color, like Cookie Monster or the LA Dodgers.

Those eyes of hers were wide. "Are you a demon?"

Neil was surprised there was no disgust or reproach in her tone. In fact, she seemed fascinated by him. He wanted to tell her no.

"Well, there are demons and then there are *demons*. I'm the first kind."

"What's the difference?"

He panned his hand across his body like a game show model. "There's me. You know, handsome, charming. I was a person before I died." He smiled brightly, and then he winced. "And then there's horrible, nightmarish monsters. Like bugs with animal heads and hooves. They were born in hell." He shivered dramatically to make his point.

"Oh." She made a face in sympathy. "I didn't know you guys had wings, though."

"Yep."

"They look so different than mine." She turned those electric blue eyes to meet his. "Can I touch them?"

He leaned into her, just inches from her face, and lowered his voice. "I'll let you touch mine if I can touch yours."

She gasped, all indignant, and Neil couldn't help but laugh.

"Don't get all nasty about it," she said in a huff.

Still chuckling, he reminded her, "I'm a demon. What do you expect?"

"Nothing about being a demon means that you have to be rude."

"Ha! Clearly you ain't never been in Hell, girly."

Chewing on her bottom lip, she contemplated his wings. "Okay, but don't get mine dirty."

He showed her his palms. They looked pretty clean to him, but she wrinkled her nose so he wiped them on his jeans. She rolled her eyes but didn't say anything. He reached over her shoulder and stroked his palm over the tips of the primary feathers.

Juliet giggled. "It kinda tickles."

"Oh yeah?" He did it again, from the first feather tip to the last one on the end. The girl looked him in the eye, her smile shyer than it had been before.

"My turn." She held out her own hands for him to inspect, like he gave a damn about how clean hers were. Smooth, pink skin. No blisters or callouses. "Turn around, please. I'm too short to reach them like you did."

Instead, Neil kneeled. He dropped to his knees in front of her and spread his wings wide enough that they touched the walls on either side of the landing.

She was tentative. Just a fingertip skated along the leathery covered ribs that made up their structure. She paused at the claw that extended out of the top joint, darted her eyes to meet his. He shrugged indicating that he was fine for her to continue. She wrapped her sweet girl fingers around that claw, and Neil thought he was going to die.

Again.

He held his breath when she let go and, now emboldened, ran her whole hand along the top ridge.

"It's so smooth and strong," she said, stroking her palm down the leathery skin.

Neil chuckled uncomfortably. "And they're so warm and soft. I thought they would be rough, but no." She stepped closer and caressed her hand back over the claw.

It was a struggle to keep his hands off her. "You know I have horns, too."

She pulled her hand away from his wings and it was a relief, really. "You do? Can I see?"

His head was level with her breastbone, but he bowed even lower. "Go ahead and feel."

Her fingers tangled gently in his hair. It was longer than usual and it had always had these big loopy curls that girls loved to play with. She squeaked when she found one and moved the curls away so she could see it better. The other one was discovered on the other side. Dark bone colored, they weren't sharp but they did start to twist about a half an inch from the end.

"They're really pretty," she said, and damned if it didn't sound like she meant it. She wound both hands around them and moved her palms up and down.

His hand shot up and grasped her wrist. He closed his eyes and exhaled heavily. "That's enough of that."

"Did I hurt you?"

He chuckled uncomfortably. "No. It felt really good. Too good."

He'd never expected stroking his ugly wings and fondling his awful horns would give him a hard on. Had never been in that situation before, but there it was, making itself known as much as his wings were.

Juliet took a big step back and had the good sense to look afraid.

He released her wrists and stood up. Collapsing his wings would hopefully settle down other things, too. He'd never forced a girl to do anything she didn't want to do when he was alive and being a demon wasn't going to change that. He still felt plenty of humanity. There were lots of things to regret, and he wasn't going to add to the list by hurting this innocent girl. "Don't worry. You're safe."

Blue eyes blinked at him, assessing, before giving him another tentative smile. Damn, she was so pretty, no matter that her perfect wings were put away. Finally, she said, "So, why are you coming upstairs?"

"Looking for the Devil's dog." He shoved his hands back in his pockets. "I'm supposed to be watching the stupid bastard, but the crazy thing keeps getting away."

She narrowed her eyes at him. "What does he look like?"

Neil snorted. "Can't miss him. Big ugly fucker, three heads. Drools a *lot.*"

"Cerberus!"

Both of his eyebrows shot up. "Yeah."

She nodded and her grin was even bigger. "He's up there. The kennel master, Hugh, watches out for him. He's got a girlfriend and they had puppies. Two-headed puppies. They are so cute, you could just die." She rolled her eyes. "Well, you know."

"You have puppies?" No wonder he couldn't keep track of the dog.

"With two heads. Oooh, they're so cute."

Yeah, right. Adorable, he was sure. "Well, I've got to get him back or my ass is dust."

"How are you going to do that? I don't think you can get into Heaven, can you?" Even her wrinkled forehead was pretty. It made her look smart and he really liked the idea that maybe she was concerned about him.

"I don't think so. I was going to worry about that part when I got up there."

"Well," she twisted her lips to the side again. She seemed to do that when she was thinking. "Maybe I can help you."

Frankly, he could use all the help he could get. "How?"

"So, I wasn't sure that these stairs went all the way down, you know. But I guess they do. That's good, because I need to get down there."

"For fuck's sake, why?"

"It's a long story."

Neil sat down on the steps and patted the spot next to him. "Listen, it's so much cooler up here than down there. I am in no hurry to show up without that fucking dog and get my ass kicked by Scourge and the rest of Duke Valefor's cretins. Tell me your story so I can tell you all the million reasons why you're not going down there."

So she sat. "You hungry?" she asked, pulling a candy bar from her pocket and handing it to him. "I have a couple."

Neil almost cried. His hands were shaking as he opened the wrapper. He closed his eyes and savored the melting chocolate, the buttery caramel, the pieces of peanuts. It was the best thing he'd ever had in his mouth.

"Good, huh?" she said, and then told him a crazy-ass story about Lucifer and the first daughter, Rachel.

She turned those eyes on him again and watched and waited. "Do you believe me?"

"I guess so. I never heard that before, though. I don't know if it's true."

She nodded and patted his arm. "It's true. I found Lucifer and asked him about it."

What the—. "You found Lucifer?"

"Yup. It took a long time, but I found him." Then her eyes got all soft. "He's really sad. He still misses her, all the time. He lives in this horrible place in Heaven, all alone, like totally pining for her."

"A horrible place? In Heaven? Yeah, sounds fucking awful."

"Oh, yeah." Now she rested her hand on his knee. "Compared to what you have to deal with, I'm sure... Well, it's bad for Heaven. And then if you think about it, Rachel is stuck down in Hell longer than anyone and she didn't even do anything."

He threw her a look. "Obviously she did do something or she wouldn't be down there. Everyone is down there for a reason." He ought to know.

"You're right, she broke God's rule, but," she leaned in closer and whispered, "it was a stupid, bad rule and an unfair punishment. She's down there all alone."

Neil couldn't help looking up at the ceiling when she said that, hoping no one in power heard her. "Shhh."

She waved him off, but still kept her voice low. "I promised Lucifer I'd see if I can find her."

"You can't get into Hell any more than I can get into Heaven."

"I think you're right. I didn't really have a plan when I found these stairs, I just got excited." Now she bumped her shoulder against his. "So I was thinking I could find your dog in Heaven and bring him back here and you could see if you can find Rachel down there."

He let his head fall forward. "Hell's a really big place. I've never—." He couldn't even think of the nightmarish punishments they could cook up for him. He tossed his candy wrapper on the floor.

Juliet clucked her tongue and picked up the wrapper with a reproachful look. "We're not littering."

That made him laugh. Here she was, telling him this story and trying to rope him into helping her do something totally rebellious, but she was gonna yell at him about littering.

"You're killing me," he told her. That irony wasn't lost on either of them.

"Will you try?" She trained those blue eyes on him and, damn it, she was so pretty. "I'll bring you more candy."

"And chips?"

"Sure, chips."

"I can't promise anything."

"Thank you." And then she kissed his cheek. "Thank you."

Damn it.

CHAPTER TWENTY-ONE

L uke had to concentrate to ignore Jeb. They had taken one of the company Town Cars to the meeting at Virtus Templum so, as his assistant put it, "they wouldn't have to tackle parking." Now they were on their way back to their office in the same car. The driver paid them no mind at all, but Luke found it more and more taxing the longer they sat in traffic. They sat side by side on the soft leather seat. Luke stared pointedly ahead, his hands in his lap, nursing a slow internal burn. Jeb, however, sat as far into the corner as possible so that he could angle his body toward Luke's, Jeb's knees just centimeters from his own. Luke didn't need to look at him to know that his arms were crossed and that he wore a mutinous expression.

A highly dramatic and overplayed sigh filled the cabin of the Lincoln. Jeb's legs were crossed and recrossed and then the huff came again, more theatrical this time, if that was possible.

Luke ignored him, although if this kept up, they were going to have to roll down a window or die of suffocation.

A set of long, delicate fingers passed into Luke's peripheral vision. A microscopic fluff was plucked from his companion's knee and then the fingers disappeared again. Luke could sense more than hear Jeb wind up for another emphatic exhalation, and that was the proverbial straw.

"I swear to everything you hold dear, if you let out another of those ridiculous, hysterical sighs, it will be the last noise you ever make." Luke did not look at Jeb. He trained his gaze on the taillights of the car in front of them, afraid if he saw Jeb's outraged expression, he wouldn't be able to stop himself from launching across the car and wrapping his hands around his granite neck.

Not in the least bit cowed, Jeb said, "Oh, no."

Luke also knew without looking that Jeb was wagging his finger at him. Jeb might well be made of stone, but Luke knew that the rage bubbling in his gut would give him all the power necessary to snap it right the fuck off.

"Don't you get all wrathful on me." Jeb launched into full histrionics. "You did this to yourself. I cannot believe you stood right there and cut her loose. What is wrong with you? Seriously, Luke, what? Because I have done everything I can to make this transition easy for you. Believe me, you're no cakewalk." Jeb flopped back against the upholstery and then shot back up again to make another point. "When the other guardians complain, I laugh. I actually laugh, Luke. Last week, Lust's was complaining to me about how intolerable her Sin is, losing his underwear all the time. I was like, 'Boo hoo, Esther. So you have to go shopping. That's a goddamned tragedy.' I should be so lucky."

Luke clenched his jaw and his hands and even curled his toes inside his loafers. "Shut up," he growled.

Jeb snorted. "Or what? You're going to do some brutal thing to my person? I've heard it all already." Those slim fingers came back into view again while he ticked off a list. "You're going to strangle me. You're going to rip my head off. You're going to break my neck. Of course, sometimes you're not very creative and it's just the simple old you're going to kill me. I've heard it all before and I get it. The little prince has a temper."

If Luke wasn't so wrung out over what he'd just done, he actually would have found Jeb's conniption fit funny. His gargoyle had expressed his displeasure in countless ways during their tenure together; it had never been a secret when Jeb had felt maligned. He'd just never done it in quite this way. Previous irritation had been expressed in devious and passive-aggressive ways: Hiding all of Luke's right shoes or putting a parental lock on the cable box. But he'd never launched into a full-on shrieking fit before.

Jeb gestured wildly, his arms waving about in the cabin. "I know you think you've done this as a way to give your father the finger, but you've made a huge mistake. I honestly cannot believe you're this imbecilic. The only person you're hurting here besides yourself is Mia, and that lovely woman does not deserve this."

Luke tuned him out again. He let the tsunami of insults roll over him without acknowledging them, like boiling water over stone. Nothing Jeb could say to him would be worse than what was going on in Luke's head, anyway.

From the minute he'd left the Devil at the restaurant, the rage had been relentlessly churning. More than blind outrage, he felt keen betrayal on behalf of his mother who was so naively led into an unconscionable situation that only death allowed her to escape from it. If she had been alive when his father had been selected... Surely that would have killed her.

"...almost thirty-years-old. There's no way for you to escape this. What did you think, you could just refuse Mia and then the curse wouldn't affect you? You know better than that." Luke tuned back into Jeb's tirade. "You will have a son when the time comes. It just won't be with Mia. All you've managed to do is alienate the one woman who would have made you happy." When Luke finally looked at him, Jeb's arms were crossed, and he was shaking his head back and forth. "I wash my hands of you."

"You promise?"

"Bah," Jeb flicked both hands at him like he was dismissing a truant child.

"I don't need to explain myself to you," he told Jeb, who rolled his eyes and pursed his lips. "Mia is too..." Too what? "I can't... Not to her." Luke couldn't manage to complete the sentences. He didn't know what Mia was too much of, but every time he thought of betraying her innocence like his father had done, it made him crazy with—

He didn't know. Whatever emotion it conjured up, it felt different than the usual wrath that consumed him. It made him feel desperate and...afraid?

All Luke knew for sure was that he hated this feeling. If he cut Mia loose, let her escape from the horrors that being with him would bring her, the feeling might subside. He hated hurting Mia, but in the long run the relatively mild pain from today would easily make up for the devastation that being with him long-term would bring her.

He knew he had all the right motivation the second she walked into her office. He could smell her before he saw her. Womanly and beguiling but with an earthy undertone that he would forever associate with her.

It was like a gut punch.

He tried to explain, to take the blame, to tell her it was all him, but of course she was angry. For once, an emotion he could completely identify with. But in the end, there was no way he could explain. He'd hurt her and he felt awful.

"I hate to think what's going to happen when your father finds out." Jeb didn't sound like he hated the idea. On the contrary, it sounded like he relished the aftermath of his discovery.

"I don't care."

"Umm-hmm."

Mia had told him to go to Hell. The irony was rich.

In reality, he might already be in Hell.

She'd said the words with furious tears in her eyes. A fierce pixie of a warrior. He'd never wanted to protect someone more than he had at that very moment. He had to remind himself that protecting her was exactly what he was doing—protecting her from Luke Mephisto, a Prince of Hell, the Son of the Devil, and if the omens were to be believed, the Heir Apparent.

"I did the right thing," he told Jeb.

Jeb's expression softened. "I know you think you did."

"No, I did. She cannot get mixed up in this diabolical shit show."

The gargoyle watched him for several heartbeats before sighing and crumbled his shoulders. "I should have known. I should have seen this coming and taken precautions. I just never imagined that the great and powerful Wrath would fall in love. It simply never occurred to me. Stupid really."

He rolled his eyes. "I'm not in—"

Jeb patted Luke's forearm and gave him knowing eyes. "Just as sure as God made little green apples."

Luke shucked off the sympathetic hand with a jerk. So incensed that he couldn't even form words and shaking with the intense ferocity of his emotion, he roared. As if a tiny nuclear bomb detonated, all the windows in the car exploded outward, sending tiny squares of safety glass out into the world. The driver, rattled from the oblivion Jeb had settled on him during the drive, brought the car to a screeching halt. Luke threw open his door and crunched through the glass. He stormed off through the city, desperate to be alone, like a miserable Godzilla looking to punish himself more than anyone else.

FOR MAYBE THE TWELFTH TIME, Mia watched the video rendering of her building. Her favorite part was when the view sped up like a bird and rose from the ground level into the center and turned towards the sky shining through the glass ceiling. She'd been rewinding that part for the last three days, over and over. The ritual had her feeling overwrought. First her heart would sing as light streamed in, blessing her gorgeous apple trees and allowing photosynthesis, but then it would flame out as soon as she remembered the only reason Luke caved in and gave her exactly what she wanted was because he felt guilty for dumping her.

She was still furious, which was a far sight better than feeling pitiful, which she assumed was pessimistically waiting just around the corner. To keep the wallowing at bay, she stoked the fury. Every time she remembered his bullshit come on about fate, she wanted to hurt something. Or someone. What kind of loathsome person came up with something like that? Not even Cassie had heard that one, and she thought she'd heard all the lines.

The final specs and cost analysis was delivered several days after the train wreck of a meeting, and Mia rang up her father's assistant to get a time to show him everything. It was kidding herself that she wasn't afraid of what her father was going to say. The end result was as dramatically different from what he'd originally requested as heaven was to hell. It was entirely possible that he'd hate it. Wouldn't that be a bitch? If she had to go back to Luke and his team and tell them to put it all back?

"You will not be wishy-washy, Mia," she told herself in a stern voice while riding the elevator. She clutched the thumb drive with the presentation and counted along with the floor indicator as she rode up the floors.

"Hi, Mia," Yvonne was waiting for her outside her father's office.

Yvonne linked her arm through Mia's and escorted her towards her father's inner sanctum. "It's holding steady. He had a call earlier that put him on edge, but he settled down pretty quickly."

It was always a good idea to get a barometer reading before venturing into her father's office. A person was wise to be prepared. It wasn't a big deal if he was in a decent mood, but if things looked black in there, it might be best to just leave and try another day.

Mia's insides clenched up at the thought of dealing with the man when he was already ruffled. One would think she'd have the inside track on how to work through her father's mercurial moods, but she didn't. Where Mia's skill set lay was in damage control after the fact. Once her father and his temper had run roughshod over the top of everyone's feelings, Mia could come in, mop up the carnage, and apply metaphorical bandages.

Placing a soft-knuckled rap against the wood, Yvonne opened the door. "Your daughter's here."

Mia plastered a smile on her face that she hoped didn't let on to her anxiety and strode through the door. "Hello, Daddy. I have the final renderings and cost evaluation for the new building."

In a move that was almost smooth enough as to not appear clandestine, her father dropped a stack of papers in a desk drawer before eyeing her from across the desk. "I hear there have been changes." His baritone was intimidating even without the glare to accompany it.

Even with the stern expression, her father was still a handsome man, a fact that made her mother furious. Get a couple of martinis in her and she'd rail on for hours about how his gray made him distinguished and more dignified, while she was forced to spend her alimony money on chemical peels and exotic creams just to maintain.

Mia supposed Luke would age the same way.

Inhaling through her nose and exhaling through her mouth, Mia used tricks to keep her nerves calm. "Yes, but I think you'll really appreciate the result." She rounded his desk and handed him the thumb drive.

Once the presentation started, she held her breath. The camera circled the flagstone floor of the lobby, lingering on the lush, fully grown trees and paused before the security desk camouflaged within the foliage. Her father sat back in his chair and thrummed his fingers on the armrests. She no longer watched the footage, which she knew completely by heart by now. Instead, she watched his expression. Lips pursed in annoyance. Brow furrowed with deep lines that merged into the beginnings of a scowl once the view shot up towards the windowed ceiling.

The footage ended and there was silence. One heartbeat. Then two. Mia couldn't take it. She put her hand on her heart, ostensibly to keep it from bursting out of her chest, but also to state her opinion emphatically. "I think this is a powerful statement about Veritas Templum."

Her father continued to stare at the computer monitor, and Mia couldn't read his body language. "What the hell happened to the original plans? Were they scrapped completely?"

Mia didn't hesitate for even a second before she started her pitch. "No. The automated systems are still in the functionality of the building. I thought Veritas deserved more than a simple, stark building. The original plans were amazing, but stark."

"They were intimidating. That's what I liked."

Gulp. "Yes, but not what I would call distinctive."

Her father's leather chair swung so that he faced her. She took an involuntary step back. His gaze pinned her down. "You understand that I hired that firm because they're well-known for designing intimidating structures. We are one of the largest pharmaceutical firms in the country and we should look the part."

Breath in through the nose...

"You've built a very influential company, and others in the industry look towards us to lead the way. We are huge," she agreed. "Our primary goal is health management. What says that more than a garden?" He wasn't yelling at her which was more unsettling than if he had been. Her father was listening to her. She rushed onward, speaking quickly, hoping not to lose him. "What this building says is that we're at the forefront of technology, but we know what's important. We're growing literally and figuratively. We're trustworthy and stalwart. We will feed your health."

He narrowed his eyes at her for a moment before spinning the chair back to the front and restarting the presentation. She stood behind him, focusing on the back of his head, willing him to grasp the significance and beauty of her masterpiece.

"Well, it sure as hell isn't like anyone else's."

"True," she agreed and walked around to the front of his desk to face him again. "Think of the publicity. The technological aspects of it are astounding—the water filtration system, the solar commitment we'll be making. All of those things above the aesthetic nature of the structure."

She watched her father's mind work and kept breathing.

"They're going to call it genius, Daddy."

"Yeah, how much is this genius going to cost me?"

"Genius is never cheap." She sat in the club chair in front of his desk and folded her hands in her lap. "The tax breaks will be phenomenal."

He clicked on that folder, and she remained quiet while he ran through the financials. There was nothing she could say to excuse the outrageous cost. She had to sell him that the expense was worth the distinctiveness of the building. If there was one tool that always worked with her father, it was a good ego stroking.

"I know it's expensive," she conceded, "but it's going to be the Chrysler Building of this age. As famous as Frank Lloyd Wright's Fallingwater. You're going to be considered a pioneer in the environmental age. The free publicity will be immeasurable."

Her father raised an eyebrow and gazed across the desk at his daughter. "That's a lot of smoke you're blowing up my ass."

She remained mute, breathing in and out, heartbeat racing at breakneck speed.

He continued, "But you're right. No one will ever forget this."

She wanted to dance and scream and raise her arms to the heavens. "They will not."

"Have them send the final contracts. I'll sign them."

She tried to smother a smile, but her lips wouldn't behave. "All right." She reached for the thumb drive, but he waved her away.

"No, I'm going to keep it. Show it to a few people who can start leveraging it."

Of course he would. She was going to trot right down to her office and have Jason get those contracts so everything would be solidified.

Before she reached the door, he called out to her. "Mia, wait a second."

Damn.

"This is good." He indicated the renderings which were playing on his screen again. "I was right to let you take point on this. A brilliant tactical PR move. Well done."

She didn't try to suppress the grin this time around. For the first time in her life, she'd impressed her father.

And the angels wept.

CHAPTER TWENTY-TWO

L uke's Aunt Claire swanned into Ethan's spare bedroom where he'd been camping out for the last week. She was like that, graceful but dramatic in all things. She never entered a room like a normal person. You'd think all that gliding and breezing would irritate him, but it didn't. Aunt Claire might be his very favorite person on Earth, and he was willing to forgive her almost anything.

A surrogate mother after his father left, she was the only person who was able to find the scared little boy hiding behind all the Wrath. Perhaps, she'd been the only one who'd tried. Lord knew he hadn't made it easy. When Luke came to live with his cousin Ethan, he'd been a fierce ball of fury, prickly with animosity and nearly rabid with antagonism. Claire had wrapped her arms around him and held him tight while he literally and figuratively gnashed his teeth at the world.

"You didn't eat your lunch," she noted while inventorying the food left on the tray. There was an uneaten roast beef sandwich and a scoop of potato salad with parsley on a china plate. "Oh, I'm mistaken. You did eat the cookies."

"I almost didn't. They have raisins in them."

She didn't even try to hide a smile. "I'm sure you can use the iron; you need to eat better."

"That sounds great," he said from behind his laptop. When he checked his email this morning, there were three hundred and thirty-seven of them. He'd expected Jeb to have weeded some of them out, but the snotty bastard must be punishing him. Luke hadn't been in the office or even to his own home since he'd stormed out of the car after breaking off with Mia. He'd shown up at Ethan's house sixteen hours later, stone cold sober and seething.

The laptop closed on top of his fingers. Glancing up in surprise, he found Aunt Claire standing in front of him. "I'm done being ignored. We all are."

Luke opened and closed his mouth several times, not sure of what to say. He landed on, "I'm not ignoring you."

She lifted an eyebrow.

"I'm not ignoring *you*," he said, emphasizing the last word. "I am ignoring Jeb, my father, work, and probably Ethan, but never you."

The eyebrow came back down, a sort of concession. She walked to the other side of the room and sat on his unmade bed, giving the spot next to her a pat in invitation. Luke slumped backwards in his club chair.

He knew what she wanted. "I don't want to talk about it."

She resettled her hands in her lap and gazed across the room at him. "My boy tells me that you've been here a week."

"It won't be a week 'till tomorrow."

"Um-hmm. He also tells me your gargoyle has called and been by countless times."

Luke exhaled through his nose. He didn't want to see Jeb. He knew exactly what that experience would be like and wasn't in the mood to be berated. "He brought my work laptop by."

Luke had instructed Ethan's gargoyle, Mordecai, to take whatever Jeb brought but not to allow him in the house. Mordecai had rolled his eyes, reminded Luke that he didn't answer to him, and strode away.

Luke's blood pressure had risen but he'd managed not to throw anything at the retreating blockhead. Still, hours later the man had rapped on Luke's door and handed over a laptop bag and a huge manila envelope overflowing with papers.

"Jeb says to call him."

"Right." Luke had tossed the envelope on the bed and slammed the door in Mordecai's face.

"I've been in contact with work," he assured Claire, as if that would alleviate her concerns when she was faced with the evidence that he was holed up at his cousin's home like a war criminal hiding from the authorities.

She stood up from the rumpled bed and began gathering clothes from the floor. "I called Jeb," she told him, glancing up to gauge his expression. "He told me what happened."

"I'm sure he did." Little asshole loved to gossip. He probably already told everything to that cabal of gargoyles who hung out together all the time.

"He said you have a young lady." She sat back on the bed and folded a shirt.

He left the comfort of his chair across the room. He snatched the folded shirt from the bed and the rest of the dirty clothes and threw them back on the floor in an unruly pile at the end of the bed. "Had. The important word in that sentence is had."

"Ah." Claire folded her hands, her expression still calm. "And now you're hiding at Ethan's because you have a broken heart?"

"I don't have a broken heart." Was what he felt love? Or was he confusing that emotion with the feeling of completeness she gave him? They'd been so wrapped up in that whirlwind— He didn't think he'd loved Mia already, but even if he had, it hadn't been long enough to be heartbroken. "And I'm not hiding."

"Avoiding, then," she amended.

Acknowledging the truth with a tilt of his head, he closed his eyes for a long second. "Jeb only sees things from one point of view. He's been on my ass because he thinks Mia is the one and what that means is quite impossible for me to contend with."

"Is she the one?"

He kept his expression neutral. "Probably. Jeb thinks it's true love. After what he's told the others, they probably all do, too. My father has already determined that she is the one for me, like he has any say in the matter."

"Sure," she said, "and you're pushing back against your father. You know, I understand your impulse to rebel, but is it in your best interest? Who are you really punishing? Your father or you and your pretty lady?"

He rubbed his temples and then pinched the bridge of his nose. He had such a headache. "I'm not trying to punish anyone. Trying to punish the Devil would be foolish."

"It would," she agreed. "And you know that wouldn't work anyway, right? So here you are, miserable and alone, hiding in your fort just like you used to when you were a kid."

Luke snorted. He hadn't thought of his fort in years. He and Ethan had built it on the furthest corner of his uncle's estate. It was a monument to tetanus. Poorly built by two boys with no construction skills, the fort was more a ramshackle lean-to than an actual building. Still, the boys had added on and repaired boards when they rotted out, dedicated to preserving their hideout. Luke had once spent five days in there the summer he was thirteen. He'd been plagued with confusing and terrifying bouts of rage symptomatic of a terrible cocktail of puberty hormones compounded with the curse of Wrath. It had been a shitty time in his life when he'd never cursed his father more—except for maybe now.

"So I ask you again." She looked at him pointedly. "Is she the one?"

Luke knew the answer to this question without even thinking about it. Every atom in his body recognized Mia was his. He nodded. "I'm certain she hates me at this point."

Mia had told him to go to Hell, and she'd meant it. She didn't even have any idea the irony of that suggestion. Her last words to him had been spoken with fire and assertiveness he'd never seen from her before. Under other circumstances, he'd have been proud of her.

"Well, if she's the one then I'm sure you can get her back."

"I don't want her back," he insisted. "I want her as far away from all of this as she can get. We're a plague, Claire, a plague that destroys people. There is no fucking way I'm getting her mixed up in this freak show." He realized his hands were clenched in fists by his side. They hurt; he was squeezing so hard.

Claire sighed and slumped a bit before saying with a soft voice,

"Honey, you realize if she's really the one you want forever, you don't have much of a choice. Sometimes the Sin never finds someone and he simply fulfills his duty by having a child without love. But other times he does find love and, when he does, that connection is magical in all the best ways. It's the one little reward you might get out of the bum deal of being in this family."

Luke's hands were still balled into compact fists. "I don't care. God gave man free will. Every man, even the fucking Mephistos. That has to mean something. Curse or no, I'm not subjecting Mia to this horror."

"John and I have been very happy," she pointed out, referring her to husband and Ethan's father. "Our lives have been very fulfilling."

He threw his hands in the air. "Of course, you have. John wasn't chosen." He bellowed, something he'd never done to his surrogate mother. Claire had always been a soft place to land even when he'd been overcome by Wrath. "It was my dad who left. The only good thing about it was that my mom was already dead, so she didn't have to suffer."

Claire's eyebrows rose at the same time she stood from the bed. "Luke—"

Her tone was placating, and Luke couldn't stand it. He didn't want to be soothed or coddled or made to think this horrible situation was anything less than it was. He wanted to rage and throw things and spit fire at the injustice of it all.

She tried again. "Your father adored your mother, and she him."

"How can you say that?" Fury coursed through his muscles so that even his skin heated. "What honorable man would lure an unsuspecting woman into this train wreck? I thought I missed my dad, but it turns out he was just as much of a bastard then as he is now."

Hands on her hips, his aunt's expression morphed from patient understanding to anger. "What the hell are you taking about? We're not doing revisionist history here. Your father fiercely loved you and your mother, and Felicity loved him back. Is your sticking point here that you think your father lured her in with some crafty bait and switch? Felicity was a dear, sweet woman and my very best friend, but she wasn't clueless. She understood the rules."

"Not according to the Devil," he spat out.

"What?"

It should give him no pleasure to prove his aunt wrong, but for some perverse reason, he enjoyed setting her straight about this. As if somehow making her feel bad would ease his agony.

"He came up to see me. We had lunch. I couldn't figure out what he wanted at first, but it turns out he just wanted to mess with my head. He'd found out about Mia. In fact, the bastard had already visited her in a dream." Clair made a satisfactorily distressed face. "Exactly. So like an idiot I tried to talk to him like he was my parent for a minute. I just wanted a little advice on how he handled it with my mother. You know, how did he tell her about the curse? How did he convince Mom that he was worth the risk? He said he never told her." He paused for a heartbeat to let that sink in. "That bastard just lured her into this biblical freak show without telling her that her husband might be the Devil one day, and there was a one in seven chance that her son could also be. What the fuck? He tricked her. He had to because what sane person agrees to that?"

She reared her head back in indignation. "Excuse me?"

He threw out a hand, palm up, an admission he'd misspoke. "I don't mean you. Although, you know, maybe I do. Why would you ever agree to that scenario?"

Now she glowered at him. Great, he'd royally pissed off the one person who was always on his side. She spoke in clipped words. "John and I were very fortunate in that we had one of those incredible, mystical connections. Love can overcome a lot of sins, Luke."

"Holy shit, you did not just say that."

Her eyes narrowed at him, and her words turned to ice. "Watch your tone with me. You don't know everything there is to know in this world. Do you think you're the only ones compelled with this curse? The Mephisto Men stand alone," she mocked with a curled upper lip. "If you're lucky she'll take you back and give you a son and you'll be able to share that with her. If not, it's a possibility that you'll still have a son with her anyway, or some other woman," she reminded him of the terms of the curse: Every Sin has a son the year they turn thirty to populate the next generation. "You obviously didn't take that into consideration or you wouldn't have decided for Mia. What you're doing is forcing her to go through it by herself. Awfully goddamned selfish, Luke."

The fury that kept him going, the motivation that fueled him, ebbed. "I'm trying to make it easier for her."

The ice thawed enough that his aunt smiled at him sadly. "That's admirable, honey, but sometimes it's what's hard that makes it worthwhile."

Unfortunately, it all came back to that undeniable truth from his father, and it rubbed ceaselessly on something broken inside him until he was raw. "My mother didn't know."

"Of course, she knew." She reached out a hand and pulled his fingers into her grasp.

"But the Devil said—"

"The Devil is a liar, don't you know?" She squeezed his fingers. "Do you really think I'd let her go into this without knowing? The Sins also aren't the only ones who stick together."

Luke swallowed hard. For the first time in over a week, there was no churning, furious bile egging him on. He felt bereft without it, rudderless. "You did?"

"Of course. This is not an easy choice, and there are many times when we second guess ourselves. Still, there are many rewards. She got you, and your mother loved you more than anything. Your parents had an amazing, passionate love affair that was cut much too short."

He bowed his head. "What do I do? I feel like I cannot have her, but I need her." If he loved her—if it was true—then how could he bring her into this?

Aunt Claire shrugged. "You cannot know the future. Consider there is only a one in seven chance that you'll be chosen. You could have a long and happy life together. What would you give for that?" Luke deflated even more, and she pulled him into her arms for an embrace. "Go to her. You'll know what to do."

He very much doubted that. But the pull to Mia was powerful. Would he be dragging her down to Hell with him?

HEAVEN & HELL VIII

N eil had a hop in his step that not even descending back into Hell could quell. He could still taste the Snickers bar Juliette had given him. It was the best goddamned thing he'd ever eaten. He would let that memory, and the promise of more to come, sustain him as he attempted to find Lucifer's missing lover.

As the atmosphere grew heavier and the heat lay leaden on his skin, he couldn't stop thinking of the beautiful angel. For that brief period of time with her in the stairwell, a miracle had happened. Neil had felt a trickle of hope, something he'd been without for an unbearably long time. His whole existence had been bleak at best, atrocious the bulk of the time. But somehow even now, he carried with him an incandescent bead of hope, hidden in his chest where the Duke's minions wouldn't defuse it. He would defend and shield it from all the horrors of Hell if it killed him.

He was insane for agreeing to help the angel, but man, she was so convincing. In truth, it was a Herculean task. Juliet was positive that this Rachel person was stuck in Hell. To be honest, Neil had never given the old urban legend any thought at all. What did he care if some woman was down there? There were lots of women down there, and each and every one of them deserved it. That's the way

Heaven and Hell worked. People went where they were supposed to go.

Juliet was sweet and pretty and, Neil had no doubt, pure of heart and conscience. Beyond a shadow of a doubt, she belonged in Heaven. He, on the other hand, was heading right back where he belonged. He'd had a short lifetime on Earth to make all the wrong decisions and it seemed now, even with no hope of ever getting out of Hell alive, helping Juliet was the right decision.

He just had no idea how to go about it.

Hell was a big place, and there were legions of inhabitants—some were souls sent to suffer like he was and many, many more simply belonged there. The Devil ran the place with the help of seventy-two demons like King Bael, who topped the hierarchy. Of course, each of them had their own army of imps, goblins, and fiends to do their dirty work. What that amounted to was a multitude of inhabitants who had no desire to help Neil in any way. Most of them would be more interested in harming him, actually.

It turned out down was considerably faster than up, and he arrived back at the first landing in what seemed like no time. The room was empty, just as he'd left it. He half expected to find Scourge and the rest of his filthy crew waiting for him in there. He closed his eyes, counted to ten, and opened the door a crack. Swinging the door wide on its hinges, he was hit with the blast of heat like a...a... He couldn't even think of anything hotter than "the fiery pits of Hell" since that's exactly what it was.

It wasn't just the heat that afflicted him. The stench coated the inside of his nostrils as well. He swallowed against his gag reflex— there was no point in getting squirrely about it now—and pushed himself out into Hell.

He figured under the auspices of his continued search for Cerberus he could loop in the further districts and lower levels. Also, there would be the added benefit that Scourge and his band of cretins wouldn't be tolerated in other territories. Though it occurred to him that those he found out there could be worse than Scourge.

Afraid if he lingered too long in the hidden room, some hideous creature would find it and take advantage, he headed across the barren ground at a fast pace, anxious to get away from the staircase to Heaven. He wanted to knock out his task quickly and return to the meeting place first. The thought of Juliette waiting for him all alone when any abominable thing could skulk around in there and do her harm was not something he wanted to linger on. Best to do his chore, find Lucifer's woman, and get back there right away.

As expected, expediency wasn't on his side. He knew Duke Valefor's territory pretty well and believed that Rachel wasn't anywhere nearby. But where to start? Neil knew the basic layout of Hell even though he'd not visited most of it. The place was gigantic. Everything flowed in a pitched arc downward. Following the lava flow as it descended, your calves would ache and eventually your toenails would turn black from rubbing against your shoes. Each level inevitably flowing into the next one if you were crazy enough to keep trekking along the spiral. Neil didn't even want to consider it. The distance was prohibitive, and he'd never been one for hiking.

The elevator was the best place to start. Starting in Limbo, the shaft ran all the way through the levels with stops on each. Neil supposed it ran all the way down to the bottom, to the Devil's mansion, but of course he'd never been there himself. The lift was the preferred way the few souls who had the freedom to move around traveled from level to level. But there were still challenges.

First and foremost, the elevator operator was terrifying.

Even the children of Hell like Scourge dreaded dealing with him.

Charon required payment. In the old days, back when all he did was ferry people across the river, Neil heard that he only accepted coins, but now days, you could negotiate a deal with him if you had the cajones.

Neil patted his pockets for tradable items. Not much. He still had the dog leash in his back pocket, a useless ring full of keys to things on Earth, and a cell phone. That last one was particularly useless. Obviously, it didn't work to call or text anyone. Surprisingly, Siri still worked, but only about as well as she ever did. You could ask her questions, but she'd never give you a usable answer. When he hailed her and asked who Rachel was, the electronic bitch said something about a main character on some stupid television show who was on a break with a dude called Ross. What the hell was he supposed to do with that? Fucking useless.

There was also a piece of chocolate he'd saved from the bounty Juliette had provided. Man, he really didn't want to part with the chocolate, but it might be his best option. Hopefully he'd get more. And maybe some chips. That kind of stuff would be more tradable than gold down here.

He wound his way through the badlands of his home circle, Gluttony, towards the center and the elevator, keeping himself near cover as best he could to avoid Duke Valefor's minions. If he could get to the elevator without getting caught... And convince Charon to let him ride the elevator... And find this Rachel woman...

This was a fucking lot to ask of a gang banging junkie.

The elevator was just ahead, past the barracks and Duke Valefor's home base. This was the trickiest part—the nasty little bastards could be anywhere. Even with the sweltering heat, he broke into a trot as he rounded the low cinderblock construction. They must have all been out on patrol, probably looking for him or some other pathetic loser, because he made it to the far side of the building without anyone noticing. A lazy Siamese cat lolled on a wall and judged him while he trotted low next to the duke's windows.

"Where is everyone?" he whispered to it as he paused to catch his breath.

The cat swished his tail in response and glared. Neil stood slowly with the thought that he'd peek over the wall and see if the coast was clear to the elevator, but as soon as he got within striking distance, the blasted cat lashed out with his paw, claws extended, and swiped at his face. It stung like hell when the claws tore open his cheek.

"Ow! Damn!" It stung even worse when he touched the place with his fingertips.

The cat arched his back and hissed in response.

He glared back at the cat from a safe distance and wiped the blood off with the back of his hand. "Son of a bitch."

The cat's tail swished madly, back and forth, and Neil moved away with alacrity. Blood was still dripping off his chin when he climbed two stairs up the riser to the kiosk that surrounded the elevator shaft.

He pressed the call button and looked over his shoulder to make sure no one had spied him. The cat eyed him malevolently from afar. Neil gave a shiver.

All his life he'd had a vague fear of dogs. He couldn't even count how many times he'd been chased over chain link fences by dedicated and very serious Doberman pinchers and rottweilers in the middle of a B and E or, that one time in the process of committing a particularly felonious arson, a German Shepard. That's most likely why he was assigned Cerberus-sitting duty. Oddly, he wasn't even remotely afraid of the three-headed-dog. He had never actually formed an opinion of cats when he was still alive. Cats just were. He'd never realized what assholes they were.

He narrowed his eyes and squinted at the cat. Yellow eyes glowered back at him. He heard the ding heralding the arrival of the elevator just as the cat leaped down from the wall and stalked in his direction like an evil, malicious lion.

"Where in Hell are you going?" The voice was as ancient as dust.

Neil hated to turn his back on that cat, but he needed to get in the elevator in a hurry before someone wandered by.

"Charon, dude, how are you?"

The ancient man holding the elevator doors at bay wore equally ancient and tattered robes. The fabric was probably black at one time, but now the color was a faded and washed out gray. The cowl was thrown back on his neck revealing a slack-skinned, heavily lined face. His skin was as thin and fragile as parchment paper and so transparent you could see the shadows of his bones. Red eyes still sparked with malevolent intelligence, though, as the ferryman took his measure. Neil's skin crawled like it was desperate to get away, as if his body had more sense than he did.

"Where in Hell are you going?" he repeated. Neil wasn't sure at first if he heard the words with his ears, or if the sound just filled his head, but as the pressure grew in his skull it became clear.

He thought of corn chips and Hershey bars and swallowed his fear.

"I really dig the uniform." Neil used his index finger to indicate the red collarless blazer he wore over the robe. In addition to gold epaulets on his shoulders, brass buttons and black velvet trim decorated the front. On top of wispy, white hair sat a jaunty red bellman's cap.

Charon sighed. "My master does have a sense of humor."

"Makes you look spry." He glanced back and that cat was still watching, and he was definitely closer. It occurred to him that maybe the cat was a spy. "So, hey, I'm looking for Cerebus and I need to check the other circles and see if he's wandered down there."

"That dog—" Charon spat out the word with derision "—has not been in my conveyance."

"Right." A quick peek over his shoulder showed the cat was closer yet. "He probably wandered down the long way and I don't have that kind of time to fuck around, you know. I'm gonna need a ride down a few floors to see if I can find him."

With deliberate slowness that sent Neil's anxiety skyrocketing, Charon lifted his palm for payment.

The moment of truth. "So how much does it cost these days for you to ferry me down?"

"A coin." The voice was definitely in his head, which was creepier than Neil could have ever guessed.

"I have these." Neil dangled his keychain in front of the ferryman, causing a merry jingle.

"It's always been a coin."

"These are better than coins," Neil assured him.

Charon's hand didn't falter. His fingers were long and boney with giant arthritic knuckles as big as marbles. His palm hovered there, expectantly.

"Do you have any idea how many coins it would take to buy these keys." He gave them another enticing jingle. "This one right here was for my motorcycle." He finagled it off the ring and set the silver key in the leathery palm.

The fingers curled around the token. "One circle."

"Great!" Neil pushed in beside the ferryman. When he turned and faced front again, the cat was sitting only feet from where Neil had been standing. He was lazily washing a paw, as if uninterested in any of his surroundings, but he knew the beast was probably enjoying a snack of Neil's own blood off his claws.

The doors slipped soundlessly closed and a sinking feeling suggested they descended. Another oddly cheerful chime indicated their arrival and Charon voice filled his head.

"Fourth Circle, looters and hoarders."

CHAPTER TWENTY-THREE

"You understand that Carrie Underwood song would get you arrested for vandalism or worse." Cassie transferred the shopping bags from her right hand to her left and grabbed the escalator handrail. "It's not a how-to instruction for getting even with your ex."

Mia waved her hand dismissively. "I'm not sold on the idea. I was just spit balling."

Cassie put her free hand on Mia's shoulder and patted. "I know, babe. You have every right to be super pissed off, and he deserves punishment. I'm in on whatever shenanigans you come up with, but I'd just as soon not get a mugshot for doing it."

"This is not okay."

"What isn't? Are you hungry? We can go over to that cupcake bakery. Sugar always helps."

Cassie had grown tired of Mia stomping around the house in a state of high dudgeon and had forced her to the mall for some retail therapy. She hated to admit that the change of scenery had helped. She'd looked for peace in the Daughters of Eve's garden, but it was elusive, or she was too restless to find it. She'd felt power in storming around, growling and snarling at the world.

"Yes, to cupcakes." Mia paused to look at some cute strappy

sandals in a store window. "Things must be really bad if you're being the reasonable one."

"Okay, reasonable to a point," Cassie conceded. "Luke Mephisto was a complete dick, and I think reparations are in order, just not ones that come with a felony mischief charge."

Mia didn't care. The last week had been transformative. She kept catching Cassie giving her strange looks, and Mia suspected she knew why. She barely recognized herself. Her entire life she'd been the one to ease other's guilty consciences when they'd wronged her. Those words would come out of her mouth, *I'm fine, don't worry about it*, whatever it took to keep the peace.

Not this time.

Fury simmered just underneath her skin, and it didn't take much to set her off. In fact, this week she found herself looking for trouble, any opportunity to test out this new kick-ass-take-names life philosophy. She wasn't letting anyone off the hook ever again.

She kept remembering an old line she'd heard her father say one time during a particularly tense business negotiation: you mess with the bull, you get the horns.

By god, Luke was going to get the horns.

Mia shrugged. "You'd bail me out." She took Cassie's hand and pulled her towards the store. "I want to try on these shoes."

Ten minutes later, Mia was posing her feet in the mirror, admiring the Louboutin heels from every angle. These were take-no-prisoners, woman-in-control-of-her-life, afraid-of-no-one, woman-warrior shoes.

"Wow," Cassie said for the third time. "Those are amazing, seriously. Can you walk in them?"

Mia nodded. You'd have thought she would have felt precarious balanced on four-inch stiletto heels, but she didn't. Everything about these shoes made her feel powerful. They were sexy, but not cloying. More bad-ass than sex kitten. Candy-apple red leather with two wide buckle straps around the ankle, they also had pointy toes and a cross section of see-through vinyl that made them seem even fiercer. These were the kind of shoes she imagined a dominatrix would wear. Or a

Spartan warrior-woman stomping through a killing field impaling the enemy on her spikes. She told Cassie as much.

Cassie looked at her in mock horror and giggled. "Jeez, you're getting bloodthirsty."

"Find yourself some man-eating shoes. We're going out tonight." Before Cassie could comment, Mia was already texting Beth and Lucy.

She ushered the three of them into the restaurant Luke had taken her to during that early meeting. Mia had this fantasy running in her head she couldn't seem to get rid of—one of the few that didn't involve bodily harm to Luke. She stood at the entrance to the dining room looking for the impertinent waiter from before.

"Who is that waiter?" she asked the hostess and pointed at him across the room.

There might have been a momentary twinge of animosity on the girl's face when she recognized who Mia was indicating. Or maybe not. Mia could have been projecting. "The waiter? That's Gerald."

Mia's smile was filled with venom. "We want to sit in Gerald's section."

The hostess gathered her eyebrows together. "All right. That may extend your wait time."

"I don't care. That's where we want to sit. In Gerald's section." She gathered her warriors with her and signaled to the bar. "We'll wait in there."

Lucy lagged behind, trying to peer into the dining room as they passed. "Who's Gerald? Is he cute?"

"Hell, no, and who gives a shit?" Mia signaled the bartender. Taking in the array of call liquor behind the bar, her gaze landed solidly on the Fireball cinnamon whiskey and the red devil on the label breathing fire. She ordered a round of shots.

Beth took her glass of amber liquid and grimaced. "What is this?"

"Fireball Whiskey," Mia told her and raised her own short glass. "A toast. To not taking shit anymore." She threw back the liquid in one gulp, welcoming the alcohol burn, compounded by the cinnamon flavor, as it went down. When she opened her eyes again, three sets of

AMYLYNN BRIGHT

eyes were trained on her and no one else had shot their whiskey. "What?"

Cassie stared at her with her mouth agape. Beth was still looking disgruntled at her drink.

Lucy waggled her index finger at Mia, up and down, encompassing her outfit, her personality, everything. "What's happening here? Don't get me wrong. I love going out with you twice in two weeks. We never see each other enough anymore, but this is weird. You don't look like you. You're not acting like you. What's going on?"

"Do your shots," Mia told them.

Beth pouted. "I like drinks with umbrellas and fruit."

Mia reached over the bar and fished out two maraschino cherries from the container of garnishes and plopped them in Beth's shot glass. "There."

"And umbrellas," Beth reminded her.

Mia's voice dropped an octave. "Take your shot."

"Okay," Cassie intervened. She took Beth's shot glass and put it on the bar. "Order whatever you want." Then she turned to Mia. "You're going to have to take it down a few notches there, killer."

Lucy took a sip of the shot and frowned. She reached between her friends and set her glass on the bar next to Beth's. Mia immediately scooped it up and drained it. Lucy turned to Cassie and asked, "Will you please tell me what the deal is?"

It wasn't easy telling the story in the bar with the background noise, but Cassie got the gist of the last week across with Mia's interjections of pertinent information.

"That guy from the street fair last weekend?" Beth clarified. "What's his name again?" She immediately started googling on her phone.

Lucy said, "All of this happened in a week? That's, ah, kinda crazy."

"In my defense, it wasn't exactly a week. Cassie and I went to see him fight—"

Beth interrupted by showing a picture on her phone of him in the ring and emphasized this with a wide-eyed expression of awe. "Get a load of this," she exclaimed.

Mia couldn't help looking. He might be a complete asshole, but he

256

was an asshole with a magnificent physique. All six foot four inches of glowering, glorious asshole.

"— and I took him out with me apple hunting."

Beth whistled, a long appreciative note, as she scrolled through everything Google images had on him. "Was he a good kisser? He looks like he could kiss like the devil."

Mia didn't really want to think about his skills—which were legion. She wanted to stay angry. She'd managed this entire week to not let the melancholia get a grip. If she allowed herself to give in and romanticize their time together, she would be lost. There could be no contemplating the slope of his back as it curved into his firm, muscular ass. No picturing the delineated lines of his abs or the sharp edges of his jaw.

The truth of it was, she was hanging onto this fury like a lifeline.

Lucy gave the picture a quick admiring glance, but then ignored Beth. "This was still kind of a whirlwind, though, right? I mean, I think I know what's going on here. The connection was instant, yeah? Hot and heavy right from the get-go, pretty much. You spent one long weekend in bed fucking each other's brains out, and he said all the pretty words, and then BAM—" she exploded her fingers in the air like a chrysanthemum firework, "—he gives you the it's-not-you-it's-me speech. Anyone would be furious."

They followed the hostess to their table and picked up the conversation when they were seated.

"Why would he start in with that fate bullshit?" Mia asked with an emphatic gesture. "What the hell kind of M.O. is that? How many girls has he pulled this 'fated lovers' horseshit on? I'm furious that I fell for it. I'm furious on behalf of all women, everywhere."

"I, for one, am very appreciative." Cassie said.

Beth was back on her phone. "I say get right back on that horse. You need a rebound guy."

"I do not need a rebound guy," Mia announced just as the waiter rolled up. She waited for him to recognize her, but his eyes just scanned right over her, dipped briefly to her cleavage and then on to the next faceless pair of boobs at the table. Mia felt the simmer in her gut tick up a notch.

"That's a shame," he drawled. "I am happy to apply for the position of rebound guy for any one of you."

He clearly hadn't learned how to read a table any better since the last time she was here. He received four sets of raised eyebrows in response.

"What can I bring you ladies to drink?"

They ordered more drinks and Mia watched him with laser intensity the entire time. Even when he was talking directly to her, there wasn't a glimmer of recognition. That could only mean he was such an unmitigated misogynist prick to so many women he wouldn't even remember a specific instance. The simmer was nearing a full boil by the time he'd left.

"It's a really good thing you're not able to set him on fire by looking at him," Cassie told her. "You remember Liz from Hell Boy? How she could spontaneously combust when she was furious? That's how you look."

Mia reminded her about the incident with the waiter and how Luke had taken him out during that early meeting.

"Oh, my god," Cassie said, looking around for the waiter again. "That's why you wanted to sit in this section. A little transference. Oh, this is going to be good. You channel all of that animosity into eating him alive. I will get arrested with you for that."

"Or instead of jail, we can get her a rebound guy." Beth piped back in. "I signed you up for Tinder."

"When?" Mia shrieked. "No!"

"Just now. It's fine." Beth waved a hand dismissively in the face of her reluctance. "All right, ladies. Let's start swiping."

Beth extended her phone to the middle of the table where they could all see the guys who came up in her feed. "Nope. Nope. Oh, look, this one's cute."

"No."

"Okay, how about this one?" Beth asked.

"Look at the size of his nostrils," Cassie said. "You could fit carrots in there."

"Okay, no, no, no." Beth continued swiping left. "Oh, I like this guy. He looks nice. Look, he has a dog."

Lucy screwed up her face. "And what looks like a cold sore on his lip."

Three faces inched closer to the screen and then recoiled.

"Ew."

"Ohmygod."

"Gag."

"Calm down," Beth said. "Clearly, he's a no." She swiped her finger.

The waiter showed up with their drinks and some more smarm. When he asked if they were ready to place their orders, Mia smirked. She requested the same meal she'd done the previous time, exorcizing the morbid curiosity of whether or not her convoluted request would trigger his memory. It did not. However, this time she was actually hoping he jacked it up.

"I dare you to show up at this table with raw meat," she told his retreating form. Tonight, it was take no prisoners.

"I don't get it." Cassie shook her head. "If you want to yell at the guy, just yell at him."

"No," Lucy interjected in horror. "I don't want any spit in my food."

Mia laughed. "I don't want to just yell at him. I want to eviscerate him, but I'd like him to hang himself first. He needs to earn it. Otherwise, I'm just a bitch."

Cassie gestured towards Mia like a game show hostess. "See. Bloodthirsty."

Beth wiggled her phone. "Shall we keep looking?"

"God, no," Mia told her. "Seriously. I'm off men. All I want to do is nurture this burning fury. There is no Y chromosome individual who would stand a chance with me right now."

"I'm not giving up on you," Beth told her, but she tucked away her phone.

Lucy patted her hand and shrugged, sounding like a little Jewish grandmother. "So you get through this stage. You get all the angry out first. Finding your empowerment is brilliant. You're always too nice, if you ask me. The person you should really be yelling at is Luke."

Beth played with the umbrella from her fruity drink. "What are you going to do about work? Don't you have to finish this project together?"

That just brought up another sore point. Now that the contracts were signed, she couldn't escape. She put Jason in charge of all communications with Luke's team that weren't on paper. She was also furious at herself for getting involved in a work romance. She absolutely knew better than to get involved with a colleague, but she'd been led astray by fantastical words and a beautiful body.

She was a fool. A fool who should have known better.

"Enough." She wiped her hands across the tablecloth as if erasing the entire topic. "Tell me about your week."

Mia did her best to listen and participate in the conversation, but underneath her outrage, she was exhausted. She hadn't been sleeping. Well, actually, she'd been sleeping, but not waking up rested. She'd wake up in the morning, her head full of the craziest dreams that seemed to disappear like fog as she came awake. She'd brought a journal with her to bed hoping that if she wrote them down immediately after waking, she'd remember more, but as she read back over what she'd written, she was even more confused.

They weren't nightmares exactly, but her recollections were full of terrifying imagery that certainly signified they should have been. She always woke up sweating and breathless, but not screaming. She tried to organize the themes from her notes into something cohesive, but none of it seemed to make sense. What the hell would a therapist think of dreams filled with red-skinned creatures with horns and tails, pits of fire, and unbearable heat? Probably that she was crazy. All of it fit into a classical description of hell. One thing that didn't fit into the whole scheme was the man. He was in every dream. Remarkably handsome and full of charisma, he met her every night. It wasn't sexual, though. He would loop her arm with his and escort her though the horrific landscape as if he was the smoothest tour guide taking a nun through a prison camp. She couldn't remember any of their conversations, but that's all they did: talk. Then she would wake up in the morning with the strangest combination of unease and contentment.

A plate appeared in front of her, shattering her reverie.

The slow boil ramped up as she looked at it. As opposed to last time, at least this time there was pasta on her plate. Not angel hair pasta. Of course not. How could a restaurant of this caliber have a waiter this inept?

Honest to god, it was like he was doing it intentionally.

"What is this?" she asked him, daring him to respond to her like he'd done before.

"Pasta."

"I ordered angel hair. This is linguini."

Next to Mia, Cassie sat back in her chair, crossed her arms, and allowed Mia to do what they'd come here for. On the other side of the table, Lucy and Beth followed the conversation like they were watching a tennis match, moving their head back and forth

"Linguini pasta with light tomato and extra carrots," the waiter recited, looking up at the ceiling as if the words were written there.

"Not even close," Mia exclaimed. "I requested pasta pomodoro with angel hair and no onions. This is the second time you've screwed up my order."

He pursed his lips together, and there was the slightest flair of his nostrils. "It will take longer to have it remade."

Mia raised her eyebrows and maintained a calm tone. "Are you suggesting that I should just shut up and eat the wrong meal because it would be inconvenient for you?"

All three ladies' heads followed the volley back to the waiter.

He paused one second, then another, before replying, "No. I will have the kitchen redo it."

He extracted her plate and left in a huff.

Lucy watched him walk away with her mouth hanging open. "Is that how he was when you were here before?"

"Exactly," Mia said, her eyes narrowing as she watched his back as he made his way through the dining room.

"Only last time he brought a barely dead cow," Cassie informed the other ladies. "And our Mia was just going to let him get away with it. That was her and Luke's first date and—"

"It was a business meeting, not a date," Mia interjected.

"—and Luke ripped him a new one for her." Cassie finished and raised her hand to Mia, "Not that doing that redeems him in any way, but it was nice that he stood up for you."

Mia made a face. "I always got the feeling that he enjoyed that little scene for his own benefit, not for the sake of defending a damsel or something." She gestured to the other's plates. "Please don't wait for me. Mine may never show up. Eat."

Cassie told the ladies about the weddings she was helping to plan, and Beth told a story about her brother that had them all pealing with laughter. No one touched their plates, the others too polite to eat while she had nothing. The time stretched on and their sauces congealed.

"Really, you guys, eat."

"No," Beth shook her head. "We're all in this together."

"Absolutely," Lucy agreed.

Half an hour later, the waiter showed up, his expression a challenge. He placed the bowl in front of her: angel hair pasta with fresh tomatoes and what was very clearly onions.

"Do you have a problem with me or just women in general?" Mia asked him, but all he did in response was stare back at her blankly. "I'm going to need to see the manager."

He turned on his heel and marched away. The manager appeared moments later. Gerald was nowhere to be seen. Mia succinctly explained the situation, detailing her first experience and the one this evening. "Truly, I cannot imagine an establishment of this quality allowing this. It's not just that he can't get an order correct, it's that he is also unbearably rude. It's not possible that I am the first person to complain about him."

"I'm so sorry you've had such a frustrating experience." The manager's smile was pained. "Yours is not the first complaint. Unfortunately, there's not much I can do about him."

"The answer is simple. You fire him." Mia couldn't understand why this was up for debate. The man was a liability.

"I really wish it was that easy. The owner of this restaurant is Vaso Georgiadis. Your waiter's name is Gerald Georgiadis."

All four women responded at once, "Oh." Well, that explained everything.

The manager not only refired all of their meals since they'd all waited so long, but also comped the entire table and sent over a bottle of wine. She personally delivered Mia's correct order to the table less than five minutes later.

Mia's blood returned to a gentle simmer. She felt like she'd stood up for herself even if the waiter wasn't going to get fired. They finished their dinner with laughter and jokes, and Mia's mood was much improved with her victory over one of the blights in her life.

She hardly thought about Luke once.

Until she went to sleep and the mysterious man met her at the edge of her dreams. For one astonishing moment, she thought he was Luke.

CHAPTER TWENTY-FOUR

L uke growled and hit the end button on his phone and shoved it back in his pocket. This time he didn't leave a message in the void. It wouldn't do any good. He needed to come up with a different plan.

"She's still not taking your calls?" Ethan asked, with a sympathetic shake of his head. "You know what they say, Thirty-second time's the charm."

"Do you think she blocked me?"

His cousin shrugged. "Either that or she's exceptionally good at ignoring you."

"Honestly it would serve him right." Jeb was unrelenting in his criticism. "If I were her, I'd never talk to you again," Jeb told him and threw Luke's dry cleaning on the living room sofa instead of putting it away in the closet. The clear plastic bags which held the suits began a slow, slippery slide down the arm of the couch until they hit the floor in a shiny heap. To punctuate his point, Jeb walked away and left them there ostensibly to rot.

Ethan sipped from a tumbler of amber liquid, one leg crossed lazily over the other knee. Luke had finally decamped from Ethan's home to his own and Ethan had followed along because he didn't have anything else more entertaining to keep him busy.

"Send her flowers," Ethan said. "Chicks always appreciate flowers."
Jeb appeared at the edge of the living room. "Surely you're kidding. This is Mia, not some floozy Luke wants to get back into bed again sometime soon."

Ethan smirked. "I'll bet he does."

"You're not helping," Luke told his cousin. "Don't get him riled up, please."

His cousin laughed. "But it's so easy. Look at him twitch."

Jeb turned to face Luke, ignoring Ethan completely. "You cannot do anything as pedestrian as send Mia flowers. You need a grand gesture." He drew a big circle in the air with his hands. "Something magnificent."

"Send a lot of flowers then," Ethan said.

"That could work." Luke pulled out his phone and googled florists. Ethan always had the pulse of what was new, big, now. "If I send enough of them, she can't ignore that."

Now with his hands on his hips, Jeb's voice lowered an octave. For a moment, Luke felt a twinge of what a gargoyle would be like when pressed into battle. Gargoyles were protective by nature, and they could be fierce when necessary. "Fine. You do whatever you're going to do and hopefully you don't fuck it all up beyond repair. When you're serious about getting Mia back, you come find me." He turned on his heel and was gone.

"Shit. He's so dramatic. Mordecai may be a pain, but at least I don't have to deal with—" Ethan waved his hand in a big circle, mimicking Jeb's gesture earlier, "—that prissy bullshit."

Luke considered running after Jeb and asking for help, but reconsidered. He was a grown-ass man and he should be able to figure out how to get his woman back. Besides, Ethan should know. After scrolling through the florist websites, they picked one with a five-star Yelp rating.

"This one." Ethan poked his finger at a review for Glory's Garden. "Says, 'magical floral artistry.' These are some hella, magical flowers. And you can order them right online."

Luke scrunched his nose, unsure. "But how big are they exactly? I can't tell from these pictures. There's nothing to give them any scale."

"Good point. It would be very helpful if they had like a bottle of wine or something next to them so you could tell." Ethan scrolled up with his finger. "Jeez, flowers are expensive."

"I don't care how much they cost," Luke closed down the phone. "I want to make sure they're done right. I'm going down there in person."

Ethan tagged along because, well, why the hell not.

The florist at Glory's Garden was damn near as tall as Luke and certainly bigger around. He wore a massive oilcloth apron the color of moss with snippers sticking out of the front pocket, but stretched across his bulk it looked like a napkin. The man gazed at him from across the counter, expectation in his expression. "How can I help you?"

"I need some apology flowers," Luke told him and pulled out his phone. "On the way over here, I googled which ones I should get. There is a whole language of flowers, you know."

His pleasant smile morphed into one of patience. "I did actually."

"That makes sense," Luke nodded and looked at Ethan who had wandered to the other side of the small store and was smelling various plants. "I made a list of what I want. Let's start with a dozen filberts."

"Filberts?" the florist repeated. "Why?"

"It says here they mean reconciliation."

"Do you know what filberts are?" the other man asked. When Luke consulted his phone instead of answering, the florist told him. "They're hazelnuts. Or rather the tree where hazelnuts come from. Are you sure that's what you want?"

"You should get her some hazelnut chocolates," Ethan suggested from behind him.

"That'd be better. Okay, forget the filberts." Luke scrolled back through his list. "Instead, how about a couple dozen star of Bethlehem'? They're also for atonement and reconciliation."

The flower guy screwed up his forehead. "What now?"

Luke turned his phone towards him, and the other man peered at it. Moving along the counter, he pulled out a well-worn glossy catalogue. He licked his finger and started flipping through the pages.

"Hmmm. Here we go. Star of Bethlehem. *Ornithogalum.*" He looked up at Luke and then back to the page. "Southern Europe and southern Africa. Yeah, I don't have these."

"Oh. Can you get them?"

"No. These are not the normal kind of flower that you'd come in here for. There isn't anyone in town who has these."

"Money is no object," he told the florist.

He frowned back down at the page and shook his head. His tone was disintegrating from helpful to vexed. "I wouldn't even know where to start. I guess I can try, but we're talking weeks, maybe months, until I can get them in. If I can find a distributor. And they're in season."

Ethan rejoined the conversation. "That's too long. Hey, what flowers mean hot monkey sex?"

Luke gave him a look and spun his finger in a circle suggesting that Ethan and his smirk should turn around and go back to smelling flowers. Back to the florist, "That is too long. I need her to forgive me now."

Ethan had teased him about it, but Luke had no real desire to defend himself from his cousin's accusations. Yes, maybe Mia had made him squishy and soft, but if that's the way it was, then Luke was good with it. He was turning into a giant teddy bear. He didn't want to be anything else.

"Any chance on a lotus flower?" he asked, expecting the worst. "They mean estranged love."

"Well, dude, I don't have them in the shop." The florist consulted the catalog again. "But I can get some for you. They would only take about a week to get as many as you're asking about."

Maybe he was a teddy bear with itchy stuffing because this was making him grumpy. "Is this a flower shop or what? Is there someone else, an owner perhaps?"

The huge man pivoted and pointed to a large, framed newspaper article behind him. Luke wasn't about to squint at the entire article, but the headline and picture accompanying it suggested the man in front of him had once been a star football player, Carl "Glory" Wilson, who'd been injured while making some miraculous touchdown. Apparently it had been a game-ending injury and now he'd opened a florist shop. Luke gazed back at the corpulent fellow and found it unlikely Glory had ever run anywhere.

"You don't have any of the flowers I'm asking for." Luke tried to keep the whine out of his voice. Magical or no, this was troubling.

Glory Vanna Whited the show room with a grand sweeping gesture. "We have lots and lots of plants. I'm certain I can accommodate you if you ask for a normal flower. What else do you have on that list?"

"Just get her hazelnut chocolates," Ethan called from inside a walk-in refrigerator.

Luke gritted his jaw and scrolled through the list again. "Primroses? Hyacinths, purple ones? Gladiolus?"

"Now you're talking." Glory came from behind the counter and gestured for him to follow. When Luke turned, he whacked his head with a hanging plant. How the hell did that giant manage to walk through the place without violating all the displays? "Primroses are usually in the form of a plant. Here." The owner pulled a potted plant with sweet lavender flowers from a grouping of ferny-looking greenery. "Primrose."

While it was a cute little plant, it wasn't really the showstopper he was looking for. "I'd need like a thousand of these."

"Well, hold on to that one." He directed him towards the walk-in. "Hyacinth and Gladiolus are bulb flowers. They're really very striking and dramatic. Probably what you're going for. Let's see how many I have."

In a big bucket on the floor, Glory plucked out four light purple hyacinths. "What color for the gladiolas?"

"It doesn't say. Any, I guess."

Glory grabbed the entire bucket of flowers. Upon exiting, Luke slid a cotter pin into a slot on the handle, locking Ethan inside. It only took a second for Ethan to start banging. Luke chuckled at him from the warm side of the glass door. Ethan flipped his cousin his middle finger and mouthed threats before Glory made Luke let him out again.

Back at the counter, the three of them surveyed what they'd gathered. About thirty multi-colored gladioli, four purple hyacinth, and a potted pink primrose. "I need a lot more. Like a lot, a lot."

"I don't know," Ethan said. "All of this and some chocolates. That should make her happy." Luke shook his head and Ethan held out his hand. "Okay, give me the list."

Glory started grouping the flowers on the counter. "I can make a great arrangement with these. It will be big and impressive."

"Here you go. This is totally perfect." Ethan told them. "Fleur de Lis."

"Those are actually irises," Glory told them. "We have a bunch of those."

Luke was suspicious. Ethan was staring at him with a totally straight face which was clue number one. "What do they mean?"

"Flames. Burning," Ethan read from the list on Luke's phone.

Luke narrowed his eyes at him. "You need to stop talking." Luke looked to the professional. "What else do you suggest?"

"Good lord, dude. What did you do?"

"He's a moron," Ethan volunteered, "of monumental proportions. Elephantine." He spread his hands wide. "Colossal."

Luke rolled his eyes. "This moron is correct."

"I get a lot of guys in here buying apology flowers. Usually they're satisfied with a dozen roses."

Luke bowed his head, resigned. "Fine. All of the roses you have or can get your hands on. What's that look like?"

"I'm sure I can get twelve to fifteen dozen," Glory told him and Ethan whistled.

"Great. With all these, too." He gave him his credit card and Mia's address. "Deliver by the end of today?"

"Throw in the irises," Ethan said as they left. "I'll pay for those."

Now all Luke had to do was wait until she called.

At eight o'clock, Luke sat in his car looking at Mia's house across the street. He knew the flowers had been delivered. Glory had sent him a text when it had been completed. It had been four hours and nothing from Mia.

He didn't know what to do. Should he call her? Was it possible she didn't know about the flowers? He checked for the millionth time that there weren't any new texts and his ringer was definitely on.

Jeb was AWOL, so he couldn't ask him. Ethan was busy being an asshole. He was embarrassed to ask his aunt again after all she'd already done.

He saw figures moving behind the drapes in her living room. "All right," he said aloud. "This is ridiculous. Go ring the bell and beg."

He combed his fingers through his hair, straightened his shirt, and took a deep breath before ringing her bell. Insane barking sounded from the other side, a deep woof that made the window vibrate. No one answered the bell even after Luke had counted to sixty and the dog had settled down. A sense of dread filled his gut like cement. It was stupid, but he rang the bell again anyway. The dog started up again, barking like a psychotic monster. He was almost ready to walk away when the door finally yanked open.

Mia's friend Cassie pushed the dog back, a giant black and white creature with a rabid look in his eyes. "Was this you?" she demanded. He opened his mouth to answer, but she talked over him. "All these flowers? This is ridiculous."

He braved getting closer to the house and closer to the dog so he could look past her into Mia's place. Every surface and much of the floor was covered in roses.

"I'm downing Benadryl like Tic Tacs." To emphasize her point, she sneezed.

"Bless you," he said, because that was the polite thing to say. "Is Mia here?"

"She doesn't want to see you."

The concrete in his stomach shifted. "I just want to talk to her for a minute."

Cassie paused for a heartbeat and looked, if only for a second, like she was going to take pity on him. She shook her head. "I'm sorry."

"Did she get the chocolates?" He was definitely an idiot, but he had to ask. As unlikely as it was, what if that was the thing that nudged him into the clear.

"Yes, the chocolates and eighty thousand roses."

He swallowed. "And the purple ones and the Gladioli? And the cute little potted one?"

She raised her eyebrows. "Yes. Every flower in this town is here. How much did this cost you?"

"It doesn't matter," he told her.

"Knowing her like you do, I can't believe you sent her dead flowers."

"In my defense, the primroses were potted." Her expression didn't change. He bent his head. "I just wanted to get her attention."

"Well, that did it. And you fucked yourself royally with them. Honestly, flowers? So stupid."

His heart sank. "What? Why?"

"She never told you? Oh my God, she never told you." Cassie sighed. "Her father used to send her mother flowers every time he screwed up, which was all the time. It was a hollow, meaningless gesture from him, and I know that's the way Mia took this, too. There honestly couldn't have been a worse move you could have made."

Luke scrubbed his hand over his lips and squeezed his eyes shut. Shit, shit, shit.

Now there really was pity in her eyes. "So, what's Plan C?"

He had no idea and now he was going to have to go apologize to the person who *would* have a plan. "Please tell her to call me."

Cassie shrugged and shut the door on him.

Fuuuuck. Now he was going to have to beg Jeb which he should have done from the get-go. He clamped his jaw tight and stalked to his car.

"You really sent her flowers?" Jeb asked, shaking his head. "Why would you send her dead plants?"

Jeb had been waiting in his kitchen when Luke got home, smug and self-important.

Luke swallowed back some nasty retorts. He needed Jeb's help, so he was going to have to suck it up for a few minutes. "I was just trying to get her attention. I sent hundreds of them."

"Why would you listen to Envy," Jeb asked, referring to Ethan. "What the hell does he know about romance?"

Truth be told, Luke had no idea why he listened to his cousin, except that Envy always knew what other people wanted. This time Luke had hoped it could work in his favor. As usual, Jeb was right. It was possible Ethan meant well, but it's not like he was a role model of successful love affairs. But then again, none of the Seven had any long-term relationships.

"In my defense, it would have worked in a romantic movie."

Jeb just rolled his eyes, hands on hips, looking petulant. Fortunately, he was easier to placate than Mia. Luke slid his Black Amex card across the counter. "Buy yourself something pretty."

Jeb pursed his lips and snatched up the bribe. He tucked the card into his pocket and then perked right up. "Fortunately for you, I will help."

Luke told Jeb what he'd found on Google. After Jeb's jaw hit the floor, he declared Luke brilliant and then took over on the laptop, making arrangements. In less than a half an hour, Jeb handed Luke his passport. A carryon suitcase sat by the door.

It was an ingenious, if complicated idea. It involved thirty hours of flying, counting air time and layovers, and four different planes. He managed a fitful nap in the Dublin airport before his connection to Cardiff, Wales. From there, he paid a fishing trawler an exorbitant amount of money to take him out to Bardsey Island, a wretched, nausea-inducing ride on choppy seas.

Once he stepped foot on the tiny Welsh island, he was swamped with anxiety. It was as if the island itself wanted him to know he was not welcome. He pushed back against the feeling. He was here for a specific task, and nothing was going to stop him.

He quickly discovered the only vehicle anywhere on the island was a tractor, one, and it was currently busy on the farm, singular. He managed to borrow a bicycle from the lighthouse keeper and obtain iffy directions to *Plas Bach* house. Once he got on the thin, worn track that sufficed as a lane in the erstwhile town that had no other motor vehicles, he peddled towards the site. Although it was less than a mile across the entire island, his trek was miserable going. He wasn't sure if Welsh lighthouse keepers were small as a rule, or if it was just his dumb luck to be stuck on the bicycle of the world's shortest civil servant. Unless he pedaled with his knees spread akimbo it was impossible not to bang them against the handlebars on every upstroke. And the back tire might have been flat. If there wasn't what the internet promised at the end of the journey, he would be bruised for nothing.

His destination was relatively easy to spot once he drew close. There were only about eight buildings on the entire island, including the lighthouse. This one was a two-story, stone home which Luke had to admit looked warm and inviting in contrast to the salty wind whipping his hair and flapping his jacket lapels. Near the house, hunched over like an ancient druid sat the crumbling remains of a thirteenth-century abbey. Only a stone tower stood in the center of a graveyard to mark where the ancient building had been. He steered the bicycle away from the cemetery and the sacred site. There was no place like a holy one to remind the Sins they had been forsaken and were wholly unloved by God.

He knocked on the door to *Plas Bach*, painted a curiously cheery red, and was pleasantly surprised when a gentleman opened the door and not a berobed monk of yore. "Good afternoon," Luke said.

The man raised an eyebrow, looking every bit like he was cast by a BBC production of Luke Goes to Great Britain. He wore warm-looking flannel pants and a tweed jacket over a workman's shirt. His hair was as wild as it was white, and his cheeks were ruddy, wind-blown, and chapped. Luke imagined the wind and rain dictated most fashion choices on this bleak and comfortless island.

"*Prynhawn da,*" the man said. His expression was amiable enough that Luke assumed the incomprehensible words were friendly.

"I've come very far, from America, to get apples." Luke blinked at the man who blinked back. "Apples. You know—" he cupped his hands in a reasonable facsimile of the size of an apple. Then he pretended to bite it. "Apples."

"*Afalau,*" the man said and nodded. "*Dod gyda mi.*" He stepped over the threshold and jerked his head to the side of the house. Luke hopped to and followed the man across the yard and around the corner.

There, growing in a recessed corner of the house, grew the world's rarest apple. Rumored to be a thousand years old, the tree was gnarled and as weathered as everything else on the remote island. It flourished there, crammed up against an inverted corner of the house, protected from the brutal salty wind. Dozens of pink-striped apples hung from its scrabbly branches. This was the only tree in the entire world which grew the Bardsey Island Apple.

The man plucked a fruit from the tree, pulled out a pocketknife, and cut a wedge from the apple which he offered to Luke. Dripping in juice, the crisp sweet flavor filled his mouth and made him smile. Only weeks before, he would never have detected the faint lemon aroma or the pleasantly crisp finish, but Mia had been a good teacher and Luke a rapt pupil.

It took a lot of hand gestures and the flash of cash, but eventually Luke filled a basket with fruit and convinced the Welsh-speaking caretaker to gift him some cuttings. The man wrapped them tenderly with some sort of foul-smelling compound and then in newspaper. All the while, Luke babbled to the man about Mia and her splendid knowledge of apples. He told him how she was an apple detective herself and would be so excited at the prospect of growing her own Bardsey Apples.

Balancing all of this on his bicycle, he rode against the wind, banging his knees, back to where he'd left the fisherman. The trip had been hellish, long, and exhausting, but Luke had never felt such a sense of righteousness as he did while undertaking this Herculean effort to bring Mia something she would truly value.

The roses and candy had been a massive miscalculation. An insult, almost.

This had to work. It felt right.

Luke didn't know what he would do if this failed, too.

HELL IX

With a disconcerting shudder, the elevator door creaked open on the Fourth Circle pausing the elevator music, a bunch of third-graders playing Ring of Fire on kazoos. Neil peeked out. The landscape stretched further than he could see, a rocky expanse with no discernable features.

"It doesn't look so bad," he said to Charon. He moved to the edge of the doorway and peered around the side. More boulders. "Kinda rocky. What's that all about?"

Charon did a bored, one shoulder shrug. "Don't know. Don't care."

For the first time, Neil noticed a desk set to the side of the elevator platform. Letters hung from the front in peeling paint. Information esk. The "D" was missing and the "f" was askew. He turned back to the elevator operator. "What's with the desk?"

Charon blinked at him. "Information."

"Duh. Is there one of these on all the circles?"

Again, with the shrug. "Yeah."

"I never noticed one on Three before." Granted, Neil hadn't spent much time at the elevator on his own circle, but he really didn't remember seeing an information desk there before.

Charon leveled his dry gaze on Neil. "Maybe Gluttony ate it. Look, are you getting out here or not?"

Neil tossed his hands up in surrender. "Yes. But if I don't find the dog here, then I'm gonna need to go further down."

Charon put his finger on the close door button. "Ring for the elevator. Make sure you have payment." Then the doors slid shut with a thunk.

Once outside the cabin of the lift, Neil immediately noticed the rise in temperature. It was at least fifty degrees hotter down here. He flapped the front of his jacket to create some ventilation, but it didn't help.

Intrigued by the idea of an information desk, he skirted a couple of boulders and clambered over some of the bigger stones to stand before the desk, which was really more of a counter. Reaching down he grabbed the "D" from the ground and brushed the dust off to reveal peeling gold paint. There was no one at the desk, and Neil didn't know what to do with the retrieved letter.

He leaned over the counter to see if anyone was down there. You never knew in hell. Some of the lesser imps and goblins were pretty small. No one was hunkered down behind either. A bell sat on the desk with a hand-written sign that said, Ring for Service, just like you'd find at a regular office. He couldn't resist and tapped his fingers on the plunger in a rapid staccato rhythm. Nothing happened. No uniformed information desk person appeared.

He glanced around the Fourth Circle to confirm no one was around before walking around the back side of the desk. He didn't know what he thought he was going to find there, but it was a letdown, nevertheless. The caps of some old pens, crumpled-up paper, and what looked like fingernail clippings were scattered on the shelf under the desk.

"Eww." He plucked a pen cap from the shelf with the tip of his fingers and poked at the clippings, intrigued and disgusted at the same time. He counted sixteen of them, thick and yellowed with age before he realized in horror that they weren't actually fingernails, but claws. He straightened with alarm and threw the pen cap back into the pile. "Gross."

Still, there was no one in sight—not only no one to man the desk, but no one anywhere. No ghouls, no imps, no goblins. It was kind of weird. He wondered if Four was always like this, because if it was, he'd consider relocating. Would anyone notice if he picked up his stuff on Three and just disappeared? Scourge would, and he'd probably narc him out, the little bastard.

Absently, he jingled the plunger on the bell, playing the rhythm of Jingle Bells, which he found hysterical considering where he was. It was in the middle of a rousing rendition of Mary Had a Little Lamb that he noticed someone was responding to the summons.

Or something was responding.

The wind created by the flapping of its massive wings caused his hair to ruffle into his eyes.

Neil had always secretly loved having wings. He shouldn't; they were part of his punishment. But they were truly badass. He wished his boys back on Earth could have seen them. They'd have shit their pants once they got a load of them, especially when the leathery skin was stretched tight when they were wide open. And the chicks. Man, based on how the little angel had responded, he'd have been beating the live girls off with sticks. Being dead sucked. Then again, he wouldn't have had wings when he was alive.

Or the dreamlike chance to let an angel pet them.

Still, his had nothing on this demon's wings. Easily three times larger, these wings were leathery like his own but blood-red instead of black. With one last massive beat of those terrible wings, the creature rose vertically in the air before settling a pair of hooves onto the rocky dirt behind the desk. Trying for nonchalance and hoping that he didn't look like he was retreating, Neil scrambled to put the surface of the desk between them.

"You rang?" the demon growled, the sound coming from deep inside a gargantuan chest. Neil was used to the imps on Three. There wasn't anything intimidating about the pesky goblins like Scourge, at least on their own. Only when they got together in a pack were they dangerous. This monster, though, it was scary as hell. He looked like the Hulk, if the Hulk was red.

And had whopping big, twisty horns.

And huge, hairy fucking goat legs with honest-to-God hooves.

And wings that created their own weather system.

Neil ogled, too gobsmacked by the sheer size of the behemoth to speak.

"Was that you?" One heavily muscled arm as big around as a tree trunk extended to point to the bell.

Unable to lie, Neil found his head nodding almost of its own accord. "Yes."

He watched in fascination as the bell was swallowed up inside the demon's fist and then disappeared down the monster's gullet.

"Need anything to wash that down with?" Neil tried for flippancy, but inside his jacket he was quaking.

"I hate that bell." The tenor of his voice resonated like the thumping bass in an old lowrider.

"Right. Uhh, sorry about that." He heartily hoped the bell hit the spot, because Neil sincerely did not wish to be eaten in the same manner. In another life, Neil would have made sure the bigger, badder banger was his friend, or attempt to make him so. He made a fist and extended it to the creature in lieu of a handshake. "I'm Neil."

The demon stared down at him without blinking. Ten treacherous seconds ticked by while the fiend stared at him before an absolutely enormous fist came toward him and they bumped. Neil exhaled.

"Mammon," the creature growled his own introduction.

Neil nodded and smiled at him. "Dude, I've heard of your work. You're famous, even on Three." Smile and flatter, he repeated the mantra and resisted the urge to flee. "Where is everyone? Is this place always this dead?"

Dead. Ha. Neil absolutely did not laugh.

Mammon's gaze moved off Neil, and it actually felt like there was less gravity, the demon's attention had been so heavy.

"It's beating day," Mammon said, his tone so matter-of-fact that Neil thought he should already know what that means.

"Well, that sounds...horrible."

"You're late," Mammon's expression darkened. Now his skin wasn't just blood red, but the color of blood after it had darkened and coagulated.

"For what?" Neil asked and then it dawned on him. "Oh, no! No. No, I'm not here for the beatings. I'm here to find the Devil's dog.

Have you seen Cerberus? I'm supposed to bring him back with me, and if I show up missing and there's no dog, either, well, then, the Devil is going to be very put out. You know what I mean?"

"No beating?" The colossus deflated the tiniest bit, his disappointment evident.

"Not this time. Maybe I can come down again, though, huh? When I'm not in such a time crunch. That sounds like something I should really take my time with, if I want to enjoy it properly. I knew a guy on Earth who used to take all day to kill someone. A real artist, like you. I'm sure I'm really missing out on something fantastic. Like I said, you're legendary on Three." He made himself stop babbling and turn the attention back on the dog. If they could talk about Cerberus, maybe he could figure out a way to shift the conversation to Rachel. "So, have you seen the dog? Big, three heads, vicious and mean?"

"I know that dog," Mammon said. "He crapped in the dungeon."

Neil had to clench his jaw to keep from laughing. This infamous demon whose sole job it was to torture the greedy sounded like a put-out grandmother whose puppy refused to be housetrained. "Yeah, he's an awful dog. Has he been around?"

"No. If he was any other dog, I would eat him."

No laughing. "Perfectly reasonable response. I just thought he might have wandered down here the long way. Maybe he has a friend or someone he likes to visit. A lady?"

"No one likes that dog," Mammon assured him. "Try Scorchy's. Someone there would know."

"What's Scorchy's?"

"Demon bar on Six."

"You're telling me there's a bar? On Six? For Demons?" How the hell did he not know about this? A fucking bar? All this time there'd been a bar. Damn it!

"No humans." Mammon shook his head. Smoke trailed off his horns.

Oh, there it was. Part of Neil's Hell was obviously that there was a bar he wasn't allowed to go to.

. . .

WHEN THE ELEVATOR opened on Six, Neil was grateful. The current entertainment consisted of a pan flute rendition of "The Number of the Beast" by Iron Maiden. A wave of heat filled every inch of the elevator, as if it was a sentient being. He stepped out, lighter this time by the key to his old studio apartment thanks to Charon, and looked for the Information Desk. A weathered iron table covered in rusty patches burned at the edges of the elevator platform.

In fact everything burned. It looked like the entire Circle was on fire. Buildings blazed all around without the risk of collapsing. Red and orange flames licked the feet of sinners digging in the distance. Black, charred trees continually burned.

When Neil had been a little kid and the nuns talked about Hell, this was what they were talking about. This fucking sucked.

A demon with his hair literally on fire manned the desk. He raised one flaming eyebrow when Neil approached. "What brings you to Six?" Black smoke escaped his mouth as he spoke, as if he was even on fire on the inside.

Neil watched with fascinated dread as a smoke ring morphed into the shape of a ghastly clown and then dissipated into nothingness.

"Scorchy's."

"No humans allowed."

Neil leaned forward and whispered. "Mammon sent me." It was worth a shot.

Old Flaming Hair squinted at him and adopted a sarcastic tone. "Did he show you the secret handshake?" When Neil remained silent, the demon continued. "Where do you think you are? A speakeasy? Some kind of club? This is Hell. You're with the heretics now. Six isn't some cakewalk like Four."

Neil felt heat licking his ankles and realized he'd miscalculated. "Oh no, sir. I can see that. You are definitely scarier than the others." He shifted in his boots trying to pull his toes away from the source of heat. There wasn't any feeling in his feet already. "I'm trying to find Cerberus and Mammon thought Scorchy's was the best place to look."

The demon sat back and the heat on Neil's feet and legs eased slightly. "You're the keeper of the dog?"

Ooh, he needed to be careful here. Mammon hated that dog almost as much as Scourge did. There was an excellent chance that this demon would, too. "Mostly, I'm the dog seeker. No one really 'keeps' that dog."

"If you go to the bar, will you find that dog and take it with you?"

Neil would promise the world if the burning would stop. "Yes. Definitely."

The fire demon relented and gave him directions that consisted of hiking through the fire field to the Highway to Hell. Scorchy's Roadhouse was across from the tombs. Neil didn't hike, he trotted. Walking was too slow. He didn't like leaving his feet on the ground that long. He kept checking the soles of his boots, expecting them to be melted, but they weren't. Yet another of the pleasantries of Hell. Here, you could burn forever.

"You should use your wings, asshole," he told himself. "What would that angel think if she knew you were too scared to fly with those wings she thought were so fucking cool?"

But he wouldn't fly, no matter how much he loved it. He cast his eyes to air above them and shuddered. The sky in Hell was full of spine-tingling terrors that equaled the monsters on the ground. Winged cats, demons, and other creatures he didn't even know the names of circled lazily above. No, he had these amazing wings, but he stayed on the relative safety of the ground where he could use his wits and avoid talons.

Scorchy's looked like every roadhouse on Earth. The building was held up by will alone. Paint peeled from the fascia in long strips and the windows were cracked. The door sat propped open. Neil couldn't tell if that was to let the heat in or out. Music leaked from the doorway, bluesy riffs that seemed familiar.

When he got to the entrance, he saw ancient posters nailed to the walls and doors.

Tonight and every night – The Crossroads Tour – Starring Robert Johnson

Inside, the place was only about half full. Demons and imps and ghouls sat at the bar or tables. Others lined the stage area getting close to the young Black man playing guitar. When Neil tried to enter, a thick, hairy arm barred his way.

"I'm the Dog Keeper," Neil told the troll like the fire demon suggested he do. The arm came down and the jerk of the troll's head granted Neil permission. He made his way through to the bar where he could get the lay of the land and then try to figure out how he was going to locate this Rachel person.

CHAPTER TWENTY-FIVE

U nable to sleep on the plane as it winged home across the Atlantic, all Luke could think about was how to present the apples to Mia with some flair. It had been a week and a half since he'd seen her, and he missed her terribly. There was no one who would appreciate the saga of getting this apple like she would. He couldn't wait to tell her about the bicycle torture, and the smelly fishing trawler, and the mystical beauty of the old abbey. Her eyes would crinkle at the edges when she smiled at his stories. Her cheeks would grow rosy when she really laughed and, if she found something especially amusing, she would inevitably snort. Luke rubbed his chest and looked out the window, as if he could recall her better if he gazed into the blue void.

What had she done to him? The great and powerful Wrath had turned all smooshy and romantic. Luke sighed.

While a child screamed and tortured the first-class passengers, Luke envisioned and dismissed scenarios where Mia took him back, rushed into his arms, kissed him like she loved him. He would be happy if she would simply allow him to talk to her. He would force his thoughts in a different direction as soon as his fantasies got around to the part where he had to explain himself to Mia.

How in the name of all that was holy was he ever going to explain this horrific situation he was dragging her into? Well, *into* if she agreed to take pity on him. He'd deal with it when he had to. He had to get her back and eventually he had to tell her, but for now he just wanted to hold her again.

He hated flying. You were always at the mercy of other people when flying. You couldn't control the weather or the airline being on time. And worst of all, you were stuck with strangers in a tube hurtling through the air, spreading their diseases and stupidity like missionaries.

The flight attendant came by and Luke ordered a scotch, hoping it would dull the sounds of the little kid. The small human ran by him for the seven thousandth time and Luke nailed him with a look. The kid stopped in his tracks, staring back at Luke.

"Where. Is. Your. Mother?" Luke spoke low, his voice vibrating with menace. The tot shrugged. Great. "Go. Sit. Down."

"I'm Kyle," the boy told him. There was what looked to be chocolate smeared across his face. In the beginning of the day, he probably looked like a well-behaved child, but now, after hours in the sky, boredom had taken over. The tail of his little button-down shirt was hanging out from under the sweater vest and one of his knee-high socks was pushed down. His shoes were long gone. He looked like a ragamuffin.

"I'm tired," Luke answered.

"That's what Patty said, too." The boy pushed hair out of his eyes.

"Who is Patty? More importantly, where is Patty?"

Kyle stuck out a pudgy finger and pointed towards the back of first class. "Patty's my nanny. She's with my baby sister."

Luke used his most menacing voice. "You should go sit with her."

The brat wrinkled up his nose. "Melanie's no fun. All she does is cry. Babies aren't fun. I'm *not* a baby. I'm four." He held up three fingers to prove his point.

"Um-hmm," Luke hummed. "I'm not interested."

The boy ignored him. His beady-eyed gaze locked onto the hamper on the seat next to him in first class. "What's that?"

"A present."

"For me?"

Luke glared. "Why would it be a present for you? I don't even know you."

"Who's it for then?" He inched closer.

Luke shifted his knees away from the boy. "My girlfriend." Lord, he hoped he could make that happen. He would have prayed if he'd had any confidence at all that would work.

The boy had inched close enough that he could reach out and touch the basket. Luke pulled it away further up the seat. "Lemme see."

"No."

The boy's bottom lip pushed out. "I wanna see."

"You should go sit down."

"I wanna see."

"No."

There was a bit of a quiver to the lip and Luke thought a temper tantrum was eminent. "Lemme see," he wailed.

"If I show you," Luke asked, "will you go sit down and leave me alone?"

Kyle nodded and inched closer. "Is it a puppy?"

"No."

Now the kid was crawling across Luke's legs to get to the basket, his grubby hands leaving smears on his jeans. "Is it a pony?"

"How would a pony fit into this basket?"

"Magic."

Well, things could happen. "It's not an animal."

"Girlfriends like animals."

"Well, if this doesn't work out, I'll take that under advisement."

The boy was entirely in his lap now. He clapped his hands. "Open," he commanded.

Once the lid was open, Kyle leaned over and peered inside. He reached his hand in and Luke grunted. "No touching." That would be just the thing. Give Mia apples with Ebola germs.

"Oh." The boy breathed out in excitement. "Sticks." He seemed to genuinely marvel at the fact that there were sticks in the basket.

"And apples," Luke pointed out. "Hopefully she's going to like it."

"I love sticks," the boy told him.

Luke looked inside the basket, their two heads touching as they surveyed the fruit. "Mia loves apples. Hopefully she'll let me give these to her."

The boy's head turned and now their faces were only inches apart. "Why?"

"She's angry at me. I did something very dumb. And I want her to know how important she is to me."

Kyle's shoulders deflated a little. "Did you make her cry?"

Luke closed his eyes and pictured Mia's face the last time he saw her, standing in her office, expression fierce with ire as she told him to go to hell. He didn't see her cry, but he suspected she probably had. He was such a bastard. If only she'll let him talk to her. "I think so."

"Patty says I'm not supposed to make girls cry."

"You should listen to her. That's excellent advice."

"You have to say 'I'm sorry' when you make people cry." Kyle's face, chocolate and all, was earnest.

"I'm trying. She's really angry. I flew all the way to England to get these apples for her and now I have to figure out a way to make her see."

Kyle sat back on Luke's knee and looked him in the face. "You just have to knock on her bedroom door and ask nicely. Patty says you have to mean it."

Initially, Luke had been trying to think of some spectacular way to get her attention, but maybe Kyle had the best idea. The most important thing at this point was that she knew how sorry he was that he hurt her. Then, afterward, he could prove to her how much she meant to him.

Now, after all the hours across the Atlantic, he sat outside her house and tried to be optimistic. Well, if Mia wouldn't accept his gift, Kyle said he would take it. He must have reminded Luke five times how much he liked sticks and even suggested any girl that didn't like sticks wasn't really worth knowing.

It was six in the morning and the early sun was casting a warm glow across the foliage hanging over the street in front of Mia's house. The basket of fruit and clippings looked ominous, sitting on the bench seat next to him in the car. Across the street the door opened on the side of the house, and that black and white beast that barked at him so viciously bounced out and cavorted around the yard. Luke's breath hitched when he saw Mia exit the house as well and cross the enormous expanse of lawn towards her greenhouse. She looked gorgeously casual with her hair tied up in a ponytail and worn jeans tucked into the cutest work boots he'd ever seen.

"It's now or never," he told himself out loud. He made an attempt to smooth down his hair. It was useless, so he grabbed the basket and headed towards the greenhouse after her. The dog—was it a dog?— bounced ahead of her and she disappeared inside. Luke took a deep breath and knocked on the metal door before opening it. Mia was standing off to the right, hose in hand, and she was laughing at her animal. She turned around at the sound of the door and her face fell.

Luke shuffled the cumbersome basket under one arm and held up the other hand as a sign of peace. "Just give me one minute, please. I just want to talk to you. Please."

With a perfectly emotionless expression, she lifted her arm with the hose and threatened, "One step closer and I'll let you have it."

Instead, Luke crossed the space in several strides and took the hose, squirting himself in the head and chest. Once the onslaught stopped and he'd dropped the hose, he sluiced the water from his face with his free hand. "I've been on a plane for thirteen hours and desperately needed a shower, so thanks for that."

The goofy animal came bouncing up one of the aisles between the plants. His attitude mirrored Mia's in that the instant he spotted Luke he growled. He went from a frolicking doofus to a menacing beast in seconds flat.

Mia stepped back to intercept him, putting her hand on the dog's collar. "Sit, Godfrey." She glared at Luke. "What do you want?"

"I was a fool," he blurted out.

Her face could have been sculpted from marble—it was that beautiful and that blank. "Yeah."

"I've been wracking my brain to come up with ways to apologize to you." He gave her a tentative smile, the water was still dripping from his eyebrows so he also might have winked, which gave his whole demeanor a flippant air that he was not going for.

AMYLYNN BRIGHT

"You had better not have any dead flowers in that basket." Her
eyes didn't smile.
"I learned my lesson with the flowers. I'm sorry about that, too.
They were my cousin Ethan's idea." The basket was getting heavy.
"These are not flowers."
"Whatever that is"—she indicated his bundle—"I'm not
interested."
He moved closer and the dog growled low in his throat. "Please let
me say what I need to say and then I'll go if you still want me to. I'll
even leave the present."
She stared at him for forever, it seemed, while the basket pulled
down at his arms and the water dripped from his hair and earlobes.
She heaved a sigh laced with impatience and animosity, then rolled
her eyes. "You have twenty seconds and then I'm letting the dog
loose."
He exhaled and then pushed forward. "I could give you a bunch of
explanations and excuses, but they would all come down to one
thing: I was afraid. I am a stupid man, Mia, and all of that stuff
doesn't really matter. I am so sorry. So, so sorry. I need you. I missed
you so much, I hurt." The dog was still growling, and it took super-
human strength not to break eye contact with Mia to look down at
him. "You fit me exactly. I never thought in a million years I'd find a
beautiful, brilliant woman who filled in the holes of my furious soul
the way you do."
Mia blinked her eyes. It was possible her expression had softened.
At least the thin line of her mouth had relaxed. She sniffed once and
her gaze flicked to the bundle in his arms. "What's in the basket?"
Luke allowed a smile and he stepped forward two more paces.
The rumbling from the dog vibrated in terrifyingly close proximity to
his crotch. "Hey there, puppy. Nice doggie."
"Go off and play," Mia told the dog. She let go of his collar and
Luke tensed, expecting an attack. The beast must have taken a cue
from the change in her tone, because he did not lunge in and chomp
on his nuts. Instead, the dog looked from his owner to Luke and then
bounced off to play.
He closed the gap until he stood directly in front of Mia, the

basket filling the space between them. "I wracked my brain to come up with something, anything that would convince you. This"—he indicated the basket—"took me on a major expedition."

She glanced at the basket and curled her bottom lip into her mouth. Her words were breathy when she asked, "Where?"

He leaned down slightly and told her just above a whisper. "A little island in Wales."

She gasped and met his gaze. "Bardsey Island?"

Now his mouth stretched wide in a grin. "One of the reasons I adore you. You're so brilliant."

She ignored his compliment and zeroed in on the basket. "You went to Bardsey Island?"

"It took several airplanes, a terrifying boat ride, a mile on a treacherous bicycle, and hand signals with a very strange Welshman, but it was all worth it to bring the other half of my soul a Bardsey Apple." At that, he flipped open the lid.

Inside, nestled in crumpled Welsh newspaper, sat one dozen Bardsey Apples and the cuttings Luke had convinced the man to prepare for him.

"You even brought me scions?"

"You mean the cuttings?" When she nodded, he grinned. "Well, I figured you'd want to grow your own Bardseys, too."

He watched her face as she touched the fruit and pulled the twigs from the basket and inspected them. She smelled the apples and grinned, then she put everything back and closed the lid. Clasping her hands underneath, she relieved him of the burden and set the hamper on a work bench before turning back to face him. She closed the gap and Luke held his breath, too afraid to hope that the plan had worked. She reached up and pulled his face down to hers, and then she wrapped her arms around his neck.

He whispered against her lips, "I'm so sorry."

"Shhh." And then she kissed him.

Her lips were soft against his, like a prayer. He wrapped his arms around her waist and pulled her tightly against him, molding her body flush to his, her body completing him as well as her soul did. Something tight in him came loose and relief seemed to liquify him.

Luke deepened this kiss, remembering her taste, her feel, the way the churning fury seemed to settle when she was near.

Finally, their lips came apart, but they stayed tight in the embrace. He tucked a lock of hair which had come loose from her ponytail behind her ear.

"That was the worst ten days of my life," he told her.

She agreed. "It sucked. I was miserable." She kissed his chin. "You know, you look terrible."

He chuckled. "I wasn't kidding about the odyssey. I came here right from the airport."

"Come on," she said and tugged his arm towards the door. She whistled and the dog appeared out of the greenery, tongue lolling out the side of his mouth. He whipped by at top speed, a watering can in his mouth. Luke was shocked when the crazy dog ignored him entirely. One minute he was literally threatening to chomp his balls off and the next he was a slobbering doofus.

"Is your dog bipolar?"

Mia laughed. "He's really just a puppy. I've actually never seen him behave like he did earlier. I didn't even know he could growl. Grab my present and come on." She took him by the hand and pulled him towards the house. Luke's heart sang as he tucked the basket against his hip.

MIA PUT him in the shower and while he was washing off his travels, she made him breakfast. Waffles, eggs, and bacon sat on the kitchen table when she went to go collect Luke to eat. She'd heard the water cut off to the shower ten minutes ago. The door to her bathroom was open and steam was still curling out into her bedroom. Luke wasn't in there, though. She paused and turned back to her bedroom and located him immediately. He was crashed out on her bed. The covers had been pushed aside and he was still wearing the towel around his waist, looking dead to the world. The best part was, her vicious attack dog was asleep right alongside him, his head resting on Luke's knee.

Mia tiptoed to the side of the bed and took him in. As huge as he was, laying in her bed, the still-wet ends of his hair curling around his ears and on his forehead, he looked like a little boy. Well, not exactly. He was definitely a man, one with muscles and tattoos and scars, but he did look peaceful.

She blinked back the dampness in her eyes and smiled. He was back, and as much as she'd charged around like a rabid bear for the last week and a half, declaring that she didn't need him and he was the asshole, she'd been morose without him. He'd tried to give her some ridiculous song and dance about why he'd done what he had, but really, Mia didn't want to hear some lame story. They were always the same: I was scared; I was stupid; I made a mistake. She didn't care what it was so long as he didn't do it again.

She ran her palm over his shoulder and lightly tugged at the towel. He sighed in his sleep, and she managed to pull the wet towel out from under him when he rolled to the side. She convinced the dog to move so she could pull the sheets and comforter over him. Then she kicked off her boots, shucked off her pants and T-shirt, and crawled into bed beside him. She'd just gotten settled with her head on a pillow, turned so she could watch him, when his muscular arm reached over and pulled her into him. He tucked her head under his chin and kissed her hair.

"I love you," he whispered, holding her tightly to him.

CHAPTER TWENTY-SIX

When Mia woke up, the sun coming through the window was high in the sky. She was still wrapped up in a Luke cocoon. One arm draped across her middle and one leg was nestled in between hers. She'd had so many plans for the day and tasks that needed to be completed—all of which had been thrown to the wind the minute Luke walked into her greenhouse. Well, that wasn't exactly true. When he'd first walked in, she'd wanted to drown him with her hose.

And then let Godfrey eat him.

She shifted and turned underneath his heavy limbs until she was facing him. She ran her nose along the top of his chest and inhaled deeply. There it was. That exclusively Luke-like smell. Tears welled in her eyes and she swallowed hard. It had been a horrible, soul-crushing week and a half. She'd had to work so hard to stay angry because, in the quiet moments, the sadness would descend, and Mia feared that she'd be smooshed underneath it. Anger was empowering. Desolation was a killer.

But he was back.

And he said he loved her.

She traced her index finger along his bottom lip. Gently skimming her fingertips over the scruff of his beard and brushing away the heavy locks of hair that had fallen over his forehead. Down the slope of his nose, and yet he slept on. He probably hadn't slept any more than she had while they were apart. Selfishly, she hoped he hadn't. It would only be fair that he be as miserable as she had been. After all, it was all his fault.

And he loved her.

She kissed his chin and watched him sleep. This extended nap was the first real rest she'd had since they'd gotten together that she hadn't had a dream. Her subconscious must have been really working overtime because her dreams had been bizarre.

Using her fingernail, she followed the dips and rises of the muscles in his shoulders, arms, and chest. He finally stirred when her path led her down past his navel. Even then, his eyelashes only fluttered against his cheeks before his hand flattened against her back and he dragged her in tight against his body again.

Either he'd come to her completely tapped out or he was the most intense sleeper ever. If he'd really flown all the way to Wales and traveled to Bardsey Island and back all in one weekend, then it made sense he'd be knackered.

Mia sighed and stroked her palms over his back and down to the rise of his butt. She tickled her fingertips along his rear. He stretched his back and lifted a knee to nestle between her legs, but still he didn't wake up. She pressed her lips to the divot in the center of his collarbone then along the ridge of bone and up the column of his neck. Encouraged by a humming sigh, she moved her lips to the top of his pectoral muscles and traced the space between the planes of muscles with her tongue.

He lifted his knee higher between her legs and arched his back. She gave her hands free rein to stroke his shoulders, tangle her fingers in the soft hair on his chest, and test the ridges of his abdomen. Slowly she brought him back to the land of the living. He didn't open his eyes, but his breathing hastened and he gasped when her fingers slipped under the covers and followed the deep-ridged vee of his obliques. She wrapped her fingers around his wide-awake cock.

"I thought I was dreaming." His voice was gravelly from sleep. It was ridiculously sexy. "But here you are."

With his palm flat against her spine and his fingers stretched out, he covered most of her back with warmth. He flexed his hips, pressing her against his thigh. His cock nestled in her fist between their bodies.

"How did you sleep?" she asked from the crook of his neck.

"Like a dead person." He slid one hand between them, palmed her breast and massaged. "I'm so sorry I fell asleep. I was even more wiped out than I thought."

Mia squeezed his shaft and moved her fist up and down. With each rise she ran her thumb over the head, smearing the precum before sliding back down. Luke moved his hips in tandem, joining in her rhythm as Mia rode his thigh. In one quick movement, he pressed her flat to the mattress and rose over her. With hands on either side of her shoulders and his knees pressed between her legs, he gazed down on her.

"I was a wreck without you," he told her.

She smiled. She didn't necessarily want to hear his excuses, but it was satisfying to know he'd been as bad off as she'd been. Misery loved company, right?

"Good," she said and used her free hand to pull him in for a kiss. She sighed at the feel of his lips and the slide of his tongue before he broke the kiss and filled his mouth with her nipple. Arching up to him, she pressed her head into the pillow and wrapped her legs around his waist. He sucked and massaged her breasts, gently scraping his teeth along the sensitive flesh. She used both hands on his cock now, cradling his balls and stroking the shaft until he hissed and raised up on his knees.

"Condom?" he asked.

"Drawer." She gestured to the nightstand.

He pulled it open with such force the thing came all the way out and crashed to the floor. "Goddamn it," he cursed.

She gave a surprised shriek and giggled while he leaned over and rummaged around on the floor. While he was searching, she continued her dedicated ministrations, paying extra attention to the sensitive vein running underneath before circling her thumb over the head.

"Take pity on me, woman," he cried.

She responded by taking a nip out of his bicep and another on his rib cage. Finally, he came back with a condom between his teeth. She pulled it free and tore it open. He sat back on his heels to give her easy access. Instead, she dipped her head down and guided his penis into her mouth as far as it would go before it hit the back of her throat. He plunged his fingers into her hair and groaned. She bobbed up and down several times before he clasped both sides of her head and pulled her up.

"You're killing me," he said. He angled her head and kissed her, fast and hard, sliding his tongue along hers and along the roof of her mouth before pushing her back down on the bed. He plucked the condom from her fingers and rolled it over himself. Grabbing her under the knees, he yanked her down to him. Mia yelped, exhilarated by his need, that she'd done that to him.

"I'm never letting you go again," he declared.

"You better not," she agreed.

He spread his giant hand over her stomach and used his thumb to rub her clit. Mia dropped her head back, mouth open, breaths rapid and needy. She couldn't hold her hips still and, when he slid one finger inside her, she nearly launched off the bed.

"Mia," he groaned and added another thick finger.

He clutched her hips, pressing his fingers into her flesh to hold her still, and thrust home. He froze on a groan, gripping her body so tight to his he might leave bruises. Mia flexed her internal muscles, reveling in how he filled her. Slowly, he began to move. They moaned in concert, hips rising together and falling away. Mia fisted the sheets and held on as Luke drove them both towards the edge.

"Oh, God," she called. "Now." And she dropped over.

On a roar, Luke followed. Moments later he collapsed next to her on the mattress, the condom in the trash next to her bed.

He kissed her shoulder. "Thank goodness I got a nap before we tried that."

Mia lay like a wrung-out towel, limp and satisfied. "Take another nap. I'd like to do that again in a bit."

Luke chuckled and kissed the side of her head. His stomach growled loud enough that Mia lifted her head and stared at it.

He rolled over on his stomach and sucked her nipple into his mouth and let it out with a loud pop. "I'd love to make a joke about eating you, but I really am starving."

She ran her fingers though his messy hair. "You know, I made you breakfast like seven hours ago."

"You did?" He raised up on his elbows.

"Yeah. It's probably still sitting on the table along with the mess in the kitchen. As soon as my bones grow back, I'll get up and find us some nourishment."

Luke hopped up and strode to the bathroom. Mia found the strength to lift her head and watch his perfect naked ass walk away. The water came on in the shower and then Luke reappeared at her bedside. Before she knew what was happening, he'd scooped her up and was carrying her towards the water. He set her on her feet on the tile and her head under the water and climbed in with her.

Her house was an older one, and the shower stall was much too small for a man of Luke's size. She giggled when he had to keep his elbows in while he washed her hair and banged his poor bruised knees on the walls. There was definitely not enough room to get frisky in there. As it was, they had to mop up the floor with the towels when they got out.

"All group showers will occur at my place from now on," Luke informed her with a scowl and rubbed his elbow.

"It's not my fault my shower wasn't made for moose. Come on, grumpy. Let's find something to eat." She led the way to the kitchen but stopped in the doorway. She'd expected a disaster but the mess had been cleared away and there was a note on the table.

Based on the basket of apples I'm guessing you let Luke back in.

Well done, you big ass. Don't fuck up again.

Let me know when it's safe to come back home.

XOXO - Cassie

Luke scowled and Mia laughed with a shrug. She plucked one of the fruit from the basket and took a bite.

Luke loved her enough to travel across the world to fetch her an impossible apple.

LUKE CARRIED two cups of coffee out to the greenhouse, trailing along behind Mia and her crazy-ass dog. There was a nip in the air signaling fall, and he wished he'd remembered to put on a flannel before going outside. Once inside the greenhouse, though, the moist warmth enveloped them.

He was excited this morning to learn how to take the sticks he'd brought from Bardsey Island and turn them into a tree.

His woman was wearing work jeans and chambray shirt. She'd tied her hair up into a messy bun on top of her head. She looked fucking adorable.

"Saw," she said and held out her hand like a surgeon.

"Saw," he said and gently placed a small-toothed saw in her hand, handle first, because you don't mess around with saws.

She showed him the optimum location for the graft and how to cut the cleft in the trunk. Using another tool, she pried apart the cleft and he helped wedge the scion inside. She left him to cover the entire cleft with the asphalt water emulsion while she went to discover what shenanigans that dog of hers had gotten into.

He was just finishing up when she appeared from the far aisle with about five chewed-up lengths of garden hose. "I don't know what Godfrey's beef is with hoses, but this is the fifth one this year." She inspected Luke's work with a smile. "Well done. Now we wait."

Luke stepped back and looked at the larger tree that now included a branch of the one and only Bardsey apple tree in existence. Wow, this was so fucking cool. "How long will it take?"

Mia slipped her hand into his and entwined their fingers. "Years."

Years? "Well, that's disappointing."

She chuckled. "I know. The next several years we'll be trimming the scions and making the graft strong. You'll see. Before you know it, we'll be eating our very own Bardsey apples."

She'd alluded to their future. *Their future*, and it made him warm and squishy. Luke stood back and took in what he'd done—what *they'd* done. With all the projects he'd completed, all the buildings he'd designed and erected, was it weird that he was prouder at this moment than he'd ever been? He raised their clasped hands to his mouth and kissed hers.

He pushed down the nagging and insistent voice in his head, the one that sounded an awful lot like his gargoyle. He still had a lot to tell Mia, but it was so tempting not to tell her yet. He wanted to bask in this rosy glow of happiness he'd known so few times in his life.

Later that afternoon, using a recipe from the Daughters of Eve, they turned some of her present into apple butter. While peeling and coring and chopping, Luke told her about his journey. The interminable airplane travel and the retching boat trip from Cardiff to the island, including the fisherman who smelled as ripe as his boat. She was laughing so hard she was doubled over when he described his bicycle journey over that windy island. He told her how cool the tree was, all gnarled and scrappy, huddled against the side of the house to protect it from the salty sea air. She begged him to stop, tears of laughter making her eyes glisten, when he detailed his encounter with Kyle.

"He gave good advice," she told him.

"Thank God you're a girl who likes sticks," he told her and kissed her in front of her stove.

At midnight, naked and sweaty, they ate apple butter and toast in bed. Luke had never been more at peace.

On the third day, Mia came back into the bedroom, cups of coffee in her hand, wearing his shirt as a robe. "We're going to have to get dressed eventually. At some point we're going to have to interact with other people and go to work."

"I don't like other people." Luke took a deep pull on the coffee.

She shucked the shirt and crawled into bed next to him. "All right, well, eventually we'll run out of food."

He put his coffee down on the nightstand and pulled back the covers. "We'll have some delivered."

He started with her toes, then kissed her ankles and the supple skin of her calves. He heard the clink of her cup settling on the wood of her own nightstand. By the time he got to the back of her knees, she was making those little noises he loved so much. He crawled further up her body and gave the inside of her thighs a little nibble.

Half an hour later, their coffee was cold, but they lay hot and panting in the tangled covers. "See," he said, "we don't ever have to leave this place. Everything I need is right here and everything else can be delivered."

She turned her head to gaze at him. "You're going to have to take another shower in my tiny bathroom."

"Son of a—" he cursed and flung a dramatic arm over his eyes when he realized his plan wasn't foolproof.

Mia purred and sucked his earlobe into her mouth. "It won't be so bad. Don't you want to see me in something besides work clothes?"

Muffled underneath his arm, he pouted. "I'd rather see you in nothing."

"How about if I get all dressed up and fancy? I'll put on something slinky, barely any panties." When he raised his head, she wiggled her eyebrows enticingly. "Super high heels?"

"No panties."

She laughed again, low and inviting. When she did that lusty laugh, sweet Lord, it was like a direct line to his dick. He was already hard again.

"Deal," she said, "if you promise a night of sin and debauchery."

"Well, I can deliver the sin," he said.

He would tell her. He would, soon. Just not right this minute.

HEAVEN & HELL X

Neil took in the roadhouse. Still shocked that there was an actual bar in Hell, he waited until his eyes adjusted to the darkness before he ventured too much further inside the place.

It smelled. A fact Neil found oddly comforting. Sweaty bodies, stale drink, and whiffs of brimstone hovered in the stagnant air. It smelled like every trashy bar he'd ever used a fake ID to get into on Earth, just substitute gasoline fumes for brimstone. He'd bet his favorite boots that the bar was sticky and the bathroom required hazmat suits.

Neil could live here. Not even the cretins inside could sour the fact that he'd found a real bar. Man, he was so freaking happy to have found this place. Things were really looking up. Between finding his sweet little angel and now this honest-to-God bar, Neil was feeling good. Well, as good as he could feel in Hell.

He jostled his way past a gremlin or two until he found an empty stool in the curve on the bar. Sliding onto the torn vinyl seat, he hooked the heels of his boots on the foot rail. And the stool teetered. No matter how he shifted his weight, the stool rocked to the other side. Shit. One leg was at least a half an inch shorter than the others. He tried to balance by putting his ass in the exact middle of the seat and holding out his arms. Immediately he tipped to the left.

The bartender lumbered to a stop in front of Neil, dropped hands as big and hairy as an orangutan's on the bar, and grunted at him. "Drink?"

"There's something wrong with this stool." He tilted to the right.

"Nah. S'fine. Drink?" Red eyes trained on Neil, waiting.

He adjusted his ass on the stool. What to drink? He closed his eyes and pictured an ice-cold pilsner, beads of sweat rolling down the side, an amber brew with a frothy head.

"What's on tap?" he asked.

"Don't have a tap. Special on room temperature lime Kool-Aid for happy hour."

What the hell? "Huh?"

The bartender sighed, wafting breath wretched enough to singe nose hair in Neil's face. He slapped a laminated list on the bar. "Decide by the time I get back."

Neil perused the list. The type was smudged and the yellowing laminate made it very difficult to read in the dim light. Also, there might have been blood splashed all over the back. According to the makeshift menu, the drinks were broken up into categories. At the top and in bold font was the heading Hot Drinks. Who went to a bar in the Sixth Circle of Hell and ordered a hot drink? Hot toddy? Neil didn't even know what that was, but the first word in the name was a dead giveaway that he wasn't interested in it. Misplaced curiosity had him squinting at the next item.

Unsweetened Cocoa.

He looked up from the paper and scanned the others in the bar half expecting them to be laughing at his expense. Surely this was a fucking joke, right? But, no one was paying him any attention at all. Either they were involved in their own conversations, or they were whooping it up at the stage where the blues guy was playing.

Skipping the rest of the hot drinks section, he simply couldn't bring himself to read the rest of that horror. The list of Not Cold Drinks was considerably shorter. Right at the top was the room-temperature Kool-Aid that had been mentioned earlier. Lime was on special tonight, but apparently Tuesdays were slated for orange. They couldn't even have cherry-flavored Kool-Aid? Flat ginger ale followed, with curdled buttermilk and cough syrup. Neil thought he might very well cry, right here in this bar, on a wonky goddamned stool.

Orangutan Hands was back.

Neil handed him back the menu. "You don't have any beer? None at all?"

Snagging the laminated sheet with a yellow fingernail, he flipped it over to the bloody side. He used his hairy palm to swipe across the droplets, smearing the red liquid across the page but revealing more words underneath. Now the page was streaked with blood and stray orange hair. Neil flared his nostrils in disgust.

"Beer," the bartender directed.

Neil wasn't about to try and read through that nightmare. "I'll take one. Whatever you got."

A dirty glass with a chip in the top sloshed on the bar in front of Neil. He took a moment to relish the saliva that flooded his mouth at the thought of a beer after all this time. Now he wished Juliet had given him some chips. It would have been almost like he was still out on Rosecrans Avenue, joking with his boys, chugging a cold one and eating a bag of Doritos. Well, he could have closed his eyes and pretended. It would have been the closest he'd been in a long fucking time.

His eyes drifted closed, he licked his lips, pressed them to the glass, and took in a long swallow.

And nearly spit it out.

When his eyes flashed open in surprise, the bartender was standing right in the line of fire. Neil choked down the warm, flat, skunky swill, feeling it slip down his throat like he'd actually drank piss. He gave the bartender a thumbs up and a manic smile.

The demon shook his shaggy head and revealed teeth as yellow as his claws when he smiled back. "Didja want anything to eat?"

Neil couldn't suppress a cackle. "What's good tonight? Airline food?" he joked.

"Nah." The demon wiped the spilled liquid off the bar with his wooly forearm. More hair stuck to the wood and Neil felt the warm alcohol give a nasty swirl in his stomach. "Yah gotta get here earlier in the week if you want the airline food. We might still have some school lunches left. I can check if you want."

Neil stared at the bartender for several long beats, digesting the concept of canned spinach and more bologna sandwiches. "I think I'll give it a pass for now."

When the creature nodded his head, stubby horns gleamed through the hair. "Check back with you later. Let me know if you change your mind." Then he lumbered off.

He scrubbed a hand across his face, then surreptitiously ran his palm across his tongue but not even the soot on his hands got the skunky taste out of his mouth. He couldn't bring himself to put that crap in his mouth again, but he didn't want to piss off the bartender, either. He shivered. He turned himself on the barstool. It gave him a jaunty, wobbly ride until his back was to the bar and he could face the crowd.

What a motley crew. Denizens of all sizes and breeds made up the group. He recognized goblins of Scourge's ilk, but there were other ghouls he wasn't sure he'd seen before. To be fair, he'd never been down this far, either. The bigger beasties he identified as trolls and ogres, but there were others he wasn't sure of. A group in the far corner didn't really seem to keep a shape and he thought they might be wraiths. Either way, he wasn't keen on finding out. Looking at them too long gave him a headache.

He swiveled to look at the other side of the room and noticed a collection of fiends sitting around a table, looking very self-important. He suspected they were higher up the food chain, maybe Dukes or Marquis, like Duke Valefor from his own circle. He made a mental note to stay away from them, too. No good could come from the sadistic bastards being aware of his existence. Either they'd send him back to Valefor or, worse yet, take it upon themselves to punish him.

He spun back to face the bar and his glass of puke-inducing drink and considered how he was going to get from here to where he needed to be, considering he had no idea where that was. He wasn't even a hundred percent sure this Rachel person was real, but Juliet sure seemed to think so. If she was a prisoner of Hell, she could be literally anywhere down here. The whole place was a dungeon.

He propped his elbow up on the bar and settled his head against his fist. The angel had told him a long, complicated story where Rachel was supposed to have been Lucifer's lover. Lucifer was supposed to be down in Hell running the place, right? Anyway, that's what the nuns had been jabbering about all the time. Thanks to that Catholic orphanage, he knew all about the fire and brimstone Hell. Neil had never seen him down here, but that didn't mean anything. He'd never seen the Devil at all, but he damn well felt his influence and knew he was real. According to Juliette, Lucifer and the Devil were not the same person. Wouldn't that shock the shit right out of old Sister Bertha?

The bartender shuffled by and dropped off a bowl in front of Neil. There was no way they were peanuts or pretzels, but he couldn't help but look. Yep, that was dog food. And if he'd learned anything by his time in this hell, it was store brand dog food at that. He briefly considered if that would clear out the taste in his mouth, but to what end? Which taste would be worse? What if all it did was add to the mixture and then he would be stuck with piss-beer and dog chunks. Better the devil you know... He skipped the bowl.

So back to Juliet's story. The legend implied Rachel would be the mother of the Devil and all his generations.

Neil sat up straight and tilted to the right.

Holy shit.

She was the Devil's grandmother. Neil didn't care who you were, you didn't put your granny in a dungeon.

"Ooh, ooh, ooh." He gave an excited little wiggle on the stool. He was on to something here.

So where in Hell wasn't a complete shithole? He cast his gaze around the crappy little bar and realized that these spooks loved it here. This was their happy place. Duke Valefor's house was set up pretty sweet, for a demon. Probably the higher the rank, the higher the privilege, right? The princes probably lived in nice fucking penthouses. Well, actually the opposite of a penthouse, but whatever, it would be really fucking tight.

He nodded in excitement and made two fists.

The Devil himself would have a motherfucking castle, and he'd bet his next bag of Doritos that's where he kept his grandma.

Neil's mind was whipping around at a zillion miles a minute. In his excitement, he didn't even realize that he'd reached for the drink again. He took a giant self-congratulatory gulp. He stared at the glass in horror. *Ah, fuck it.* He shoveled a handful of dog kibble in his mouth and chased it with the last of the brew. Hopping off the stool, he saluted the bartender whose name he realized he never got and headed for the exit.

Charon demanded his other motorcycle key and the shoelace from one of his boots in order to ferry him all the way down to the bottom. Neil had convinced the elevator operator that he'd heard on excellent authority the loose Cerberus was down there, so Charon had pursed his lips and shoved the payment in his pockets and clanged the elevator shut.

The ride down felt like they were arriving on the sun, it was so fucking hot. Neil actually removed his motorcycle jacket at one point, afraid that he would broil inside the leather. Charon eyed the jacket greedily, but Neil shook his head. The saliva in his mouth boiled and sizzled on the elevator floor when Neil spit it out. It was no use; his guts were cooking and his blood seared the inside of his veins. He could almost feel his brain sautéing inside his skull. All the while German techno music serenaded them on the way down.

And then the elevator door dinged.

The minute the doors parted, a cool breeze wafted in and Neil thought he would cry. He threw himself out of the oven and into a grassy expanse, chasing the cool air.

"Good luck," Charon called as he beat a hasty retreat, wiggling his fingers as the doors closed, leaving Neil alone on the Devil's lawn

CHAPTER TWENTY-SEVEN

W hen Luke had finally left her house that morning, it was with the promise that they were going out to dinner that evening. He made Mia renew her promise to wear something slinky. But when she and Cassie had stood in her closet, Mia wasn't satisfied, and nothing in Cassie's closet was any better.

It was a shame, but they'd have to go shopping.

Besides, Cassie demanded some girl time. "I need to know all the details," she'd urged. "What did he finally do to get you to forgive him?"

Mia recounted the details of the Apple Odyssey, as Luke was now calling it, to Cassie over lunch at their favorite coffee shop. "You should've seen the bruises on his knees from the bicycle."

"Well, apples." Cassie nodded in understanding. "That's a hell of a lot better than all those damned flowers. At least he put some thought into it that time."

"I just threw the last of them away today." Mia had been weeding the dead flowers out bit by bit, combining the zillions of roses into fewer and fewer vases until just the last one remained. "I'm sure he paid a fortune for those flowers, but they sure did die quickly, huh?"

"Whatever," Cassie said with an eyeroll. "I thought I was going to have to move out. I'm telling you, I couldn't even breathe with all that pollen."

"But I haven't even told you the best part," Mia continued. "He brought me cuttings from the original tree. Can you believe that? It's not just that he went on this crazy expedition to get me the apples, which of itself is incredibly thoughtful, but to bring me scions is above and beyond thoughtful, you know what I mean? It's like he really, *really* understands me."

Cassie propped her chin up on her upturned palm, her elbow on the table, and sighed wistfully. "I knew he had it in him."

"Let's be honest. Most people's eyes glaze over when I start talking about apples and emulsions and all my crazy cultivating nonsense. I mean, you love me, but even you have your limits when I drone on." Mia paused while Cassie rolled her eyes in agreement. "But the thing is, Luke never does. He trots along with me, listens to my babble, asks questions. He even wanted to help graft the cuttings." She paused for effect. "We've already secured them onto a parent tree."

"Seriously?"

Mia grinned. "Seriously."

"Wow," Cassie said with a mirroring smile. "A man who listens *and* who looks like Luke. You've hit the motherlode there, sister."

"I know." And Mia did.

"The man is an urban legend." Cassie snatched the bill when their waiter dropped it at the table. "It's my treat. Don't protest. You always pay. I got this."

They found a fabulous devil-red dress that clung to her body and dipped very low in the back but was high enough in the front to be deceptively chaste, at least until she turned around. They went to the same store where she'd bought her warrior shoes and found a pair of sky-high silver heels that shone so brightly, they seemed like chrome. Put together, the shortness of the dress and the height of the heels made her legs almost look long. Cassie styled her hair in a messy updo that suggested she'd just gotten lucky in the back of a car on the way to the restaurant. Finished with sparkly chandelier earrings, smoky eye makeup and red lipstick, Mia felt like a movie star—or one of those gorgeous party girls that were always pictured in society pages.

"You tramp up real nice," Cassie told her with a smile. When Mia shot her a questioning look, she explained. "You know, the opposite of cleaning up real nice. You always look cute and ready to meet someone's mom. Now, though, you look hot!"

Mia took it as the compliment it was intended.

When the doorbell rang, Cassie ran to answer it while Mia stowed her cell phone, a credit card, house key, four condoms (because you never know), and her lipstick in a tiny silver purse. One last assessing look in the mirror, front and back, and then with a burst of bravado, she shucked off her thong and strode out to meet her guy, commando.

She was gratified that before he could speak, Luke had to clear his throat when he first saw her. His greeting kiss was fiery and carnal. He had driven over in his Chevelle instead of taking one of his company's Town Cars. Mia hadn't ridden in it before, but it fit her mood to a tee. It was fast and dangerous and there was something inherently sexual about the rumble of the engine.

She was blindly staring out the window when they pulled up to a stoplight. In the middle of a fantasy that involved climbing over the stick shift and straddling him, the steering wheel at her back—when she felt his gaze on her for real.

"You are gorgeous," he told her. His eyes were dark and his voice husky.

"So you've said." He'd already complemented her several times. She reveled in the power of feeling sexy.

He reached across the console and ran his fingers up her leg, smoothing along her skin from knee to mid-thigh, sliding half his hand under her dress. "Are you sure you wouldn't rather go home and let me take that dress off you?"

She raised an eyebrow but didn't remove his hand. "No. I'd rather sit in a restaurant full of people, wearing this dress, and watch you deal with the fact that I'm not wearing any panties."

His mouth fell open and he drew a shaky breath. Before he could investigate, the light turned green and she pushed his hand off her thigh with a laugh.

"No panties?" he repeated, darting his eyes from her lap to the road and back.

She pushed her skirt down towards her knees and crossed her legs. "Nope. By your request, if you remember."

His fingers plucked at the red material, but she smacked his hand and he pulled away with a playful yelp.

She tossed him a suggestive side-eye. "If you're a good boy, maybe I'll give you a peek later."

"How long is 'later'? Like during the salad course? Or would I have to wait all the way to dessert?"

She liked who she was when she was with Luke. She'd never been this forward or brave before, and she loved the rush. She barely recognized herself, but it was thrilling.

"We'll see."

Luke stomped on the gas and the powerful engine in his hotrod roared to life. She threw back her head and laughed. This Mia was exhilarating.

The valet opened the car door for her at the restaurant and Luke was beside her in flash. He wrapped his arms around her and tipped her back slightly with a fast, hard kiss before taking her hand and escorting her inside. The maître d' greeted Luke as if he was known in the place and they were immediately escorted to a half-moon booth tucked in a corner.

Luke slipped in next to her side and waggled his eyebrows at her. "This was good, huh? Nice table and we didn't have to wait at all."

"Mr. Mephisto." She adopted the tone of a schoolteacher. "Are you angling for a reward so soon?" He nodded his head enthusiastically. "Well, you're on the right track. Keep up the good work."

His grin never faltered. "When I get you alone…"

Mia giggled, low in her throat. The wine list was in a leather-bound folio and was quite extensive when she opened it. "Are you in the mood for red or white?"

"Are you seriously asking me that?"

It took her a second, before she got her own unintended joke, proving to herself that underneath the sex kitten, she was still just Mia.

Luke ordered a bottle of red wine from the waiter, his hand on her naked back the whole time. She blinked and maintained a serene smile while his thumb drew lazy circles between her shoulder blades.

"I checked in with the office today. Well, all I really did was check my emails from while I was gone. Looks like the plans and permits for our building have all been submitted to the city."

"That's exciting. How long will that take?" she asked.

The palm on her back slipped a little lower. "Six to eight weeks, depending on how busy they are down there, if any revisions will be called for, that kind of thing. This is the slowest part, while you wait for all the paperwork. Still, we'll be breaking ground before you know it."

"Maybe we'll even have a Bardsey Apple tree to put in the lobby."

A grin stretched across his face. When had she ever thought he looked mean? Her Luke was playful and boyish and beautiful. She felt a glow in her chest that she'd feared had been extinguished during that horrible time when they'd been apart. He hadn't told her that he loved her again, not since that time when he'd been almost asleep. But she could feel it, like waves coming off him when he looked at her, or smiled and teased, or touched her simply because he couldn't not touch her.

They ordered dinner and sipped from the wine. Cuddled up in the booth, they talked of nothing and everything while she let all the angst she had been holding on to melt away. Luke laced his fingers in with hers and Mia let herself fall back in love.

The waiter arrived with another bottle of wine. "This was sent over by the table in the corner." He gestured to a table of gentlemen on the opposite side of the dining room. Mia thought she recognized Luke's cousin with three other men. He gave a nod and a salute.

"Is that Ethan?" she asked.

Luke groaned. "Yeah. Those others are my cousins, too. Let me go over and say hey or they'll insist on crashing our dinner. Then I'll never get rid of them." He kissed her and slid out of the booth. "I'll be right back. Don't put any underwear on before I get back."

AMYLYNN BRIGHT

She raised an eyebrow. "Depends on how long you're gone."

He held up his hand, all five fingers extended. "Less than five minutes," he promised.

Mia watched him move. He was such an anomaly: both large and graceful. Any man who looked as good in a suit as he did naked...

She leaned back in the booth, the leather cool against her skin, and took another sip of her wine. She toyed with the hem of her dress, smoothed the material across her thighs, rolled her ankle under the table. The restaurant was crowded, and she took the opportunity to look at the other diners, amazed that she and Luke had been so oblivious to all the other people in the room. Luke stood at ease at the table with the four other men. One of them laughed about something while another one glanced across the room at her. He raised his eyebrows as if in wonder and then smiled at her. She watched a waiter deliver dinner to a table with older diners, two couples who looked in their seventies. Another couple looked to be having an argument far enough away that she couldn't hear the words, but their expressions told a story.

When she glanced away from that little tableau, she noticed a man walking towards her. She hadn't seen him just a second ago, but now he was there, and his gaze was locked onto hers. She couldn't seem to look away from him as he came closer even though she wanted to. He was so familiar, yet it took several long seconds, his stride bringing him toward her like an advancing tide, his attention threatening to swallow her up, before she realized he was the man from her dreams. But that was impossible, wasn't it?

Diabolically handsome, his smile more smirky than friendly, he was dressed in an expensive black suit. Glossy ebony hair was styled away from his face and he was clean-shaven. The word *impeccable* came to mind. His black gaze never wavered.

Her heart pounded and she swallowed the mouthful of wine before she choked on it. Even then, the acrid taste of metal filled her mouth. He was only three or four strides away from her when she tore her eyes away from him long enough to throw a panicky look in the direction of Luke. Still with his cousins, he didn't seem to notice what was happening. The man in black recaptured her gaze and Mia felt the oddest sensation of a sob stick in her chest. She held her breath as he took the final step to their booth, unsure why her body seemed to be struggling with its fight or flight response.

The handsome man extended his hand to her and, as if she wasn't controlling it at all, her own hand stretched before her and he clasped it like an old-fashioned courtier. He bent in a half bow and brought her hand to his lips.

His voice was velvet, the smoothest brandy, heavy and yet soft like a fog. "Please allow me to introduce myself."

"Apples?" Ethan shook his head. "Okay, dude, if that's what works, then it works. Whatever. Just glad the long, dark, night of your soul is over."

"She's lovely, Luke," Asher said, without a single ounce of lust in his tone. "Really."

"So what are you guys even doing here?" Luke asked. The seven cousins traveled in a pack most of the time, so it was never unusual to encounter them in clumps of three or four. Not that long ago, Luke most likely would have been with them.

"This place has a wild mushroom risotto that makes my heart sing," Seth told him like he was talking about a lover and not food. "Paired with an Italian Nebbiolo"—he grabbed his heart—"outstanding."

Benji eyed Seth like he was from another planet then shook his head and rolled his eyes. "I came along because I didn't have anything better to do, and apparently, I am not allowed to lay around and watch television and be happy."

"If you don't get up and move around once in a while, owls are going to nest in your hair," Ethan told him in annoyance. "You're not happy; you're bored."

Luke laughed. There was a great deal of comfort in the never-changing ways of his cousins. Each of them filled their role as it was ordained and had been for centuries. He saw himself like a ghost, the Luke of old, sitting as the fifth at this table not all that long ago. Seth would probably have been rhapsodizing about some new thing he was overdosing on, be it food, wine, or women, and Luke would have been throwing off fierce, menacing vibes like radio signals. That was before Mia. Now, it was crazy, but the world didn't seem so hostile, and he was driven to that feeling like a junkie.

Asher glanced behind Luke and blanched. "Luke," he said with an edge in his voice. "Look."

All five of them turned around.

"Fuck," Luke said, and it was chorused by the four men behind him. "Stay here," he commanded.

His father was sliding into his booth, Mia's hand in his. There was no way Luke could get to her in time to run interference. He turned on his heel, controlled his walk from breaking out into a run, and weaved through the tables to get back to her. That sense of calm that he'd just been marveling over was devoured as his blood turned to acid. His old friend rage coursed through him at the thought of his sweet Mia being terrorized by that unholy bastard.

"...and I said to myself, 'Isn't that the lovely Mia?'" The Devil had captured her hand and held it sandwiched between both of his. "And of course, it is you. My son is a lucky man, indeed."

Luke tamped down his rage because he was more afraid of frightening Mia than he was of angering his father. "Let go of her," he demanded through clenched teeth.

His father finally blinked, and the connection to Mia seemed to have been severed. He did not relinquish her hand. Instead, he brought it up to his face and brushed her knuckles across his cheek. Mia whimpered. A supernova spun wildly though Luke's gut, like a dervish of wrath.

"There's no need to worry, my boy." The Devil's voice was smooth. "Mia and I are old friends, aren't we, my dear."

Her voice was tiny when she replied. The sound of it made his heart bleed, like a cancerous ulcer. "You've been in my dreams." Luke saw the clarity in her yes. "They haven't been dreams, have they?"

"No," the Devil confirmed with a seductive smile.

"That's enough," Luke growled and shoved himself through the other side of the booth so he could sit next to her also. "Let her go."

His father turned his wicked attention to Luke. "She has free will," he reminded him. "I've never made her do anything against her wishes. You know how this works."

"What are you trying to pull off here? Do you want to ruin this for me?" Luke accused his father. "You want me to be miserable and alone like you were?"

The Devil barked out a laugh, but he let go of Mia's hand. Luke wrapped his arm around her waist and hauled her flush against his side.

"Don't be an idiot. I'm never alone unless I want to be." The Devil brushed some imaginary lint off his sleeve, then raised his gaze back to Luke. "Frankly, I'm not all that concerned about your love life. We both know that there is zero risk that you won't fulfill your role in the prophesy. How far Mia's participation extends is, of course, up to the Powers That Be, but your bouncing baby boy will show up at the appointed time. Whether this one"—he flicked his index finger in the direction of Mia—"loves you then or not is really not anyone's concern."

"It sure as fuck is my concern." It was everything that he could do to hold himself in check and not resort to physical violence.

"What?" Mia seemed to come back to herself. She looked from his father to Luke. "Did this man call himself your father?" She turned back to the Devil. "Are you his father?"

The Devil flashed a movie star smile at her. "At your service."

Mia stared at his father and Luke could almost feel her brilliant mind sorting it out. "But I've seen you in my dreams. You're... You can't be... No, that's crazy."

"The Devil?" his father prompted with a smirk. He did that thing where the temperature in the booth ratcheted up to searing temperatures for an instant.

Luke cursed a string of invectives under his breath.

"The Devil," she repeated, with realization and understanding coloring the words. She spoke clearly, outlining the things she understood. "You're the devil. And you're Luke's father? And I've been to Hell?"

"Mia." Luke touched her arm and said her name gently.

"No, I'm trying to understand this." She shook him off. "I know he's saying the truth. It's completely insane, but I've been there. It didn't make sense, what I kept dreaming, but now I see it."

"It's very complicated," Luke told her. Son of a bitch, he wanted to get her out of here. This was not how he wanted this to come out. He would have been gentler. *Fuck.*

"Complicated." His goddamned father laughed at that. "Mia, darling, it's not complicated. I'm the Devil. Luke is my son." Mia turned to look at Luke, and he knew his expression confirmed everything she feared. "It won't get complicated again for another, what is it Luke, twelve years?"

"I'm sorry," Luke breathed into her ear, and she flinched.

Luke couldn't read her. Was she angry or afraid? Her body language was confusing. He knew he wasn't confused. He knew exactly what he wanted, and he was fucking terrified he was never going to get it now.

It came out of nowhere, a spasm of wrath he could not control. It detonated out of him like a sonic boom before he could get control of it. The entire restaurant was affected. A cacophony of angry words and broken dishes rose up as the dining room roared to life.

The Devil smiled, obviously pleased at the chaos. He lifted his cuff and took a look at his Rolex. "I'm going to have to dash. I have an appointment I don't want to be late for." He leaned in and kissed Mia's cheek. She didn't flinch, or even really move. "As always, it's been a pleasure, sweetheart. If you need anything, you know where to find me." He guffawed at his joke, a wisp of dark smoke trailing up his jawline and circling above his head before it disappeared. He rose from the booth and turned back to Luke as if he was an afterthought. "Son." He turned the corner and then he was gone.

Luke reached for Mia. He was desperate to do some damage control, but she yanked her hand back and scooched around the bench seat before he could get to her. She held her hands up, palms out, ready to push him away if he advanced.

He implored her with his eyes. "Don't. Please let me try to explain."

"I think I'm going crazy," she told him. "None of this can be real."

He swallowed but said nothing. It was crazy. And it was true. He had no idea where to go from here. If she would just let him hold her...

But she wouldn't.

"Is this a joke?" she asked.

Luke shook his head, because obviously the time for lying and half-truths was over. She finished sliding out of the booth. Keeping his eyes on her, watching for any indication of what she was thinking, he came out around the other side and stood next to her. Her phone was out and she was already dialing her friend.

"Let me take you home," he said.

She recoiled from him like he was a leper. "No. I don't want to see you right now." Then she spoke into her phone and walked away. "Cassie? I need you to come get me. I'm walking down the street."

Luke let her take three tiny strides, her opportunity to storm out hampered by the high heels. He looked to his cousins, all of whom were watching the scene with various expressions of anger and dismay. Ethan threw up his hands, his gesture asking what the hell Luke was waiting for. Luke started after her.

Mia whirled around, radiating thunderous fury and he stopped in his tracks.

"Do not follow me," she growled, her voice formidable and low as she slipped off her heels.

If he didn't know better, he'd have thought he'd given her a push of Wrath, but he hadn't. It was all Mia.

CHAPTER TWENTY-EIGHT

"What happened?" Cassie asked as Mia threw herself into Cassie's car and slammed the door. Her friend had found her two blocks from the restaurant, storming down the street, talking to herself. She had been much too riled up to stand at the entrance to the restaurant and wait for her.

Mia was so angry she was practically vibrating in the seat. She reached over and snapped the radio off, not interested in hearing any stupid poppy songs about love. "Just take me home," she demanded.

Cassie eyed her from across the console. "I thought everything was good. You seemed really happy before you left."

"I didn't really know what was going on, did I?" she snapped. "Just drive." Her friend opened her mouth to ask another question and Mia yelled, "Drive, Cassie! Drive!"

Blinker on, Cass merged back into traffic. "Seriously, what happened? Did you get into a fight? He's a big guy. Did he scare you?" When Mia didn't answer right away, Cassie kept guessing. "Oh, my God! Is he married? He's married, isn't he. That bastard."

"He's not married. It'd be a lot damn easier if his being married was all it was."

Steering around a corner, Cassie concentrated on the road before turning her attention back to Mia. The silence lasted for several long blocks. "Are you going to tell me what happened, or what?"

"He's the Devil." Mia blurted, her voice harsh with fury.

"I'm sure, the asshole." Cassie nodded in empathy. "Men can be total dicks."

Mia raised her index finger to clarify. "Actually, I misspoke. It's his father who's the Devil. Luke is just the heir apparent."

"You met his dad?" Cassie looked away from the road.

Mia threw her hands in the air. "Oh yeah, I met his dad, all right. Apparently, it wasn't the first time."

"Honey, you're not making sense. Is his dad someone we know?" Cassie gasped. "OH. HOLY. SHIT," she yelled. "Is his dad your dad?"

When Mia laughed, a touch of hysteria sent the sound into a scary-high register. She sounded like one of those crazy zoo birds. "That actually might be better."

Cassie sped around another corner and onto their street. "What exactly is worse than incest?"

"His dad is the Devil, Cassie." That wasn't a statement a person could warm up to. Luke never warmed up to it for her, no easing gently into that conversation. Nope. *Just dive right in, Mia.*

Cassie's head bobbed up and down in agreement. "Okay."

Her realization that Luke's father was the Devil had been a slow epiphany. As he'd approached the table it had been a déjà vu moment. Then he'd taken her hand and it was like she had opened an oven door and a fierce heat escaped and the skin on her face tightened like it was trying to recoil.

The reality of it didn't make sense.

The Devil wasn't real. He was a construct of religion, a fairy tale told by priests. A cautionary fable.

And yet...

Mia had felt his draw from the instant he locked on to her. He'd held her in his terrifying thrall. If he'd taken her hand and pulled her down to Hell with him, she feared she couldn't refuse him. She would have followed that man down into his pit on her own volition even though she was horrorstruck by what she already knew was down there, even though terror consumed her.

They pulled up into their driveway. Cassie shut off the engine, but Mia made no move to get out. "No, Cass, he's the Devil. With like horns and smoke. Well, actually I don't think I ever saw horns. But smoke for sure." Cassie blinked at her. Of course, she didn't believe her. The very concept was outrageous. Totally absurd. "Never mind." Mia yanked at the handle and flung open the door.

Cassie threw open her own side and popped up to talk to Mia over the roof of the car. "No, wait. I want to understand and properly hate him with you. Explain what happened to make him the devil."

She opened her mouth, but before she could get a word out, the throaty rumble of Luke's car pulled up at her curb. A new sense of heat engulfed her, as if someone had set fire to her shoes and the flames were rising like a bonfire until her hair blew back from her face with the wind of it. With strength infused with rage, she hauled back and slammed Cassie's car door, causing the car to rock slightly to the left from the force of it.

Whirling around, she stormed down the driveway. "I told you not to follow me," she yelled before Luke had even exited his vehicle.

He rose up on the outside of his car opposite her, his height giving him an advantage that only fueled her rage. "Please give me a minute. Just let me explain," he pleaded.

She spread her arms wide. "What in the hell could you possibly say? What, Luke? What? Are you going to explain Hell?"

Cassie appeared at her elbow, her fists on her hips, giving Luke the evil eye. God love good friends.

Apparently, the two of them weren't scary enough, because he'd rounded the hood of his car and was approaching. "I know this seems crazy, and it's certainly not the way I wanted to talk to you about this."

"Crazy?" She was still yelling. The front lawn of her house wasn't the place for this conversation, but she couldn't seem to stop herself. "Preposterous, Luke. This kind of thing isn't real. It's just not."

Two more vehicles pulled up at her curb with a dramatic squeal of brakes.

"Well now, who is this?" Cassie asked over her shoulder. Mia certainly hoped it was a rhetorical question, because Mia sure as hell didn't know. Except that when the driver of the first car unfolded out of a sleek Bugati, Mia recognized him as Luke's cousin, Ethan. The other guy in his car and the two who emerged from a black Hummer were a mystery.

Mia waved her hand in the direction of the guys, a sweep of her arm that encompassed all of them before sniping at Luke, "Who is this? Why are they here?"

She could hear his forceful sigh from thirty feet away. "They're my cousins. I told them not to come."

Her laugh was on the verge of hysterical. "Why would they listen to you? I told *you* not to come, and here you are." Then she turned back to Cassie. "Men never listen."

Cassie shook her head in solidarity. "Nope. Never."

Luke put his hands palm up in a gesture that suggested his submission. "Wait right here. I'll get rid of them. Please just don't go anywhere."

He backed up slowly, his eyes trained on hers while she glared at him with her arms crossed. Convinced that she was staying put—something that definitely was not a sure thing—he turned to his cousins.

"You guys can't be here now. I need to try and fix this."

The swarthy guy from the Hummer stepped forward. "We were there. We saw it all go down."

A guy with dirty-blond hair hopped down from the passenger side of the Hummer. "That could have been any one of us in there."

"Well, it wasn't. It was me," Luke told them as Ethan and the fourth cousin joined them at the Hummer's bumper.

Ethan, the one cousin Mia recognized, stepped in between Luke and the others. "What did he say to her?"

Mia strained to hear the response.

Cassie watched the clump of guys talking. "Cousins, huh? They don't look anything alike, but I guess they wouldn't necessarily, huh? Awful pretty collection of guys, though, right?" Mia kept glaring. "What do you suppose they're all talking about?"

Mia, in all her righteous anger, turned to her friend. "How the hell should I know? Probably me and the Devil."

"Don't yell at me. I know you're mad, but I didn't do anything."
Mia returned her glare and her ear back to the men.

"—in her dreams taking her down there," Luke said.

Four masculine gasps sounded followed by sharp curse words.

"You know what," Mia yelled at the five of them, no longer giving any care at all to the neighbors. "I've had enough of this crap. You guys go ahead and have your little reunion on my lawn. I'm going in the house. If you're not gone in five minutes, I'm calling the police."

She stuffed her purse under her arm for dramatic emphasis and marched towards her front door, leaving Cassie standing on the driveway.

Faster than Mia thought any man as big as Luke could move, he ran in front of her before she'd gone more than four steps and held his arms out wide. "Baby, you have to wait and give me a chance to explain."

"No, I don't." Mia shook her head. "I don't have to do any of this." She turned her back on him only to discover that the four other men had joined Cassie on the driveway. Everyone was staring at her, watching her expectantly. She pointed to Ethan. "You all know about this?"

He shoved his hands in his jean's pockets, looked down at the grass, and then back up to her. He nodded. She waved that index finger at the other three. "You, too? All of you know about this?"

Cassie's jaw dropped. "Everybody knows what? What's happening here?"

Mia ignored her. What Cassandra didn't know would only save her sanity. This was some kind of dream, a surreal nightmare that kept winding her up tighter and tighter.

"Every one of you is nuts," Mia declared. She spun on Luke. "And I don't want anything to do with any of you."

The darker guy from the Hummer stepped forward. "I know this seems unimaginable, but we can explain."

"You can explain?" Mia snorted. "What is your name?"

The guy was big, maybe even as big as Luke. He had long black hair and even though Luke was a fighter and frequently sported a black eye, this cousin looked rougher. And yet, he seemed intimidated by her.

"Seth," he answered.

"Um-hmm," she nodded and amped up the glare. "Well, Seth, you and Ethan need to gather your boys here, including this one"—she indicated Luke with a backward tilt of her head—"and go away. I don't need any of this insanity."

Godfrey had his head shoved under the curtain in the front window and was barking his fool head off at all the strangers in the front yard. He ran from one edge of the window to the other. It was only a few feet wide, but between the barking and rearing up on his hind legs to bang against the window with his paws, it made a nice cacophony. Especially exciting when he added yelping to the mix as the curtains came down and he got tangled up in those, too.

She pointed to the window where Godfrey doubled as a poltergeist wrapped in curtain. "As you can see, I'm all full up on crazy."

"Are you going to shut up that dog?" Mr. Harris was stomping across her yard. As far as neighbors went, he was a giant pain in the ass. Mr. Harris was the president of the Homeowners Association and he was a tyrant.

Today was the day she killed Mr. Harris. "You cannot hear my dog barking from inside your house."

His smile was smug. "But I'm not inside my house now, am I?"

"No, you're in my yard."

"Obviously," he told her as he took in all the rest of the people in her yard. "I came outside to remind you of the rules regarding parking in the street." He pulled a small book from his coat pocket and flipped through the pages to the statute he was looking for. "Ah here, 'Guests shall park in front of the home they are visiting and shall not block any driveway, mailbox or fire safety area.'" He looked pointedly at the street where the Hummer and Bugati were overlapping into the neighbor's areas.

"They're not staying long," Mia pointed out. However, the minute the words were out of her mouth, another car pulled up across the street. Two men stepped out of a sleek, gray Bentley and made their way towards the cluster of guys on her driveway. They all nodded at each other in greeting.

"We got a Nine-One-One text with this address," one of them told the group.

Mia threw her hands up in frustration.

Mr. Harris made another tick in his book. "And there's another violation."

Godfrey ramped up the barking to a frenzied level. A couple walking two golden retrievers stopped to admire the vehicles and then the drama taking place on Mia's lawn.

She turned in a wide circle, taking it all in, only to pause in front of Luke and chastise him, "All of this because you wouldn't listen when I told you not to follow me. Damn it, Luke. This is ridiculous. Why is it too much for you to understand that I'm freaked out by your...issues and I don't want anything to do with this?"

Cassie, now surrounded by a crowd of Luke's cousins, raised a hand. "I still have no idea what the heck is going on here."

"And I don't care," Mr. Harris spoke up. "Whatever it is, you can't do it parked here."

Mia balled up her fists. How did this get so out of control? She was so angry it didn't take much to envision wrapping her hands around Luke's throat and squeezing until he listened to her.

Luke extended another hand, his expression pleading. "Let's go inside and talk. We can get all these people off the front yard and into the house where the whole neighborhood isn't involved."

"Excuse me," Mr. Harris interjected. "There's still these cars to deal with."

She was just about to turn the full force of her hostility on Mr. Harris when out of the corner of her eye she realized Jeb was standing to her right. When the hell did he get here? Before she could fully form the question, she understood that he hadn't been there. Only moments before that space had been empty. She was one hundred percent certain of it. Any other time she'd have blinked it away, but not after tonight. She knew what she saw, or rather, didn't see.

Grabbing at Jeb's rock-solid arm, Mia asked him, "How did you just get here? I already know you weren't here just a second ago, so don't lie to me."

Jeb waved his hand at her. "Oh, honey, I never lie. Not to you." He circled his hand in the air and let out a piercing whistle like a referee gathering a rowdy team of soccer playing toddlers. "Come on. In the house. Now."

As if they were being pulled by a string, Luke and all six of his cousins headed towards the door. Cassie met Mia's gaze, then shrugged and stepped in the line moving towards the house.

"But I don't want these people in my house," Mia sputtered. "Why doesn't anyone listen to me?"

"Just a second, honey," Jeb told her and then turned to her neighbor. "These cars will be fine here for now. They won't be long. You can go home."

Mia watched with her mouth hanging open as Mr. Harris put away his notebook, nodded to Jeb and then to her, and then turned to go into his house.

"You need to teach me how to do that," Mia told Jeb.

"Trade secret," Jeb told her with a twinkle in his eye. "Now listen to me. You have a lot of questions and we have a lot of answers, and then some. We need to go inside. Will you agree to that? I'd much rather you decide to do so on your own, but this is very important and I'm not above giving you a little push just to get you there."

Mia instinctively knew that "push" he was talking about was whatever he did to Mr. Harris. Never in his entire life had her neighbor given up an argument like that. He always got whatever he wanted because the man was relentless.

She paused for several heartbeats before nodding. "Fine."

She pushed to the front of the small crowd at the front door and slid her key in the lock. When she swung the door open, she fully expected to have to reach out and grab Godfrey before he bounded out the door. With all that panicked barking, she wasn't completely sure he wouldn't try to bite someone.

Except that the arch of the front door didn't reveal her hardwood floor or the soft rug usually in front of the door in her foyer.

Instead, the room opened into a cavernous expanse of marble. In the absence of her living room, rows and rows of marble arches ran down the side of an immense corridor all the way to a magnificent altar which ran the expanse of the far wall, towering at least one hundred feet high. Diffused colored light filtered down from stained glass windows.

Jeb strode through as if this was exactly what he expected. "Come on."

The others followed along behind him with wide-eyed awe. Even Cassie went inside without much more than a WTF expression as she passed Mia at the threshold.

Mia stood at the cusp of the door and whispered aloud, "What is happening?"

She felt Luke's hand slip around hers, entwining their fingers and holding tight. "I don't know," he whispered in reply. She was so stunned, she didn't even yank her hand from his grasp.

Together they stepped into the cathedral.

HEAVEN & HELL XI

N eil took his boots off and crammed his socks inside them so he could feel the grass under his feet. The living, breathing plant felt so cool against the blisters he could almost weep. The individual blades tickled his arches and ankles as he walked around in a lazy circle. The lawn stretched for longer than a football field, and it had those wild alternating light and dark green stripes you'd see after a huge lawn was freshly mowed. He lay down on the carpet of green and inhaled through his nose to take in the clean scent.

He wondered how long he could lay there before someone—or something—noticed him and did something about it. That thought was actually what got him back up and moving.

He was not supposed to be down here, and his excuse about Cerberus was pretty thin. Any demon with half a brain in his head would know it was bullshit as soon as he heard it.

Reluctantly, he stood and turned back to look at the Devil's house. Or mansion, actually. It was massive and imposing. The ritziest haunted house ever, and Neil couldn't imagine why the Devil needed such an enormous place to live. The roof was black and steep with decorative iron work all along the edges. The building itself was gray marble block, and when he counted the windows up, there was four stories. It was a jaw-dropping place no matter where it was located but especially so when one considered that it happened to be sprawled in the deepest level of Hell.

Neil vaguely remembered old black and white reruns of a television show called *The Addams Family* the kids in the orphanage would watch on an old donated television set in the common room. That was the kind of house he expected the Devil to live in, all spooky and dark and foreboding, not this luxurious palace of comfort. He couldn't marry the two ideas together: A classy haunted house? The place didn't look like a dungeon to torture sinners. Where were the lakes of fire and clouds raining acid? Neil kept his guard up anyway, completely aware that Hell was a tricky place and he shouldn't relax for even a moment. He didn't, he couldn't trust what he was seeing. Lounging on the grass, no matter how wonderful, had been a tactical mistake.

Taking in the breadth of the place, his shoulders sagged. How in the hell was he going to find Rachel in this massive building? And what kind of hideous, devilish creatures would try and stop him?

He could always go back and tell the little angel he couldn't find her.

But then Juliet wouldn't have any reason to meet him in the stairs anymore. That would mean no more snacks and, even worse, no more opportunities to kiss her.

"You've come this far," he said aloud and started across the lawn barefoot, his boots dangling from his hands. He kept watch for gremlins and imps and other creepy things keeping watch over the grounds. There was no plan if he was confronted. All he could do was throw his boots at them, but then he'd be shoeless. It didn't matter. Nothing seemed to be patrolling the area at all. Where were all the minions? Surely the Devil had minions.

The closer he got, the more his unsettled stomach roiled. The hair stood up on his arms in warning.

Up two stone steps and he was at the entry with the massive front door in front of him. It looked like a castle door with vast wood planks held together with wrought iron hinges that stretched halfway across the width. At least ten feet tall with a humongous metal door knocker that he estimated weighed at least fifteen pounds.

Banging on the door seemed stupid. In fact, going through the front door seemed stupid, but another glance down the length of the building and Neil knew there was no way he was going to trudge all over Hell trying to locate a back door even if the grass was soothing on his feet. He tried the doorknob and was disconcerted when the heavy door swung open on well-oiled hinges. He took an instinctive step back, preparing to make a run for the elevator if anything fearsome popped out.

Instead, all he saw was an entry with polished hardwood floors and an enormous Oriental rug. He poked his head in and listened for the sound of cloven hooves or heavy breathing.

Nothing.

Inside, he closed the door behind him with a soft click, then stared, goggling, at the fine interior of the magnificent house. Art hung on the walls, some of it really ugly which Neil assumed meant it was expensive and old. The wood was polished to a high shine, and the upholstery seemed lush and comfortable.

Neil didn't get it.

When he'd been in the duke's houses they were comfortable—for a demon. But they certainly weren't the kind of places Neil would willingly spend any time.

This place, however, was the shit.

A hobgoblin wearing a black apron and a delicate little hat stepped into the entry hall holding a feather duster. Neil nearly shit himself.

"Uhhhh," he said somewhere between a moan and cry.

The creature hacked out a cough while Neil contemplated making a run for it. Finally it gestured with the duster down the hallway. "He's in the blue drawing room."

Who was? This could not be good. He hesitated, his body in this weird limbo where he couldn't decide if he should flee or follow the hobgoblin's instructions.

"Go on," the beastie said and shooed at him with his feathery stick, "he's awful when he gets bored. I'm not cleaning up another one of his ragers." The hobgoblin narrowed his eyes at him. "You're not bringing him mescaline, are you?"

Neil shook his head. "No." He hadn't dealt in hallucinogenics even when he was alive.

The hobgoblin maid blew out an exhausted breath. "Do you have any idea how long it takes a Mongolian horde to come down off acid? They made an unholy mess."

Neil made a sympathetic grimace.

"So git but don't make a mess." Then the creature disappeared into another room, leaving Neil to the vastness of the house. A grey and white striped tabby eyed him from the end of the hall.

Does the Devil have a drug dealer? It that who that guy thought he was? Whatever the case, he didn't raise any kind of alarm that Neil was in the house. He tapped into his old B&E skills: stealthy and quiet, don't set off any alarms.

No one was in any of the rooms off this main hall. He stuck his head in all of them as he started wandering. When he came to a junction he paused, wondering where the blue drawing room was located because he'd like to go the other way. Ultimately he turned right because it was as good a direction as any, thinking he'd double back at some point and take the left side of the house later.

He wandered past several sitting rooms and a smaller room that looked to be a very small dining room, and a vast library that caused him to do a double take. The room was longer than it was wide so he couldn't take in the whole room by just sticking his head in the doorway and glancing around. Inside the room had floor-to-ceiling bookshelves with a ladder on rollers that circled the entire room in order to reach the top shelves. Against the far wall and over a massive desk hung mounted heads like in an old movie with rich people. Usually there were like lions and bears and animals with horns and maybe a fish and shit. Not in the Devil's library. The biggest one was a stuffed troll head complete with a massive nose and bugged out eyes. It was as horrifying in death as it had been in life. On the other side of the desk was a grouping of gremlins, six in total. Taxidermy was creepy under regular circumstances, but there was something so unsettling about their leathery skin and jagged teeth that it gave Neil goosebumps. One of them even had a long, wart-covered tongue hanging from its mouth. He couldn't stop himself from getting closer, compelled to see the horror up close.

He was less than three feet away when the one with the unnatural tongue grinned at him and shrieked, "Boo!"

Neil screamed and dropped his boots. The gremlins all cackled in unison.

He wiped his face and swore under his breath. "My God." If he wasn't already dead that would have done it for sure.

"We scared you," they all sang together, six voices shrill enough to curdle milk.

If he had still had a beating heart, he would have needed those paddle things to get it started again. "Is this what you do, hang around here, waiting to terrify people?"

A gremlin head with a bulbous, hairy mole on its chin growled, "It's not like we can go anywhere."

His nasty, little compatriots set off another round of snickering.

Neil picked up his boots, prepared to storm out of the room, but thought better of it. "How long have you been in here?" he asked.

"The whole time," the smallest one answered.

"You ever see a lady in here?"

"We've seen lots of ladies," they answered. "Tall ladies, short ladies, fat ladi—"

Neil held up a hand to stop them from listing off all the adjectives. "How about a really old lady."

"Sure!! Tall old ladies, short old ladies, fat—"

"Stop," he yelled. Jeez, these idiots. "This one would be related to the Devil."

"Maybe," the big-nosed one said with a smirk.

"We'll tell you," said a gremlin with tremendous acne, "if you answer a riddle."

Neil snorted. "Not a chance."

He perched on a leather sofa and put his boots back on. The heads on the wall did a demonic version of a barbershop quartet that was physically painful to listen to. He covered his ears with his hands and fled the room.

He continued peeking in doorways, looking for grandmotherly

types, moving further and further from the library where now it sounded like they were singing in a round. He passed a room with a grand piano with three cats draped over the top and a cello leaning against a straight back chair. When the hallway branched off again, he took the right fork and passed by the biggest room yet. The floor was glossed to a high sheen and a ponderous chandelier hung from the middle of the ceiling. There were only a few straight-backed chairs scattered against the perimeter of the room and a small raised stage in a corner. Neil could imagine hundreds of fancily dressed dukes and counts dancing around the room while some spooky orchestra played a waltz.

As he wandered the house, he encountered several more hobgoblins of the domestic sort. Not a one of them paid any attention to him whatsoever. On the other hand, he'd come upon at least thirty cats all of whom trained their lazy eyes on him as if they suspected he was up to no good.

One more right turn down a hallway and he discovered the blue drawing room. There was a man seated at a small table with an old electric typewriter. He was thin and nearly bald with a ring of hair around the back of his head. While Neil watched, the man inserted a cigarette into a long white holder and lit it with a match. He sucked hard on the stem and even from the doorway, Neil could see the cherry bloom on the end of the cigarette. He tilted back his chair and exhaled smoke rings towards the ceiling.

Neil wondered if this was the bored man the maid had referred to.

"Hey," the man spied Neil and dropped his feet flat to the floor, righting the chair. "What have you brought me?" He rubbed his hands together as if in anticipation.

Neil showed his own empty hands. "Nothing."

The man let loose a string of invectives that would have made Sister Agnes lose her mind. An orange tomcat looked on disapprovingly from atop a pile of paper stacked on the floor near the man's feet. "Well then, come and wait with me so I'm not so bored."

Neil shrugged and strode into the room figuring he could pump the guy for information if nothing else. "You a writer?" he asked and pointed at the paper and typewriter.

"Aren't you the observer." The man hit the space bar with his fingertips. "Even after the dark thumb of fate ended me, I'm still a writer."

Neil ignored the snark. "What do you write?"

"Past the deadline," the man said and laughed ruefully.

"I read some, you know, before. Would I know your stuff?"

Another long puff on the cigarette followed by an exhale of gray smoke. "You ever read Rolling Stone?"

Neil shrugged. "Sure."

The writer spread his arms wide, cigarette and holder hanging jauntily from his lips as he smiled. "Gonzo journalism, baby."

Neil stared at the guy. That phrase was familiar. He stretched his mind back and searched the man's appearance for clues. Tinted glasses on the table, a goofy hat on the sofa behind him, the weird affected cigarette holder.

Gonzo journalism. Then it clicked.

"Hunter S. Thompson?" Neil said with reverence. Everyone in the drug culture knew who Hunter S. Thompson was. The man was the patron saint of the loose-cannon, recreational user. "What are you doing here?"

"In Hell?" Hunter asked. "I always figured I would."

"No, I mean the Devil's house." Neil looked around, and he still couldn't put all the pieces together. Why this place was so classy and expensive. Why no one questioned him or even seemed to think it was weird that a stranger was wandering around unescorted.

"I'm hammering out a piece about it. You know, how the Devil really lives or some shit. Man, if you liked the Hells Angels piece, you'll love this." He poked the stack of papers on the floor and under the cat with his toe. "Just because I'm dead doesn't mean I stop writing."

"I guess." Neil still couldn't believe he was talking to the real-life Hunter. So fucking cool.

"How 'bout you," Hunter asked him. "What are you doing here?"

Did he lie or tell him the truth? If he was writing about the place, maybe he knew about Rachel. Maybe he'd rat him out. Nah, Hunter was one of the good guys, screw authority and all that shit. Besides,

Neil could spend the rest of his life wandering around this place and never find who he was searching for.

"I'm looking for a lady."

"Right on." Hunter nodded with a shit-eating grin.

"A certain lady," Neil amended. "I think she's here. Maybe you've seen her?"

"I've seen these fucking monsters dressed as French fucking maids. There's even one of them who wanders around wearing a pink goddamned wig." Hunter shuddered. "I swear to God, I thought it was an acid flash back." Then he scowled. "They won't let me have acid anymore. One damned party and you're cut off. Ugly damned bastards."

"Yeah," Neil agreed. Wig or no, just being dressed in a maid's outfit was bad enough. "How come there's no security here? I'm used to having to sneak around to avoid getting snatched up by the imps and orcs."

Hunter laughed. "What the hell does the Devil need security for? Who the fuck is going to sneak into the Devil's house and steal from him? A world-class idiot, that's who."

Good point.

"So no ladies wandering around?" When Hunter didn't answer, Neil prodded a bit more. She simply had to be here. It made too much sense. "Maybe a prisoner? Her name is Rachel."

Hunter bunched his eyebrows together in thought, then ruffled through an unruly stack of notes. "Rachel, Rachel, Rachel. I do remember something about that name. Somewhere in all this garbage." Finally, he withdrew a wrinkled and dirty cloth napkin with some barely legible notes written in ink. "I heard the household help talking about someone who lived in the 'cage,' they called it. I'm pretty sure it's on the other side of the house. Is that who you're looking for?"

It had to be. Unless the other side of the house was one giant prison full of the Devil's family members. This was Hell after all. It certainly could be. Neil thanked Hunter profusely and shook his hand vigorously before stepping back into the hallway and making all the turns in reverse. He passed the caterwauling gremlins in the library and the same bunch of cats he'd already seen until he discovered himself back at the start. This time he went left. That side of the house was pretty much the same; same luxuriously furnished empty rooms, cats lounging on the sofas and tables or all over the floor, random hobgoblin servants who totally ignored him. He was beginning to think this whole thing was a lost cause when he heard a voice.

Distinctly crystal clear and melodious, it was not the sound of a creature of Hell. This was a woman's voice.

He followed the sound to a partially closed door. Standing on the outside, Neil eavesdropped on the decidedly one-sided conversation. "I'm looking for a blue piece with just a hint of pink on the side shaped sort of like a fat person with one leg. You see anything like that?" A short pause, and then she continued. "No, I think that one is part of the river. This blue is more sky. I think. What do I know about sky, huh?"

A very fat black cat squeezed through the open doorway opening it up just enough that now Neil could peek in and see the woman. She was young and beautiful with long, wavy blond hair. She was leaning over a table putting together a jigsaw puzzle. The ever-present cats congregated in the room with her, and Neil could count ten just from the small view he had of the interior. Puzzle pieces littered the floor around the table. A kitten was perched at the edge of the wood looking down at the mess, then shifted his attention to another piece sorted out on the table. Unchecked, he pushed the piece onto the floor with a swipe of his paw, then he leaned over to look at where it had landed. The lady ignored him entirely.

"Aha!" she crowed. "Here we go." She clutched a piece in her hand, fitted it into the puzzle, then banged it with her fist until it fit.

All along the floor, completed puzzles lay like mismatched carpets. Actually, they weren't finished. Not a single one. They all had at least two pieces missing, making their design wholly unsatisfying. Neil imagined an obsessive-compulsive person would lose their mind in here.

A white Persian cat with a smooshed-in face noticed him in the doorway and meowed in his direction. It swished its excessively long tail, dragging pieces to the floor in its wake.

Neil rapped two knuckles against the door, then pushed it the rest of the way open. The lady paused, a piece in each hand, and gazed at him with a wide, unafraid expression.

"Excuse me," Neil said, "I'm looking for Rachel. Do you know where I can find her?" He asked the question expecting her to say no. This beautiful lady couldn't possibly be the Devil's great, great-a-gazillion-times grandmother.

She nodded, her mouth a gape. "I'm Rachel."

"An angel sent me to find you," he said as he walked into her room.

Rachel started to cry.

CHAPTER TWENTY-NINE

J eb led the way through the cavernous cathedral that somehow fit
within the floor plan of Mia's house. Luke had experienced
many supernatural things in his life—it was impossible not to
when you were one of the Seven Deadly Sins and your father was the
actual Devil—but he'd never been magically transported somewhere.

He squeezed Mia's hand, reassured that she was still there and still
clinging to him.

"Don't be afraid," he whispered to her.

"I'm not. I trust Jeb." Realizing he still had possession of her hand,
she jerked hers away. "Where are we?" she asked, her voice hollow in
the immense expanse of the room.

Marble floors and columns that blended into arches seemed to
extend into infinity with dizzying effect. Possibly endless rows of
wooden pews stretched on. At the top of the room, magnificent
gilded architecture towered to the heavens. Everything was bathed in
ethereal light filtered in through magnificent stained-glass windows.
Glorious.

"I'm not sure, but I think its Jeb's place."

She tore her gaze from the splendor before her and turned to
Luke. "Jeb lives here?"

He nodded slowly, in awe of the beauty of the building. "With the other gargoyles."

Mia stopped walking and stared, her full attention settled on Luke.

With a gentle smile, he tried to reassure her. "I won't let anything hurt you."

She snorted. "This whole thing is so *Twilight Zone*, I don't even know what to be afraid of. Based on what I just learned about you, I wouldn't consider you in the clear."

"There's nothing here to be afraid of." The female's voice was melodic with a soft accent Luke couldn't place.

Their band had come to a stop in the transept before the great altar. He was pleased to see that all of his cousins were as much in awe of their location as he was. Benji and his love of art looked like he was going to bust a nut over it. Jeb stood to the side, his arms smugly crossed, surveying the group.

Even though Luke was pretty sure he knew the answer, he asked him the question he knew they were all thinking. "Where are we? Why did you bring us here?"

With all the dignity the place seemed to inspire, Jeb stood tall and made a grand gesture. "I present to you *La maison de la Gargouille*. The House of Gargoyle. This is where we were born, where we wait, where we watch."

"Who," Mia asked, her voice tiny in the huge scope of the building. "Where who watches?"

The female's voice answered softly, "The gargoyle."

The air above the altar shimmered and the giant stone gargoyle stepped away from the gilded cornices and decorations. In all the years he'd known Jeb and his father's gargoyle, Ezra, Luke had never, ever seen one of them change from a stone guardian into a flesh being. As jaded as he thought he was, he was still entranced by the transformation. A trick of light and a flutter of mystical illusion, and the statue went from a terrifyingly carved granite gargoyle into a diminutive lady.

She wore a soft white robe that reminded Luke of a holy woman or an angel. Though instead of a halo, she had a crown of soft, brown curls that complemented a pair of ancient and knowing eyes. She extended her hand to Jeb who immediately stepped to her and nodded in deference. He took her hand and, ducking slightly, he kissed her on the cheek.

"Notre Dame," Jeb said with deference. "Everyone is here as you asked."

"Well done, Jebediah." She patted his shoulder, then turned and addressed Luke. "Wrath."

Luke nodded in response. At his side, Mia whipped her head around to stare at him.

"Wrath," she said. "That's the second time someone has called you that. What does that mean?"

He exhaled through his nose. "There is so much to explain; I almost don't know where to start."

The lady gargoyle turned her attention to Mia. "And you are Mia Hatcher." A smile filled her face, and her tone was both kind and filled with wonder. "The champion of apples."

Mia's eyebrows rose. "Do you know me?"

"I do not, but I have been watching. Your and Wrath's love affair comes at an interesting time."

"Our love affair?" Mia snorted derisively. "I don't think that's what's happening here."

Luke sighed. He didn't try to reach out to touch Mia again. That made her hostile, and that was the furthest thing from what he was trying to accomplish. His life was a monumental disaster, and he didn't know how to make it palatable for her. What words could he possibly say that would make it all okay?

"Mia has only just recently come to understand the situation," Jeb told the lady.

There was no mirth in Mia's laugh. "Understand? No, I don't understand. I don't know if I even want to. I'm not even sure if this is real."

Jeb stepped up and said, "I know you're angry and frustrated. You have every right to be. A whole lot has been thrown at you and it's all very surreal. I also know that Luke is desperate to explain to you—"

"Somebody had better explain *everything* to me." Her eyes narrowed and she glared at Luke.

Where was all his wrath when he needed it? Not that this was a situation to be resolved with fury, but it was always nice to fall back on the comfort of his anger rather than floundering in this morass of frustration and despair. It was entirely possible that Mia would never have anything to do with him again after how badly he'd bungled this.

Jeb met his gaze and gave him the slightest shake of his head before he took Mia's hand. "I know, honey. My boy, Luke, is a real pain in the ass."

Several of Luke's cousins snorted. That would have made him angry under other circumstances, but just now he was concentrating too hard on Mia to allow it to rile him up.

Jeb continued, "You'd make me feel a whole lot better if you'd give us an opportunity to bring some illumination to this dreary tale. Notre Dame has been here since the beginning of it all and she knows everything."

"Wait a minute," Mia said, holding up her hand. "I don't even know what you are. Just a minute ago she was a statue."

"Touché," Jeb said with a smile. "My name is Jebediah, as you know." He indicated the ancient lady with a graceful gesture. "Notre Dame, which means Our Lady in French—"

Mia gave him a look. "Yes, I speak French."

Jeb turned up the charm. "Of course, *you* do. I'm just working to fill in all the blanks." He gave her a conspiratorial nod and flicked his eyes toward Luke. "Luke never studied his languages. I want to make sure he's following along. Anyway, Notre Dame is the Superior of our order. We are Gargoyle who serve the Seven Deadly Sins."

Mia shook her head and looked more annoyed than ever. "Okay, people aren't gargoyles and they don't just emerge from statues. How about you explain this to me like I'm a four-year-old."

Cassie came to stand next to Mia, and together they tried to follow along as the ancient lady told the story of the Mephisto Curse. Luke and his cousins bunched together nearby and listened intently as well. Luke didn't know about the other six, but he could certainly use a refresher. They'd all heard the story from their fathers, grandfathers, and uncles, and they'd read the ancient scroll at the ceremony, but they never talked about it in day-to-day life. Who knew what important things he could learn today?

"...Lucifer is restricted to his cell in Heaven, miserable and alone. Rachel is imprisoned in Hell, to endure by herself. They are punished to never be together again. The legacy of their sin is that the first-born son of each generation assumes the mantel of a Sin. Your Luke is Wrath."

Mia turned to glance at Luke, and he was heartened to see her expression was laced with sympathy. As Notre Dame listed off each of the Sins, one of his cousins in turn raised a hand to identify himself. Mia and Cassie's eyes were wide by the time Ian raised his hand in recognition of Pride and Jacob for Greed.

"And of course, Cassandra." Notre Dame nodded at Cassie.

Cassie's eyes rounded in surprise. She looked at Mia and shrugged.

"How in the hell are you involved in this?" Mia demanded of her friend. Cassie's jaw hung open and she shook her head, clearly as mystified as Mia was. So many questions, Mia didn't even know where to start. She turned back to Luke. "You're Wrath? And Ethan is Envy? And the others do their thing? What does this mean exactly? How are you Wrath?"

Ethan barked out a laugh. "How is he Wrath? Good God! You saw him fight?"

Luke nodded. "That's it exactly. I am anger." He ducked his head and softened his voice, trying to speak only to her. He wished they were alone so he could tell her how much he loved her. Some place private so he could make her see him, not Wrath. "Except when I'm with you. I never feel the living, breathing fury when I'm with you."

"That is true," Notre Dame confirmed. "We noticed that. It seems when the Sin is lucky enough to find his perfect mate, the sin is tempered."

"Really?" Asher asked. "I've never heard that. Have any of you heard that before?"

Seth shook his head. "Definitely not. That's fucking huge, man. Like maybe it doesn't always have to be so bad."

"I'm telling you, it's true," Luke said. He reached tentative finger-tips towards Mia's arm, but she pulled her arm out of his reach.

Mia rubbed her forehead with the heel of her hand. "Supposing this is all for real, how come his father is the Devil?"

Notre Dame folded her hands and continued her story. "There is a ceremony. One Sin from each generation becomes the Devil and, in turn, the next generation takes their place in the mythos, becoming a Sin."

Luke remembered everything about that night. The smell of the leather sofa in the library. The way the material of his shirt scratched the back of his neck. The boys had been naively hoping for pizza afterwards. How when the doorway into the inner room had opened, Luke had learned the smell of brimstone.

Mia's eyebrows bunched together on her forehead. When she turned back to Luke, there was genuine concern etched on her face. "It could be you? Next?"

Luke shrugged, trying to lessen the significance of the fate he always assumed would befall him. "Not for twelve years."

Benji's mellow voice had an unusual edge to it. "That's not the whole truth, Mia. Yes, it could be him, but it could also be anyone of us. For some reason, Luke has been convinced for years he will be chosen. I want you to know, there is zero evidence of that. Zero."

Mia nodded, but didn't relax any. "But he could? I just want to be sure I understand this. He could be, or you could be, but one of you will be for sure?"

Benji closed his eyes on a long blink before he nodded.

Mia ran her fingers across her mouth. "And so could your son? No matter what, one of you is going to have a son who will be the Devil? Do I have that right?"

This time the affirmative answer came from Ethan. Cassie gave a little strangled cry and covered her mouth with a shaky hand. Luke could feel Mia pulling further and further away from him.

"And your son will become a Sin?" She shook her head vigorously. "This is insane."

"I know it's a lot to take in," Luke whispered. "I wish it wasn't true."

She held up her hand. "I don't want to hear anymore sad apologies from you. Just let me take this in for a minute." Her words were clipped, short, angry.

Luke exhaled through his nose, frustration setting his blood to a simmer. What did that mean—that suddenly the sensation of bubbling rage tickled at his gut? Was she not the perfect woman for him anymore? Was he losing her?

Mia directed her attention back to the gargoyles. "That story still doesn't explain who you are. I can't believe I'm buying in to this craziness. What do gargoyles have to do with Sins?"

It was Luke who answered. "The Devil sends them to spy on us."

Jeb rolled his eyes. Notre Dame smiled. The soothing presence of the ancient gargoyle settled over them. Luke could feel how Mia relaxed and his own tension seemed to ebb.

"We do not belong to Hell," Notre Dame explained. "We do not belong to Heaven, either. We protect the Sins. We watch over them. It is our pledge to aide each Sin as they suffer the burden of the curse."

Luke tossed a quizzical look at Jeb who smirked back at him. Everything about his expression was smug.

"Have I not?" Jeb asked with one raised eyebrow.

Luke raised one of his own eyebrows and tossed him a noncommittal sideways nod/shrug combo.

Ignoring their exchange, Notre Dame continued. "I had Jebediah gather all of you here for a reason. For the first time in millennia, we see a chance to break the curse."

A chorus of "WHAT?" echoed across the cavernous room.

"Forces are at work in the universe. The Daughters of Eve are growing a Tree of Life." She paused for effect. "An angel and a demon are working together. We aren't sure what these things mean, but it's undeniable that they are important. If the curse is ever to be broken, we feel that now is the best opportunity."

CHAPTER THIRTY

" A re you telling us you think we can break this curse? After all this time?" Luke sounded incredulous.

Mia still stood more than an arm's length away from him. He'd stuck close to her, hovering in a way she would have found comforting if she hadn't just found out the man she was in love with was the Devil. Or could be the Devil. The whole thing was confusing and surreal and overwhelming.

She fumed.

She had never been so angry in her whole life, and she was actually damn proud of herself. Confrontation had never been her thing. She was extraordinarily good at making excuses for people's bad behavior, but a person had to draw the line somewhere, and obviously, being the ruler of Hell was a bridge too far.

One of Luke's cousins spoke next. Mia didn't know who he was, but she studied him anyway, trying to figure out which Sin he represented. She should have paid more attention during roll call. Wow, her new reality was really weird.

"How is this possible?" he demanded, shoving a hand into his hair and pushing it from his face. Dark hair, dark eyes, at least two days' worth of scruff on his face. Funny thing though, he looked clean-cut underneath his artful dishevelment.

The tiny lady responded to him with immeasurable patience. Nothing about her expression altered. If she hadn't continued talking, Mia might have thought she had lapsed back into stone. "Anything is possible, Asher."

"Okay, if that's so, then how come no one has ever figured out a way before?" This guy seemed genuinely angry. Mia thought that was Luke's department. Even taller than Luke, which made him a giant, this next cousin had sandy brown hair and shocking blue eyes. She couldn't pick a Sin for him, either. None of these guys were easily cast into the role of what she'd expect a sin to look like, except that each was sexy as hell.

"We have always been watching," the lady told him, so calm in the face of so much outraged testosterone, "always looking for a way to end the curse. We believed, if we were patient, eventually a way could come clear."

Luke threw his hands in the air in exasperation. "Patient? Are you kidding me? How many generations of us have there been? Five hundred? I don't even know. How goddamned patient are we supposed to be?"

Shaking his head, Jeb stepped next to Notre Dame. "Settle down, big guy. The Gargoyles didn't make this curse. We're on your side, remember?"

Mia giggled. She couldn't help it. How many times had she worried for Jeb's safety, confronting Luke so often when he was riled up? Now it seemed like he'd never been in any real danger at all.

The lady nodded at Jeb. "We have stood as witness since the beginning. We saw Lucifer and Rachel make choices that set the curse in motion, and we watched as the Father showed no mercy. The gargoyle are the guardians, but we cannot change the course of the curse."

Cassie leaned into Mia and asked, "But why is it so horrible that Lucifer was with that woman? They were in love. Is that really so bad?"

It was Jeb who answered, for once his tone was serious. "It was forbidden."

"Oh, ladies, there are rules." Sarcasm dripped from Ethan as he

AMYLYNN BRIGHT

smirked. "We know all about that, don't we? No dying. Have your son and sacrifice him, too. Don't try to be happy because it's all going to end."

"Shut up, Ethan," Luke growled. He cast a furtive glance at Mia, but she ignored him.

"Actually," the dark man from the Hummer grumbled, "both of you need to shut up. If there's a chance to end this, I want to know what it is."

"Please understand," Notre Dame began, "we don't know the answers and there is much work to be done, but we see a chance worth investigating."

"What do we need to do?" another cousin asked. His hands were shoved in his pockets, and he stood apart from the others. While his cousins were dressed in suits and expensive clothes, this one had paint-stained jeans and a sweater with a hole in the shoulder.

"The path is unclear, Benjamin, but the time has come that you need to be aware and be prepared to act as the situation arises. We don't know what will be asked of any of you." The lady smiled. "We are confident with Mia's help, the Daughters of Eve are well on their way to resurrecting the Tree of Life. The significance of this should not be lost on any of you. Of the three trees in the Garden; the Tree of Life, the Tree of Love, and the Tree of Knowledge, this will be the first one to reawaken."

Mia gasped. She knew exactly what the lady was referring to: the massive tree in the center of the Daughter's compound they'd been experimenting with for the last ten years. At last count, the massive tree had forty different scions growing from one parent tree. It bloomed all year and there was never a time when there wasn't ripe fruit available. It was a marvel of sustainable art.

"You said something about an angel and a demon?" the disheveled one asked.

"Indeed," her stony face spread in a beatific smile. "This gives us the most hope. A young angel has learned of the curse and found Lucifer, while a young demon is searching Hell for Rachel. They are working in union to bring the lovers together again."

There was a long heartbeat of silence. Mia's gaze flit from one man to the next before landing on Luke's frowning face. His eyebrows were scrunched together in thought, and he stared off into space. He must have felt her attention land on him because he lifted his head and met her eyes. His frown eased away and the tension fell from his shoulders as he studied her back.

Without his eyes leaving Mia's, Luke asked, "If Lucifer and Rachel can come back together, the curse will be broken, won't it?"

"Or," Benji interjected, his tone jaded. "That could really piss off God and he could curse us even worse."

Notre Dame lifted an elegant shoulder. "That is unknown. Whatever it is, it will not be easy, and we're not sure how much help you can even be to the angel and the demon, but the Seven must be prepared to intervene in any way necessary."

As light as an evening breeze, Mia felt hope drift across her...soul. Was that a possible thing? She pulled her gaze from Luke's and took in the others' expressions. Luke's cousins stood in contemplative silence or exchanged loaded, questioning glances with each other. The air was so heavy with possibility, even Mia could feel it.

Cassie squeezed her hand and whispered, "Are you following this?"

"I hardly know," Mia confessed. "All of this is so hard to believe."

Jeb tucked her arm in the crook of his just like he'd done countless times before, as if this was no stranger a situation than any normal office meeting. "Don't worry, hon. I'll fill in all the blanks later. Just now, Luke is desperate to talk with you."

That peaceful feeling fled.

"I know you have doubts," Luke told her, his voice low and entreating. "Please just give me a chance to talk to you. I can try to explain."

She snorted and jerked her arm free from Luke's gargoyle. She made a big deal of it, but the initial fury wasn't there anymore. "I can't imagine how you can."

Cassie still had ahold of her left hand, and she tugged gently until they had stepped several feet away. "So, all of this—" Cassie swept her free arm in front of them "—is crazy balls. I still keep expecting someone to jump out and tell us we've been punked, but I don't think that's actually going to happen. Somehow we're in on this, and I think you need to hear him out."

"There's a curse," Mia reminded her friend.

"What if it's finally over?" Cassie whispered and pointed at Notre Dame. "From what she says, you're pretty important to breaking it."

How did she get all wrapped up in a family curse? She was just Mia Hatcher, botanist, average woman, and disappointing daughter. She wasn't the kind of person who got involved with plots to save the world.

Cassie continued, "You know as well as anyone, no family is perfect."

Mia pursed her lips and raised her brows. "They're not perfect and then there's this mess."

"You know what I mean. You never know what's going to happen. You could end up with some other man who doesn't love you nearly as much as Luke does but who gets hit by a bus the day after your wedding. With Luke, you get someone who really sees you, who really *loves* you. The question is, how much do you love him? Is it enough? Is the possibility of breaking the curse enough of an incentive to take the risk?"

When Mia raised her eyebrows at Cassie in question, her best friend shrugged and nodded.

"Talk to him and see." Cassie gave another gentle squeeze, then let go of her.

Luke reached out his hand. Mia hesitated, but ultimately stretched out her fingers to go with him.

Except the second their palms touched, they were no longer in *la maison de la Gargouille*.

THE SUN WARMED her skin and hair and the aroma of growing things filled the air with a comforting scent of mulch and blossoms and earth. Mia and Luke found themselves in a small clearing tucked inside a massive grove of trees, the greenery all but hidden by pink and white blooms.

"Where the hell are we now?" she asked.

Luke released her hand and rotated in a small circle, taking in the scenery. "Looks like an orchard somewhere."

She gave him a look. "It was actually more of a rhetorical question. I'm not real keen on this magical transportation thing you people have going on."

"That's not us," Luke said with the shake of his head. "This is a first for me, too. My cousins and I don't snap our fingers or wave our hands and then all of a sudden, we're somewhere else. That's a gargoyle thing.

"I don't like it."

He gave a small, one shoulder shrug. "Jeb knew we needed to talk alone."

She opened her mouth to say something, but snapped it shut again and exhaled sharply through her nose. "Also, pretty presumptuous."

Luke chuckled, low and sexy, and Mia resented the fact that it hit her in all the right places. She was working really hard at maintaining a righteous fury—she certainly had cause—but all the explanations from the gargoyles was turning Luke into a sympathetic character.

"You've met Jeb, right?" Luke asked when he was done chuckling. "Everything he does is presumptuous."

"Do all of your cousins have one? A Jeb, I mean." She could not say the words 'a gargoyle' because it was totally nuts.

"Yeah. From the time when we're ten and we go through the ceremony to become a Sin all the way until we die. My father's gargoyle, Ezra, still takes care of his earthly concerns."

And there we go, circled right back to the crux of the matter: Luke's father was the Devil.

He reached up and plucked a pink bloom from the nearest tree and brought it to his nose. "It's funny. I thought all this time they were spies for him, like his minions or something, and it turns out we were wrong all along."

"Yeah, weird," Mia said, dripping in sarcasm.

They stood for a moment in silence, Mia trying to figure out what question to ask first, Luke mindlessly twirling that flower between his forefinger and thumb. Finally, she just blurted something out.

"So, Wrath, huh?"

He wrinkled his forehead and peered at her. "Yeah."

"What exactly does that mean? You never seem all that 'wrathful' to me. Grouchy, sometimes, but wrath seems so extreme."

"It's hard to explain, but imagine if everything you are was colored by, I don't know, let's say, the color red. Every interaction, everything you did, was a shade of red. When you're stuck in traffic, it's maybe light red because that's only slightly irritating, but if you're seriously late maybe it's a little darker." He raised his eyebrows at her as he continued. "Or if your assistant makes a point of driving you absolutely insane. Maybe he keeps you in a shade of magenta most of the time." Now his lips formed a lopsided grin. "Say you were in a restaurant with a pretty lady who was already frustrating you, so you're kinda running a little pink. You think you're going to be able to sort her out and get your project back on track, but she turns out to be ridiculously smart and stubborn. Maybe the realization hasn't hit you yet that you've lost, but you know you're in trouble, so the color gets darker, maybe wine red. Then the waiter turns out to be a total asshat and insults the pretty lady. By that time, wrath would have really kicked in. Imagine the whole world as dyed in crimson. Or if your father shows up at dinner and terrifies the woman you love. Then it's blood red."

She got where he was going with this little story, and she wasn't falling for it.

"So, you're always angry?" How did he mask that so well? It made her feel like she never really knew him at all. What was he capable of if he let Wrath loose?

"No, I'm not. I used to be." He let the apple blossom fall to the ground with the zillion other fallen flowers. "You changed me."

Right. She changed him. What a load of bullshit.

"Um-hum," she hummed with a roll of her eyes. There was still too much to get to the bottom of for her to fall into believing all this pretty nonsense. "So, you said this zapping thing wasn't you. There must be something. What can you and the rest of your crew do? Fly? Be invisible? Read Minds?"

He chuckled again, damn him. "I wish. Sadly no. None of that. I'm like every other man."

WRATH

"Except that you're totally not." She narrowed her eyes. "Don't lie to me anymore. I want to know what the hell you've dragged me into."

"I cannot die, not until the ceremony the year we all turn forty."

She couldn't keep the sarcasm out of her voice. "Yep. Totally like every other man. I'm going to need to know more about that ceremony thing later. What else?"

He let out a sigh. "I can make people really angry."

"Like I am now?" She mocked him with as much indignation as she could muster. Disappointment rolled through her. She'd been enjoying the satisfaction of this self-righteous fury, and it turns out it was all fake. He'd been manipulating her all along, and now she didn't know if anything was real. She couldn't even trust her own emotions and that was a brutal blow to the state of happiness she'd been just a few short hours ago.

"I have no reason to want you angry. Quite the opposite, actually." He lifted a hand and his fingers twitched like he wanted to touch her, but he withdrew his hand. His gentle smile did nothing to sway her, and she maintained the hard glare. He ignored her tone and gave her a one-shoulder shrug. "Not exactly. It's like I can give a little push and infuse someone with wrath. Or a crowd. If I felt so inclined, I could create an angry mob with very little effort."

She nodded. "Like the restaurant tonight. Well, that's something to be proud of. Can you understand how used I feel right now?"

He sighed again, the sound of frustration filling the air around them. "I can't do it to you. It doesn't work on any of my cousins, either. Or Jeb. I think Gargoyles are immune to the effects of the Sins. Actually, I think we don't have any effect on any of the divine or diabolical beings."

Wait, what? "You can't do it to me. What does that mean?"

"It means that everything between us is all us. My wrath has no effect on you. I can't make you do anything or feel anything that isn't one hundred percent Mia. I don't know why. It must mean we're made for each other." She held her ground when Luke took a step toward her, then another. "You and I are real. Everything I feel for you is gospel and everything you feel for me is genuine, too." He was right in front of her now, less than an arm's length away. She could feel his warmth and smell his cologne and Lukeness over the floral notes of nature that surrounded them. "I wasn't prepared for you. At all. I made a point of never getting close to a woman because I hated what I was. I lived in fear of destroying anyone I loved."

"Oh, gee." She crossed her arms as a self-defense move, a literal barrier between them, as a last stand before she let other softer emotions run a coup. "I feel so honored you chose me to destroy."

"I couldn't help it," he said. "You're like a drug to me; I can't get enough of you. When I'm with you, I feel...calm? Peaceful? I don't know, but when I'm with you everything that is usually red and fierce is quiet and, what's the opposite of red? Blue? Not sad, but serene like the sky. This is a terrible analogy."

Mia raised one eyebrow in agreement.

"I tried to protect you from all this, Mia. I tried to let you go, you know I did, but I couldn't. I know you feel it, too." He placed both hands on her upper arms. "I love you."

She closed her eyes and took a shaky breath. "This is bigger than love. I mean I love you so hard it makes my teeth hurt, but it still all comes down to the fact that you could be the Devil. I don't know if I can live with that."

He smirked at her playfully. "You love me?"

"That's not the point."

"Of course, it's the point." Seeing that she wasn't going to be wooed by his teasing, he softened his voice and caressed the backs of her arms with his palms. "I understand what you're saying. The unknown is scary. Until I met you, I was miserable about my prospects. Ask Ethan or any of my cousins. Jeb will be all too happy to tell you about my misery ad nauseum. You know what helped?"

"What?" She almost hated to ask. The fury she'd been nursing had mellowed, and as he talked to her, it slipped more and more into fear of losing him and less about a betrayal.

"My aunt reminded me that my odds were pretty good." He tipped her chin up with his forefinger so she was finally looking up at him. "It's only one in seven, you know."

She swallowed hard and repeated, "One in seven."

"Yeah." He grinned at her, and her stupid heart beat faster. "One of those other sorry bastards might get it."

"Or maybe no one. That gargoyle lady made it seem like it could all be over." It was completely insane that she was considering this. "But Luke, if we, or more like when we, have a baby...his odds are one hundred percent that he'll carry the burden of a sin. I don't know if I can do that."

"It's scary. I understand. That's why I've never had relationships. I know my cousins are afraid to hope, but not me. Not anymore." He pulled her in flush to his body and wrapped her in his arms. "I am thrilled at everything Notre Dame said. I know this will work. You want to know why I'm so sure?"

Resisting was a lost cause. She unfolded her arms and participated in the hug. "No, why?"

"Because she said you had a part in it."

Mia rolled her eyes. "I don't even know what I'm supposed to do. I can't imagine that I can make any difference."

"My brilliant, beautiful Mia can do anything." He ducked his head and touched his lips to hers, ever so gently. "Have faith with me," he murmured against her lips. "Faith in us that we can beat this. I don't want to do it without you by my side."

Luke was compelling, with his earnest eyes and heartfelt declarations. A smart woman would run away from all of this. His story was insane. What he was asking her to do was outrageous.

And yet...

Maybe what Notre Dame said was true. She was a walking, talking gargoyle, for heaven's sake. How could an enchanted gargoyle not be taken seriously? Mia wanted everything the lady had hinted at to be true.

He pressed his lips more firmly against hers, and she didn't even pretend to resist anymore. She parted her lips and kissed him back.

When the kiss finally ended and they came up for breath, Mia was hit with a pertinent question they hadn't covered up to this point.

"Umm, Luke. How the heck do we get home?"

EPILOGUE

I t was a gorgeous day for a groundbreaking.

The Veritas Templum Board of Directors was there, nine suits wandering around, looking important. Of course, Mia's father held court with the small crowd, telling jokes and acting like a hero. The principals of Luke's firm were also in attendance, along with reporters and photographers from the news services.

Asher Mephisto, known to his cousins as Lust, had come with the rest of the Seven as moral support. Not wanting to be left out, most of the gargoyles had tagged along. Ash observed Luke and his lovely fiancée as they stood in front of an enlarged copy of an artist's rendering of her gorgeous building. It was blown up and printed on a billboard-sized backdrop to the day's festivities. An innovative blending of functional and natural, both the architecture and green engineering so unique as to be revolutionary. Like a botanical garden on a colossal scale.

This building was going to be a very big deal internationally.

Now the supernatural buzz suggested Mia's building might be the new Garden of Eden.

"I am so proud of you. Look what you've done," she was telling Luke as Ash got closer.

"Well, you know, trees. Lots and lots of trees," Luke replied with a provocative smile. "I told you we were fate." He slipped his hand around her waist and pulled her close. He whispered something in her ear that had her giggling, and it made Ash unexpectedly warm and fuzzy to be in the presence of such happiness.

"You're going to win so many awards with this," Asher said when he joined them. He handed off two glasses of white wine, one to each of them. "I'm impressed, Luke."

Luke eyed the wine glass with suspicion and muttered. "What's this?"

"Try it," Asher encouraged. "You'll like it." He grinned at Mia. "It's the apple wine you requested. There's a boutique vineyard I found that makes the best small-batch craft wine I've ever tasted."

After Mia took a sip, her mouth spread in a wide smile. "That's yummy. Crisp and sort of caramel-y." She took a much bigger sip.

Luke was less effusive. "It's all right."

"Man cannot live on beer and whiskey alone," Asher told him.

"So you and Seth keep saying." Luke grimaced.

Mia finished her glass in a gulp. "It's my policy to take all food and wine recommendations from Lust and Gluttony. You're going to find us something amazing for our wedding, aren't you?"

"You can count on it, honey," Asher told her and kissed her cheek. "I've got plenty of time to find something amazing before your venue will be ready." He tilted his head at the field where their building would stand.

"Thank you, Ash." She squeezed Luke's hand and then pulled away. "I'm going to make sure the Daughters of Eve taste this wine. I don't know if Diana & Maevis have tried making wine yet, but they should." She headed off in the direction of the nuns. She'd invited them to the event as an opportunity to showcase Veritas Templum Pharmaceuticals commitment to green construction and as an opportunity to collect donations for their community kitchens.

Asher observed his cousin watch his fiancée walk away. Luke clearly admired the sway of her skirt, and Ash grinned at him.

"She's a doll, Luke," Ash told him. "We all really like her."

"I thank Heaven I was able to pull that off." Luke blinked after her in wonder.

"I still wonder how." Jeb appeared at Luke's elbow. He was way overdressed for a morning that showcased shovels.

"Where did you get that hat?" Luke growled.

"Isn't it outrageous?" Jeb crooned. "I made one for Mia, too." Sure enough, he had a gift bag stuffed with artfully crinkled tissue paper that held a matching rhinestone hardhat. Luke rolled his eyes.

"On her it will look adorable," Luke admitted. "On you, it just looks fu—"

"Fabulous? Fashion Forward? Phenomenal?" Jeb interjected, ending with a model's pout.

"Legendary." Asher supplied.

Jeb grinned broadly and air kissed Ash. "You've always been my favorite Sin. Esther is such a lucky gargoyle, that bitch." He flounced off to give his present to Mia.

The crowd coalesced into a small herd in front of the artist's rendering. The funny little gardeners from the Daughters of Eve Convent had left their table of wares and stood rapt waiting for the ceremony to begin. The Board of Directors and Bruce Hatcher, Mia's father, gathered around in a loose arc at the front. Mr. Hatcher said some words that Ash didn't listen to.

He had noticed Luke's father at the edge of the crowd. He shot a quick glance at Luke, but he hadn't spied his father yet, and Ash didn't want to clue him in. It was Mia's big day, and Wrath would just ruin it for her.

The Devil, looking every bit as handsome and sinister as Asher expected him to, caught his gaze. The edges of his lips curved into a dark grin. He raised an index finger to his nose and tapped it gently before gesturing toward the giant illustrated building. Ash's brows came together and his glance darted to the backdrop, then back to the Devil.

But he was gone.

Ash scanned the crowd, but he didn't see his dark head anywhere. He stepped back and onto his tiptoes to see better, but the fiend had vanished.

"What's up?" Luke asked.

Ash shook his head and turned back to the presentation. "Nothing."

Mia had been invited up with the rest of the dignitaries, and they all posed with gold ceremonial shovels for the photographers. She was beaming underneath a sparkly hardhat. She was so cute and so obviously the opposite of Wrath.

The members of the Luke and Mia Mutual Admiration Society made Ash a little wistful. And jealous. But not hopeful.

Much had been made of Notre Dame's revelations that night. To the unjaded, all of this might have seemed auspicious, but for someone like Asher, someone whom God had forsaken, not even standing at the site of the next garden of Eden was enough to illuminate fate.

THE WEARY ARCHANGEL Michael watched the proceedings from the roof of a church. Seconds later he wasn't alone. He noted the arrival of his dark counterpart by the tangy whiff of ozone.

Michael grunted. "Has the boy found her?"

The demon reported, his voice guttural and foreign, "Yes, in the lowest level of Hell. Who knew he had it in him?"

ABOUT THE AUTHOR

 Amylynn read her first romance novel in 2008 after being a lifelong literary snob. By the time she was done, she was hooked. Now she pens Regency, contemporary, and paranormal romances that will make you laugh.

She in an Arizona native and lives in the same house her husband owned before they were married. Amylynn fears she will never call another state home unless someone tells her husband there are forty-nine others to chose from. In reality, she'd settle for a walk-in closet.

Her family consists of the aforementioned husband, two very loud children, two dogs, four cats, and a hankering for a panda. She'd like it mentioned she's never been in prison, but we'll see how that panda thing works out.

COMING SOON

The Devil's Descendants - Book 2

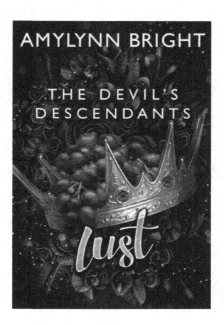

As one of the Seven Deadly Sins, Lust has its perks—certainly better than the other six Sins his cousins are cursed with. Asher Mephisto allows Lust to drive his business ventures, and Dashiell Vineyards is calling to his sensual appetites. When he meets the determined and tempting vintner Evangaline Dashiell, his attraction to her is the first thing he's felt more powerful than his curse. If Lust isn't driving the relationship… is it love?

Eva is trying to save her family's vineyard by bringing the ancient monastery and unique wines into the modern market. Wealthy, sexy, and slick Asher Mephisto comes into her life full of excitement, plans, and money to back his ideas. She is dubious. Eva believes Asher comes with strings and schemes because nothing in her life has ever been this easy. She should send him packing except his intoxicating kisses feel like so much more to her than just lust

JOIN IN THE FUN!

Don't miss a thing! Sign up for the newsletter at:

Amylynn Bright

HTTPS://AMYLYNNBRIGHT.COM

BOOKS BY THIS AUTHOR

THE BENNET FAMILY SERIES

COOKING UP LOVE

Is there anything more pathetic than a food critic who can't cook? That's Holly Darcy—secret socialite, wannabe author, lousy chef and "The Covert Connoisseur." Feeling like a fraud for critiquing restaurants when she can't boil a pot of water, Holly joins a cooking class for beginners…and quickly cooks up serious chemistry with the sexy instructor.

Mark Bennett was born to be a chef, but his foray into restaurant ownership fell far short of his dreams thanks to a scathing review from The Covert Connoisseur. Now teaching is the closest he will venture into a kitchen. Luckily the job comes with an unexpected perk: the attraction simmering between him and a curvy, clever writer with pinup-girl looks.

Flirting over pasta soon leads to passionate kisses and a sizzling relationship. But how can Holly be honest about her job when Mark blames his restaurant's failure on her review? And when Holly's secret is exposed, how will Mark be able to forgive her for ruining his life?

BUILDING UP LOVE

Five years ago, Lee Bennett's whirlwind romance with Candace Claesson ended as abruptly as it had begun, and just when he needed her the most. Since then, Lee's built a successful construction company and a satisfying, if solitary, life. When he's hired to build Candace's new veterinary clinic, Lee finds her as irresistible as ever— but he's never forgiven her and he's sure as hell not letting her break his heart again.

For years, Candace has wrestled with regret and guilt over leaving Lee. At the time, nothing was going to stop her from achieving her dreams of studying in Scotland and becoming a vet—not even young love. They'd been inseparable for six months, but anything that intense couldn't last. Or so she thought.

Reunited in their hometown, neither Lee nor Candace can resist picking up where they left off. But with so much from the past standing between them, how they can rebuild what they started so long ago?

HEALING UP LOVE – COMING SOON

Sarah Grant is holding it all together after the accidental death of her husband, the same accident that left her with a disabled child. She's doing a pretty good job of it, too, until her son gets a new therapist. While Mr. Miller is full of unrealistic—and possibly dangerous— ideas, he's also incredibly attractive. Driven by guilt, she'll never let anything bad happen to Sidney again. Unfortunately, the more she's forced to deal with Mr. Miller, the more she remembers she's more than just someone's mom. It's hard to focus on getting the man fired when she's set aflame whenever he's around.

Zachary Miller didn't expect his forced retirement from the military to be easy but dealing with Sidney's mom was more than he'd bargained for. He'd faced down the enemy in combat and survived, but this woman could oppose anyone and win with her cool, nononsense gaze. She's a force to be reckoned with even while she makes him want to forget the scars that define him. He'd bet good money that under her ice queen façade burns a fire ready to illuminate the dark future that terrifies him and keep his demons at bay. Maybe Sarah Grant and her son are exactly what he needs to pull himself into the light.

Can Sarah and Zach leave their broken pasts behind and find healing in each other?

THE SECRET SERIES

LADY BELLING'S SECRET

Francesca Belling is torn between two worlds—her past infatuation with her brother's best friend and her future obligations. She never intended to end up in the bed of her longtime crush, Thomas Wallingham, but that's exactly where she finds herself. Unfortunately, mail is slow during a war. She thought he knew everything. He had never suspected. Thomas has always wanted to be a part of the Belling's family but he was too foolish to grab the chance when she threw herself at him before. Instead, he ran off to war. Emboldened by his new-found appreciation for a grown-up Francesca, he finds that dream is within his reach. If she thinks he's running away this time, she has no idea what she's in for.

MISS GOLDSLEIGH'S SECRET

When Henry Cavendish, Marquess of Dalton, leapt to catch the fainting woman before she hit the cobblestone, he never thought that one chivalrous act would set his well ordered life on end. His ingrained need to protect her has every bit as much to do with her enchanting beauty as it does his desire to wipe the hunted look from her startling blue eyes. He thinks he has everything in hand, but the lady has secrets that put everything he loves at risk. Olivia Goldsleigh just wants to live without terror, but a gunshot in the night proves things can always get worse. The beautiful and god-like Lord Dalton swears to protect her, to make the danger go away. She wants the man, the life, the family, the bliss he promises, but her secrets are certain to destroy them all.

THE DUKE OF MOREWETHER'S SECRET

Thea Ashbrook comes to London on a mission to do right by her half-brothers — not to find a husband. Homesick for Greece, she causes an incident at a Salon lecture on Greek architecture where she is introduced to the annoyingly handsome Duke of Morewether. The gossips have told her of every deviant escapade for which he's so famous, and she is not impressed. When she discovers that his love of family mirrors her own, she gives herself permission to open her heart to him. Christian, Duke of Morewether, is infamous for his scandalous ways. He thinks his life lacks nothing, until he meets Miss Althea Ashbrook and, for the first time in his life, he finds himself tongue tied. When his past comes back to haunt him, it will take all his powers of persuasion to convince Thea he is worthy of her love. The duke has a secret – one that Thea thinks she could never forgive and sends her racing for home. To find redemption and win her back, Christian must realize mistakes can't be ignored forever. The secrets you keep can change your life forever.

MISS SINCLAIR'S SECRET

Anna Sinclair is an English lady who refuses to settle—not if all her friends have love matches. When she receives notification that her father, General Sinclair, is missing and presumed dead in America shortly after the War of 1812, she knows she has nothing to lose by going to find him. In an untamed country, she'll need to navigate the Mississippi River, miles of wilderness, earthquakes, Indians, and one absurdly attractive American sea captain. Nathaniel Johnson is an American patriot whose only goal is to return to the country he loves with his recently located brother, a sailor impressed by the British.

The money offered to escort a young English woman to the United States is too much to pass up when he's desperately trying to save his family's shipping empire. The beautiful lady spins a ridiculous tale about looking for her father, but Nate has powerful reasons to believe she's a spy for the Crown. He'll help her on her quest, at least until he can prove her villainous intent. Will Anna's secret destroy his country and be his undoing?